Wherever the Grass Grows Greener

A NOVEL BY ZACH CROWE

The Witch and Walter Monroe
Part 1 of 10

1st Run released August 2019, Hampton Roads, VA.
Copyright Zach Crowe 2019.

1st edition ISBN: 9781708077693
2nd edition ISBN: **978-1-952773-17-4**

"We can be heroes
Just for one day."

~ David Bowie

"Gen X have a lot of the psychotic entitlement
that Boomers have. They know enough that
they should feel bad about it, but they have
enough Boomer in them to never do anything
about it. Just believing that 'feeling bad' is its
own punishment is what makes Gen X (more
than Boomers) the most American generation."

~ Felix from Chapo Trap House

Senior year of high school in a dysfunctional household can be confusing enough without sharing a remote stranger's memories.

For two young men in middle America, it's just another Monday. Walter Monroe was a kid known as a wrestling prodigy. Now a teenager, he isn't known as anything. He's ready to move on from being an addictive personality who picks unnecessary fistfights – graduating and self-respect are the two things he thinks can fix him. He's unaware that across state lines, an identical
Walter Monroe views himself the exact same way.

The underprivileged Walter Monroe has committed his life and his reputation to running a racket with a dozen of his schoolmates. Their ringleader is scheming with the boss of their school's largest gang. This massive coalition of students have a reputation for imitating an empire – and they exert the cruelty of one. Walter is adapting to keep up: his role is now robbing other students. Being an expendable enforcer isn't all winning, as his dual loyalty makes him a target for betrayal. His girlfriend is distant, his family is shattered, and his friends might put a knife in his back. After a lifetime of lashing out, he's fueled only by the desire to survive.

Born with a silver spoon in his mouth, the other Walter Monroe is a member of the well-connected elite by birthright: a guaranteed lifetime of bathing in luxury and ignorance. Walter's teachers complain that he is as apathetic as he is devoid of ambition. Unbeknownst to all, his parents are raving mad, and he is without a single adult role model. His girlfriend is his saving grace: the ice-cold Hitchcock blonde, Brielle. She leads him by the hand on a constant adventure, and the two are engrossed with one another – resulting in a twisted screwball comedy.

Set on Monday, October the 4th of 1982, this novel tells two stories of polar opposite experiences from the same perspective: switching off every chapter.

The 1st in a 10-part series that spans two weeks, both Walter Monroes will be followed as their lives each get upended. Cracks form in the reality that separates the two distant people; amid the chaos, one commonality emerges:

THE WITCH

AND WALTER MONROE
PART 1 OF 10

Wherever the Grass Grows Greener

*

*

"Reality doesn't have to look this way – it could be as simple as stick figures

against a white background and it wouldn't matter. So long as something exists from one

moment to the next, the universe can be sure to forget every other detail. All I want

is to be able to believe there's some complexity working behind the lives everyone receives, but

I keep coming back to the slack-jawed excuses that people piece together: there are the ones

who talk like they've been placed on this planet for the sake of another person, or for their god,

or because of the great thing that they might accomplish someday. Nobody dares to voice the

legitimate concern that we're cursed as vessels for the things we can see hear and feel, because

everyone is so entrenched in their own mortal nature. We're all caught in this battle

against feeling disposable and each individually losing by the day, so it seems worthwhile

to drop faith into this thing that's supposedly worth waiting on, just to arrive out of thin air someday.

Nothing's coming. Nothing will ever come. They need to stop waiting and just be.

Walt – You know I'd never lie to you, but I don't think I chose to love you

by my own will. It had to be this way, always – from the very beginning.

The way we just… The way we can just… be."

*

*

I – A

The flat analog clock sitting on Walter Monroe's bedside table began screeching a two-tone alarm in rhythm to the flashing of **7:00** across the harsh neon red seven-segment display.

Walter's unconscious thoughts blew backwards through his mind, carried as though they were riding on the tip of a traveling bullet. Whatever lengthy chain of personal realizations he had encountered in his dreams that past night found itself dissolved in the immediate rush of anxiety flooding him over the awareness that Sunday night had ended and the unthinkable had arrived: Monday morning. The peace of sleep was a basket that tilted just enough to roll him over the edge, and he fell into the sudden sensation of his skin touching against warm bedsheets. One shock was all he received before his emotions subsided into mounting confusion and distress; the alarm blotted out all other senses. His arm jolted to life out of a spontaneous reaction and his hand slapped down onto the flat clock. Buttons clicked, getting pressed in as he gripped his fingers into the top of its plastic surface.

The alarm switched off over to the sound of a woman's voice broadcasting on the radio.

"*The death of Jack Bannen has shocked the neighborhood of Briarwood in which he grew up. On Luka Street, he was known by his friends and family to be a thoughtful boy who loved sports, and not the type to choose a path of dangerous criminal behavior* just in the onset of his young adulthood," the woman's voice said flatly.

Walter rolled over onto his side and used his elbow to hold his torso off the bed. He smacked his tongue to wet his mouth and flared his nostrils as they made cavernous, rattling breaths. The dim morning light in his room was enough to keep his eyes blinded shut. He flexed his legs from under his covers, and as he stretched out his body and moved around, his sheets clumped together in a wadded mess.

"*I had known him since his folks settled down here in the summer of '76,*" an older, raspy male voice said in a slow drawl, coming from the radio. "*It's a mystery to me why the Lord above gives us people like him… the ones who don't want anything more in life than to ruin someone's day. He was only eleven on the first day of school that year but age didn't matter to him, obviously, because he picked a fistfight between just him against boys who were tall enough to be passed off as a-dults…. Jack turned and sprinted off the other way once he ate the third or fourth punch, and he came back to the bus stop the next day with some stitches and a learnt lesson. The block all realized right away that it had gained an outcast: he kept himself apart from the crowd and made sure people only saw him with his head down. I knew I was watching a brooding little devil… but I ain't never expected him to turn out a gangster.*"

Walter's eyes peeled open gradually enough for them to adapt to the sunlight coming through the window facing him. A shade was covering up the glass, causing outside light to project down onto the floor in a faded tan prism. His vision was clouded, but there wasn't much to see in his room apart from his decrepit wooden dresser or the busted-up framework of an ancient bookshelf. Waking up was requiring more energy than he had to give, so as soon as he could comprehend the voice from the radio, he began to focus on the news story instead.

"*Unfortunately, by the time police arrived at the scene on the afternoon of this past Friday, the situation had already gone too far.*

Bannen had been loitering along the trail leading to True Hope Chapel with members of his gang when an altercation broke out. Two men were stabbed in the fight and Bannen was subsequently chased into the section of walled-off forest along a trail starting behind the chapel. Once detained by police, the gang members claimed Bannen had sprinted far ahead of them and was already well into the woods by the time they had first even made it up to the trail. According to their alibi, a gunshot rang out as they were still running in the woods, and it took five minutes of searching to find the spot behind a tree where Bannen's corpse rested, magnum in hand and his head blo-"

'That's enough,' Walter thought.

He held the alarm clock in his hand, having had just picked it up and shut it off. He placed it back onto his nightstand, swung his legs over the edge of his bed, and sat up enough to hunch forward. His bare torso felt gripped by the frigid morning air, which rested densely in the space between his four walls like how a freezer filled with water will trap the contents in place. Stillness soundproofed the room so that the only noise he heard was his heaving breath, but the blood coursing between his inner ears turned the silence into a crashing of waves.

Rage stacked within him as he was managing to recall each of the individual words that he had time to yell out in reaction when meeting Jack Bannen for the first and only time:

"Shithead! You spat in my potatoes!"

It was the seventh grade and Jack had managed to break away from the staff who were transporting him out of class through the cafeteria when he made the snap decision to harass yet another stranger. Walter didn't even need to hear a name that day in order to instantly identify who and why this person was running up to him – the rumors that circulated the hallways all described him as exactly the wild-eyed lunatic who had cracked a wide grin at the sight of Walter lethargically eating alone. He berated himself for how pathetic he seemed in hindsight. His food had slobber dripping over it one moment, then the next, a cackling Jack went sprinting off quicker than Walter could get to his feet, but apart from hearing the spited name echoing the halls as a part of the gossip that infected them, he never saw sign of the pariah again. On the first day of high school, he learned that Jack was zoned elsewhere, meaning his chance at revenge had finally been snuffed out.

'What a bastard he was,' Walter thought, 'to make the whole world his enemy and then surrender. God, I just wish I was able to cut myself the same fucking break....'

The analog clock's display flicked from **7:06** to **7:07**, which caught the attention of the corner of his eye. What should have been a gentle reminder that Walter's time to get ready before the bus came was gradually running out instead caused panic to swarm him. He could feel his neck tighten up under the grip of existential fear and his stomach sicken, boiling like broth out of anticipation for the inevitable heap of stress he would face from the coming day. Desperation took hold, and his mind went to scavenging itself for the one saving thought, the one memory that could quell the surge of chemicals which had him incapacitated.

In a moment of delayed awareness, he leapt from his bed like the sheets had caught fire and bounded across his room to the closet. Instinct took control of both his hands, gripping the two rounded wooden knobs and pulling the double doors open. The floor of the closet hosted a scattering of dusty memorabilia and trophies from his days on the wrestling team, but his interest was in the single shelf perched above his head. Walter lifted his heels up off the floor, suspending himself on his toes, giving him just enough height to reach onto the shelf and grab a brown paper box from the back of it. The tips of his fingers siphoned pure relief from the polished surface of the cardboard. In the center of the box's lid was a small rectangular card held in place by a thin metal frame that fit the card within itself snugly, which read *Notes from Alina* in a precise black ink sign. He held it out in front of him with both hands and was staring at the three penned words intensely as he sat his heels back down onto the carpet, turned, shuffled back to his bed and sat down again with the box in his lap.

Walter's fingertips gripped either edge of the box lid and pulled up ever so slightly. It slid off and a gentle pop of air poured out from under it. The box contained a sea of paper scraps all lying intertwined together, filling its volume about two thirds of the way up from the bottom. Each piece of paper had a handwritten message on it, either scribbled in pen or printed in pencil, and they all featured the same distinguished heart and sign at the bottom of each one. Walter glanced over at his bedside table and grabbed an index card off of it, of which was filled with dates and instructions and bright blue marks beside the completed lines – the furthest one down that wasn't marked off read *For Monday read my Nov 3rd note – the one with the 4-stanza poem* in a messy scribble. He glanced back into the box and noticed a full sheet of notebook paper labeled *Nov 3rd* was resting on the very top of the entire pile, completely uncovered.

'...Did I really forgot that I had already went through and found it?' he thought. 'I must've dug it up on Friday after work, I think.... That could explain why my memory from before the weekend is so cloudy: because that night I was exhausted enough to be pronounced a corpse.'

Walter shut out his thoughts, grabbed the piece of paper, and set the box down gingerly away from him on his bed the same way he would a cat haranguing him for attention. He read the note:

Dear Walty,
This English class is murdering me in my seat, so I made my knee-jerk reaction of choice and decided to write another note. I must've already written you a hundred of them (don't expect me to stop ever ever ever, though) and it's been what, a month and a half? So much happened so fast... and I'm grateful for it, don't get me wrong! I just get afraid sometimes that since you haven't known me for that long – maybe you're not used to me yet? Maybe I'll say something that catches you off-guard, and you won't know what to say or think? It seems obvious to me that the only logical decision is to be as extremely 'me' as possible so that way I can break down

Crowe

your every expectation for me and you won't have anything else left to expect!... Except there's nothing interesting about me at all, but I can't quit worrying about my dad right now because he's undergoing his first surgery later today, and he did once say that he sees me as a reflection of him. I just so happen to personally believe that he has done some of the most interesting things I could even conceive of, so instead of talking about anything that might interest you, I'm going to copy his latest poem because it's freaking the ever-living fuck outta me. Please something Holy intervene and make it so that me writing this poem causes first period to end faster. Here goes:

Up over the valley and down by the crick
Through bushes and brambles and branches all thick
There was an old man who lived in his home
And it was every day he would read memories from his tome
Because it was his mistake to be left alone

When he was younger and chose to play a thief and a trick
He caught hatred for people and he made himself sick
He wanted to forget where he had come from
He cursed his loved ones and was thrown out to roam
And then he realized his fate to be left alone

The world got harder and his skills did not stick
He lost all his blessings and he'd lose himself quick
But the anger and sadness kept his mouth at a foam
He lacked any direction and had an attitude like stone
But all only once he had let himself become left alone

And now he is ancient – in his head there's a nick
He let the world destroy him by making himself an easy pick
And he has to face Hell; it's not looking well
Only by the curse of being left alone

P.S. It didn't make English period go any faster

Walter's brow furrowed. He read the note again but when he got to the poem, he ignored it and looked at his shaded window to keep his eyes away from the scribbled text. A cold feeling in his gut reminded him that she *had* stopped writing him notes a little over a year ago, and resorted to having him reread notes that she remembered as being significant. He grappled with himself as to whether he should search for a different note in the pile, if only for the chance that his spirits could potentially lift even slightly: on the average day, chasing a grim note with any other note that contained plenty of *You're all I desire*'s and at least one *The universe will make space for us* would have been enough to balloon his mood after having been put through a dreary poem like the one on the page he was holding. But today, Walter felt particularly unmoved; it was as though he had gone to sleep with some fantastic possession and woke up to realize it was gone without any trace. His patience was elsewhere, and reading that poem had deflated any eagerness he had to pick out any more of the notes that were in the box. Even still, just hearing her voice narrating in his head brought warmth to his pallid thoughts. It was a bittersweet thing to be able to read Alina's vibrant feelings from years ago; the two of them had long since realized that there was never going to be any returning to those times.

He watched his clock flick from **7:12** to **7:13** and a second wave of fear swept him: nearly half of the time he had to get ready was spent sitting comatose on his bed with only his boxers on. The threat of having to walk to school on a Monday peeled him off his bed and sent him to the other side of the room. He looked blankly into his dresser as he began flinging drawers open and slamming them shut again. It wasn't as though he had expected to find a decent outfit from the few clothes he owned, but his disbelief built upon itself as his search for suitable clothes dragged on and he continued to come up with nothing. Everything was baggy, faded, and tawdry: even his socks. After he had finished going from top-to-bottom through each drawer, he begrudgingly picked out a medley of clothes that barely suited him, but would at least last him until the end of the day and threw them on. He took his wallet off of his brown work shirt from atop his dresser, putting the former into his back pocket and folding up the latter, sliding it into his backpack.

Walter, fully clothed, turned to face the open box sitting on his bed. He wanted to blame Alina for being inconsiderate and not giving him a more heartfelt note to read, but she had never slighted him before when it came to his needs. It seemed like she had his emotions planned out weeks in advance, and she was tactical in her treatment of him like a general to his troops. Walter was sure to be swift as he dropped the sheet of paper flat into the box and set the lid back in place. He took the box over to his closet and put it up on the shelf again. The doors to his closet shut when he pushed them into their frame, and as the magnets that connected the two surfaces clicked back into place, he could feel his will melt slightly.

'You're being a victim – what good is that?' he thought. 'You bitch; you've went your whole life with the awareness that the world isn't watching to see if you succeed, so why is it breaking you right now? No one cares; it's just another morning. Conserve yourself.'

He stood directly in front of the closet door, bowing his head slightly as though he were before a king and begging for his life, eyes closed and fists balled. Cold tears were caught in his eyelashes.

'You're not dropping out of high school…. You won't get to the point where you'd even consider dropping out. You're not quitting your job, either. Because it's the only way you can ever get better. And there's only one way to see if things will ever get better, and that's to suffer through the moment. Hold the fuck out. Just be strong enough to survive today; long enough to make it back to this room tonight.'

He took a sharp breath through his nose and pulled it all the way to the bottom of his lungs, not stopping until they were filled.

'Just hold out.'

His lungs emptied in a sudden gust from between his lips.

'Okay – get going.'

He walked out of his room and into the hallway bathroom on the right.

The first thing Walter noticed about his bathroom as he stepped inside it was that the air wasn't any less cold inside there as it had been in his room. Morning air doesn't seem to realize that the sun has come out for at least a few hours after it first rises, so even though it was as bright outside as it would be all day, he felt as clammy and as unwelcome in his attempt to get out the door as though it were still the dead of night. He studied his eyes in the mirror as he gripped the stubbornly tight faucet to the sink and struggled to turn it on. Water poured out and gathered in Walter's cupped hands; with a flick of his wrists upwards, he splashed cold water against his face. His skin stung with the raw reminder that he was awake. His every thought was directed in the attempt to deduce exactly how long of a day he would have to endure before he'd be able to get back to catching up on sleep. Despite his exhaustion, he felt a slight boost of energy out of the gripping dread that was pumping through him at the sight of himself in the mirror. He felt a slim shadow of how happy he could vaguely remember once feeling, and he looked the part.

Walter's hands grabbed his toothpaste and toothbrush and took to brushing. His cheeks would bulge around as the brush jerked back and forth inside of his mouth to clean his teeth, but his eyes were cemented on their own reflection. He was aware of how quickly you could check someone's eyes to get a sense for whether or not they were happy, but Walter had never thought to made it a point of checking his own in a mirror during the few times that he could still clearly remember when something had him legitimately joyous. The truth was that he had no idea what his happy eyes might look like, but he could at least be certain that the hollow morning routine wasn't doing anything for his mood, just based on what he saw in the mirror. When was the last time he felt satisfied enough in his life to be able to get ready for school without it being a crushing and repetitive process? Well, never, technically, because getting ready every morning was repetitive by nature, and the repetitive nature of things doesn't require much time to become crushing on a person who isn't allowed a break from them periodically. When had been his last break? He always told himself the same answer to that question: it had to have been last Halloween with Alina.

Sex had become a forgotten practice due to how locked up she chose to become upon taking her hospital job, primarily because she began doing her schoolwork during her shift every day. The subsequent stress from stacking worksheets and readings on top of cleaning up after dying patients across a whole building had rendered Alina decidedly impotent in the sense that her sexual urges had been practically erased, similar to the way poison ivy can destroy a person's fingerprint. The memories that she would normally share with Walter while musing about their sensual history didn't cycle through her thoughts anymore, and she had no further desire to attempt any of their old habits. Last year's Halloween had been a much-needed break in that reality. Walter would attest that he rarely came in contact with pleasure, but on that evening, it practically strangled him when the two of them were shaded by the black curtain of night and spent what could have been ages pressed into each other on a small grass bank within a cove of trees at the edge of a forest. Time had lost all meaning during that shag – they assumed that it must have lasted close to the entire night because both of them agreed afterwards that it was easily already 4 AM, meaning he must have fucked her into another time zone. Whether it really had went on for hours or the two of them had simply just packed an amount of sensational satisfaction that went beyond all belief into a deceptively-long thirty minutes, it didn't matter, because it was the single last good fuck he could recall.

Walter filled his mouth with water from the sink, swished it in his cheeks, and then spat the mixture of water spit and foamy toothpaste out down the drain. He looked back up at the mirror.

"Quit your moping," Walter told himself out loud. "It's only been what? Almost a year now? And that memory is already wrung

completely dry because I'm always letting it sit out on my mind...."
He gripped either side the sink with his hands and looked down into
the drain. "Just cut it out." The lights flicked off in the bathroom as
he grabbed his backpack from off the floor and hit the switch.

*"I don't think you understand, Flint. Those two are criminals
– my job as a man of the law is to apprehend them and your job as
a citizen is to assist me!"* a mature male voice with a staunch British
accent spoke dramatically from the television in Walter's living
room.

*"Now, under any other circumstances, I might be willing to
play along with that, but Tophat, I've been digging up clues to keep
me on the trail of these two from the moment I touched down back
in the country,"* replied a gruff, equally-aged, stalwart male Texan
voice. *"You don't need to explain it to me – I already understand
exactly how well it would work for you if, for the sake of the law, I
just decide to forgive them for robbing me of sixty-two million
dollars, my ranch, and any chance to ever come home to my wife in
this mortal plane ever again. And you yourself, lawman; you
shouldn't be too quick to forget that you're the one who built the
case against me that stuck me with the only two choices of whether
I wanted to fly overseas or rot in a cell. You were the problem that I
was given in the first place – you're dead,"*

*"And I will temporarily overlook the fact that you flew off to
Taiwan while your case was still pending and that you never served
your sentence for drug cultivation and mass distribution from the
location of said ranch!"* the Briton continued. *"Right now, however,
these two are about to blow our bloody fucking brains out if you
don't assure them that you've given up your tremendous hunger for
revenge!"*

*"On the contrary, both of you are dead as all fucking get-out,
no matter what gets said,"* a third male voice spoke, this one deep,
young, and through a thick Yankee accent. *"I just need to make sure
the old man doesn't kill me first."*

"You're high on the list, son," an elderly Italian voice rasped.
"You could have turned in Burbank, or Maury, but your own father?!

And you dare still walk this earth after confessing to a crime that lost me five years of my life? Tophat dies, then I'll be taking those years back from you not long after."

"You calm yourself, Moretti!" commanded the Briton. *"And you, boy! You'll be coming with me, straight to a cell! Your father might have funded the criminal acts that stole from hundreds of properties down south, but he served time and paid out his entire estate to the law in fines as reimbursement for his ill-gotten gains. You, on the other hand, have done nothing to atone for your participation in the chain of home invasions that the two of you orchestrated, including the raid you assisted in on my friend's ranch over here."*

"I'm not doing any kind of atonement; no way, no how," the Yankee growled through gritted teeth.

"You were part of the raid on my ranch?" the Texan asked, pain sticking to his voice like hair on flypaper. *"That means you were there the day my wife was killed."*

Simultaneous to the voice finishing the final sentence, Walter walked out of the bathroom to see the rough-looking Texas man flick his thumb back on the hammer of his pistol, and an instant later a shot rang out and the Yankee's skull blew back outwards through his black head of hair, brain matter spattering out from just above the view of the camera. Four more shots exploded from all around in disjointed, immediate succession in the moment that he finished his sprint over to the television and then jammed the power button into its face. It shut off with a diagonal white flash across the screen and a zipping static click.

Walter stood petrified in front of the television, the silence in his living room being nearly as haunting as the sudden image of carnage that he had just involuntarily witnessed. He turned around and saw his mother laid out across the couch in a deep sleep. She was wearing the same linty turquoise bathroom that she put on every time she got back home from work along with her light pink slippers: the only pair that she owned. Walter didn't understand the first thing about how or why his mother was able to operate the way she did. She slept all day, worked all night, and watched men kill each other in movies when she wasn't doing either. But as he observed her, he noticed the slight tension in her brow and the way her lips creased downwards into a subtle frown. Walter could feel remorse simmering within him suddenly on the hopeless Monday morning that it was: he knew that as a boy struggling through high school, he had very little power to help his overworked mother reach a more dignified state of living, apart from keeping the pantry stocked with a job of his own. There wasn't a single day in Walter's childhood when his parents didn't have food for him and his sister on the table, but it seemed as though just about everything else around the house needed to be paid for with money that didn't exist. Nobody was there anymore to help his mother manage all the burdens in her life, and the frustrated look on what would've otherwise been her neutral slumbering face couldn't have made that somber reality any clearer.

Walter stepped up to the couch and gently reached his arms under his mother, who was sleeping so soundly that she wasn't even disturbed in the slightest as he picked her up. His right arm supporting the top half of her body and his left arm hooked under her legs at the knees, he carefully tread out of the living room and across the kitchen. The air conditioning unit was blaring cold air out into the hallway – he couldn't imagine why she even had it turned on at all. The doorway to what was once his parents' room had been left open. Inside the room, all the windows were covered up by thick shades that his mother had installed over them a day or two after she started working nights at the pharmacy so many years ago. Walter gingerly lowered her into her bed, first putting her head against her pillow and then taking care to not jostle her at all as he laid down the rest of her body. He pulled the covers to her bed over her and planted a gentle peck onto her forehead.

"I love you, Ma," he whispered to her, and then walked out back out of her room. He pulled the door shut behind him, and the sound of his mother lightly snoring was silenced as the doorknob clicked and a hushed gust of air blew out from between the door as it came to rest in the doorframe.

Walter walked back into the kitchen and checked the clock on the wall just above and to the right of the kitchen window, noticing that the minute hand was directly over top of the 4. On the face of the refrigerator were two sticky notes that had titles written in pen across the top and tally marks scribbled below them. The first read *7:00 AM's since we last saw Sandy* and the second read *7:00 AM's since we last saw Dad*. Walter took a pen out of a plastic mug on the counter and added a tally to each of them. He put the pen back in its mug and read the totals: the first note came up to eight marks, and the second note came up to one-hundred thirty-three.

Walter reached his arm across the notes, grabbed the handle to the right of them, and pulled the refrigerator door open. He peered inside only to find a carton of juice, of eggs, of milk, and a bagel bag. He took the bag from off its shelf and plucked the top bagel out of it, then set the bag back before closing the refrigerator door. His fingers pulled bite-sized chunks off the bagel, which he popped in his mouth intermittently without looking, reveling in the sensation of each crumb as it would make contact with the impoverished walls of his stomach. The view from the kitchen window matched Walter's emotions: regardless of however early in the morning it was, the pavement was just as gray and faded as it would be all day, the grass was yellowed and sickly, and without the veil of night to cloak the houses on the other side of the street, it was visibly apparent that all three of the rusty huts would need to be demolished if the value of the crowded, sprawling trailer park was ever going to increase. Instead, Walter kept his eyes and ears away from the window and up and to the right of it instead to immerse himself fully in the plain white face of the kitchen wall clock.

'Mornings are a special kind of hell,' he thought while watching time pass at the rate of the ticking second hand. 'They shouldn't have to be so awful – you wake up every day of your damn life. I don't know. It's the only time of day designed to swipe every personal comfort out from under you, is what I think it is.

That's to say that you're asleep and in your own business for hours, but then at a totally arbitrary moment, it's all over and you get dumped out of your dreams. It has to be the biggest slap in the face from the universe to people everywhere that our imaginations go wild the whole night long, creating little movies and stories in our heads just for us, only for it all to evaporate once the sun rises.

'Getting up, getting dressed, and getting out the door aren't difficult tasks at all in themselves; it's just that having to arrange yourself immediately after the death of your own little mental world could be considered poetic in the way it takes people's unique thoughts and emotions and rips them right out every day on schedule. Morning emerges from night without warning, the threat of failing to meet your responsibilities marches you on out the door, when suddenly, however you look or feel becomes the concern of the entire world, and it's your job to just bear it. It really is torture in its own way if you consider how this goes on in endless twenty-four-hour rounds, because I've never met the person who didn't claim to be beaten down by the feeling that they're only keeping up with their week by rushing through it – by the time you've had a complete thought to yourself, it's not surprising if the sun has already ducked out and back in again.

'One second it's up and you're up with it, and then before you even have the chance to go searching for hope: darkness. And so the cycle repeats. That's how mornings seem to string together – but it gets real scary when the sense sets in that your entire life has become trapped within the breaking of dawn, because before 8 AM, memories take it upon themselves to come back to you with laser-guided accuracy, and there's no defense from the ghost of every past morning that you ever let get completely fucked as they return to haunt you....'

As he swallowed the last chunk of bagel, he became overtaken by a new hunger which cemented his attention on the wooden fruit bowl sitting under a hanging wicker planter.

'It's funny, really, how staying home is just as awful of a way to spend the day as is going to school,' he thought. 'Regardless of the outcome, regardless of the events that will make my future, today will be shit, and not from a lack of trying.'

Walter walked over to the fruit bowl, moved aside a dented orange and a blackened banana to reveal a tightly-wrapped joint. His hunger turned ravenous. 'Frankly, there's only one way to save myself from wasting away unnecessarily.'

He held the j upwards in front of his nose, admiring its resemblance to a baseball bat.

'No matter how I spend the next eleven hours before the sun is gone and night returns, I'll have been effectively miserable from dawn 'til dusk... unless.'

He wanted to save it. He really did. He didn't want to waste even a crumb of weed that could otherwise be saved for another day, but this was about survival.

The front door shut behind him and his sneakers scraped the ground as he walked the brief cement pathway that led away from his house and up to the thin, winding street. Crisp fall air blustered through his clothes and hair. He looked to the tops of the withering trees that peppered the surrounding neighborhood, noting the gray sky behind them.

'Sobriety has nothing to benefit you. The world around you is practically falling apart – it always has been. There's only one solution, and that's a forced change of outlook.'

He plopped himself down on the curb, then slipped off his shoe and retrieved a matchbook from under the sole. After tearing one match off, he dropped the book back in and pressed the sole into place. Fitting his foot back into the shoe, he observed his surroundings. There were no cars on the street; no people around at all. It was as if he had been trapped inside a rejected concept for a snow globe. Not giving himself any more time to think, he struck the match on the pavement and lit the tip of the joint – the other end resting between his lips.

With a single inhale, the surrounding trailers transformed into a benevolent paradise. He flexed his muscles, admiring his own health.

'Why haven't I ever tried running a marathon?' he pondered.

The smoke he exhaled smelled like sweet pine, and as he continued to inhale from the joint with intermittent ashing, he found himself becoming more and more distanced from the dreary road that he was sitting on. Turtle Creek Ridge at the state line was a gorgeous sight to behold last March, when he and Alina had the chance to take a bus out that way. If he had to be honest with himself, he had never considered a day trip into the forest could become anything remotely enjoyable at all, even up until the moment they went to disembark with the other passengers at their stop. In the end, it only took them but a moment to a secluded spot by the bank, and they were smoking and laughing and kissing like they had just bought the place.

Walter spent the better part of his days regretting that the two of them had to become employed around-the-clock. During the week, he would leave school and go directly to the post office where he worked past sundown, but when Alina left school, she wouldn't waste even an hour outside of the hospital that she stayed shackled to – including weekends. She shadowed surgeons there when she wasn't doing chores or cleaning up spills at the discretion of the nurses. The staff had developed a dependency on her willingness to perform any and all upkeep across the entire building at the order of anybody with a problem, meaning the same voices were constantly attempting to dissuade her from the path of learning surgery so they could overwork her as a nurse instead. However, she never worked out of naïveté, nor ignorance. The red tape that the rest of the staff laid down for years did effectively nothing to prohibit her, as she had either sat in on or helped with every surgery her father had undergone to date, so the disapproving grown men in green scrubs had since realized that they could do very little to keep her out of the operating room, or to dampen the restless desire she had to find a career within it.

Napping throughout the day was the only way she managed to prevent crashing on the job, but this habit resulted in her dozing off in enough of her classes to force her teachers and the principal collectively to determine she would have to attend daily lunch detention in the auditorium for all the hours she needed to make up just to prevent preliminary failure of the school year based on attendance. Walter had complete awareness of how sore he made himself in his attempts to try and conceive a way around the grim reality that he wasn't going to be getting any chances to get to see Alina that day if he couldn't get into the auditorium during lunch. Regardless of that he still chose to fantasize about spending whole hours at a time with her the way they used to be able to, even though the memory based fiction being conjured up in his head by utilizing scenes of the past only ended up playing into his illness of heart during the present.

It was possible for him to manage a miracle on rare days, spending all of lunch with her, and the chance of that happening did by itself give him hope – even if his options were few and the odds at success meager. If he took the hallway that started at the far corner of the cafeteria, he would be able to sneak into a side door to the auditorium, but he ran the risk of getting caught by the wandering eyes of any of the semi-omniscient coaches who liked to stand around outside the gym during lunch. The most reliable method involved merely approaching whatever faculty member they had stationed out front and try to convince them that he should be allowed in to see Alina, but that required someone being at the door who either didn't care about the rules or was sympathetic to Walter's cause. His heart was put up on a daily basis on a single gamble that he'd just have to take his chances on when the time came, but until then, he knew to ignore the thought of it because of the way it built on his anxiety.

He flicked the burnt paper butt across the street and closed his eyes. 'Survive until Friday, skip the full moon and the clocktower entirely and go straight to the hospital to see her. You can take cold comfort that if you get nothing else from the world to sustain yourself by the time the week ends, you'll be with her for that night in the very least,' he thought, barely able to maintain the train of thought itself over his intense sensory stimulation: the gushing of blood in his heart as his mind lapped itself every second. Like demons, fear manifested inside him and danced to the tune of his high hopes. He tried breathing through his nose until his lungs were filled, exhaling fully out of his mouth while counting the spaces between each breath.

The roaring sound of the yellow school bus coming around the corner snapped his eyes open, and he found himself engrossed in reality yet again.

'You can be stronger than this;' he thought, 'you have to be.'

II – B

Walter came down in a spiral like a plane missing a wing, his dreams fading to the back of his conscious and his awareness slowly surfacing.

"Walter."

His brow furrowed: a twitching muscle reaction. He was still deep in his mind and had no awareness of his own frustration even as it was occurring.

"Walter."

The bubble of his slumbering bliss was cracking.

"Walt."

A face devoid of eyes, ears, or a nose appeared before him, calling out.

"Walt."

The ground dropped out from under him and he took to plummeting.

"Walter!"

His shoulders shook as his mother gripped them and yanked him back and forth. He took a sharp breath and his eyelids peeled wide open, his ears flooded with noise from the blood rushing into them.

"Yeah?" he asked meekly. His pupils were flashing from left to right as he studied her fearful countenance. She was wearing her usual blue suit and her hair was done up stiff like a corpse.

"Brielle will be here any moment – were you up late last night? You were sleeping like a rock." Her tone was weighty with worry.

"I think? I can't remember, really." His memory was riddled with gaps and contradictions, forcing him to throw out faces and details that were flashing in pictures of the past he was certain never actually took place.

Walter's mother dropped his shoulders out of the tight grip that had been holding them and suddenly pulled him into a nonconsensual hug. "Oh, you must have been caught up in the trauma. It's alright; we all have to deal with grief in our own ways. It'll all get easier once the anniversary passes this Friday, I promise." She was speaking in a voice strained with emotion.

He had not the first fucking clue what she was on about, despite him frantically trying to conjure up the context to what she was in fact saying.

His mother whispered from over his shoulder, "Everyone misses Rachel; don't feel guilty for trying to move on past the tragedy."

Walter's blood froze in his veins. "Yeah, I must have lost sleep last night over the thought of her missing from our lives," he spoke robotically. "I keep reliving the day it happened."

"Oh Walt," she said, beginning to sob, "I'm so sorry, I'm so sorry –" her voice hollowed out into a whisper "– I'm so sorry." Her breath reeked of red wine and there was a splotchy stain on the edge of her shoulder.

"Mom, are you going to be alright to go into work today?" he asked her.

"Huh? What do you –" She traced his eyes down to the spot on her shoulder. "Oh! I didn't want you to know – your father is too afraid to tell me that I should know better given the time of year. This is just for today: I promise it's not going to become a habit," she said in a tone that was almost pleading.

"Alright, if you say so Mom," he replied warily. "Do you think I could –"

"Yes; please do get ready," she said, reading her son's mind. She got up with a start and vanished from his room.

The sudden absence of anyone in his room created a vacuum of energy that was in complete contrast to the raging wildfire taking place in his brain. He was trying to pace out his breaths, he being full of adrenaline due to his sudden terror. He scratched his eyebrows and his eyes blinked rapidly as he scanned the posters and decorations scattered around his room – all the while his thoughts tumbled down a mountain of realizations to reach the ground of actuality.

Walter's dresser mirror caught his attention, and his covers flew off of him as his feet planted on the floor, and in a hustled stupor he made his way up to it. All along its trimmed wooden border were polaroids tacked up of him with family, friends, but primary among them was the radiantly-blond girl who possessed a vibrant array of facial expressions that couldn't be described as anything less than angelic, and it was that girl who was evading identification by his lapsing memory. Walter plucked off a scenic picture of the two of them located on the deck of a beach house, laid out on pool chairs, clinking colorful margaritas in ornate glasses, sporting tropical outfits, and beaming ear-to-ear in unison. He looked into the background and saw a winding lake cutting in front of a pine forest. In an instant, he could recall piping her in three different spots across those woods during a single day. He stared in awe at his massive smile: he never could've imagined himself looking so satisfied..

"Brielle..." Walter softly spoke, his eyes drifting up from the photograph. Back behind him, he turned to notice posters of movies over his bed that were foggy in terms of the details he could remember. There was *Death Toll*, with a phone booth that was splattered with blood along its inside. *Double Time* featured soldiers wading through a muddy trench in the rain as lightning crashed across the sky. Among the others was *Low Whisper*, one with a woman who had red hair in a bob and was placing an index finger vertically over her lips, her spaced-out eyes staring dead ahead.

Wherever the Grass Grows Greener

      To say that Walter felt out of sorts would have been an understatement – he might as well have been the first man on Mars: a vagrant in an alien land. This room was the only place on the planet he could think of that was familiar to him, but entirely despite that he felt as though he had no business being there. Voices from all over the house played over radios and television sets as usual, but he felt like he hadn't woken up to any noise at all in years. The activity buzzing all around him seemed to mesh together in a carnival of sound, cheering in unison for a celebration of the moment.

      He knew, however, that it served as a poor distraction from a much grimmer reality. His mom wasn't going to wrap up her drinking that morning, he figured to himself: she'd be drunk that afternoon, late into the evening, and for a good majority of the coming week so long as her stomach could keep up with her.

      Walter tried to imagine what life had been like back before Rachel had even left for college, when she was in the marching band and that meant Walter would go to every football game with his parents to cheer on the team and his sister. Back then, he thought so loftily about what high school must be like due to the way Rachel kept so busy with extracurricular gatherings. Fast forward just a few years and now he can barely survive his classes, or any of the sporting events that drew in his whole neighborhood like floodwater down a storm drain. He knew the silver lining to his current living situation was that someday soon he'd be off at college or doing something occupational, sharing a place with Brielle: the two of them building towards a future so rosy that even the most resolute pessimist would place his hope. His heart ached at the realization that his parents would be left to ruminate over their lost past until the end of their days.

      It immediately struck him that he had on only boxers and that his ride to school would be pulling up with his girlfriend in mere minutes, if that. He tore open drawers, flipping through layers of clothing. All the while, he made thoughtful pictures in his head of what might look satisfactory together, and he had arranged his outfit in an instant. Dressing himself, he looked himself up and down in the mirror. His hair held its shape without him having to brush it, his shoulders squarely back to pop his chest out through his white t-shirt, and his jeans loosely fit over his legs. It was nearly unbelievable how he was staring at a person who looked skin-level to be perfectly content and well-put-together, but really just under a sheet-thin barrier was a stew of revolting issues of identity.

Walter wanted to fit into his own skin so badly, yet he would only be satisfied if he could to change places with someone more deserving of his spot in the world: someone who would do his life proper justice. He didn't know what living up to one's potential meant; he didn't even know if that was something the average person ever got to do for a single time.

Being yourself was like a horror show, because the individual details are never going turn out the way you'd ideally want them to, but your only option at any moment is to divulge in numbness and resort to just holding out hope that maybe the stars will align in your favor and that you might move another little step closer to final sanctuary. Watching himself in the mirror, he didn't think there was a such thing as sanctuary – not for him. He was a wandering soul, cursed to dream the unattainable, and to attain only more dreams.

He emerged from his bedroom toting his backpack and trotting jauntily like a thief through a crowded marketplace. Sunlight pouring in through the front bay window refracted in the glass chandelier hanging from the top of the foyer. He passed through the second story hallway where they kept the busts of his great aunt Eunice and his great grandfather Jordan. Against the opposite wall that faced the front of the house was the life-sized painting of him, his parents, and Rachel.

Rachel.

Walter couldn't reconcile his own ignorance: how did he forget about her crash? Rachel had been gone for nearly two years and his lack of conscience dissolved him into the assumption that she was still out in the world, learning and loving at college. The news that a truck had ran her off of the highway was still as fresh in his mind as it was incomprehensible. Time seemed to have stacked up against itself and was resisting its own expiration, everything occurring and reoccurring in a tumbling cycle like history.

It felt in an instant like his whole past was coming back to him: his pony rides at Ballah's Ranches, his cousins teaching him to wrestle in their family gym, fishing with his sister on a placid Rabbit Woods Lake, and drifting around in a restless stupor all weekend camping down in the Northwoods due to his inability to go to sleep as the harsh winds whipped the canvas tent around. Conversely, the current moment of him moving through the hallway, caught up in times elapsed, seemed to be a vivid memory; already over before it even had a chance to happen. Did it come to mind that his anxiety was a product of his feelings of unworthiness? That he was only unable to move on because he felt like he deserved nothing but was bestowed with more than he could ever fantasize of having? The harder he tried to rationalize his place in the world, the more it seemed like some glaring oversight of the universe that he was alive for another day.

The morning air that Walter smelled was sweet like Dutch chocolate and fresher than the produce aisle. Was it a coincidence that the seasons echoed his moods? That he'd spend the better half of the year in a wistful stupor, devoid of fear until autumn settled in when he would come face-to-face with the reminder that he hadn't changed or evolved in any form? He had always assumed that he would someday have personal growth to show for his time spent lounging around, because his sister was constantly expanding her horizons, growing into new incarnations of her unique self, and all his life foolish bliss led him to believe that he'd one day be out and doing things how she managed to do them, if not for a miracle than any other reason. It was commonplace for her to discover new passions and display them for all to see, successfulness coming second only to personal exploration.

Walter frequently wondered how the two of them were even related by blood: she had been exemplary in her ability to adapt to a volatile and ignorant world, whereas he was a doddering, complacent excuse for a student that claimed to be learning but was actually just biding his time for his chance to perish. He knew that he wasn't gathering momentum – it's a sorry situation that one finds themselves in where the only viable path appears to be complete incompetency and nostalgia for days that weren't even noteworthy the first time through. Was he supposed to have faith that he'd someday change for the better? Or was he merely to blame himself as he slowly capsized into his own heightened expectations? The only certainty that he could hold onto was that everyone around him would continue to forge ahead, undaunted by the inequity beset upon them. It drove him mad how he could have virtually no idea who he was but was still told to stay true to himself, whomever that was.

"We're always at the doorstep to our perfect selves – you just have to get your bearings before you can take that final step through," Rachel once told him when he was a child as he was crying over a comment that Uncle Marcus had made about how he needed to figure himself out if he was to ever become anything.

His surroundings were eerily in oneness, which unnerved him slightly. He didn't fancy the idea of there being a conspiracy of infinite size and scope in motion around him – in fact, he preferred complete and utter chaos over that, for at least godforsaken debauchery would request neither morals nor ethics from its occupants. There would be no ultimatum of character, and his composition of self would never be called into question: he could be as lowly as a hog and he'd never have to answer to a higher power regarding his justification for such sins. What of morality commands a need for truth or righteousness? Were these not just words to describe the collective vanity project constantly under construction by those who command the masses? Public sovereignty was just dinner talk between the people determining the quality or even existence of such a thing, and he shuddered to consider the reality that even still there existed people who believed the world to be innocent and accommodating, like how a boy who had never been on a farm might be foolish enough to mark a coyote as being a docile creature. No, it was nastiness that kept clocks ticking.

A wave of clarity swept over him: Walter was consistently concerned regarding his reassurance that he wasn't in someone else's shoes entirely, but he had a sudden awareness that if he didn't want to put up with the trouble of being unique in the world, then the world must not want to put up with the trouble of him trying either. It was just as well that he kept his expectations subdued, because the one characteristic that all tragic figures share is unstifled anticipation. At the same time it was difficult for him to believe that he didn't really want anything for himself – because when he considered his girlfriend, he wanted to earn the Moon and give it to her to hold onto. Brielle had expensive tastes – well, no, she just had an expensive background. The truth was that she was pacified by the things that came and went without the exchange of a single cent but was infinitely mired by the price that was attached to every motion, every usage of energy.

The concerning idea that Brielle was just putting up with him for the sake of passing the time did occasionally cross his mind. It was entirely unclear to him as to whether his concern derived from the fact that she outclassed him entirely as a mate, or if she was actually using him as a springboard to find an even better boyfriend, or if she had no interest in him altogether and that instead she had some sort of masochistic complex that made misery taste like honey. In a perfect world, he'd live around the clock being convinced that she really did love him, and that their relationship was something genuine, but it was her teetering moods that tipped him off. If he really was the boy that she longed for, why couldn't he bring her stability and comfort?

He couldn't imagine himself being anything more than a sideshow figure to her tumultuous time on the planet: an extraneous filler that's only purpose was just to make things pass more pleasurably. He had never once heard her say "I wasn't sure, but you've made me come to my senses. Thank you, Walter. Things seemed broken before, but you've reassured me." She had never said anything to that effect – not that she had ever come close to saying the opposite, however. As far as he could tell from the signs she gave off, he himself might as well have been the root of her existential anxiety. She was flowy and drawn-out when she'd speak, but her cards were always kept close to her chest: there was no procuring information from her that she wasn't ready to willingly hand over.

That unfortunate Sunday during Makers' Weekend was the closest he had ever come to losing his temper with her. She had spent their whole time there that day parading him around the campground like he was some kind of ornament, making her best effort to get reactions out of him and the horde of girls whom were fishing, painting, and playing music. Maybe it was all because he was the only male within a twenty-mile stretch that she felt like making a minstrel out of her boyfriend, but at every opportunity she had, she would be hanging off of him and fondling him and making him swoon for her. To say that it was humiliating would be a tragic oversimplification of the torment that was entertaining her charades. The entire time, she was doing everything in her power to force him into an erection, but he was resisting her on all counts. Despite the fight he was putting up, his balls were bluer than a folk singer. The campfire come-together at sunset had turned out to be the tipping point for him. They had been setting up string lights on posts as it got dark, and, having been the tallest one of the harem, he had been in charge of attaching the cords into the small indentations at the top of each post. As such, his arms had been up the whole time, holding and placing wire. He had nearly put them all up when Brielle leapt to her feet, pulled Walter's shirt up over his face, and began sucking on his nipple. The bench he had been standing on rocked from side-to-side due to his shock and he was a single misplaced toe from slipping off. Meanwhile, the whole mob of girls were in stitches, just falling amongst one another and pounding the ground as they gasped for air. The only thing that had been more swollen with blood than his penis was his face, and he had half a mind to chew her out for being so insensitive. He didn't even consider

Crowe

putting his hands on her as an option: he'd never have made it out alive from the whole legion of girls that surrounded them, amongst any of the endless other reasons as to why that would be a fatal course of action. No, the only option was to just take it – not like a man, but like someone trying to feign dignity and failing at all turns.

Brielle wasn't normally like that at all, however. For him, she was the most fair-tempered and just person he could ask for in his life. He'd have no concept of right from wrong but she'd tirelessly labor to keep him on his best path, guiding him like a stable keeper caring for a blind horse. It was her grace with which she conducted their union that impressed upon him the necessity of human charity and goodwill to meet one's ends, for if she wasn't there as his shepherd, he'd surely lose himself to his cantankerous and jaded inclinations. A sensitive heart hurts twice as hard, and it was one wicked burden that she had been stricken with from her childhood onwards: levity was something that evaded her entirely.

See, she had a sensitive composure much like that of a foxhound or the creatures that it might hunt. Her ear was always to the ground and the slightest rumble displaced her into a state of dismay that could only be described as shock caused by the cruel nature of human indifference. Every worldly interaction carried the weight and momentum of a cannonball, simple interactions being strict diplomatic relations in terms of severity in her mind. She took her place in the world seriously, as it took her as well: she deserved every ounce of her stature, but she pushed herself to the edge and stayed there for the sake of pleasure and excellency alike. Her rogue nature made her hard to reach at times, but she told him the truth and he kept it with him.

He could only beg reality to permit Brielle some joy or relief, but her every step was accompanied by a lash of times past that scarred her empathy in ways that couldn't be healed. She was thoroughly convinced that she was the only one in the world who felt the way she did, and she was further convinced that if anyone was to take her place, they'd display all of the ethically and morally reprehensible behaviors that she did – as well as be as cold and cutting in her speech as she could be at times. Frankly, she didn't think it was an issue if she hurt anyone's feelings – as far as she was concerned, she was doing them the favor of toughening them up for free.

Observing the silvery dust that lined the surface of the black floor vase which held a tall, three-leaved fern made Walter appreciate the intricacies of average living. If he could, he'd carry a camera with him everywhere he'd wander to record each and every one of them, but he realistically couldn't do so without risking coming across as being queer. He didn't want to lose all the brief moments that would inevitably slip through the cracks in his memory just days after making them, because the way things seemed presently, he didn't have the first inkling if they even had any value or purpose. If he at least could again and again revisit the days he had already survived through photos, then he might gradually be able to deduce what the meaning of all the collective moments was. The way things stood, there was no telling why events occurred down the avenues that they chose in his life. Why was it that he'd go days without seeing anything of any significance, and then a day might come along that would drop him to his knees? It all felt so needless that he didn't even want to know what the reasoning was for such torture.

"Walter – are you getting ready? Are you awake yet? Brielle will be here any moment now!" his mother called from the other side of the house. He heard her voice through the woodwork, muffled.

There was no reason for him to reply. His mother wouldn't remember his answer, just as she didn't remember waking him up herself. There was no dealing with her: she was as stony as an inmate, but had the disposition of a character straight from the theater. She'd become unhinged at the most minute comments and it barely took more than a few minutes for another crisis to pop up after one passed. The house suddenly had become a list of unpleasantries that needed tending to in the last two years, and she ran him and his father around on a whim – usually for cleaning purposes. If they weren't busy with her chores as she directed them, then she was alone, brooding, as it brought her bittersweet catharsis in the indulgence of begging reality to give her another try at the things that she could no longer help. She was stuck at the top of a lighthouse on the rocks, staring out at a gray sky over choppy waters and keeping watch for a ship that she already knew had long capsized.

Sometimes it occurred to him that his parents were bankrupt when it came to hope. They had put up the largest stake that two people can ever come together to make, and they got swindled out of the only part of it that truly mattered to them, only moments after the eternity they spent getting everything right. It was just as crushing to their egos as it was their mental health, as Rachel had been the star of the show for them. If it didn't relate to her, it wasn't worth considering as important, because she was naturally just going to be successful in all ventures she undertook. Her opinion was worth its weight in gold; they'd have sold the house if she would've went so far as to convince them of such a thing. Without her to prop the two of them up, they soon realized she had been the only person keeping their spirits aflame, and her void rendered their patience and benevolence emaciated.

Emancipating himself from his cumbersome and unbearable thoughts with a shake of his head, he began to ponder what the clocktower would have in store for them during the full moon on Friday: a lot of possibilities open up for partying when an alternate dimension is accessible for a night. It was almost like renting out an island, except instead of the open sea being what would surround them, it would be the highway that stretched around Cobey Pond and the strip mall on the other side of it – just devoid of any occupants, and completely still.

It amused him to try and reason out how the occurrence even came about: did everybody temporarily leave the planet for the evening, or did reality split in two, leaving the people around the tower in another space entirely? He was practically certain that time didn't break in any way or do something strange, because everything looked exactly the same around them when they'd get there as well as when they'd leave. The only thing he knew for certain was that having sex out there was particularly gratifying, because it meant he was the only guy he knew outside of his friend group who could say that he was able to get it in another dimension. Brielle always seemed more laid back when they were out there, but maybe that was just because the location was scenic and remote.

Walter approached the top stair, peering down below him. In the living room, his grimacing father stood leaning back against the bar like a cowboy out of a Western, toying around with a whiskey glass and dappered down in a gray pinstripe suit. Walter shuffled down the rounded staircase, sliding his hand along the banister, and hurried towards the door.

"Come here, boy," his father ordered without shifting his view.

"Dad, I really need to –"

"I said come *here*." He pointed to the floor and planted both of his feet, clicking his soles against the wood.

Walter hung his neck and dawdled up to his father. Off in his mother's study on the other side of the foyer from where they were standing, he could hear a light jazz melody being played from a record. Cymbals were being tapped in pace to the warm voice of the singer.

'Cause it's a loooud cir-cus and it's a wiiild pro-gram.
We've got a looot to ask for and our heaaarts: we must fill them.'

He didn't know what to expect. That was the worst part of it all; how unpredictable his parents always had to be. It was their way of proving themselves to him, it seemed, because if they telegraphed their intentions, it might make them seem weak or compromising. No, they had to be windier than a dirt road and keep him guessing just to maintain some sort of image in the same way a politician wields an atmosphere of clout to keep their constituents in line. His feelings regarding the relationship between him and them did, in fact, frequently feel like how an unwilling participant must regard some professional that's been appointed to their life, such as a parolee and their officer. They had a business to run, reputations to build, and stature to seek. They had no time for anything if it didn't improve their standing in the rat race.

"Sir?"

"Hello, son," his father said, his face directed Walter's way but his eyes glued to the record player across from them like it was an ex-girlfriend sitting at the far side of a restaurant. He then set his head completely forward in the same direction as his eyes. "Be straight with me: how well was your mother holding it together when she woke you up?"

Walter looked at his dad to speak. "If I'm being honest, not very. The first thing she started talking about was Rachel." He decided to face the record player as well. His voice dropped to a low whisper and he said "I had forgotten about it already. It almost seemed typical of you guys."

His father sipped his whiskey and smacked the inside of his cheeks against his gums as if he was swishing down cola. "She's drunker than a toddler, and not even bothering to come up for breath. She's careening down a steep cliff, Walter."

"I worry about her too," Walter murmured.

"I didn't ask for you to be sorry," his father barked, then downed the glass, faced the bar to place it down, swallowed hard while frowning like a two-year old brat, and gripped the counter, leaning over and watching its polished surface. "I don't have to wait for you to tell me to know that she doesn't do much for you, because you practically live with your girlfriend –"

A horn honked twice outside. His father didn't even flinch, his eyes stuck in position.

"Brielle," Walter said wistfully, looking to the door and then back again to his father. "Dad, sir –"

"Quiet, I'm talking." His father cleared his throat. "But for me, having her versus not is the difference between night and day, and I need to know that when she needs something, she can get it. Do you follow?"

"Uh – Yes, I follow."

"Let me be clear: she needs us to be there for her to satisfy her every need. She's on her last legs, and if she snaps, it's going to plunge this house straight into hell, mark my words."

"I'll do anything you want that'll prevent that, sir."

His father took a seat at the bar and began passing off a frosty bottle of brandy between his hands like he was an infant with a guinea pig. His gaze was tactical and measured how a sniper's or a chemist's might be. He analyzed the space in front of him as if someone was about to leap out at him, then finally poured some brandy out over the ice in his glass and observed its tense surface. "Like water passing over a stone, your mother's exterior is wearing down as a result of time. There is no returning to the past, as you know, so once the day comes that she separates from reality, neither of us will have the capability to pull her back. Any opportunity conceivable we have to deescalate the circumstances of her situation must be taken without consideration for the consequences."

"Flowers."

"What?" his father exclaimed, snapping his stare straight up and yelling right into the wall.

"Flowers – Mom is always going on about the wildflowers that Rachel loved to go pick."

"The ones in Tailcreek Woods?"

"I think so," Walter answered lightly. "She'll want to bring her some."

"Flowers...." He was shifting his jaw around. "Yeah, that's good. Tell her that they're from me."

"Yes sir – Of course."

His father turned to face him for the first time. "I won't even get into the fact that you were out all last night with the car," he stated plainly, absorbing his son's reaction: Walter's expression went blank and his face turned pale like the moon. "That's right; I'm onto you," he declared sternly and solemnly.

The horn honked twice more, the second time being several seconds long.

Walter did a double-take from his father's face to the door, his eyes as frantic as a rodent's, when he suddenly blurted out like an auctioneer: "I'm-so-sorry-but-I've-got-to-leave." In an instant, he turned completely and bolted through the front door.

"Don't get lazy on me!" his father called from behind him, his tone ominous like a black cloud on the horizon.

Forever and always, running away seemed to be the only appropriate solution to Walter's problems. He wasn't just fleeing from his mother's icy love, or his father's dictatorial grip over the household: he was on the run from every accusation that had ever been slung his way. Because to him, he wasn't capable of contending any attack on his character. He deserved the criticism just as he deserved any doubt that might befall him. There is no such thing as a beautiful machine in the same way that there is no such thing as a noble animal, and in regards to Walter's single-sided nature, he was devoid of complexities and resembled a pauper to someone with any sophistication. Was it just unfortunate circumstances that caused him to be an underwhelming creature, writhing and begging for distinction? He just wanted to arrive at a place where he wasn't expected to be full and detailed like a resumé or impressive in any manner that would put him out of sorts to maintain. It was irrelevant either which way, however. For everyone that was keeping score, he would never match the leading contenders, because he was swiftly striding in the opposite direction of the race and heading straight for the way out. It wasn't that he didn't desire supremacy over the competition – quite the opposite, in fact: he wanted to lord over his peers just out of spite. It was the desperation of it all that repulsed him to his very core.

III – A

The yellow school bus whipped directly in front of Walter and the double doors opened with a jet of compressed air.

'Try not to make it too obvious,' he thought, struggling to get to his feet. He stepped up off the ground into the bus and dropped down on the first seat across from the driver, who suddenly stood up and turned around.

"You reek kid – get to the back," the bus driver declared, his arm outstretched and finger pointed.

"Wh-What?" Walter paused for a second internally, wondering if confrontation was the answer.

"Back. Now. Go." A few seconds passed, after which the bus driver dropped his jaw and looked at Walter with shocked disbelief. "Do you not speak English all of a sudden?!" he asked incredulously.

Walter got up and began trudging down the aisle amid the noise of jeers and cackling from the other kids on the bus.

"Wal-ter's a dope fiend, Wal-ter's a dope fiend," chanted a girl twirling her two long braids.

"You just get dropped off from a Grateful Dead concert? Pahahaha," exclaimed a lanky kid as he slapped his thighs.

"Jah, mon – really week'ed stuff, mon," said a redhead boy who was leaning in as he rotated his fist around, holding out his pinkie and thumb.

"Different cultures," Walter hissed while passing, getting in his face for a quick second, "you pale fuck – but nice try."

The bus was almost entirely full, every seat filled by two occupants as well as consumed by unending conversation, except for a single row towards the back that was empty on one side and had just Leland on the other – it was no surprise that Leland of all people had a row to himself.

'Fuck,' Walter thought as he begrudgingly took the open seat across from him.

"You know they sell spray-on deodorant, right? It really helps if you plan on frying your brain before school without reeking like dogshit," Leland said, chortling. "Alright, come on, I'll stop; just talk to me."

"I've got fuck all to say to you, Lee – just leave me be," Walter replied, looking out the window. His neighborhood of decrepit trailers and obtuse drainage ditches made the feeling of hopelessness double down.

"You know, Alina practically lives in the hospital?" he asked, trying to sound as invasive as possible. "I think she'd have something to say about your smoking habits if she caught you."

"She knows," Walter grunted.

"And she still doesn't dump your ass?" scoffed Leland as he reared back his head. "Pfft, I almost can't believe it, but it's not surprising that she has no standards."

The school bus leapt upwards as it went over a bump in the road. Metal creaked as the tires slammed back down.

"So, what do *you* think happened to Abe Carelin?" Leland asked Walter. "Do you think it was the mob, or an old enemy, or –"

"What in the hell are you talking about?" Walter exclaimed the moment before realization struck him that he had just unintentionally made a fatal mistake. "Forget I asked," he quickly said with a swish of his hand, as if to undo his question.

"You don't know who Abe Carelin is?" Leland cracked into a large grin, sucked in his breath, and stood up to face the front of the bus. "Hey, everyone: Walter doesn't know who Abe Carelin is!"

This statement was met with intense laughter from all over the bus, preceded as well as followed by unrestrained chattering.

"Walt, I guess you just don't follow these sorts of things, but Abe Carelin was a director who released over a dozen full-length films last week and then went missing on Sunday. The police still have no idea where to begin looking," said Leland, matter-of-fact.

"OK? Great? I really couldn't care fucking less," Walter grumbled, arms crossed so that his bicep was flat, making the muscle appear much wider than usual while still staring out the window and wishing he could afford cigarettes again. The bus was going down a thin stretch of road that cut through a forest.

"Gavin Winchester was his best friend, and he's going to be on the radio today during third period to talk about what he knows so far in the investigation," Leland stated.

"You want to know what I'll be doing then? Nothing, because I'll have third block." He shook his head, unable to believe the idiocy he had to endure.

"The two of them have went from being nobodies like yourself to 'the hottest film producers of an era,' is what people are saying – how can you say that you just don't care? Walt, don't you know what culture is?" He was speaking at Walter like he was a halfwit with a political opinion.

"Culture? Culture doesn't have shit to do with me and I don't have shit to do with it." He couldn't help but to frown intensely.

"You know that they spent years making these things, right? And then a single week after his films to get released" Leland extended out all of his fingers to mimic an explosion "poof. Think about that: you're in his place and you spend years directing films and don't even get to see how anyone feels about a single one. Can't you at least appreciate how mysterious that is?" Leland asked.

Walter faced him and held out his hand like he was expecting a handshake. "Lee, I'm going to put this into terms that even a troglodyte like you could understand: these bigshot Hollywood phonies not only don't know that you exist, but even if they did, they'd forget about you so quickly that your fat mouth couldn't even get a single word in edgewise. You – don't – matter. Not to them, and certainly not to me," he said, and turned around.

"You know that the same applies to you?" Leland replied, pointing at him for emphasis.

"Uh, yeah. Yes, dickleaf, I do," he said contemptuously with a nod of his head. "Don't get it twisted."

"You don't even care that he's probably dead? This guy goes through the trouble of making hours of films for average people everywhere that he plans on brightening their lives up with, he disappears, and you can't even give a shit less. You're unbelievable Walt, absolutely unbe–"

"Lee, you're missing the point," spat Walter, beginning to lose his patience. "Even if he was still alive, he doesn't care if we discuss his life's work. Hell, he could be a ghost watching us talk about him right now, and it wouldn't even occur to him. We're just nobodies in a sea of nobodies, you complete fruitcake."

"That's so typical of you, Walter, to not understand the significance of something like this: not only is this the first time something like this happened in our lifetime, but this is the first time anything like this has ever happened and likely will ever happen. Try to imagine any other director who completely enveloped the public eye in a single week – the fact that you didn't know who he was before I told you just goes to show your true and undeniable ignorance," Leland stated enthusiastically.

"I'm fucking done, by the way. I really meant it when I said I've got jack shit to say if it involves you," he snarled.

"You know," he said, posturing himself like he was verging on groundbreaking new information, "it actually makes sense to me now that I stop and think why you're such a tepid bore: doesn't Alina have as much of a social conscious as a sea lamprey? From what I hear, talking to your girlfriend is like starting a conversation with someone who has Alzheimer's: she got less of a clue what other people are saying to her than what it even is that she's talking about. When you take to humping her like the two of you were a couple of dogs, does she just communicate in grunts or does she manage to fit in a word every now and again?"

"Pff, I thought the last thing you'd bring up is sex: you've got about as much of it as Mr. Clean has head lice," Walter guffawed. "And fucking watch it, by the way – I'd hate to have to hospitalize you because you said one too many things about my girlfriend to my face. Seriously, I won't like it, but I'll brain your ass – just test me," he said.

Leland adjusted his spot in his seat slightly, realizing he'd have to make a change in course if he was to keep pestering Walter. "So... Jimi Hendrix – do you think I could buy sometime?" he asked gingerly like a soldier toying with a grenade in his bunk.

"Can you do anything but be asinine and utterly mindless?" Walter asked flatly. "No, I will not give you anything, no matter how much cash you pretend to have," he said flatly. "Not that I have anything to sell, but that's beside the point – you're a snitch through and through, no matter what you say or whatever your reputation might be. I know your type: stir up shit and tell authority as soon as the situation gets unmanageable. The day I tell you when and where I'm getting anything at all is the day that I have an inclination to go to jail – if you think I'd go so far enough out of my way to *sell* you something then you have more mental deficiencies than either of us have even considered."

Horns honked, the sounds passing one another as cars flew through the intersection they were crossing.

"Oh, please," Leland scoffed, "you really think that I'm some threat to your safety? You don't give anybody but yourself an ounce of credit – why would you expect me to be so poisonous that I'd intentionally abuse your trust?"

"Yeah, you'll have to forgive me for this one, Lee, but you're a fantastic, double-dealing bitchboy who really doesn't care what happens one moment to the next so long as somebody is getting slighted or insulted." Walter replied, so filled with hostility that he was practically geared up for a brawl. "I remember you going to Conrad's party out in the boondocks and you told Sonya who poured that keg of warm beer on her head from the second-story window just so that she'd start a fistfight with someone. You're about as principled as a mining director in the Congo. So take your little business proposition, slip it down your urethra, and twist,"

"You're free to cut the shit," Leland said snidely, talking right past what Walter was telling him. "I know what the real crux of the issue is here: Lando and Cisco are so paranoid that they refuse to admit anybody outside of twelve people on the planet have any needs at all or even exists for any reason apart from being targets to rob and goons to borrow, and I don't make the list of those dozen people. But that doesn't mean that you have to treat their every order like scripture – try actually thinking independently for one time before old age finally takes you."

"Apparently I haven't been clear enough," Walter started, ready to close out this conversation, "so let me *really* dumb shit down here: no one sells to you. Anything – nothing at all. You get zero deals from anyone on anything because you rival child molesters in how low you stand socially. Nobody wants to do you any favors, nobody wants to look out for you, and most definitely of all, nobody wants to have you rely on them. Any association with you is a liability, and I'd have to be thoroughly out of my mind to do anything but tell you to go fuck yourself, because I'd never hear the end of it if anybody even had the most minor inkling that we were on any kind of amicable basis with one another. You want bud? Grow it yourself – or steal it, or do something unfathomable and grow a likeable bone in your body. Making a single friend might not be such a bad decision for you – I could see not running up and trying to slap people in the face with your three-incher and just talking to them instead as being a very fortuitous change in tactics. But don't expect me to lift a fucking finger for your navel-gazing ass – and if you mention either of those two again to me by name I'm going to punch you in the throat just to save me the trouble of being asked later why I was talking to you about them. You're not one of us, so don't even try to mention anyone that has anything to do with the people I take orders from."

"Aw, c'mon – you go so far as to do your damn Fist List every year with the rest of the group and you don't even feel slightly inclined to use the privilege it earns you for anything fun? You lot are out and out psychopaths: any group that requires itself to get revenge on a scheduled basis is straight-up demented," remarked Leland.

"It's an exercise in discipline: if we can keep track of people who have done us wrong and get back at them in turn, then that speaks to our resilience as a cohesive unit," Walter riffed back at him, staying calculated in his cadence. "But it's definitely not just us – go check out any other school district in the city and ask if it's standard fare. Ringleaders have to find some way to maintain exclusive membership. People like you are just after free rides and appearances, so to all of us: if it means we each have to get back at five people every year in order to keep the leeches off, then all the more reason to join up. Because, Lelend, if you can't be reactive and comfortable in conflict, then you don't deserve to keep the company of people who can."

"But isn't it true that you yourself aren't doing your Fist List for the year?" Leland asked. "So being around the group shouldn't be completely restricted, because, let's be honest, you're nothing special."

"That's irrelevant: me being excused of doing my List doesn't mean just anybody can come into the fold. We're still only reserved for the people we know and trust," replied Walter dismissively.

"Don't act like you're not going to just be lounging around at the full moon on Friday: you all don't even party, just fill couches," stated Leland.

"You're actually insane if you think we'd actually want you around for the full moon – and I'm almost certainly not even going, because I'm going to be with Alina in the hospital that night, so I don't know why you'd expect me to be able to get you a ticket," Walter told him, irritated that he had to be his group's newsboard for overly-obnoxious plucks.

"Can't you just ask if I can come around sometime during the day for long enough to buy?" Leland insisted. "Why would that put you so far out of the way?"

"I feel stupid for saying it, but I guess we're really at this point: it doesn't fucking work that way. If you could understand what a relationship built on respect for boundaries requires, you wouldn't have to ask inane questions like 'Why don't this group of people who look at me like a flattened roach on the bottom of their shoe sole not want to risk their neck just to do something for my own benefit solely?' Seriously, you've got rocks in your head if you think pure persistence is enough to make people stop despising you overnight. You've got no contacts, no connects, and no way out of your sorry standing as a bottom feeding, pig-headed wastrel." Walter was glowering with rage, ready to cut down the next line of conversation that he was going to inevitably be force-fed.

"You're doing a poor job of disguising your intentions: you're just fearful that your ass is going to get cut out of the picture, so you try to act like you play from the sidelines and are all mysterious and your loyalties are reserved, but in reality, you're a scared little bitch who doesn't know what he'd do if he didn't have his handful of acquaintances around to protect and take care of him," Leland said with a chuckle, obviously pleased with himself.

Walter suddenly realized the error of his ways and remembered he had an out for the very standoff he was caught in. "You really think you can ride with us? Something actually has you convinced you could keep up? Want to know what happened to Joey Garcia?"

"Huh?" Leland blurted, caught completely off-guard. "He got both of his pinkie toes broken and has to stay home until he can walk again – everyone knows that, you out-of-the-loop louse."

"Hey, dumbass," Walter replied devilishly, grinning like a hyena covered in gore and staring across the aisle with the predatory eyes of a gunman, "you're missing a key detail: he's not coming back. He never is – not to our school, anyway. You want to know why?" He paused, waiting for a response. Leland had said nothing, instead allowing for the raucous chatter of the bus to overtake them. Walter leaned in so he could whisper: "Because they're finding a new school for him: one for the blind. You think that when the people he blackmailed finally caught up to him that they were just going to let him go with a minor impairment? One that would have only kept him out of the system for a few months at the most? No – you clearly haven't heard about Charlemagne the way that I have. He does one thing for the clout and rumors that then becomes public knowledge and he does another for hard results that only a select few get full disclosure on." He sat back against the window, looking through slit eyes like a detective on a hunch and locked his jaw to shift it back and forth.

"That's bullshit if I've ever heard it," exclaimed Leland, distressed at how out-of-control this talk had gotten. "You don't know that – it's story after story with you types of people. All of you act criminal but you're just little sewing circles gossiping. He crossed his arms defiantly as if that gave him a stronger position in the situation.

"Well, again, dumbass, you don't know one thing that *I* do, but I can let you in on it – just this one time." Walter reared forward, yanking his tightly-stuffed leather wallet from his back pocket and then sitting back down while he casually flipped through its contents. "See," he sniffed and rubbed under his nose with his free hand "because of the two names you mentioned earlier – the same ones that should not be repeated in my presence – I got given a gift to get any hecklers away from me. They realized that I was a weak link for mosquitos like you who are always trolling around for a plug, and if I was ever going to convince people to really fuck off, I'd need something easily recognizable that I could show the freeloaders to prove they had no business with me or with the rest of us if they don't pay the entry fee. So they gave me this –" he flipped out a polaroid.

"Jesus! Oh, fucking Christ!" Leland cried, covering his mouth.

"– to hold onto. " Walter snorted to clear his nose. "If it's not obvious, those are Joey's eyeballs, and –"

"His glasses..." he whimpered.

Walter stashed the photo and replaced his wallet. "Good, so you do know. I was afraid you might not catch on – it's one of your weakest characteristics, if I have to admit."

"But Charlemagne and L-"

"Don't say my people's fucking names to me," growled Walter.

"Charlemagne's crew and your lot don't get along; you're two groups of people who are notorious for being uncooperative," Leland figured, trying to do anything to calm his unnerved state.

"The interesting part of that, too, is that these kinds of things shift around daily, so two people might not have a single thing to say to each other for years at length, but then one moment more passes and the people they respectively listen to the closest say that both of their sides are going to get friendly, and everybody had best make chums with one another. It can last for a week, for a day, for an afternoon, for a meal, for a sale, or even just for a single blunt. But when these coalitions do happen, it's not circumstance or random odds how it comes together, because the people at the top stay busy, scheming. Maybe I don't affiliate with people who ever speak to Charlemagne, or even appreciate him as either an individual or a leader, but when he thinks he'll need something from someone, he'll always end up getting it because he'll have already found something that the someone needs and have gotten it to them by that time, on the house and with an open tab of gifts to come, and it just so happened that I was the squeaky wheel who got picked out to be given the grease. All of this starting to make sense?" Walter stated chillingly.

Leland swallowed hard. "So all that to what end? Just to save you the trouble of explaining to people why you can't sell to them? We're not talking about very charitable people here, Walt: it's unusual that they'd look out for your feelings of all things."

"You're thinking about this from a very narrow point of view," Walter said, tenting his fingers. "If you have it in your head that nobody else has been shown this photograph by me, then you're damn wrong, because it's been around the block. The single reason you haven't heard word one about it until now is because I only show it when someone *really* needs to know who they're brushing shoulders with when it comes to dope-dealing territory – I'm just a third party that benefits from the whole process. I get tossed around, called this or that, but when the time comes and the other guy needs to know why he should watch himself, I clue him in on what really goes on behind the scenes.

"You hear all kinds of nasty truths when you shut up, don't speak unless spoken to, and do what you're told – but I know you wouldn't believe me because that's about the last thing you could conceive of as being worth doing. When I come around to talk to somebody, it's because one of us, someone more important, has other matters to attend to – or they don't want to risk their neck. Nobody's going to lay a finger on me: there's just nothing to gain from it. I lift the veil, it becomes obvious what's going on, and everybody takes a step back for a second. Sure, people get mad and treat me like an extension of some mob or a gang, but really it's just a careful little operation that we've all got a stake in protecting. All of us, except for you," he finished speaking with a contemptuous growl.

"You think you're special, then?" sneered Leland. "You're just a pawn to them. One day you'll cease to have any function as a member and they'll cull you just as quick as they did Joey."

"I don't think you've been listening: I'm as compliant as a show dog and if it wasn't for me, they'd have to expose themselves to constant hazards. They send me into some meetup and I don't have to worry for my safety, because an attack on me wouldn't be anything more than a waste of manpower. I'm not going to say that they need me, because they don't need anything, but I've got my place, no matter what it seems like – and believe it or not, you've got your place as well. Some people are just born useless, is all," Walter commented.

"Well I'm so glad that you've found peace serving the beck and call of gutter scum who only keep people around that they can use, abuse, profit from, or some combination of the three," said Leland critically. "Do you really think you're better than anybody because you take orders from some other kid? You're worse than any henchman, any pig: you chase knuckle-dragging, doped-up morons and do whatever they think makes for a good afternoon. You're going to grow up – assuming you grow up – and tell yourself that you were a monumental tool for the better part of your youth – " Leland slowly leaned in, hysterically grinning and muttered, "I can't imagine that it'll feel satisfying in any form to reach the end of your road and realize that rather than doing anything to develop your malnourished, fractured character, you catered to other sociopaths like some kind of ghetto butler. You'll croak regretting being the underling to underlings: a lackey from cradle to grave."

Walter just laughed. "Yeah, okay, I'll really look back on these days and tell myself 'Lee sure was right: I should've been a circumcised golden boy in the ways that he preached to me about – hypocritically, at that. If only I had thought of him as being more than a mite burrowing into the fuzzy nipple of a dead orangutan and chose to put him on even half of the mile-high pedestal that he lived on. What a fucking hero he was.' Seriously, just think for a second: you came to me for weed, and then you start talking all this good shit about how everyone who does what I do is just another deplorable excuse for a human being. You couldn't be less consistent if you had multiple personalities."

"I'm just passing the time – but you know what this really is?" Leland asked suddenly, riding a new wave of confidence. "Just one big complex to prove to yourself that you're not the sniveling wretch that everybody knows you really are. You do what people tell you to because you don't want to get stabbed in the back for forging your own path, and you can't step out of line because all you can think about how it's going to get back to you, and it utterly terrifies you: it really does. I've heard about how things go between you and Alina: you're so whipped that you don't dare contradict her on even the most obtuse issues, and you roll over so often that you might as well be a log. You don't even have enough of a spine to tell her that she's a loony bint who doesn't know what's good for her. She's off of her rocker ten ways 'til Sunday, and you're perfectly comfortable with your balls in her purse."

Walter had a moment of clarity: everything seemed so straightforward, so obvious. He had let the scene play itself out for far too long, and it was time to put a cap on it. He wasn't an enforcer by any means, but if it was between just taking being called chicken-hearted or losing his temper for a quick moment, he didn't even need to think about which of the two paths he'd take at this fork. A moment passed after he looked up to the front and saw the bus driver honking on the horn insistently while shouting at the car in front of him to move and then he pounced with the velocity of a cougar onto Leland, tackling him.

"What – the fuck! You freak!" Leland gasped, tearing up and barely able to speak as Walter grappled with him and put him into a chokehold.

"Yeah, fucker," Walter hissed into his ear, "you blow over like a paper man as soon as someone puts a little pressure on you. Say my girlfriend's name to me one more time and the tip of your nose is going to touch your bottom lip. Fucking try me." He detached and leapt back to his seat. A quick scan of the bus informed him that nobody was paying even half enough attention to have realized what just transpired around them, and as such, his battery went unrecorded. He wasn't sure if Leland continued talking or if he actually shut up for a change of pace, as he had set his focus completely in the other direction, transfixing it out the window for the first time in the entire ride.

The bus was stopped at an intersection, convenience stores and empty, dusty lots surrounding the space; dying trees and chain link fences separating them, but when the light turned green, traffic didn't move. The piercing, wailing cry of sirens came from the horizon and battered Walter's ears as four police cruisers raced through the intersection from the right and turned down the oncoming lane, two by two. The beating of his heart spiked back up in an instant and he felt the space behind his eyes tense for a moment – he had a few instances of the past come back to him of the few times when that siren had meant his ass, but he had just barely eked out an escape each time.

The most recent and worst of all the encounters had been in eighth grade when Walter went down by South Central. He wouldn't have gone outside at all – let alone to the worst part of town – if he had realized that day there was a large-scale drug bust going on up and down every street. He was only there because the McCarthys needed a whole array of party supplies, and he had been strolling through the eerily silent, run-down block of boarded-up buildings; a plastic bag stored in a baseball cup in his briefs that was filled with tabs and all sorts of uppers and downers alike.

He had nearly arrived and was feeling confident as he rounded a corner and started passing through the L-shaped lot which wrapped around the side of a seafood joint. He had been hustling towards the sidewalk across the lot when he had spotted a patrol car: huddled around it had been three officers wearing puffed-up jackets and pointed caps that had rounded badges on the front of them like a jewel on the forehead of an Egyptian noblewoman. Amidst the panic that had taken him over, it had occurred to him that he could just walk off – but it had been one moment too late, because when he did decide to once more go back behind the wall he had emerged from, he had heard a quick whoop of the siren from around the corner and doubled back once more to confront the officers.

"What are you doing out and about, kid?" the cop with black hair, pink skin, and squinty eyes had asked. He had placed his hands on his hips. "Didn't you get the memo from your other dealer buddies: we're weeding you out today, root and stem."

Walter had stammered out something to the effect of flat out denying he had any affiliation to people like that, but before he had a chance to make up an alibi about some friend or relative's house that he was on the way over to, the one with blond hair and a tan had stepped forward. "You've got your eyes down and your hands in your pockets: that's awfully suspicious," he had said, speaking in a tone akin to what a parent would use who had just deduced what lies they were being fed by their child. "If you really aren't up to no good, you won't mind us patting you down for weapons then, right? I mean, let's not be naïve: this is a bad place to be without a car or a bike, and since I don't see either on you, you probably aren't in a rush, especially given the way you were dragging your feet."

"You know, concealing a gun or any kind of deadly weapon is a felony, right out the gate," mentioned the stocky black officer, who had moved in front of the other two. "We'd be doing the community a disservice to let you walk without a quick search – get over here, boy. That is, unless you're willing to just come right out and admit your *real* story."

Walter, realized that he had been chased down a dead end in this encounter, went to face his fate with dignity and courage, or else he would seem even more guilty than he already did. He stood in front of them and put his hands out to the sides like an action figure or a man crucified. A quick swipe of his clothing had caused his cup to fall slightly forward, making an unusual tent shape in his pants.

"Huh… easily aroused, eh?" the squinty-eyed cop remarked. "Kidding, of course. I can see your cup moving – all you had to do was admit. Bad move –"

"Joe, come on, hurry your ass!" the tan cop had frantically called from the middle of the street, his revolver in hand.

The black cop had already closed the gap to the other sidewalk before he unholsterstered his pistol. "Stop! Get on the ground!" he had yelled at a group of five or six gangbangers wearing do-rags and mesh shorts, each of them toting either Uzis or Glocks with extended magazines, all of whom had been sprinting the other way, everyone trying to outrun the others.

Wherever the Grass Grows Greener

Like that, Walter had avoided the closest thing to a life-ending moment of peril, because he knew he wouldn't be represented by anybody trained or experienced in court, and he'd hang himself with his bedsheets if he showed up at prison. He had bolted in the other direction, then made the sell and ran off as soon as he was done, not breaking pace until he was back in his neck of the woods. Having gotten back home, he promised to himself that he would never again make the mistake of travelling in public with anything that put him at risk when the eyes of the law set their sights on him. He kept good to his word – until he went back on it, as always, of course.

The row of run-down townhouses on the other side of the street reminded Walter of his father, and in an unusual moment, he actually wondered to himself if his dad was still somewhere in town. There was no reason to even make an attempt at rekindling any sort of relationship between the two of them: his father was the exact opposite of a homebody. If something had him indoors, he took it upon himself to find someplace new to travel to, and once he started to get comfortable, he'd get his hopes up that this time would be the one, and the only way he could avoid the tragedy of realizing otherwise was to run off once more.

His mother told him that at one point, this made his father incredibly attractive: whenever he suspected a single hint of danger, he'd take them and move someplace safe. They were in and out of states on a monthly basis, and it was the furthest thing from mundane that she could imagine, as she had spent the better part of her young adult life towing the line. Suddenly she had a one-way ticket to excitement and stimulation, but when she tired of his flighty nature, she forced him to settle down for long enough to get married, and then not long after, she had convinced him to have a child with her.

Still to that day, Walter had no idea how his mother had persuaded him to actually go through with such a decision: from what he heard, his father had no responsibilities that weren't related to him or people that he was currently having sex with. But then

Sandy was born, and he left not long after. It took a few years for him to return, and when he did, he was so sorry that he made it up to her in the only way his creativity permitted him to think up: making Walter. His conception had only just begun when his father realized the mistake he had just made for a second time, and it only took him one good scare before he fled the scene without even telling his wife why he couldn't fulfill his commitments. And like that, Walter had just met his father a few dozen times in his life, only for days at the most before he couldn't sit still anymore and ran off yet again. It made him think: how much of his father's predisposition did he inherit? He just assumed that once he got old enough, he'd be so anxiety-fueled that he'd use travel as an opiate the same exact way as his father continued to do. However, it occurred to him that he'd do anything for Alina; to stay with her was the only thing that even registered with him as important, and he spent every moment trying to convince himself he'd never abandon his heart and soul. As the bus pulled up to the school, his only thought was of her, and he could only wonder where his beloved was in that massive part-time penitentiary. The door hissed open and students funneled out while it entered his mind that there was nothing to be gained through this torment, but ultimately, he could only tell himself that he played no part in his decision to be at the place in which he was being forced into. Swallowing the pain was his eternal occupation.

IV – B

As he stepped outside, he felt a warm blustery breeze push past him like the moment after opening an oven. Every lawn grew lush green grass that densely filled out the allotted space and was separated by adjoining white picket fences, and across them all, the whole block was alive with activity. Across the street there were the youngest of the Turner children playing in the branches of their orange tree, Mister O'Malley was wearing his usual bucket hat fitted with fishing hooks and lures while watering his bushes with a hose, and Miss Susan and Betsy were walking their dogs down the sidewalk in-step as they chatted.

"Hey, dummy!" called Brielle from the back seat of Powell's red convertible parked at the curb, her hands cupped around her mouth. "You take any longer and we'll be later than Cleveland's second term!" The sun was shining off of her flowing blond hair while Powell downed a steel hipflask, his head tilted back and his eyes to the sky.

Walter clambered down the front brick stairs, sprinted across the lawn, and leapt over his mother's rosebushes.

"Late?" Walter asked eagerly as he vaulted over the side of the car. He dropped down into the tan leather seat next to his girlfriend, resting his arm across the flat rear headrests before smooching her on the lips. "Late like how I used to be every morning freshman year 'cause you 'd kidnap me out of homeroom so we could talk in the stairwell up until the moment that the first bell would ring? We've been punctual this year so far, right? So, what then – we might not be on time to Rickard's class for just this one Monday? I think you need to be more like Powell: he's a fierce Christian but still manages to be neck-deep in his flask with Sunday being only hours off at this point." He said pointing at the driver, "I'm friends with very few guys who are able to be *that* bold."

Powell chugged the last of his flask and after tossing it aside onto the passenger seat, empty, he jammed the gas pedal down with a resounding kick and floored it away from the curb. "Up yours too, Walt," he burped.

Walter and Brielle jerked to the side as the car sped off, with Brielle toppling right into Walter's arms. She was staring directly up, deeply into his eyes.

"He's drinking to make up for the time we spent waiting on you to come out: you've had us waiting so long that Powell's alcoholism is developing," Brielle said mystically. She was wearing a grin as wide as an open doorway.

"That's not true – Powell's alcoholism is already developed like film," Walter replied. His bottom jaw was poking slightly out and he was matching her expression with a smug smirk.

Powell was lighting a cigarette with his left hand and on the right, he put his middle finger up for the back seat to stare at.

Brielle's gaze was distant and scattered across Walter's face like she was watching two cars collide at an intersection. She opened her mouth to speak, taking in a sharp breath, but paused and exhaled instead. "I feel resurrected just having you next to me," she grabbed his arm and managed to whisper at last.

"Was last night that long ago?" Walter pondered out loud as he traced his fingers along her back. "This morning came so fast; I must've slept like a dead man."

The surrounding neighborhood melted into a section of road that passed a hill on one side and a broad lake on the other. Willow trees leaned from one side of the road to the other like ribs wrapping over organs.

"I was still high enough to be a dust cloud against the Milky Way when you dropped me off and I didn't come down for hours," she said, immersed in the details of Walter's face. "I was lying in bed with my eyes on the ceiling the whole time being mesmerized by tiny details that were coming back to me one by one, and at some point, I let my thoughts wander to the wrong place, when suddenly I had myself convinced that the world had something real bad in the works on its way for you."

"For me?" Walter asked, his tone comprised of disbelief.

"For you!" Brielle declared as she sat straight up. "This thing was gonna be what took the boy I loved away from me forever. There were all these small little hints that came together to made me think you weren't gonna be alright in the morning, and they had me so convinced that I couldn't make myself rest because of how worked up I was. Just now when you took so long coming out, I started to get concerned that something really had happened, and for a brief second, it felt like everything was over for me... like the universe had swallowed you up and I wasn't ever going to see you again." She paused, and the two of them merely watched each other's expression mirror one another's to the sound of the engine roaring.

Walter suddenly leaned in, pressing himself against Brielle, and then pecked her on the forehead. He dropped back in the seat, putting his arms up around him like he was sitting in a corner booth, and began to look around at the surrounding scenery through observant eyes slit with focus as though he was alone in the car. "Don't get so twisted up; you know I'm not going nowhere," he said before coming out of his slouched position and matching her posture. "Hey, by the way, I don't think I'm really gonna have time to fool around today after school – have to run by Tailcreek Woods."

"Do you need to get flowers for Rachel?" Brielle blurted. "I can help out, Walt –"

"No, I'm sorry, hun," Walter said in the tone of a parent letting the kids know they won't be keeping the dog. "Mom is going to want them a certain way and Dad needs her to get her way. I can't let myself get put into a tough spot on this one, Brielle, I just can't."

"Walt, c'mon," she complained, pushing him by the shoulder. "You know I keep my plans cleared almost around-the-clock so that you can always see me if you need to. I bet I can get flowers that'll make your mom happy."

"Nothing makes Mom 'happy' anymore; things can only satisfy her for the moment and that requires either my dad or myself to do something that alleviates her of some responsibility. But the homework I've been getting lately has me in chains, so I doubt I'll even be able to leave the house," he replied, studying his nails.

Powell rounded a corner, launching Brielle back into Walter's arms.

"Then I bet I can get flowers that'll satisfy your mom, how's that?" she asked as she poked his pect with her forefinger like she was picking something out from behind a glass case. "And you're silly, Walt, if you think that you'll be getting work today and I won't be. We go to all but one of the same classes today and get all of our homework done together anyway, so what's your point?"

"No, I mean that Dad doesn't let me out of the house until my homework is finished, even to run errands, so I won't be able to go get flowers 'til late late *late* tonight because homework has been fucking me lately," Walter said. "and you know he won't let you over because he damn near hates you for the stunts we've pulled." He was averting her gaze, scanning the surroundings like a prairie dog while he tried to suppress an impish grin.

"Well... ask." She sensed his difficulty but rather than call attention to it, she skirted around the issue from behind a polite disposition. "If you really can't go straight to the forest, fine, but please at least ask for permission to leave when you get back to your house today, because I'll be waiting either way. We can go home after – my parents won't be there to disturb us," she replied in a voice that was cool and cordial like iced tea.

"Thanks for being understanding, love," Walter said through a sigh. He tugged her towards him with his left arm for a quick second in a momentary embrace.

"Of course – I don't know how vivid your memory is of the Eighth from last year, but that Thursday you told me your mom had been grieving from wall to wall all week leading up to it, your dad had been needing you to get everything done around the house, and you were so drained by them that you didn't know if you were gonna survive the weekend at home," Brielle recalled profoundly. Her boyfriend merely remained hushed while his forgotten words were fed back to him. "That morning we sat out back on the tennis court so you could sneak a cigarette before first bell, and you told me that you only needed one thing in the whole wide world, and that one thing was someone who was going to not just support you through the moment, but someone who you could also trust to not stack their personal problems on top of yours to add to the stress you're under. Well, I'm stuck with a trove of personal problems like a Times Square cake shop is stuck with roaches, but if I could, I'd rid myself of them faster than the contents of an ashtray being dumped from a third-story window, just for you. Even though I don't think there's been a force yet discovered by humans that's capable of separating Brielle from her many, many issues, for the next five days I'm going to try my hardest to make it seem as if me and them are a million miles apart, that way I can be your help and not your handicap," she proclaimed. "Were your parents managing alright this morning?"

He displayed surprise, taken aback at her poignant memory. Sometimes she caught him off guard with how intensely she was capable of holding onto the past: it being an affliction as much as a gift. "Well, Mom's manic and strung-out, but what's new? Dad didn't yell at me or get harsh at all before I went out the door, which has me shocked because in the reality that I come from, he would never have let me leave the house without giving me hell first for being out with the car so damn late on a Sunday night – especially if he knew the real reason was 'cause I was out with you on a reefer run,"

Walter said. He sounded more accusatory with the end of that last sentence than he meant to be.

"I'm sorry, baby, I'm sorry. I can't apologize enough, apparently – yes, I got us lost and instead of being out for an hour we were out for three," Brielle said, her words coming out in an avalanche. "If I had known that trying to give you directions to Todd and Mary's apartment would have been so catastrophic then I wouldn't have made us go out that way at all, and instead of trying to get away with smoking an entire blunt in the middle of Wilkin Park to save time on the way, we could have just taken the time to walk over to the forest and smoked it behind the billboard since there's no one there to bother us."

"Hey, hey; calm down, dove." Walter was easing back into his seat and gesturing with his palms to make himself seem harmless like he had been caught in the wrong apartment. "Smoking in the park last night turned out to be a mess, but we got away 'cause we always get away anyway, so what's it matter? Plus, I was the one who didn't want to walk the entire distance across the park to get to the forest in the first place, and I had the idea for us to go see Todd and Mary, as well. Like I said, it's all alright as of right now: Dad didn't say I was in any trouble so if my day is going to get torn to shreds by him then it hasn't happened yet," he replied, proud at his ability to defuse her on a whim.

"Okay, I can let it go – but I wanted to ask you about something that's been bothering me," Brielle said. She was blankly staring out over the forested lake that was to their left. Her eyes fell down to her twisting fingers when the surrounding country was cut off by the bustling scene of a shopping center.

"Anything." He was adoring her undisturbed disposition: the way she was removed from her environment made her resemble something of an impressionist portrait.

"Do you remember what that old man was yelling at us as we were running to the car?" she asked, suddenly snapping her gaze to meet his.

"He wasn't that old. He was middle-aged." He was scratching his eyelid, effectively blinding himself.

"Anybody who walks their dog in the park at night and decides that the sight of two kids sitting on a bench sharing a blunt is something worth getting so furiously angry over that it's required to start yelling must be at least seventy years old... and a massive piece of shit," Brielle declared.

"That guy wasn't a year over forty – he might have just been ugly as hell which is why you thought he looked so old," Walter said with a stretch and a yawn.

"Walt, come on – do you remember or not?" she asked as she pushed him again.

"Do I remember what that screaming fat dude was saying to me as I threw a lit roach in his face and sprinted away to my dad's car? I can't say I do," he said with a chuckle. "I can barely remember what he looked like – was he fat and ugly or wasn't he?"

"Why aren't you ever listening? And I have no idea what that person looked like – I just turned away and started running when I realized that the guy yelling wasn't a cop," she said, rolling her eyes and trying to ignore the busy street around them.

"Well *I* wasn't listening because I was focused on throwing the roach properly, otherwise none of the embers would have got in his fat ugly face and we might not have had such an easy escape," he remarked.

"So you really don't care at all that he called us hedons?" she asked pointedly.

"Is that supposed to mean something offensive?" Walter replied dismissively.

"It can mean a few things, but I think that guy wanted to scold us for being obsessed with pleasing ourselves," Brielle sucked in her breath as the car passed a small park, preparing herself to launch into a tangent. "I think of it this way: this sad, pathetic geezer is taking his yippy little dog on a midnight walk, for whatever reason, when he catches two young people smoking themselves to a state of bliss in *his* park. He can't fathom the idea that there's not one, but two people on this planet who aren't perpetually in furious agony with the chaos of life the way he is and are fighting back against it instead, so he loses his mind and tries to break reality to us by telling us just what we are: hedons."

"Is that all that means? How's that any worse than being called 'spazz' or 'faceache'?" Walter rubbed the bottom of his nose and yawned again. "I got called 'chickenshit' by Rob Ramos for accidentally stepping on his sneakers in the hallway and I had half a mind to kick him in the shin for it later."

"What the old man called us isn't about it being an insult – what if he's right?" Brielle asked hysterically.

"Well yeah, isn't he?" He raised one eyebrow, finding their current conversation hard to believe.

"Wh– How can you say that?!" Her expression was that of someone who had just gotten their toes smashed. "Why would he be right? Just because we spend all day trying to make each other happy?"

"I guess...?" He was grimacing at this sudden confrontation; the chaotic scenery of busy shops around them mirrored his inner turmoil. "I'm not really sure. I've never bothered to question myself over whether or not I spend too much time seeking my own pleasure since I feel like I spend all my time trying to please everyone else in my life anyway, so what's the matter if I also try to take a little for myself? Now that I think about it, I don't think I'd want to be in a relationship with a girl who wasn't at least a little obsessed with her own pleasure, because what would I do if you weren't happy? You know that I'm not capable of finding any enjoyment in this fucking life unless you've already taken the lead."

"Happiness has nothing to with pleasure, though – happiness is just simply having satisfaction with the way someone lives," she said, speaking with the astuteness of a professor. "Pleasure is all about doing things that happy people are rumored to do, because you hope it'll be what makes you happy. A happy person can be someone who doesn't ever get any pleasure, and someone who is always getting pleasure may never actually be happy."

"Wait," Walter interjected, holding his two forefingers up in front of him like goal posts and staring between them, "I think I'm beginning to understand what the core of the issue really is here: you're worried that this guy was calling us unhappy – am I right or am I wrong?" He then pointed at her with both hands, biting his lip.

"You're...You're right," Brielle huffed, upset at being found out and slumped back into her seat.

"...Okay." He dragged his fingers over his chin. "Yeah... the more I mull it over, the more I understand why this guy's accusation might be bugging you. It was an ugly thing for him to have said to you in particular since you have an inclination to not allow yourself to feel decent about yourself, even though you deserve nothing less every waking moment of every day. I've never met anyone who's capable of being even half as genuine or selfless with the love they give out, and if that guy could have just seen that for himself then he would have taken it all back, I'm sure of it," he said triumphantly, overwhelmingly pleased with himself for all that.

"Well fuck all of that –" she slapped her thighs and shook her head "– it's Monday morning and I want to feel good. That old man has no power over me."

"You think so? That's relieving to hear." He put his foot up on the seat so that his knee was beside his head.

"Get your goddamn shoe off of my leather," Powell hissed.

Walter flinched and sat straight up, brushing the spot on the seat where his shoe used to be with his hand.

"Hun, that's not even the real relief." She dug her thumb into her waistband and slipped out a lengthy, rolled paper that was filled with dark ground material, resembling a used coffee filter.

"Is that the Chocolate Thai you set aside?" he asked from a position of desperation. "Brielle, we're on the way to school, you can't be –"

"Can't be what?" She smacked his words out of the air like she was Patrick Ewing getting his fifth goaltending of the

Crowe

championship. "High for English class? We're just reading in there today, and this stuff doesn't really last for longer than a few hours: it's a brief high. By the time third bell comes around, it'll have worn off enough for us to focus on math."

Walter put his eyebrows up and sucked on his lips, just trying to absorb her sudden shift in mood. "Shit, I'd smoke it just to keep my focus on anything else other than class. But you don't wanna just play it safe and conservative at least until the afternoon? You said that you wanted to save *that* joint in particular out of everything else you brought for us to smoke last night because you knew you'd need it for another time."

"Another time?" She tsked, her eyes squinted. "Bitch, it *is* another time! Come on, Walt: the top is down, summer is dying but not dead yet, and this ride is only going to last for another five minutes at the most – if we're looking for an opportunity to enjoy the moment, then this moment is our last good chance for quite some time... And thank you again for the wonderful drive, by the way, Powell." She squeezed his shoulder from over the seat.

"You're very welcome, Brielle," Powell replied, speeding through a left turn as the light turned red, passing parking lots on all sides and emerging in a residential area.

Walter shrugged. "Fuck it; you're right." He slipped off his sneaker, flipping up the sole and procuring a matchbook. "Let's live while we're alive."

She held it in her teeth and shook her hair around, then put it all behind her. "The rush might knock you back at first, but you should be completely clearheaded by the time the taste of chocolate leaves your mouth."

"I can only think of one way to find out." He struck a match on the bottom of his shoe, then replaced the book under the sole and fit it back onto his foot. Gingerly holding the tiny wooden handle and cupping the flame with his other hand, he burnt away the twisted paper cap, both of their eyes analyzing it closely.

Brielle took one lengthy inhale and then passed it off. She held it in and waited a few seconds, watched him take his own drag from it, and then let the smoke pour out through her nostrils. She shut her eyes and swayed to the music coming from the radio: a big band playing behind the swaying voice of a talented diva. She felt the lyrics coming at her a word at a time, reciting them mentally before she heard them.

'Does it – ever come back to youuu, that you've never changed?
Just – rearranged, something strange – without a name.
I can't – take your nerrrve, this is something – I never deserrrved,
my thoughts – all turned up burned,
but only 'cause I should've just – learrrned.'

  It didn't quite occur to her that she was at peace, because she was so exhausted from the typical anxiety of running from place to place that she was merely aware of herself resting, and that was all. How did it come to be that she felt stricken by her own fluctuating nature but still she seemed to have permanent relief provided to her by the forgiving conditions of the life that she was undeservedly fortunate enough to receive? She hated her wicked spirit, because she knew cruelty was just something that she had just been born with, but rather than resist it, she gave into it and made it a pillar of her character. She'd never alleviate herself of her critical nature – not until her time was long passed and society had lost track of her lengthy list of sins.

  Walter tapped her on the shoulder and gave her the joint. She took it and began hitting it without opening her eyes. He rubbed his face. It was flush with blood, and his surroundings were spinning. His tolerance was so low that he had to guide his breathing or else it would lose control. Suffering like this was always interesting experience: should he be grateful that he was allowed to bear witness to such an overwhelming sensation? After all, people pay good money to ride roller coasters and skydive – he was practically at the same place as a tuxedo preparing himself for his day at the altar, drunk off champagne and sick to his indecisive, aching heart. He did consider life after marriage sometimes. If he wore a ring tomorrow, he wouldn't treat Brielle any different. Actually, he might lead her on less: she deserved a break for always responding with the utmost patience when it came to his games, something for which he never even bothered to properly thank her.

He pulled his hand off of his forehead and looked at Brielle as she pulled her own away from her mouth and finally opened her eyes to see her eternal point of interest.

"Hello Walter," she said robotically. She forced the rolled paper into his hand. "Up," she instructed after a moment of him merely holding it in place. She puckered her lips and kissed her index finger and her thumb, which were pressed together at the tips. "Do that."

"Brielle, I –"

Brielle grabbed her boyfriend's shoulders, causing him to jump as well as become forced to stare at his girlfriend, who looked to him like she was at the end of a tunnel of color and light due to his impaired vision.

"I know what you're going to say, and all I can reply with is that you need to grow some nuts. It'll be okay; just think about Britcher Cabin – that water bed on a hit of T's and Blues was the most intense thing I've ever felt." She suddenly smiled and lightly smacked his cheek twice. "Okay, now go."

"Jesus," Walt said. Or maybe he actually thought it – it was hard to tell. Regardless, he inhaled as much as lungs could carry, and shot his arm out when he was done.

Brielle took it from him, giggling. She closed her eyes once more and began puffing from the joint.

Walter collapsed on the seat behind him. "You're finishing that thing, Brielle," he gasped.

"Your wish is my command," she said, smoke pouring from her mouth.

Walter covered his mouth and winced in pain. He was twisted up around and over by his eyeballs and his every thought was merged with another, his total memory showing him scenes from his own life but also one that was completely fabricated by his imagination. It was hard to distinguish one from the next, so he was in a dissociative purgatory, deceived by the very things upon which he relied. It was likely what King Louis XVI was experiencing when he realized that the Tuileries Palace was being sacked: a complete severance from the world he used to consider his own and the acceptance of unbridled isolation.

Brielle had been huffing away and managed to blow it down to just the paper filter. She reached her hand out over the side of the car and dropped it in the street. She sighed. "…You don't sometimes get that sense all at once that you're not just a hypocrite, but also that you're actually a hypocrite on such a grand and massive scale that there's no way you could ever explain it to anyone without sharing mortifying personal details… do you?" She was sucking her teeth akin to someone sitting on the front steps of a courthouse, waiting for the verdict to break the outside world.

"No – I feel like a hypocrite every moment of the day anyway, so the sense never gets the chance to sneak up on me." He scratched beside his nose, trying to play off his extreme disorientation. "But I think you should try to distract yourself with something that might make things even the slightest bit more pleasant, because you don't deserve to feel mortified – not ever."

Brielle lurched over and fell into Walter, dropping her body directly on top of his and scaring him considerably. She wrapped her arms around his shoulders and nuzzled her head into his chest. The great, deep ocean mirrored the vast loneliness that was humankind, each person just a testament to what could be if goodwill was a requirement and not a luxury. Hopelessness was standard, and hatred seemed to come with everything as a side dish. None of that mattered to her, however. She was spitting in the eye of her creator, taunting him to punish her. She was invincible. She was unconquerable. And nothing could disturb her sanctuary. "Walt I think I'm so in love with the person sitting next to me that it's got me going out of my mind."

"Do you want to know what's got me *furious*?" he exclaimed, slamming his fist on the seat.

She jumped back in shock. "What?" she asked, less interested in his answer than she was in resolving the situation that had just befallen her.

"Do you want to know what's got me absolutely raging?" His eyes were wild and he was practically foaming at the mouth, his hands up and fingers poised as if he was tearing apart a sheet of paper.

"No; I'd be too afraid," she whimpered like a politician facing an assassin in a hotel room.

"Well I'll just come right out and say it then –" he leaned into her and got right in her face "– you stole exactly what I wanted to tell you."

Brielle reared forward and planted her lips onto Walter's. He embraced her, pressing himself into her, and the two of them grappled one another in a lengthy, drawn out kiss, sliding all over the back seat of the car. Eventually, he pinned her down and was sucking on her neck while rubbing her back with one hand and grabbing her ass with the other. Her moaning was high-pitched and gentle.

"Do you two want to keep that shit to a minimum? There's only a few minutes left before we get there and I'm trying to keep my focus up – the ganj reeking is only slightly distracting, but you two being plastered all over each other is grossing me out enough that I don't even wanna check the rear view." Powell had just stopped at a light and was lighting another cigarette as he spoke. He flicked his lighter close and began shaking his head, his eyes straight up, and then scratched his eyebrow with his thumbnail while grimacing.

The two of them clambered off of one another and sat straight up, fixing their clothes.

"You're right; I'm sorry, Powell," Brielle said in a kind, diplomatic tone.

Walter cleared his throat. "Yeah, my bad, man."

He sprawled out in the back, legs splayed with his knees pressing into either of the front leather seats, his spine propped up against the corner like a rake in the crux of the wall in a garage. Brielle had her legs hanging out over the edge of the side of the car, her feet bobbing back and forth in rhythm to the somber song playing over the radio.

'It's a shameful thing that we've got to keep meeting like this;
how I can only wish that you didn't
need me like this, need me like this.
Because we're built for chaos, that's all us, so callous;
but all we really do is
refuse to wilt, refuse to wilt.'

His arm was wrapped across the petite frame of her chest and his hand was fondling the round part of her shoulder, flicking her bra strap and tugging it back and forth. The neighborhood became spread out and trees took up more total space than the houses did. They passed an extensively decorated mansion, a wide garden out front with Crape Myrtles densely packed along the road. Bees were whirring overhead, creating a constant, low hum as they dashed between the clusters of pink, fleshy flowers that were drooping down out of the canopy. Birds were dancing and singing throughout the winding branches, each one chasing another, their calls overlaid against the whirring of the wheels pressing into the ground at breakneck speed, creating a symphony of atmosphere that was being subconsciously processed by the occupants of the car, the three of them focusing in on their racing thoughts and letting the noise of the world fall on their muted ears. Sunlight peppered the ground, raining down through the leafy roof of the road, each beam decorating the surface it fell on, bright splotches scattered throughout shadowed areas, creating a pattern like the fur of a jaguar.

"The world is deafening," Brielle commented. "It's a waterfall of activity, everything crashing over itself all at once. There's so much going on that you can't pick out any one noise; it's all just a cacophony of endlessly ringing through our ears." She was rotating her head around to have the whole street in her visual scope.

Nothing was unexpected this way, and she found comforting security in such a fact.

"You never realize how much there is to hear until you ride in a car with the top down. It's like TV static coming at you from every angle: it has no start or stop, just this continuous stimulation that's the same as holding a needle to your skin." Walter was coming down, completely disconnected from the car and ever-present off in the distance that he was staring out into. "It's a feeling that's so constant that it numbs itself out," he said spacily.

She was grabbing at her hair one hand at a time. "Do you think that this sound is what dying is like? A perpetual sensation that smothers itself out as if it were a fire inside a sealed building?"

"Dying must be like sinking underwater: first you feel everything all at once and the shock overwhelms your senses totally, but then once you get deeper into it you get this awareness of the situation that only comes in the aftermath of your last path to salvation getting closed off." He lost control of his speech in a way that could only be described as a blackout, losing touch with his intentions and becoming automatically operated, uninhibited like a drunk at the end of the week. When he spoke, he didn't check with himself if the things he was saying were appropriate; he was too deep in his own noxious thoughts to be able to consider such a thing. "The further you get into it, the more you panic until it levels off and the reaction plateaus into a gradual darkness that becomes indistinguishable from the vacancy of reality."

They both stopped talking, Walter still immersed in his subconscious ramblings and Brielle sitting straight up, appearing ill.

"Walt, you're terrifying me," his girlfriend whimpered.

Without even moving his eyes, he reached down and gripped her hand in his. "I don't mean to. I wonder what death is like whenever my mind has a spare moment, because ever since Rachel took her accident, I can't help myself but to visualize what her last few minutes were like. The truck flew into her car and off the highway at 11:09. The paramedics got there at 11:37 and she died on the way to the ER at 11:44. The car got sandwiched along the middle, front side up against the back, but it didn't crack her skull or break her neck; her chest was crushed so the last thing she felt was ribs breaking and puncturing her organs and lungs. I can't fathom what that must be like: tasting iron as delirium sets in, just wondering if you're experiencing reality or if you're drifting through a bad dream. I keep picturing her bloody teeth showing through the spot where her cheek was torn away; her eyes marbly and unfocused.

"She must have thought she was only sleeping but it was all real: every last gruesome moment. She never had any idea how unlucky she really was, because her every thought must have been going in circles like a fish with just one fin, bouncing back between awareness of the pain, wondering what there even is to do, and the grim acceptance that there's no surviving. Her heart was perfectly intact, meaning it was working like a sweatshop to stabilize her sorry state. It had no idea that she was just bleeding all over the dash; that she wasn't retaining a single drop. I think about how she was just drifting out of reality like light on the other side of a tunnel." His voice had been cracking near the end and two streaks of tears were forming down his face as he slumped deeply into the car seat.

Brielle had her head on his stomach, using it as a pillow. She looked forlorn enough to be a barfly. "She must care that you're always worried about the way she went out."

Walter shook his head and put his hand back over his mouth. "If I could just know she was somewhere, anywhere, thinking thoughts still, it would set my own soul at ease. I'll be tormented with knowing the truth until my own end meets me," he said, struggling to keep his composure.

"She's out there, Walt. I just know she must be." She grabbed his thigh, as though to reassure him. "I only met her that once out at the beach house, but I could just tell that she was made of something immaculate: that she breathed love and lived with the grace of a saint. She's waiting for you, Walt. She always has been. She was born an angel and died that way. I can still see her face from the few conversations that we had – her charisma shone through on every word. Nothing about her life was accidental." Her eyes were starry with wonder; she was amazed that she was interpreting with such clarity.

"I just can't imagine Rachel suffering. She spent her every moment lifting spirits, defusing hot-headed boys, and guiding younger girls. Nourishing the well-being of the world was her pet project, and she added to it every day." Walter swallowed hard. "...I can't wrap my head around it: I'm still here as a full-time disappointment and she's keeping a grave." He held his head in his hands like a man who had just rolled down a hill in a barrel.

Brielle propped herself up on her hands to get a good look at him. "Walt – can't you understand that this is bigger than you, her, or anyone else? There's a plan in all of this. It might not show itself right now, but when things play themselves out, you'll be at peace, as will she. That is the only thing that matters." Her hand cupped his cheek.

"We're at a disconnect here, Brie. My parents aren't the same people anymore. The day that they lost their favorite, something snapped inside of them. They put a white veil over her face and went down in the casket with her. They look at me as a sickly shadow of the exemplar they had as a daughter." He was biting his lip and glancing off to the side, refusing to return her stare.

"If your dad didn't have you around to boss you up and down the block, he wouldn't be fueled by pride the way he is," she said, beginning to speak with some ferocity and impact. "You say you're not the apple of his eye, but you're entering the prime of manhood as he's being phased out of it."

"Dad kicks shit just to pass the time," Walter replied, suddenly feeling like he had to defend himself and snapping out of his melancholy stupor. "I have no idea how my mom ever ended up staying with him, 'cause she loses sleep every night on his insanity. He starts seeing red and will rant and rave at hell and holy fire. He goes berserk at the moon for shining at night and does it twice for it hiding during the day. Mom just keep her eyes low whenever he falls back into his spells; Rachel was the only person who made him happy."

"Happy? Fuck 'happy', Walt." Brielled spat back at him. "Everyone is just waiting 'til they get the next thing that they want then they die. Your dad has a volatile spirit in him because he cares, or else he wouldn't waste his breath." She was scowling like a boxer who had just gotten clapped on the ear.

"Sure dad cares, but he's so misled that he blames the world for making him and blames himself for not having the solution." Walter leaned in to impose himself over her. "Mark my words: he'll lose it one day and that'll really be when things fall apart. He gets so close each time – he's like a rabbit leaping for a carrot hanging from a string. There's only so many places for him left to go."

She leaned in as well to match her boyfriend's posture. "He's *doing* the best he *can*."

"How can you know?" he asked, easing off and putting his elbow on the side of the car and resting the side of his chin in his hand, staring at her from a distance.

"You want to know how I know?" She pointed at him and then to her with both fingers.

"I know you don't know." He pointed at himself with the hand that wasn't propping his head up and then at her.

"I do know. I really do," she replied stubbornly, arms crossed.

Walter shook his head slightly, squinted, and looked at her spitefully like someone had just asked him for some of his time. "I don't believe you?" he scoffed, trying to egg her on.

"I've had premonitions, Walter. I've seen your dad in my prayers," Brielle said with the utmost seriousness.

"Oh, come on…." He threw his hands up like he had just lost a gamble on the back of another, incredulous that he had ended up in the same place for yet one more time.

"I'm serious, Walt! I ask for signs from the future and I get visits by images of the present. If you can't –"

"No, please, stop," he begged, pinching the top of his nose and shutting his eyes as if he had a migraine. "For the sake of anything sacred, don't start on this again. Not now. It's 8 fucking AM."

"I'm sorry," she muttered, more frustrated than hurt.

Houses whipped by, first appearing whole but gradually feeding into a blur of color as they passed them. Each one of them stood out in their individuality; each one was its own testament to the people who lived and lounged inside it. Like mountains, no two were formed the same, personality distinguishing one after the next by minute flourishes and beauty marks. Some were white with red shutters, or blue with purple trim; a few were forest green topped by a range of different shades of gray. Porches would sometimes jut out, giving the house a bottom jaw and space for homebodies to watch the world taking place out on the street from an exterior shelter. Other times, there would be a balcony, either built into the roof or propped up on Roman pillars. A few even had a small bridge on the second story connecting the main house to a garage. Walter's personal favorites were the three-story houses that had a cylindrical column that popped out of one corner of the building, giving it a shape in the same way a nose defines a face.

Walter considered the way each family they passed all worked their hardest to be normal, satisfactory. Everyone wanted to be exceptional at how well they managed to fit a certain mold. They all laid down at night and dreamt of kings and rodeos and outer space and true love, then they woke up and rode out to their respective desks, building towards a brighter future. Their discomfort was merely a sign that they were doing the right thing; their wish for constant change meant they'd never have to truly become new people.

Brielle had calmed down considerably; her rage being swapped with sentimentality. She began to crave reassurance. "Walt?" she asked gently.

"Yeah?" he replied, locking eyes with her and examining her innocent, doe-eyed expression.

"Am I speaking for the both of us if I told you that riding down the street next to you makes me feel like I might be the safest person in all the nation?"

Walter cracked a smile. "You make me feel so safe that sometimes I think I'm dating a bank vault," he said boldly.

She cackled, pulling away from him to place a weak punch on his chest. "If you just called me massive, cold and heartless, then you're getting your ass kicked," she said, gasping for breath between snickers.

"No, but I do think you're filled with wealth," he said, leaning in and holding her.

"Oh, stop," she replied softly, reaching her arms around his neck and gripping his back.

"Baby but I'm barely started."

"Tell me something," Brielle commanded, prodding his chest.

Walter merely picked at his face. "No, you."

She moved back into her corner and sat up to face him, as did he, then she thought for a second. "Did you know that we must be some of the only people to ever smoke that strain in a joint? The growers and distributors who come in contact with Chocolate Thai almost always end up just making it into Thai Sticks," she said matter-of-factly.

"Are those similar to Chinese spring rolls?" he asked, genuine in his question.

"...No," she replied like she was declining an offer for prom.

"Oh."

"They're cigars that are only worth making from the best quality weed. They take the stem of the plant and skewer the cigar on it lengthwise, then wrap it all up cannabis fibers taken from the stalk." She slid her finger down the length of his nose. "Just in case you wanted to know."

"Weed cigars? How potent must those be?" Walter was excited like a televangelist. "Shit, I can't wait for those to become popular on the block – I'm gonna be able to watch people lose their fucking minds! When do you think we're gonna try some?"

"Try it?" Brielle scoffed. "Walter, you'd die; most people are convinced that these things get soaked in opium water that they're so potent. Not to mention the fact that I had to bust ass to get us that single joint: Jones Corey made me pay thirty dollars just for a dub, and I was even the one who stitched up his dog after a Cressida hit her going down the street. What's happening is that the Asian drug pipeline to America is either closing or being better controlled, because everyone is starting to notice Chocolate Thai becoming a strain that's talked about more and carried less every day." She began watching the horizon, taking note of its fragile form, in constant upheaval with the sudden rush of the world coming from before them and disappearing just moments later.

"Where are they going to get the weed from instead then?" he asked, curious as a pupil.

"I have no idea – wherever the grass grows greener, I guess."

"So what you're telling me is that we should really appreciate the high while we've got it." Walter was vacantly staring up into the clear blue sky.

Brielle put the side of her knuckle under his chin and pulled his head down with her thumb so that they were facing one another dead-on. Her expression was sultry and craving, resembling a cat witnessing its next meal scamper in front of it. She pushed him back into the seat and slid on top of him. "I think that you should really appreciate me," she murmured, her lips just inches from his.

He couldn't do a thing but whisper: "You're so right."

V – A

Pale, dimpled pillars lined the opening to the school, welcoming in the flowing student body like how the bared teeth of a coyote greet a crippled rabbit. The American flag waved atop the flagpole at the helm of the building, the dainty school flag just under it. Walter never understood the meaning of it: a man with the head of a boar stood triumphantly on the crumpled carcass of a lion. He was certain that one of the original faculty must have thought that it would make for an inspiring image, but mostly it just confused him: was the boar-person supposed to represent the power of man over the wild, or was it a commentary on the endless cycle of carnage that is existence, or was it was merely a broad-brushed attempt at generating a culture for the glorified juvenile hall that a few thousand kids were forced to attend along with him?

To him, the flag symbolized the fever dream that was his adolescence: his middle school had been even more barren, even more stunted, and at that pitiful shack he used his training from wrestling practice to commit regretfully heinous acts on other students that even still to that very day tortured his deepest subconscious musings and kept him blacklisted from athletic functions. Now he attended a school that was, in comparison, sizable and even, daresay, grand in its own gothic manner, and it flaunted its lordship over the surrounding cityscape with its comically contrived crest in complete ignorance of the horrors that

Crowe

Wherever the Grass Grows Greener

Walter had emerged from just mere miles away from it. It was all irrelevant, however, he silently figured to himself. Nobody even ever bothered to look up at the flag; he went so far as to wonder if a single person just once took the time to squint their eyes up at the confusing banner to try and decipher its cryptic implications.

Instead all eyes were set down. The student body was a gushing waterfall of individuals: never running out, supplied from some obscure source both unknown and irrelevant to anyone involved. Tall girls flipped their hair and chortled at the jokes that the broad-shouldered boys would poke at one another. Bunches of underclassmen huddled together, murmuring to one another in cautious tones that reflected a perpetual need to not say the wrong thing; to not perjure their carefully crafted outward personalities. Then there were the loners, the drifting spirits who trudged forward because they didn't know any other option. They were the people who fascinated Walter out of everybody, because as the mob was funneled into the tiny set of double doors, he could only wonder what the collective sum of all their racing thoughts might possibly be: there were artists, entrepreneurs, dreamers, politicians, actors, workers, musicians, fighters, lovers, and combinations of all the above wandering in the same direction, herded like a field of cattle being prodded by red-skinned cowpokes on trotting horses that were kicking up the orange dust of a lifeless prairie, lit only by the bloody embers radiating from a dying sun.

Walter was obsessing over the one thing that always had him in a trance: where could Alina be? The whole rest of the school could vanish like a touring band from a cheering stadium and he would be all the more pleased, because it would mean that he could find her with complete ease. The way things stood, he couldn't find her through the crowd with a pack of police dogs and a pair of roller skates: the school was so superfluous with bodies that it was practically a French catacomb. And yet, if he had to, he would fight his way through the horde and take his chances being trampled if that was what he needed to do to reach her.

There was no opportunity for heroism, however. This was life, and life is far too ordinary and humdrum to allow for such theatrics. No, he had to take his lumps and make his way to the same room that he arrived at five mornings out of every seven, because that was the rule instructed by social order. He could only imagine what Alina might be occupied with – likely reading over notes or rushing through homework due in the coming hours, if that. She was overloaded with work like how a yak scheduled to climb a mountain is packed with food and furs. It wasn't fair – nothing about it was. Alina deserved to be able to patiently parse through her responsibilities, taking a pace that suited her and functioning with the same grace and majesty that characterized her person. No other face came to mind when he considered the concept of beauty: her expression was the way snow crested the arch of a bridge. She flaunted skin a shade of caramel that rivaled the polished surface of rich mahogany. Even on the most somber of days, she would wear her hair in the fashion of a horseback charging knight's plume flowing in the breeze: effortlessly and embodying such power that she caused the eyes of spectators all around to be instilled with wonder and awe, unable to resist helping themselves to the draw of her presence.

As Walter obsessed over his day-by-day purpose for continuing, he mindlessly sifted through the masses when he began to notice that the faces he was passing were entirely obscure in their identities to him. He began searching for a familiar set of eyes, trying to locate a single person that he could attach a name to, but as he continued to fail, an unsettling panic set in as though he had somehow gone back in time to his first day of school. Alien voices crowded out his thoughts and he struggled to make his way to the side of the hall so that he could have a chance to recoup himself. He stood in the corner, humiliated by his vacancy of mind.

"Oh, look who it is."

Walter spun in place to find a group of four standing in the corner opposite from him. He studied each of their faces intently, realizing whom he was looking at and instantly becoming anchored in recollections of the past.

"Why d'you look so confused?" asked the tallest of the bunch as he walked over and rested his elbow onto Walter's shoulder. He had on a plump beanie and several bracelets. "You lost?" He smirked. "Tripping, maybe?"

Walter batted the arm off of him. "Cut it out, Trevor. And you should know better than anybody that I'm done fucking around with my mind after you made me walk from one end of Cap Creek Woods to the other on salvia. That shit traumatized me."

Trevor threw his head back and cackled. "I had forgotten about that, actually. Thanks for the good memories."

"Walter," said a girl in an airy voice, wearing a shawl and magenta lipstick, "what did we ever do to make you hate us?"

"Hate you?" he repeated. "I don't hate you and I've never hated you, so I don't know where you're getting that from."

"You used to come with us to Bateman's treehouse every day and get absolutely bombed – what changed? Being high is too good for you these days?" asked the nasal voice of a stocky boy fit in a leather jacket and plaid pants.

"I still get high – I'm even high right now, somewhat; I just don't have the same kind of money that I used to," Walter spoke as though he were on trial. "You'd be surprised what responsibilities do to a person."

"Oh, so you don't have a spare second for anyone, not even the only people who bothered to make your life bearable for a good solid few years, and we're not supposed to take it personally?" The girl talking had on large hoop earrings and a ruffled pink skirt.

"Suck yourself off harder, please," Walter said, allowing contempt to ooze out through his tone. "You guys made alright company for a while, but things are different now. I'm not the same person and I don't do the same things."

"Oh yeah? So what do you do these days?" Trevor asked, his arms crossed in a defensive stance. Walter frantically worked to think up a decent response, but his mental state was so cluttered that he couldn't make sense of his actual memories against the backdrop of dreamlike scenes, devoid of any meaningful context to his lived experiences. As his thoughts rambled onwards, it dawned on him that he was silently standing in front of his crew of former comrades that were just staring at him while donning expressions more and more bewildered by the second.

"I don't know," he blurted out, and proceeded to dart back out into the sweeping flow of students rushing by, its riverlike current rushing him up and along the central stairwell. He was swarmed with disbelief at his own social ineptitude, something he didn't consider himself to be characteristic of, but then again, he never would have predicted himself to have handled such a straightforward situation so poorly. He hustled up the stairs, trying to force the freshly-branded memory from his consciousness by focusing on the hurry of the present moment. Reaching the top, he glanced around, sizing up the small clusters of people conversing in their own little sections of floor. He felt a set of eyes baring down on him, and he snapped to attention to see a blonde girl wearing a striking white outfit, complete with a denim jacket, a denim skirt, a whispy scarf, a beret, and tall leather boots.

"Walter?" she called out. "Walter Monroe?"

His blood turned cold. As she beckoned for him to come over, he realized that he had no choice, and trudged over to her and the group she was inhabiting.

"Oh hiiiii, Walter," she cooed, putting one foot behind her and waved at him by bending her fingers into the palm of her hand and then extending them back again like she was checking for a broken knuckle.

"Hello Ashley," he replied, trying to not sound downtrodden but failing in his attempt.

"How come Alina doesn't ever answer the phone when we ring the hospital? It's like she doesn't like us anymore," she asked, feigning sadness and pouting.

He knew that the very first thing she was going to ask about was his girlfriend – they all had some kind of an obsession with the quiet outsiders that were so common at his school. "I don't know; I can't control her," he muttered. "And regardless, she probably doesn't have the time to talk – she barely has time to eat."

"She works so hard, Walt," said another girl in a tight red dress, peeking out from under a straw boater hat. "How does she do it?"

"Yeah, I've never met someone who is so focused on their goals. It's like her every thought comes straight from the future," commented a girl with long auburn hair and silky-looking bellbottoms.

"It must get tiring having to be so nice to her all the time," said one with piercing black eyes and a lusty voice. "It's almost as if she takes you for granted."

"I can assure you that she's the nice one," he responded, rubbing the back of his neck with his hand. The group tittered.

"How is she by the way? It feels like I haven't seen her in weeks," Ashley asked. She was twisting from side-to-side ever so slightly in place.

"Uh – yeah. She's doing alright," Walter replied. "To be honest, you've probably seen her more recently than I have – she doesn't ever seem to have time for me."

She popped out her bottom lip. "I'm so sorry, that must be really hard for you." Fidgeting around with her hands, she was obviously considering what she wanted to say next. "How do you manage to keep your sex life alive?" she inquired, giggling hard. "You two seem to be the type of couple that would be banging eight days a week."

Walter froze up, mortified by the question. His eyes locked dead ahead past the collective of hilarity that was characterizing the group in front of him. Without stopping to consider his options, he turned slowly and meandered off, heading in the general direction of his class, but primarily just trying to get away from the echoing laughter that was erupting behind him.

Stunned by the continued humiliation he was seemingly constantly forced to endure, he felt exhausted already before the day had even started. It was nearly unbelievable how little respect he could garner from the people he was familiar with; it was as though they couldn't help but ridicule him for his helpless nature, and it made him wish desperately he could carry more strength in his interactions. The hallway tightened up as he left the central atrium, and he was forced to walk shoulder-to-shoulder with the crowd sweeping in either which way. Suddenly, a pair of hands reached out and gripped his shirt by its collar, yanking him around and up into the air.

"Would you fucking look at that," growled the tall boy with a chinstrap and a thick green winter jacket who was holding him, "it's a lying bitch."

"Parker," Walter gasped, struggling to speak, "I wasn't lying – I just haven't had the chance to pick up."

"Oh yeah?" he replied. "Well you said Friday – it's Monday. You know that I've got bad nerves, and it's been one hell of a weekend. Looks like you're fucked, Smokey."

"Listen, I'm going to buy with Lando tomorrow. I can give you a gram or two for free the next day, just let me go, please," Walter begged.

"Really, you'd do that?" Parker asked, his mood lightening up.

"Yes, absolutely. I'm sorry that I misled you – I had no idea that things were going to end up this way."

Parker nodded, lips pursed. "Alright, that's fine with me."

"HEY!" a balding, mustachioed man yelled out from the other side of the hallway, pointing as though he had spotted a robber. "Get off of him, you!"

Walter shoved back on Parker, dropping himself to the ground, and he scurried off in a moment of distraction as the teacher began to chew his assailant out. He hurried into homeroom, breathing heavy and full of fear. Without considering where he was going, he fell into the first chair he saw, and heard a voice call out from behind him:

"Hey, Walt."

He spun around in his seat to see Simon, with his neat hair square glasses, and generally arranged decorum. "Oh, hi," Was all Walter mustered. He could feel the immediate tension coming from him.

"So, any reason why you didn't come out to ride on the boat with James, Lou, and I like how you said you would?" Simon had a way of emphasizing his words so that they hit with a certain pointed harshness.

"I'll just come out and be honest: after work on Friday I was so spent that I ended up forgetting about it, but even if I had remembered, I wouldn't have had a ride out anyway," Walter replied, on the defense.

"Lou drove James over – he could've come pick you up as well," Simon pressed. "Why can't you just cooperate with us?"

"I'm particular about how I spend my time," groaned Walter. "It's nothing anything against you guys – seriously, man. Don't read it as anything personal."

"Okay, that's all fine, but you told us you'd be there at 3:30. We waited until 4 for you to show up – don't you think you have some kind of responsibility to follow through on your commitments?"

"Didn't it occur to you I was just saying yes to get out of the conversation? And besides, why do you even want to hang out with me?" Walter asked in a guilty tone, glancing around like he was tweaking so as to break eye contact. "I'm barely even good for company."

"That's the kind of thinking that'll do you in – and I bet it's that line of thought that kept you at home when you actually wanted to get out," Simon said with a roll of his eyes.

Walter looked at him dead on in an instant. "I'd appreciate it if you didn't try to read my mind."

"Walt, I'm sure you think you're reserved and mysterious," he began professing, "but people are surprisingly simple creatures. You say one thing and do another – it doesn't take a doctorate in psychology to deduce that you're at odds with yourself."

"I ask you to quit mind-reading and you just keep on doing it." Walter thought for a second. "And what's that shit about humans being simple creatures? You sound like a serial killer."

"Keep on resisting me," Simon sighed, his head shaking. "You know that I've always been on your side, ever since we were kids. If I haven't changed since a decade ago, then you sure as hell haven't."

"Let me play to expectations and say I have" Walter replied with a smack of his lips. "I stick around stoner crews but that's about it."

"Here we go again: nope, no different. Standard, canned Walter, off the same shelf as grade school," cackled Simon. "You look down to the people one below you and try to make pals. What a hero you are – there's no mental complex you're playing to. Why do you bother with them, after all? It's not as if they actually care about the company they keep – they're just out for quick kicks," he asserted. "Once you stop entertaining them, they'll just toss you to the side. Full stop, man. Grow up."

"Gee, Simon, tell me how you really feel," Walter scoffed.

"I'm just saying – anybody who associates with other drug users exclusively is only out for themselves." Simon put up his hands to indicate impartiality, trying to pull himself out of the situation.

"You're one of those people who calls weed a 'drug'," sneered Walter snarkily. "If it's a drug then why doesn't it poison your body?"

"Oh fuck's sakes," Simon groaned, "I'm not having this argument with you. If you're actually convinced that it's in your best interest to become invested in that group of people, then I can't even begin to change your mind."

"It's pretty unfair that you don't like them just because of the way we choose to pass the time."

"Unfair?" Simon repeated, losing his temper. "You want to know what's unfair? The fact that you can't keep your word to anyone who isn't your girlfriend – who doesn't come across as anything but a narcissistic, air-headed twat anyway – or the degenerate thugs you try to be one of. You – all you do is...." He was forced to take a pause, frozen for a moment, then gasped, eyes wide, suddenly realizing what he had just said. "Shit – Walt, come on, I didn't – I didn't mean it like –"

Simon's unhinged ranting was just not enough because he eventually froze up, himself, but Walter was petrified from the start, blushing intensely, his ears flushed with blood. Rendered unable to respond, Walter merely tuned out Simon's voice as a source of noise entirely. Purely shocked that a normally-placid Simon would try to take a jab at him, he focused ahead to the front of the class and tried to put the unpleasant start to his day out of his mind.

"Alright class; is everyone here?" asked Mrs. Colley. The class continued to talk amongst themselves. She began counting heads before finally throwing her hands up with the energy of a conductor starting up the orchestra. "Alright, quiet down all! Do you want to listen to the announcements or should we just skip them?"

"Skiiiiip," called out a collective voice from all around the room.

"Okay, well continuing from last week, we're deep in the midst of the Cold War, and today we'll be covering the Cuban Missile Crisis and the disaster at the Bay of Pigs that led up to it. Read chapters twenty and twenty-one and then I'll call up a few volunteers to present a summary of the events."

A girl with wavy hair and large hoop earrings shot her hand up into the air.

"Yes, Claire?"

"Can we work in groups?"

"No, not for this. It's important that you really absorb the material, because there's so much complexity involved. Any other questions?" The class was deathly silent. "Okay! Get to work!"

Walter dug into his backpack and cracked open his textbook. If he had to be honest with himself, he hardly paid attention to anything his teacher had to say, and was usually just trailing the other students to figure out what was going on. He skimmed the pages explaining the situation: how America poked around the world with surveillance and reconnaissance to maintain tabs on friendly and enemy factions, how slip-ups corroded international trust and heightened the stakes of the situation, and how it required both sides to swallow their pride to dismantle their offensive capabilities. He was surprised at how aggressive the United States political staff chose to be, as at every turn they came to the conclusion that an all-out confrontation would be the best course of action. "Walter," called out Mrs. Colley.

His reaction delayed, Walter barely realized how much time had actually passed, and did a double take from his book to his teacher. "Yes, Mrs. Colley?"

"Why don't you come up first and talk about what you've found out," she said, her voice rosy.

Reluctant, he got up to his feet and shuffled to the front of the class. Clearing his throat, he began: "The Cuban Missile Crisis began as a result of the U.S. spying on Cuba using U-2 planes in the wake of the failed Bay of Pigs, when it was revealed that Russian missiles had been installed on the island. The United States, not prepared to deal with such a situation, felt forced into responding with an act of war: a blockade. This was after much deliberation on the part of government officials, most of them believing a military strike would be the best solution. In the ensuing exchanges, the U.S. was forced to adopt some humility and accept that they were operating with a lack of communication, and if they didn't cease their belligerence, it would mean annihilation for the world. In short, the Communists didn't see there being any other option than the one they took, and only because of Kennedy's patience that the situation was resolved peaceably."

The class was unnervingly quiet.

"Uh – That was… That was very good, Walter, I just don't think you're fully grasping the immense pressure that our nation was put under," said Mrs. Colley.

"What she means to say is that you sound like a sympathizer," called out a boy from the back of the room. The class erupted with laughter.

"Quiet, Butch!" Mrs. Colley snapped. "You did alright, Walt, just next time try to understand the context to the situation better. Alice, you're next."

Walter hobbled back and dropped into his seat, exhausted from the mere moment he had to spend in front of the class. They were ravenous, as any group of young people would be, and coming across as a weak target was grounds for immediate harassment. He slunk back into his chair, tapping his fingers and stretching his legs. He reached into a pocket for a piece of gum to calm his nerves, but was surprised when he touched a crisply folded piece of paper. He pulled it out, wondering if it had been left in his jeans overnight. Once opened, he saw a copy of the note from that morning, the top and bottom sections scribbled out in black marker and the poem in the middle circled:

Up over the valley and down by the crick
Through bushes and brambles and branches all thick
There was an old man who lived in his home
And it was every day he would read memories from his tome
Because it was his mistake to be left alone

When he was younger and chose to play a thief and a trick
He caught hatred for people and he made himself sick
He wanted to forget where he had come from
He cursed his loved ones and was thrown out to roam
And then he realized his fate to be left alone

The world got harder and his skills did not stick
He lost all his blessings and he'd lose himself quick
But the anger and sadness kept his mouth at a foam
He lacked any direction and had an attitude like stone
But all only once he had let himself become left alone

And now he is ancient – in his head there's a nick
He let the world destroy him by making himself an easy pick
And he has to face Hell; it's not looking well
Only by the curse of being left alone

As confused as he could possibly be, Walter flipped the paper over, and noticed a line of writing at the top in neat, tiny letters: *That was awfully rude of them, wasn't it?*

Walter blinked several times, unable to comprehend what was happening. He turned the paper back to the front side, which remained exactly the same, but when he went to the back again, there was a second line: *You're just going to ignore me like that?*

He couldn't believe his eyes.

What are you? he wrote. He sat patiently staring at the paper, studying the careful pen markings intently. He heard Alice talking about Robert McNamara and looked up to watch her face as she spoke. He got bored in an instant and glanced back down.

'What' am I? Last I checked I am a person, thank you very much. the fourth line on the paper read.

Okay, then what's your name? he scribbled down. He shut his eyes for a few seconds.

Brielle read the next line when he opened them again.

Walter's heart began pounding, overflowing with xenophobia. *Where are you? Do you know me? How are you doing this?* he jotted at a breakneck pace. He flipped the top cover of his binder over the paper and then closed it again.

At the movie theater with my boyfriend. We're watching this film about a crime syndicate and it's badass. No, I don't know you, but I think it's better that way. And I'm just doing the same thing you are, I would think. were the words that appeared on the paper.

He thought frantically for things to ask her. He wanted to find out every last detail about whoever was defying reality to communicate with him, but he had no idea where to start. *Are you*

Crowe

happy? was what he finally settled on, and slid his hand over the paper.

Kind of. Everyone in my life is so great and supportive but I don't even know who I am practically every hour out of the day. I don't think there's a better word to describe it other than to just say that everything feels bittersweet. It's like, you love the universe but it doesn't want you back, so you just kind of float around wondering if there's any purpose at all. I guess the short answer is 'no'.

It occurred to him that such a response was so close to something he would say that he nearly considered he might be having a conversation with himself, but he quickly told himself that there was no way this could be anything but a miracle. He analyzed the paper and he composed his response in his head before writing it down: *I couldn't have said it better myself. This one girl makes my whole world rotate and I'd lay down everything I'll ever have to give just to keep her safe and secure, but it's like she's forgetting about me more and more by the day. We haven't had sex in months and she doesn't even seem to miss me anymore. It has me going out of my mind but I can't risk losing her so I just keep it all to myself.*

He read the instructions for tonight's homework on the whiteboard before turning his attention back to the paper.

What's your girlfriend's name, if I may ask? And I know what you mean: it's like my boyfriend is constantly sinking further into himself, and I don't think I'm losing him, but he just doesn't trust me the same way anymore. I remember back when he wasn't afraid to laugh or cry in front of me, and we'd even lay in the dark sometimes just talking about what scares us most. It was the closest thing to having myself as separate person that would love me in my place, 'cause I can only seem to find the faults in me.

Alina. he wrote. *She's training to be a surgeon, but she could be a model if she was about three inches taller. I have no clue what she sees in me, but she used to tell me all the ways that we mattered on this planet, and that this was all just one big plan set in motion. She would say that if we give up, we only really are giving up on everybody else, because we might not matter to ourselves, but we all only want to watch the rest of us succeed. She could give me a reason to hope even on the grayest day of the year – now she doesn't even mention love when I talk with her about the both of us.* He pursed his lips, letting the weight of his statement sink in fully, then rolled his pen over the top of the paper.

That's a wonderful name. She sounds like an astounding individual – I wish I could meet her. But just know that she still thinks all of that stuff deep down, even if she doesn't show it for a single instant. It sounds like she's falling out of religion, and I only say that because I'm finally finding a God that I can believe in. It truly changes you once you can allow yourself to be caressed by holy love. Suddenly there are no such things as fuck-ups; there are just hiccups on the road to destiny. You should give her time – she'll come back around; He tells me so.

Walter gripped the end of his pen in his teeth and thought furiously. He was afraid he'd say the wrong thing and no more words might appear on the paper. It seemed as if every question was presented in front of him but not a single one truly mattered, and he was stuck in a limbo of indecision. *What do you do about the pain?* he decided to ask. He put the side of his forehead on the palm of his hand and dropped his fingers in front of his eyes, then pulled them through his hair and sighed.

Smoke weed by the zip, fuck all the time, drink when I can, drive around with the music blasting, and watch movies where people get cut in half and heads explode. Yourself?

I smoke when I can get it, but most of the time I just reminisce on an easier past and plan out an improbable future. Money's been real tight around the house ever since Dad gave up on us for the thirtieth time. A contradiction popped into his awareness. *How did you know what just happened in class but you don't know a single detail about my private life?* He checked the ticking clock on the wall: 10:09. His eyes flashed back to the paper in an attempt to watch the words appear on it but he was too slow.

I get premonitions and can see bits of the present and future (believe it or not – my boyfriend thinks it's all horseshit) but I can only see so much. *I couldn't see anything of you; what do you look like?*

Walter read the question and insecurity sunk into him. *Kind of dumpy. I get told that I have bad hair and a plain face. But at this point, I'm inclined to believe you, because this is supernatural front to back.*

He peered around to the seats surrounding him to see if anyone was watching his strange behavior. Of course, everyone was half-asleep in their chairs, staring ahead or down at their desk and paying him no mind.

Have you ever seen anything else supernatural? read the next line.

He bit the inside of his cheek and cracked his knuckles while he wrote: *Not to my knowledge, no.* Taking a deep breath through his nose and then out his mouth, he shut his eyes for a moment.

Well you will soon. Please be careful. were the words that greeted him when they opened.

Walter went from being intrigued to intensely frightened. *What's going to happen to me?* he authored in under a moment. He observed the clock again to try and quiet his nerves by noting the passage of time, but three minutes had barely even passed.

I don't know. I can't see that far ahead. the next line read.

The magnanimity of his situation was only just setting in. *Is it only me? How many other people are going to be affected by this?* he penned frantically. His eyes drifted upwards, studying the chips in the ceiling tiles.

I can't speak to the scope in which this is occurring; I only know that you are being searched for. I think that's the reason why we were connected: for your protection. he read when he looked back down.

He scribbled down *Am I going to die?* All sound in the room suddenly became shut out, the only noise being his heartbeat echoing in his ears. His gaze floated around, unable to focus on anything, but then finally settled back down onto the paper to read the next line:

I don't think you're in any kind of danger, but try your hardest to stay safe.

Can't you tell me what I've got to look out for? he wrote, becoming frustrated at his defenselessness. He began fearing all sorts of people from his past, picturing the faces of those he wronged, wondering to himself which would be the one to make him meet his undoing.

You'll know it when it reveals itself to you. Just be strong; you can only fail if you give in. he read next.

I feel like I'm about to pass out. he penned sloppily, unable to channel his attention entirely in any one direction, and then wiped his forehead with the collar of his shirt.

Blinking rapidly, a new line appeared after a moment or two: *You're going to be alright; just don't go out the back door when you're leaving work today.*

He shook his head, impatiently jotting down: *Can't you see what I'm going to find out there?* He was pinching his bottom lip between his teeth so hard that it was starting to bleed. Suddenly, laughter broke out in the room, startling him. He looked from one corner to the other in the room trying to figure out the source of the outburst, but he couldn't make any sense out of what just happened. When he checked the paper again, he was nearly furious to find that nothing new had appeared. He began tapping his foot in rhythm to the thumping of his heart, reading irrelevant information on the blackboard merely as a meager distraction. Hollow relief poured over him when he realized there was another line on the paper:

It's not making itself apparent to me, but I can sense a strong collection of spirits. They're waiting for you, even now.

Walter didn't know how to respond. He didn't think spirits were real for one thing, but disbelief seemed to be a poor shield against this chilling information. *What do they want from me?* he scribbled back.

Crowe

He put his hand on the paper, but upon removing it, nothing had changed. *Hello?* he wrote on the next line.

"Okay, see you all tomorrow," said Mrs. Colley as the bell rang and people lined up to get out. He felt desperation akin to a man pinned to the ground by a boulder, roasting in the desert heat, and the only thing he could do was to write: *Please, answer me!*

VI – B

Sportscars, vans, and buses trickled into the parking lot through its two entrances. The atmosphere of liveliness was formed by the blaring of music intermeshed with the raucous laughter and yelling coming from all angles. The sun was just waking up and gently touching down on the chilled pavement. The lawn between and around the lot and the school was being trampled by students walking from the nearby neighborhood passing under the shade of trees and kicking up dew. There was something delightful about witnessing the congregation of youth. They didn't know it, but their comradery was that of a military company: all stuck in a certain lifestyle that was only escapable through the passage of time, and even though they grinned and bore it, they prayed that their burdens might expire soon enough for their sanity to remain intact. Faces saw other faces, hands waved across the distance, and each voice competed for dominance over the rest, making a tangled mess of noise like spaghetti. Students waded through the crowded parking lot, cutting off cars that were already rolling around slowly while trying to find a spot, and further slowing down the process for everyone involved. The face of the auditorium looked over the swarming populace like a baron's estate looming in the presence of the local serfs. There was no baron, however, just a herd of roaming souls chained at the ankles to their fleeting desires. They all looked as though they could be an acting troupe, dressed up and decorated in the most cutting and current fashion. The whole lot of them were on their last legs to keep up their image to the ones that heckled them, desperately scraping by with the leftovers of yesterday's reliefs and triumphs. Albeit heroes in their own right as teenagers facing uncertain times, nobody would ever sing their songs; their children wouldn't know of their cautious and meticulous outward personas. By the time that they had been phased out of the limelight, no one would remember their efforts: it will be like they had been adults their whole lives.

The crackle of the loudspeaker sounded off: "Everett Marshall to guidance; Everett Marshall," and then went silent with a click.

A girl wearing bell bottoms who had short, boyish hair began laughing so hard that she was practically screaming. "I told you that Johnson was going to snitch on you sneaking out!" she shouted.

The whole outside of the school was alive with that kind of energy. Boys in slick jackets slyly courted dolled-up young women. Hair was geld and finely combed, or flat ironed and flowy and silky, or curly like chocolate shavings. Broad smiles and eyes squinted from laughter and sunlight. Freshman hustled from the buses into the school, concerned to not upset older students whom were flocking around them as they entered the building. It wasn't an issue of harmony, nor of cooperation: it was a full-scale exercise that was the clicking of boots and slapping of sneakers against the pavement, and if any of them had not one successful venture their life, they could at least take pride in never having slowed down.

In any single instance, they were all proud creatures but also resolutely aware of their lowly status in the world: not even the most charming and mainstream of the bunch could attest to anything but the inequity of their situation. The truth was that no amount of gold plating, jewel encrusting, cork popping, or balcony partying could ever cover up the feeling of servitude that came with being attached to such a place. The student body overall was wealthy, and sure they felt the part, but there was something particular that haunted them in the afterhours once they had shed their clothes and resigned themselves to silence. They'd go to sleep skewered over the crackling fire of their fears, sprinting away from the filthy core to the issue: a breach of liberty. Each one of them was trapped in the eternal hunt for dignity while also fleeing from the cruel reality of young living that was always close on their heels.

Overall, tally up every regret and missed opportunity held by the immense crowd that was passing in front of the building and you'd have such an intricate platter of drama and tragedy that it might seem as if you had stumbled upon a trove of unfinished Shakespeare drafts. There was no giving the wrong impression when it came to the way each of them chose to carry themselves: if nothing else could be guaranteed, it was a certainty that no one would fail to be brutally candid or expose their inner nature to those who should question them. It was a sacrifice of unfathomable scope and dimension to take part in the eight-hour ritual that they were all forced into for the better part of every week, but it didn't come down to a decision of what was bearable and what needed to be avoided, for if nothing ever came from the time that was spent on those wretched grounds, they'd at least have stories to tell when someday questioned on the issue of being without accomplishments. They'd say that if their upbringing had just been more accommodating, then none of their dreams would have gone unrealized. But this wasn't that kind of world. There was no difference between what should be and what wasn't. The time lost was merely lost, and any patience that wound up overboard couldn't be recovered. It didn't matter if Anís rained on the beaches of Barcelona, because they'd never receive word of what it was like. Such was the procession of events: reality struck like a tax collector and took what it was owed, leaving the meager scrapings for whomever was unfortunate enough to be stuck in such a situation.

Brielle had her spot atop Walter, lying on him and the two of them quietly smooching so as to not disturb Powell.

She kissed on his neck, then began smiling wildly with her eyes closed and murmured into his ear "Well then there now, I think

I'll take you for the summer." She was barely able to control her bubbling laughter.

Walter pulled his head to the side to get a look at her. "You just missed it by a week or two – autumn is already in full swing."

Brielle gasped dramatically and slapped her hand onto his breast. "You don't know what that's from?"

His eyes snapped away from her so they could stare out into vacant space instead. "I don't like movies," he muttered out of one corner of his mouth, the other corner bent into a frown.

The engine cut off with a rumble and the keys jingled as they were yanked out of the ignition. "Hey guys we're –" Powell adjusted the rear-view mirror and checked it "– Sick! Fucking cut it out, both of you!"

The two of them peeled off each other and sat straight up with their hands on their respective laps like pupils at a boarding school, smirking.

Walter opened his mouth first: "Hey, we weren't doing anything that time – and we didn't distract you at all from –"

"Walt, shut the fuck up," Powell said as though he was finishing Walter's sentence for him, "and just go to class. You're welcome for the ride by the way."

Walter smacked his lips. "Thank you, by the way." He leapt out over the side of the convertible.

Brielle daintily helped herself up and over, one small footstep at a time. She walked over to Walt and took his arm in hers as they moved with the crowd. "Do you think we'll see Patricia?" she asked in a candid, blissful tone.

"If we see her, I just tell her that we were helping Carter with the talent show in Licker Park and she can't be mad. The real question is: do you think we'll see the Yong twins?" postulated Walter through deep grimness. His eyes were scanning the crowds, observing endless expressions and pinning voices to them.

"If you think that they're onto us, you should remember that Hope still talks to both of them and, yes, even though they know the about everything we've done and are still doing, they've still got the utmost faith in us," Brielle replied, staring blankly ahead and wearing a disaffected face like an executioner flipping the lever.

Walter bit into his upper lip. "Look, all I'm saying is we seemed suspicious not volunteering to clean up the Card Hall even though we're trying to get its address. We're being inconsistent."

"Hi, Brie!" cheered an approaching girl in tan slacks and a gray button-up.

"Hey Susie," she replied enthusiastically, cracking a large smile and snapping into an adorable pose for a moment. Her countenance dropped upon passing one another. "It's a rite of passage to be allowed there; they might have invited you or me but that doesn't mean they were being serious. Just be patient. So long as they think we're more focused on Lewell's party than being accepted into their fold then we have an alibi. They won't expect us to be targeting them; they've already got plenty of enemies."

"I sure hope you're right," he said with a shake of his head disguised as a nod.

"Leave the hoping to me," she replied sweetly.

It seemed as though the crowd was parting just for them as they passed, as if they were some kind of guests and this was an event. They could have been patrolling through a concert, or a campus, or a mall on its opening day, but instead they were in the worst-case scenario: complete submission to their environment. To put the feeling of constriction into words would be near impossible, but in short, they were all in their own separate cages, and no matter the size of the horde that surrounded them or the level of activity that was present, there was no escaping the crushing solitude of being at such a place.

Walter unhooked his arm from Brielle's as they approached the curb and had to push past the dense blocks of people standing around talking, refusing to make way. They pathed from side to side, darting around cautiously to avoid colliding with any of the stationary packs – side glances were exchanged between them and the passive ones listening to argumentative ones speak. He found it impossible to help but to look over to meet whatever set of flashing eyes it was this time directed at him, but after a brief moment of one sizing the other up, the watcher's gaze always returned back towards a larger group. There was a certain acknowledgment that occurred in that split second of connection: both parties accepting their lowly status as another peon making up the population that had been put off to the side and forgot about. They were the long guards, the ones who had to bear the brunt of whatever misery the rest of them chose to force upon them – they could only hope for the group in totality to be a peaceable bunch without anyone interested in unleashing their own form of malice. After all, it only takes one instance of Satan to produce Hell.

He held open one of the double doors for her and watched as she entered the plain institution made of large tan bricks. The inside was a long, wide hallway with the entrance to the auditorium on the right, the gym on the left, and bathrooms at the far end. The ceiling was littered with diamond-shaped windows inset in the tiles. Further down, red and gold banners hung from the right wall around plaques and cases which faced the student shop to the left. Cliques had settled in and picked their own spot, each one distinctive by the amount of noise it put out and how expensive the clothing and accessories appeared to be.

"You know what I want?" Walter asked in a genuine tone.

"What's that, dear?" she sang back to him.

"A drink," he said with resounding confidence.

"*A drink*?" Brielle sneered, her attitude turning from pleasant to completely unsettled.

"Why is that so surprising? You don't go a single day without drinking on some weeks." His voice snapped into a defensive tone, spurred on by his sudden regret for opening himself up to her potential criticism.

"That's because *I* need it to function when I have it. You, on the other hand, are a lightweight," she said in the manner of an older sibling telling their kid brother that they can't come along.

"Am not."

"Are too."

Walter almost raised his tone; almost brought disaster upon himself and his beloved. Nothing attracted ridicule the way a public outburst does, which he knew, and he made the hard choice to maintain his composure instead. "I'm allowed to be stressed out too," he hissed. "You're not the only one who has rough patches, and you're sure as shit not the only one who doesn't get their way from time to time."

"Oh, no – you're wrong about that. I do get my way. Forever and always," she replied.

"I wish I had you recorded, because that's definitely not the truth – not according to you, anyway. I can think of at least six moments in the past two months give or take that you've come close to pitching an actual fit over things going sour for you," Walter said, still irritated by her smarmy attitude.

"I just do what I need to keep you worked up – that's all I really care about. You're so much easier to control that way," she spoke nastily.

A boy to their right turned and stared at Brielle with a shocked expression through his mess of scraggly dirty-blond hair, and paused before breaking out into laughter at her comment.

Walter's face flushed with blood. "Can you quit it, please? I think that guy knew me." He tapped her on the arm with the back of his hand.

"You want me to go easy on you?" She scoffed. "Walter, where are your balls at this morning?"

"You're on some big-and-bad shit, I get it. But save it for when we're out of the public eye: for me, please." He analyzed his reflection in the trophy case as they passed it, taking note of how the two of them looked against the backdrop of the bustling crowd.

Brielle gave a reluctant frown off to her side. "I'm just giving as good as I'm getting, hun." She thought for a moment. "But alright; what do you want to talk about?"

"I think Miller, Pauley, and Ali are looking for us still. I don't think they're in a position to do anything, but I'm just going to say:

we should watch our backs," Walter said with trepidation as though they were being watched.

"HA! That's the funniest thing I've heard in a week, easily. The Hutchinsons are pushovers; they don't want conflict. They'd just as soon start a fight or jump someone as they would roll over and show their tubby undersides. If anybody is getting back at us, it sure as hell isn't them," Brielle said with self-assuredness akin to a conquering field commander.

"Okay," Walter replied, shaking his head, "if you're so certain, I guess there's nothing for me to say. I just know that if there was someone, anyone who had violated my trust the way we did to theirs, I wouldn't rest until I had closure that I had retaliated to the best of my ability. Y'know, people only play along for so long – someone realizes that they've been a chump for one day too long and suddenly you have a hero. All I'm saying is that we shouldn't just write them off like that. They might be passive, but that can change on a whim."

Brielle rolled her eyes. "Come on, we've had this discussion already. You said we couldn't stick them up because Pauley talks to Caitlyn and she knows those gangbangers, but then I pointed out how Caitlyn got laid by her girlcrush at Foxbanks because I put in a good word for her. Then you went down the route of trying to convince me that they'd panic and we'd lose control of the situation inside the house, to which I reminded you that they all watched CJ get mugged and just kept silent. I think the hill you died on was: 'They'll key Powell's car if we do', and when I heard that I practically –"

"Alright, you've made your point, Jesus," Walter cut in, him being provoked at this point. "If you're not going to even consider what I have to say then I might as well –"

Brielle stopped in her tracks. Walter froze up as well, not able to formulate a reaction to her sudden shift in behavior. He turned back to face her, the masses of students flooding around them like ants marching past a stone.

"Brielle, cut it out," he commanded of her curtly.

"You want to act all weird, and get paranoid, and not let up, then that's great. Just don't spread your bullshit to me, because I don't have the most miniscule amount of tolerance for it. Can't help but bitch? Bitch when we're in private and you can't make a fool out of me." She was standing tall and trying to suppress an indignant expression.

"Because what you're doing right now isn't making a fool out of either of us," Walter muttered back in the lowest tone he could, making an effort maintain some relative coolness but instead coming across as agitated and flustered.

Brielle flicked out her index finger and held it in front of herself like a scoutmaster scolding a liar. "I'm giving you another chance – just fucking watch it, Walt." She spun around and followed the flow of bodies that they had been obstructing.

He hurried after her, torn between defending himself and just giving in and letting her have her way. Inevitably, she'd triumph over him if he *did* decide to keep on with her, because unlike him, she was perfectly content to go straight to his sensitive issues and pull on them like braids. It seemed unfeasible at best that he'd ever be able to quell her occasional hostile indulgences at his convenience, but if they were what sated her in the long run, then he was in no position to interfere. She purposely kept ahead of him, forcing him to chase after her. It wasn't uncommon for her to test his mettle. He always assumed that she wanted to see who was the tougher of the two – but he would sooner leave her than start a conversation with her on such a topic. Anything that measured one of them against the other needed to be avoided: they did everything in their power to not mention anything related to grades when they were both in the presence of one another.

"Brie, come on," he panted, hustling as fast as he possibly could without shoving anybody to get past. The hallway had ended and they were walking through the cafeteria, the center of its roof a glass dome. Pillars as wide as tires were situated between the white folding tables that were arranged throughout the room. They walked on the right side, the kitchen on the left where people were already in line for breakfast. It was relatively spacious in there – compared to the auditorium hallway, anyway. People were sitting down in groups rather than clustering around the walls, allowing the flow of students to occur with much greater ease. As the space opened up and the herd thinned, Walter finally had enough space to run up and take his spot beside his girlfriend.

"Don't apologize," she said with the impact of a slap. "I can't take any of your groveling, not in the mood that I'm in."

"I'm not saying shit," he replied, looking at her, then, realizing she was staring forward, did the same.

They passed the main office where inside a few students sat in plushy chairs around a small wooden table that made the space resemble the waiting room to a dentist's office. There was the security desk out front where two cops talked over coffee, and then the attendance office right next to it. It was a quiet little operation how the administration conducted itself; the two of them had rarely come in contact with its inner workings, but it was well known that if you wanted something from them, taking your time would inevitably result in a quick policing of your activities. One time, Steve Lewis had to get transferred out of the wrong shop class, but he dragged his feet and made them look up all of his options, and in the meantime, the head secretary figured out that he had been called down one time for flashing a knife in the hallway and they had his backpack searched. They only found a lighter. Still gave him hell for it, though. Across the office was a small alcove with benches and a large brass statue of a turtle, the school mascot, his head cocked back like a braying horse.

"Okay, so I'll just quickly fill you in on how things are going to go from here on –" Brielle started.

"No," Walter growled, getting past his point of patience, "let me tell you exactly how things are going to go: you're going to pretend like I'm on your side and not working against you, and in exchange, I'll play along with anything you throw my way. Sound fair?" He had calmed down considerably by the time he finished compared to his first few words.

Brielle was silent for a second, just letting the sound of shoe soles slapping against the speckled linoleum and discordant chattering fill her ears. "You're sexy when you get aggravated," she said at last, giggling and slapping his arm.

Walter just shook his head, but he was grinning nevertheless. "Well enjoy it while you can, because it's really not worth it for me, or anybody for that matter, to get worked up. Personally got tired of that shit years ago…. How are you, by the way?"

"Bitter," she replied, "but I started out that way, so" she shrugged. "I need to distract myself. Let's talk future."

"What are you going to wear for the full moon on Friday?" Walter asked. "I settled on that pinstripe white and green oxford shirt and some khakis."

"I was thinking about the orange and yellow polka dot dress, but I'm on the fence about wearing my jumper with flowers on it, just in case we have to run," she replied.

"We're not going to have to run – Joe said he wasn't sure what he saw that night. We got spooked over some shadows and fled the scene before we had a proper chance to investigate," Walter spoke in his usual tone of certainty, not willing to consider that there might be some truth apart from the one he keeps.

"What about the groaning?" she asked.

"That nasty croaking sound? Probably a toad. If not, could've been a load of crickets. Nature makes noises that can't be explained sometimes." He looked at the nurse's office to his left, noting a stocky boy with a welt on his forehead and a bloody tissue stuffed up his right nostril. On the other side of the window with the sign-in sheet on it were women in white coats standing around lazily, conversing to one another occasionally. Metal shelves lined the walls in there, each one filled with boxes and bottles and jars all arranged in impeccable fashion. He had been back there once for a swollen toe: Becky Richardson had stomped on it with the back of her heel when he told her that her makeup didn't make her look oriental, just tired. The nail got mashed in and he was down there for the rest of the day, and what he learned then was that more people come down and claim to be sick than there are kids in detention, which to him, was a lot.

"Hey, Earth to Walter." Brielle snapped her fingers in front of his face. "Come in, jackass."

"What?" he grunted grumpily, then realized he had just been tuning her out. "Sorry, could you repeat yourself?"

"Somehow I fucking knew you'd say that," she tsked. "Anyway, I think you're being ignorant to the reality of the situation. We heard something that was distinctively human-like, saw someone that was distinctively human-like, and even could tell that it was walking towards us."

"It was pitch black, just like the night. Against the water, whatever it was that looked like it was coming out of Cobey Pond couldn't have been anything but a bit of fog or something of the sort. And we must have been looking at two different things, because I saw it floating towards us, not walking," he replied.

"What do you mean? I said it was moving towards us, not walking," she said with impatience.

"No, you – oh, whatever. Just wear the polka dot. Trust me, it'll feel good to be in a dress for what might be the last warm night of the year."

Brielle laughed. "You say that like it's from experience."

"Rachel used to talk about it. She loved autumn because it meant going back to school and dressing up." Walter paused, an unsettling silence falling over the moment. The hallway became the atrium, where they went up the central stairwell which was crowded with students hustling up the right side and down the left. It was the closest thing to driving that about two-thirds of the school had access to; the rest possessing freedom beyond their years. Potted plants sat on tall quartz blocks and there were glass cabinets built into the walls all around the room, each one with some scientific or artistic display in it. He realized suddenly that he had made her uncomfortable. "Anyway, I'm sure the other girls are going to dress for summer. Plus also I go ape while fucking you in skirts. I think it's a fetish or something."

"Okay, I'll do it just for you. You just have to promise me that you won't put your hand between my thighs around the boys, though," Brielle instructed him. "When we were roasting brats at Pitcher Grove you got so close in there that you got me off a little and Joe saw."

Walter laughed himself. "I'm sure his reaction was priceless."

"Shawn saw too."

"Oh," he said, disgusted.

The two of them stepped up to the second floor and walked towards the library. A thick crowd kept them back, as the most people of notable importance spent their mornings upstairs, and they attracted large crowds all trying to get involved in their conversations. Jocks with short haircuts, dealers, party animals, and trendy scene kids all had their respective group that they commanded. Eventually, they managed to make their way across, stopping next to the library's entrance.

"Hey, bitch," said a girl with burnt red bangs charismatically.

"Hello, love," Brielle replied, blowing a kiss.

"Walt," muttered a tank of a boy next to her with a jean jacket that had the sleeves torn off.

"Joe," Walter said at the same volume.

"Brie, what day were you thinking about going to the Rich-Park townhouse?" asked a second girl with wide hips and a low-cut shirt.

"We'll be there Wednesday, Lyla," replied Brielle, bouncing on her toes restlessly. "Probably – anyway. Cable television is doing news reports out in front of it all today and tomorrow. So it'll mean waiting two days, but it's because we want to make sure we have it to ourselves: undisturbed…." She was licking her teeth when she locked eyes with Lyla, and both of them broke out into giggles; staring sensually at one another.

"What do you think we'll find?" Walter meekly chimed in.

"Not any evidence of a murder," his girlfriend said, flicking her hand as though to dismiss his question. "Everyone is certain that it was just an accident."

Lyla appeared impassioned by her friend's opinion – her mood upturned. "But haven't you heard all the details?" she insisted to Brielle. "The paper said he was decaying in his comfy chair when they finally found him and everyone thinks he had been paralyzed… but by what exactly, no one can say."

"This is all getting too freaky for me," interjected the girl with bangs.

"Come on, Hope – don't be so touchy." Joe spoke over the crowd with the force of a falling tree. "Just 'cause you're too afraid to come along –"

"You wish I was afraid! I'm just not stupid is all. Why would you sneak into a crime scene? You're begging to get caught," Hope replied, miffed.

Lyla stepped forward and held out her hand. "Hope, it'll be OK. We're not there to mess anything up – as long as everyone stays on the same page, there's no way we get in trouble."

She crossed her arms, "Listen, Lyles, I love you but I'm never going to –"

Joe was rolling his eyes. "Be more like Lyla: she actually goes along with the group and doesn't spend her time whinging," he said crudely.

Hope scoffed incredulously, her mouth wide open. "Okay, alright, fuck all this. I don't choose to use my homeroom to be put on trial." She stormed off.

Lyla was looking around, her teeth showing how they would be if she was wincing through sharp physical pain. "Yeaaahhh… I think I'm gonna have to go…. Bye guys," she said, then slinked away.

Joe was shaking his head and grimacing. "She's so goddamn touchy… fuckin' – what's her fuckin' deal? Goddamn…."

It was like this most of the time: half of the group crushing on the other half, some people liking people who liked another person who liked another person who liked another person. It seemed borderline incestuous to him how the people who relaxed around one another were also having sex freely, and going so far as to occasionally flash uniquely abusive habits that platonic individuals wouldn't dare ever reveal to one another. It didn't matter to him, as they weren't his friends anyway – Brielle was the one who had the investment in them. To him, he was a child adopted into a family that despised one another in the moments that they weren't in love instead, but no wounds would ever tear them apart. For the sake of the group, they held fast and true so that they might continue down the same path together, watching all flanks and launching themselves through the darkness that they could only describe as being anarchic disillusion. They were young, they were scared, and they were the vanguard of the future, breaching the unknown and bringing with them an unrelenting ferociousness. In the end, it was the chaos that forged their kinship.

VII – A

Walter continued to shut his eyes for seconds at a time and then snap them back open, furiously studying the paper. The last lines of his writing were enraging him with their inability to garner a response the way that they were just moments ago. Palpitations in his chest rocked his body back and forth, and the only thing his ears could hear was a rush of blood.

"Hey... Walt?" the student next to him asked, tapping him on the shoulder delicately.

Walter glanced over to see Jamal, someone who drifted freely of faction and absent of conflict wherever he went. "Uh, what?" he stammered.

"You look like you're going to be sick – are you alright? What are you reading?" Jamal reached over and grabbed the paper.

Walter panicked. "It's – fuck – It's nothing, really, don't take it too –"

"Yeah, I'll say." He flipped the paper back over, showing it to Walter. The sheet of notebook paper was completely devoid of writing, top to bottom and front to back.

"Yeah... I – I was having a hard time seeing the individual lines. I think I might need glasses," Walter barely managed to speak.

"Well take it easy dude; it looked like you were really stressing out over there." Jamal passed the sheet of paper back to

Walter. "Hang in there, Walter Monroe," he said with the blank stare and tone of a man possessed, then pathed towards the hallway.

He struggled to get to his feet himself, heart pounding and mouth dry as a bone. Making every attempt he could to not trip over his own feet, he followed the last person out and went to the right. He wasn't sure if anyone could hear his ragged breathing, but to him, it felt like he had just smoked two filterless packs while fucking for half an hour tied down to the top of a speeding van. He had been moving at a breakneck pace, but had hit a snag that took all of his momentum and slammed it into the wall, shattering all sense of self apart from a primal, paranoid desire to not be preyed upon.

'Think about it,' Walter rationalized to himself, 'what could realistically hurt you? You've fought guys twice your size and wrestled knives and blunt instruments out of people's grips before – some spirit isn't taking you down. Worst comes to worst, I'll just be really conservative with my movements for the next few weeks: if I just don't take any risks and stick close to home whenever possible, nothing is going to reach me. I don't have to be afraid of being snuck up on if I keep my back against the wall.' He considered Brielle for a moment, and how much of what she was saying might be true. 'As far as I know, she's just trying to get something out of me – she could be the spirit herself, whatever that actually may be. If she contacts me again, I have to be sure to get a consistent, thorough story from her, or else I can't trust anything that she writes to me about....' He remembered that Lando might force him to go to the clocktower that Friday for the full moon with his crew, if not for just an hour at most. 'Fuck... okay," he thought, "well I might be able to cancel on them entirely. I go to the sale in the woods tomorrow, I tell them on the way out that I've got to lay low for a bit, and then I lay low for a bit. It really shouldn't be any more complicated than that.'

The walk through the hallway was calming him down marginally if at all, and it was a relief to be able to move and feel that he had some freedom and space to throw punches, even if he was actually caught in the wide net that held the entire student body like bluefin tuna packed against one another. It was refreshing to not have to talk to anybody involuntarily – that morning had practically smothered the high that he was still barely carrying forward when he disembarked the bus. His respite came to an end when he went back downstairs and into the first classroom on the left, and he resigned himself back onto terms of survival. He looked around the tired space, students still thawing out from the frozen clutches of their sleep that had only concluded a few hours earlier. Inconspicuous like a derringer, Walter slipped a small envelope to a burly kid sporting dreads put up in a thick headband in the back and then sat next to him. Corbin, that towering street fighter beside him, was his former wrestling rival from years prior – an archaic and unintelligible respect still persisting between the two of them.

"It's light," Corbin muttered, scanning the room to ensure the two of them were safe to talk.

"That's because it's just the tabs – Cisco can't get the shrooms until the Easter Basket comes in on Wednesday or so," Walter replied calmly, easing in and interlacing his fingers over his stomach. "Just take it easy, Corb."

"You trusted *Cisco* to get shrooms?" He scoffed, incredulous. "As far as I know, these are perfume strips in here," he said as he shook the envelope. "He would steal something from you, sell it back to you, and then rob you again – there's a reason Lando doesn't let him handle any negotiations, because he's as corrupt as a Hollywood pedophile."

"Look, Cisco's under the gun right now because he got caught by the Trentons trying to move their blow without telling them he was taking it from the safehouse, not the trainyard. If he crosses one more person, he'll have enough enemies that they'll have no choice but to snuff him," Walter said, coldly staring out like a general in a plane observing a strip of countryside that he had napalmed.

"People said the same thing when he took the rims off of Jesus' lowrider: that it would only be a few days before he got together with Andre and the two of them would bust up his knees and his hands like how they told everyone that they were going to.

Wherever the Grass Grows Greener

Fast forward a few months and Jesus and Andre haven't talked since, and they're keeping their eyes so low that you'd think they were walking down a staircase," replied an impatient Corbin.

"Corb, you know the difference here," Walter remarked, beginning to get his focus back. "Andre doesn't do anything when the people he fronts for tell him that they lost his supply – he's so lazy that to him, it's not even worth the trouble of tracking anyone down and taking his share back again, because he's always onto the next thing anyway and so one-track minded that he can't look back as if he was a shark." He cleared his throat and adjusted his voice. "And mark my words: if Cisco makes one more wrong move, Lando's going to lose his foothold with Charlemagne. If that merger dissolves, then a whole market disappears, and there's going to be at least a few knife fights over reclaiming that lost territory – and that'll just be the first week."

"It's all just talk," Corbin said dismissively, "nobody knows what really goes on out there. Under all circumstances, Charlemagne cannot afford to lose his latest business partners: he just suffered that huge break-in at Back Cabin. Around a grand slipped out his palm that day, and apparently, he doesn't even have enough weight to pull a profit for the next month. He's so far in debt that even if him and Lando went to war tomorrow, nobody would go down the trail that he'd blaze because his following has no reason to trust him any further."

"No – that's not true even in the slightest," Walter contested. "Charlemagne has some of the most loyal backing in the school district. He's been in worse situations: two years ago he went down to the Clock Marshes and –"

"And lost a case of handguns. Then the next day he had arranged a hostage situation and everything was back to its rightful owner by sunset. I know, Walt – he gets results, I'm just saying that if he keeps coming up empty, people are going to take score eventually and his leadership will rotate out the same way as how Trish or Channing dropped the ball one or two many times and the congregations that they had arranged over the years all dispersed like roaches in a spotlight." Corbin checked to make sure the teacher was looking the other way as she consoled an anxious blond girl before he pulled the envelope open and took stock of its contents. "There's way too much in here," he said, unable to fathom why he had just discovered what he did.

"I told you – Cisco means business. He couldn't get you the shrooms, but he's compensating for the time being. Just have some patience with him," replied Walter reassuringly. "Don't sweat it. And you want to know the difference between Trish, Channing, and Charlemagne? It's a conversation for another day, definitely, but the truth runs so deep that you could take a college course on it."

"Honestly Monroe? I really couldn't be bothered to figure any of that out – right now all eyes are on Lando. He's got all the leverage in the world, but in typical fashion, he's sitting on his hands and not letting anyone get even the first clue what he's planning to use his extensive finances for." Corbin shook his head. "I'm not saying you should stick your neck out enough to try and get the inside track on him, but –"

"Let me finish your thought for you: if I can figure out where the revenue he made from flipping tha' shipping crate of bullets is going to go, then you can make speculation in whatever he's not going to sell, because, just being honest, if everyone has to wait any longer on him to flood the market, people are going to lose out on so much business that they're going to be stealing stray wallets to stay on track for the end of the year. You yourself invested in three hundred tabs back in August, then just one week later, Channing rides into town with sacks full of the shit. If I remember correctly, you had to sell them all for ten cents on the dollar, because if you had waited any longer, it would've all been a worthless commodity. It didn't even matter that he crossed the Fishers and lost his territory in the Ocean Rock trailer park, because he turned such a massive profit that by the time he had lost his every aide, he had enough money to move into the Billboards penthouse and be a full-time middleman there. I know, you really don't want to relive history here, but you've got to understand: if

Lando even considers for a second that I'm fishing for information that's going to lose him money, I'll show up to school the next day in a neck brace, and that'll just be the first day."

"Okay, Walt," said Corbin nastily, "I'll cut right to chase at this point, because there's no point in trying to insult your intelligence and vice versa: I'm in Charlemagne's corner."

"I know: you were the one with the red hockey mask and the black Wolf Warrior sweatshirt behind him at his desk when Zeke had to make the trade for his paintings to get enough vodka for his party. I don't let those kinds of things go over my head – if I didn't know how to ask all the right questions, I wouldn't even be aware of the fact that Lando pushes drugs." Walter had his eyes closed and he was scratching the space between his eyebrows.

"That's great – I couldn't be less bothered at the revelation that people know my identity without my awareness. I'm only concerned with keeping the back of my head intact." Corbin had his lips to the side, biting the inside of his cheek anxiously. "Guess you feel like hot shit for that lucky fucking break being Lando's lapdog: you proved your capability by snitching on someone and got relieved of your List for the year. It's a fucking joke that immunity from all sides of the court 'til the end of the year just landed in your lap with a bow on it, only because you lurk in corners and have big ears." Irritation settled into him once he had fully gotten out his rant, yet Walter was silently still staring fuzzily into the space all around him and digging his thumbnails under one another, hands clasped. "Everyone's buzzing about it. Not a single one of them is saying anything except that it's goddamn ludicrous how five people who fucked you over in the past year are going to walk free of punishment, but you don't have to go a day without reaping all the benefits of being under Lando." He snorted through one nostril to show disgust but also to clear it of thick, bloody mucus.

"Listen," Walter scoffed, eyeing him lazily and wearing a dopey expression as he began talking, "man, if I'm keeping up with the ringleader's expectations, then who cares if anybody I'd have to go out of my way to get revenge on ends up just walking instead?

It's not like it actually occurs to them. People seem to forget that regardless of whether or not I'm under the public pressure to complete a Fist List, I don't go pussy behind-the-scenes: someone comes at me the wrong way? I take something of theirs and put it the wrong way." He looked off in a different direction, a grimace chiseled into his face and chin protruded. "And I include ridiculous, bullshit requests like the one you're pushing on me as coming at me the wrong way, just so you know, Corbin."

"Charlemagne isn't asking," he stated firmly, his brow creased with tension. "If I don't get back to him with knowledge of what to expect, he'll more than likely set up a plot against all of you, and trying to relay such a message back to Lando saying you heard that from me will be met with the exact same response as if they thought you were intensely schizophrenic."

"I wouldn't double-deal on you even if I could profit from it and get away, too: I know what Charlemagne's crew do to people who get on their Fist Lists and let me just say, you lot are medieval." Walter paused for a second, thinking. "But I see your point – okay, so you need to know what Lando's money is going to be invested into? Because if that's what you're saying, Charlemagne must be pretty worried about protecting his investments, and I have to assume you all are in such dire straits that you'll take any available way out no matter the consequences. Doesn't really do me much good to hand out favors for desperate despots who'll inevitably need something more of me in the near future. And I don't know if the worst 'loyalty' registers in your malnourished vocabulary, but –."

"Let me fill you in on something, Monroe:" snarled Corbin, "this was my way of being nice to you. A big mouth will get you a front row seat to the gun show. You want to know what happens now, instead of the easy way?" He paused for emphasis, leaning in. "You're going to get visited."

Walter's face dropped and his eyes appeared paralyzed like an addict who was experiencing excruciating withdrawal. He swallowed hard, "Corb – Corbin, no. I'll – I'll do it: I'll ask Lando and anyone else any questions you've got. Just don't –"

"The offer's fucking over, just like my patience, just like this conversation," he murmured back, his poisonous tone being a reaction to his trust getting desecrated in all of a few minutes. He pulled a crumpled sheet of yellow notepad from his sweatshirt pocket, flattened it out, and jotted down a quick set of numbers interspersed with words – hieroglyphics as far as Walter could tell. He finished in an instant and then held the note down low on his opposite side, away from Walter. The boy on the opposite side of Corbin snatched the sheet from his hand and tucked it away. Walter flicked his eyes at him, and in a strained moment of contact, the boy's unaffected stare told him that he had caught every word in their exchange.

"Okay class: the problems are on the board," said Ms. Aven. She suddenly noticed the gray-faced student in the back of the room who had a thousand-yard stare. "Uh – Walter? Are you going to be sick?"

"Yes," Walter said, pretending to gag.

"Good lord! Get down to the clinic!" she commanded.

He dashed around the side of the room and out the door, Corbin smirking and the class horrified, exclaiming and yelling at him to not vomit on them. For the third time that day, he was thoroughly stricken with fear for his safety. If he had to sit in that room and get boiled alive by the knowledge of it now being inevitable that what was effectively the largest gang in the school was going to grace him with its presence, he might have *actually* been sick if he didn't have a plan. This just worked into his schedule anyway, as if he could have planned such a thing. Nobody looked his way as he exited the central stairwell and passed the security office – there wouldn't be anybody manning it until lunchtime. Reaching the other end of the cafeteria, he went out into the back parking lot and passed through a few rows of beaters and rust buckets, then opened the door to the back seat of a wood-covered Buick wagon before tossing his back pack in.

"Oh, fuck – scared the shit outta me," exclaimed Annabel from the passenger side, whose face had been pressed against a round hand mirror. Her collar was undone and messy, her short, spiky hair was put to the side as usual, and her bloodshot eyes had pupils the size of dimes. She sniffled and brushed the powder off from under her nose. "Ohp – fuggin'," she said suddenly, snickering and replacing her bra over her right breast, it being covered in a scattering of round purple welts, then buttoned her shirt back up. "You didn't see shit."

"You've shown me your nipple piercings twice already – most recently being two weeks ago at that block party on Barnard," Walter replied with levity as he settled into the back seat.

"What? I didn't even fucking go to that block party," Annabel scoffed.

"Oh yeah? What did you do two weeks ago?"

"Shit...." She rubbed her head, groaning. "Okay, yeah, you might be right."

"Hello, Walt," said Zeke with the professional intonation of a receptionist from the driver side.

"Zeke." He shook his hand from over the seat.

"I hear that you'll see us tomorrow for the buy," Zeke stated coolly.

"Yeah – against my better judgment, too," Walter said, scratching his eyebrow. "I need to pay back Parker and also it's getting to be that point in the year when I need to smoke daily or else my nerves will make me feel like I'm being put through a roller."

"You mean to say: all year," Annabel remarked. She took out a pack from her shirt pocket and slipped out two cigarettes, putting one in her mouth and holding the other one over the back seat behind her. "You really should," she said insistently to Walter. "It's not good to let yourself melt in your emotions."

"If I have one now, I'll end up craving three more by the time I go to sleep," he replied begrudgingly, making a concerted effort to not second guess himself.

"I mean... I can give you four," Annabel said in an obvious tone like someone had just asked if she was on the pill.

"Really? Oh, fuck yeah," Walter exclaimed triumphantly. He let her put it in his mouth and light it from around the seat, then he rolled down the window and leaned his arm outside of it, pulling his hand back in occasionally to take a drag.

"I'm debating on how much I want to cop," Zeke said pensively.

"Well, do you think Cisco is going to come through with the Easter Basket by Friday?" Walter asked, ashing the cigarette onto the pavement of the parking lot. "If it turns out that weed is a useless commodity by the end of the week, I'd say it's better to just play it conservatively."

"The Khans said they'd come out to the clocktower if they know we'll be smoking on the full moon, and watching them box is some wild shit," Annabel commented.

"Eustace Khan is a pathological liar, Bel," Zeke cut in, looking at her. "He'll bring his family, smoke all our smoke, and run off when there's nothing left to take." He peered out the window at the gray sky that was resting behind the run-down bleachers of the football stadium.

"You just don't like him because he grabbed my ass at homecoming," Annabel snapped. "Get over it."

Zeke glanced at Walter, then back out the window. "Not now," he said flatly.

"Fuck the Khans," Walter declared. "This March, Brent Khan pushed Alina into the lockers and felt her all over, then ran off." He took a long pull, letting the crackling of material burning fill his ears. "I'd be hard pressed not to bust his head."

"Why don't you?" Annabel asked so devilishly that she might as well have been rubbing her hands together. "We could lure them out, and nobody would expect you to end up coming out to the full moon, because you told everyone that you're visiting Alina at the hospital that night. The Khans respect a good square-off: you could get the fight that you want."

Walter shook his head, his lips pushed to the side. "If I leave the clocktower and show up to the hospital bloody, Alina's going to send me back home. She can't stand it when I get into trouble. Besides, if we can go off the past, then the Khans are going to have the integrity of mealworms."

"Yeah, but if you don't start working on your Fist List, Lando is going to…" Zeke started, turning around to look into the backseat.

Walter stared venom at him, betrayal and anger consuming him.

He glanced between Annabel, who was shocked, then back to Walter. "Oh, fuck – sorry, Walt, I –"

"What do you mean…? Walter doesn't have to do his this year." The two of them were deathly silent, when suddenly she screamed at the ceiling of the car: "You weren't going to fucking tell me that Lando went back on his decision to not force Walt to do a List for the year?! Zeke, you selfish fuck!" Her fists were tightly clenched, and she was brandishing her knuckles like they were firearms.

"Bel, it's really not that serious – Lando might change his mind back again once things between him and Charlemagne work out," Zeke said, desperately trying to deescalate the situation.

"And what if he doesn't?" Annabel cried out. "Cisco only got four done two years ago and he got jumped three times in the week after the New Year – if he hadn't gotten back on Campbell to reach his full five, it would've only gotten worse from there. Once Lando lets everyone know that you pussied out on your List, you turn into a giftbox for anyone looking for an easy victim: it destroys any kind of reputation you've got. If my life is safe right now, it's only because I've already taken revenge on six people so far this year.""

"I'm at four; apparently Lando is at nine, which isn't surprising," Zeke said with trepidation, shrinking into the corner of the car. "Didn't you tackle Ken Couric in the soccer field this January, Walt? That should put you at one, which is at least something to work with."

"No – that was last November. I'm at a resounding zero." His cigarette was hardly putting him at ease, as he knew how precarious of a position his life was steadily entering into.

"We have to start planning – now," commanded Annabel. "How many other people know that you've got to do your list again?"

"Only Cisco and Zeke were there when Lando told me, and neither of them have told anybody," Walter replied, covering his forehead with one hand and smoking out the window with the other.

"Bel, we knew you were going to go mental over this," Zeke groaned while shaking his head and staring upwards at the Buick's wood-panelled ceiling. "If Walt isn't worried about it, why do we have to be?"

"Oh, he's worried about it," snapped Annabel, a defiant scowl masking her fury and a finger sharply pointed at Zeke. "He's worried about it because Lando is a fucking nightmare and we all know what's going to happen if he thinks any of us have been slacking off – and Alina is worried, too." She then gazed deep into Walter's eyes with the affection of a counselor. "Come on, Walt: think. Who can you get revenge on?"

"Well, if I don't act soon, my possibilities are going to be in the dozens," Walter said with solemn flatness.

"…Walt? What does that mean?" asked Zeke, horrified.

"I'm getting a visit: Corbin said Charlemagne is fishing for information," he sighed through a futile growl, "and I'm the unlucky fuck who got chose to get it for him."

"Corbin is an extension of Charlemagne?" Annabel snapped her stare from one of them to the other and back again, holding a hand out for everyone in the car to look at as though to take the moment and not let it pass due to her disbelief at it. "Why doesn't anybody ever tell me shit?"

"Honestly, even I didn't know that," Zeke mused. "It makes sense, though: they were always talking with Reno and Peng in gym when we were freshmen."

"I just wish I had some kind of idea about what to expect," Walter pondered vacantly. "I don't want to have a sack put over my head and get thrown in the back of a van."

"Charlemagne is humane to business partners, if nothing else," commented Zeke to prevent falling out of the conversation.

"Apparently, Eckhart's brother stole a watch from one of Charlemagne's right-hand men and once they tracked the guy down the next day, they just took it back and left him, not a hair out of place. And Eckhart and him just traffic booze together – nothing as serious as him and Lando."

"No, you don't understand – it's… a different situation, to say the least. According to Corbin, Charlemagne is ready to 'set up a plot' against all of us," replied Walter tensely, biting his lip and pinching the skin on the back of his neck like he was picking up a kitten.

"He can fucking try," Annabel cackled while landing full-force punches into her palms and absentmindedly alternating hands between each one, her eyes glazed over as she relived fond memories. "If Lando finds out that Charlemagne wants war, then it's going to get real bloody. I've been wanting to break out my knuckles again ever since I cracked Vi's jaw with them."

"I don't think it's going to go over like that." Walter was staring down, afraid to look up and see something that he wasn't ready for. "Charlemagne doesn't fight battles: he deals under the table in notes, threats, and promises. If I don't do what he wants, he'll find some way to force me to comply, one way or another."

Zeke had been furiously scratching at his throat and under his chin, disturbed by the present scenario. "Do you…." He dropped his hand and made eye contact with Annabel, both of them sharing the same uncomfortable thought and wearing the same apprehensive expression as they glanced around the inside of the car.

Annabel turned to face Walter. "Do you think they'll do anything to… to –"

"To Alina?" Zeke blurted out at last, the question having been a band-aid that neither of them wanted to rip off.

Walter rubbed at his eyes while subtly frowning. "The day Alina gets harassed as collateral is going to be directly followed by the day that I show up to school with a machete – it just isn't going to happen. Nobody is touching her; they'd have to be too deranged to feel forced to hurt her and too stupid to not fear the consequences. Charlemagne doesn't check either of those boxes."

"The only thing we have to go off of is the standoff that Trish had with his people when she made the snap decision to start stealing from him," Zeke said, working to recollect his distant memories, "and that was the last time she ever made a sale as the leader of anybody. It's not really a good frame of reference, because she had stopped vetting any of her informants, so two of them had already defected by the time she tried to make off with the Jeeps they had stored in their joint garage – he already had her playbook the same day she distributed it, so ending that day in possession of all the chips was, for him, just a formality."

"That day," Annabel continued his thought for him, "Charlemagne came damn close to pulling off the cleanest sweep of an entire faction that I could think of – if he didn't have to abandon the one Cherokee that got crashed into a tree, then he'd have absorbed every last pill, gun, and dime bag that Trish had control of before that day, but from what I heard, he could've been brutal if he had really wanted to go down that route: he had access to their safehouses and knew exactly who the traitors were. It makes sense that he didn't choose to get extreme in that case because he had everything planned out from the very onset – still something worth considering though."

"What I'm mostly worried about is ending up on people's Lists – I mean, if it gets out that I'm working both sides of the court – and it will – then everyone from our end is going to put me at public enemy #1," Walter stated grimly. "Not even *fucking* taking Lando and Cisco into account, Brax and Candy are going to target me just because they're losing money on this whole Charlemagne coalition, Alexus and Ella blame me for the .44 going missing even though I wasn't the one watching it, and Grover wanted to fuck Alina before I had gotten to her. So basically for our whole group, any opportunity to break me publicly just needs a good excuse to be taken, and that's the most valid justification that any of them could ask for."

"If you can find a way to do your list all at once, then you'll have immunity for the rest of the year," Zeke pointed out. "And that wouldn't be the first time anybody's ever done it – it just takes some planning."

"I have a better chance at fleeing the state than I do getting this finished by the end of the year at all – I think even trying to get two done at the same time would be too much to ask," dismissively replied Walter.

"Well, let's just start somewhere: Brent Khan is as good a place as any. He still has detention for the rest of the month, right?" Annabel asked.

"Him and Barry Stewens. Barry ratted on me to McAllen that I was selling to his cousin, and McAllen stole an eighth from me when I was making a sell to him. That makes a few people right there," said Walter airily, absorbing the stakes of what he was suggesting.

"McAllen plays soccer after school in the gymnasium," Zeke recalled.

"What about Odie?" asked Annabel hastily: keeping the ball rolling at top speed. "He sold fake Darvocet to a bunch of people – were you one of them?"

"No, but he sold some to Sara and her girlfriend," he answered word-by-word as the past manifested in his head, "who were my dealers at the time, and she made me pay extra that week to help make up for the amount that they lost. He walks home every day, and he lives about ten blocks away. He doesn't really associate with anybody, so if we get to him a day before everybody else, he won't have told anybody."

"And Kara?" added Zeke. "She fell on your table at lunch during that catfight and spilled all of your food on your clothes."

"If I do anything to Kara, Pearl and Holly are going to get back at me because they're all part of Kat's fold, and they take Fist Lists even more severely than we do," replied Walter.

"Well… that might not be the worst thing. All of them go to the Rink Rocket Dance Hall on Thursdays and they don't have security there," Annabel pointed out with a nod.

"Thursday is when Teller is having that house party and Caleb and Dean are both going to it; the two of them jumped me because I got assigned Elena as my lab partner and Dean is jealous like a gorilla ready to fuck, and Caleb is such a cock-riding best friend that he had to get involved," Walter grunted nastily.

"Okay…" Annabel hummed, deep in her train of thought, "so it sounds like on Thursday, we're getting McAllen as he comes out of the locker room, then Barry Stewens and Brent Khan in detention on the way out; after that, Walt has work until 8, when Gaz can pick him up with my dad's truck, and we'll have our choice of going to the dance hall when it lets out at 8:30 or stopping by Teller's house. Having Odie as a safety just gives you room to work with."

"All that's left to do is to sort out who gets what treatment," Walter stated. "Fuck – and to find a way to cover our tracks so that people don't start calling each other and telling everyone to be on the watch for us. If we can't be inconspicuous and part of the crowd, we'll get picked out just about instantly."

"Walt, when do you think Cisco is getting that Easter Basket again?" asked Zeke in a snap reaction.

"Huh? Uh – If I had to guess, Wednesday," he tentatively replied.

"If he does get it then… and this is a big 'if', people are going to want the tabs, and the caps, and the mesc, and the ecstasy, and the… and the –"

"And the DMT," Annabel listed for him.

"We're getting DMT? Oh, fuck yeah, dude!" cheered Zeke. "Okay, so if we do get all of that Wednesday, someone's going to have to do the rounds to distribute it, which makes for a great alibi to cover why we've got to keep showing up in different places; all we need is someone to ask Cisco for permission to do so…." His voice trailed off, but his mouth was still open and teeth bared, pointing at Annabel with both fingers.

"Yeah, I'll do it," she replied with a pause. "One condition on this, though: when it's time to draw, keep up." Her chin flinched to the side, causing her neck to crack as she popped each of her knuckles on the left hand with her thumb. "I'm tired of doing all the mugging by myself."

VIII – B

"Hey, I feel like this is only the third time in a week that Joe and Hope have had that exchange," Walter spoke in huffs, hustling away from the stairwell with Brielle. "You know that I'm not here to judge but fuck, if that isn't impressive. It's almost like they're practicing for a scene – you'd think that eventually one of them would look around and say 'You know what? You're awful, I don't know why I put up with you, let's stop pretending we're a couple and just break all association.' Honestly, I think that's the only healthy thing to do."

"When your career as a marriage counselor fails, you'll be glad that you stayed in school," Brielle remarked.

The two of them rounded a corner as the first bell rang and found that gathered outside of their class was a large crowd that was so dense there was no room to move through. The two of them looked at one another and then Walter stood on his toes to peer over the crowd.

"Hey, Brandon! Hey!" he called.

A boy with crew cut black hair and thick square glasses turned to the left. "Walter! Hey, everyone: make way, those two have to get to class!"

A few people glanced around and Walter and Brielle walked between the space that they formed for them to pass. They made their way up to Brandon, all eyes directed to the boy who was in the fetal position on the floor.

"Your boyfriend is *still* on acid?" Brielle asked Brandon, pointing down at the quivering ball.

"Yes; Cosmo has been tripping all weekend. Right now he's at Omega-2. Earlier he was at Terridus Maximus – and he was not ready for Terridus Maximus," Brandon said, sounding like he was giving a professional report and suppressing his Indonesian accent as best he could. "Overall, he's at a better place than he was the first day of school when he was shitting rainbows; this time he isn't speaking in tongues, though, just practicing telepathy."

"That's crazy – Brielle does that without taking anything at all!" Walter exclaimed.

Brielle's expression was the same as if she had just gotten milk spilled over her head, her chin on the floor and eyebrows pointed like a roof, and punched him in the top of his bicep with all the force that she physically could manage.

Walter shouldered the pain and just cackled wildly.

"Don't laugh so quick, Monroe!" Cosmo shouted from his position on the floor. He uncurled himself and sat up against the lockers inset in the wall.

"Oh, what the fuck," Walter replied robotically in a complete knee-jerk reaction.

"Yes, that's right – you're being searched for by her and you don't even know it," Cosmo said, eyes lazily staring in different directions.

"Bullshit. Brielle: homeroom," Walter said, snapping his fingers and pointing towards the door.

"You don't even want to know what she looks like?" he asked ominously.

"Nope, not really."

"She has no eyes, no ears, and no nose. But she'll still find you." He gasped and began laughing frenziedly as a madman. "She'll still find you! She'll still find you!"

Walter wasn't aware of what happened next, but he could've sworn that he didn't kick Cosmo in the gut before he ran into Rickard's room and slammed the door once Brielle had followed him in, but the crowd of eyewitnesses all separately attested to him later that he most definitely did commit such a deed.

The room was rectangular with a whiteboard and a blackboard, the teacher's desk at the far end of the room and a scattering of students at desks around it all reading for pleasure or for homework. Laminated posters were scattered around the top portion of the room, each one either a quote with a headshot of the famous figure who said it or advice for reading and writing.

"What the hell!" Walter exclaimed when they went to sit down. He kicked the leg of his desk before doing so.

"HEY!" called Rickard. "Just *what* on God's green Earth do you think you're doing, Walter?!"

"I'm sorry, Mrs. Rickard. I'm just heated 'cause Cosmo said someone was going to find me."

"My goodness!" she cried. "I'll phone the office at once!"

"No, he's – he was – uh, he's lying, is what. I don't trust him but he made me look weak in front of everyone in the hallway, is all," Walter stammered.

"There's people in the hallway?" she repeated, looking at the clock that hung over the whiteboard as the second bell rang, then hustled to the doorway and yelled "Go to class! Go, now!"

The sound of feet scuffling across the floor could be heard as though a dancing troupe was practicing out there. Suddenly, there was silence and Rickard reentered the room.

"Chill out or get out, Walt," his teacher told him without looking as she walked back to her desk.

"Are you worried?" Brielle whispered.

"What?" Walter asked. He scoffed. "Cosmo is out of his mind. He couldn't predict the fate of a goldfish; why would I think he knows anything about me or what's going on in my life?" He slumped down in his seat. "Fuck him, man…. He's just scared and wants to spread it someone else. There's a good a chance as any that he really thinks that thing is searching for *him* and he just wanted to freak me out instead."

"She, Walter. He said 'she'," Brielle pointed out.

"It's not a she, him, or any mix of the both, because nothing has no eyes, ears, or a nose – just a mouth. It just doesn't exist – not a person, anyway," Walter was pouting how he would if he hadn't gotten his way.

"Maybe she's not a person: maybe she –"

"Brielle, I'm going to say this as politely as I can possibly manage: take whatever cockeyed speculation you're having right now and stuff it up your ass. It's all fake – all of it. I don't believe it for a single second, so don't bother wasting my time thinking about it."

Bernard came into the room and sat in front of Walter.

"Bernard: do you think it's possible for someone to see into the future?" he asked him.

"You're talking about Cosmo, and all I can say is that if he's got the capability to tell what's going to happen to you, then I can see a unicorn that isn't visible to anyone else. He's just out of his mind; you shouldn't think about his ramblings for any longer than you would a child speaking gibberish," Bernard said while rooting around in his backpack.

"What'd I fuckin' say?" Walter said, beating his chest with the pride of a champion Oxford cricket team captain.

"Take your lips off your dick, dick," Brielle hissed.

Bernard pulled out a thin glass bottle with honey-colored liquid inside of it. Checking Rickard's desk quickly, he noted her reading the newspaper, then took a large swig from it, putting it at about one-third of the way full.

"Hey, Bernie," Walter said, attempting to sound charming. "You're on my list of beneficiaries if you're willing to share really quick with me." He gestured to himself, fluttering both hands. "Whaddya say? Willing to help me out, comrade?"

"Walter, you're a fucking nutcase," Brielle exclaimed, slapping his arm. He didn't respond so she continued to hit him.

"You can't be serious; Walt, you're too rowdy when you get drink in you. Just wait until later today – I'm not joking, don't do it."

"Can you take pictures of the soccer team with me on Wednesday?" Bernard asked. "Zoey can't make it to the game."

"Just call me Robert Riger!" Walter said enthusiastically.

Bernard passed off the bottle without putting the cap back on.

"Walter, I'll fucking deck you. Don't make me put your ass to sleep," Brielle threatened, raising her fists.

In an instant, Walter upended the bottle and began chugging it like he had just skinned his knee.

Bernard grabbed it away from him, looking between Walter and the teacher, ensuring himself that he wasn't in any trouble before he went off. "Hey, fuckface, I didn't say you could finish it. There's like, less than a shot left. Fuck it; I don't even want you to take pictures with me. You're a goddamn hog is what you are." He stuffed the bottle into his backpack.

"No, I'm a *hic* I'm a man of my word," Walter slurred. "I'll see you Wednesday." He looked over at Brielle, who was silent but appeared furious as a rabid hound, staring straight ahead and crossing her arms tightly. "Brielle," he said. "Brie. Brielle." He waved his hand in front of his girlfriend's face.

"Come that close to me again and I'm boxing your ears," Brielle said chillingly.

A shiver went down Walter's spine, him being genuinely afraid. He considered saying a lot of things: it might have been a good idea to apologize, or to say 'I'm fine,' or 'I forgave you; can you forgive me?' but he knew that trying to smooth over his sins would only inflame the issue.

"Okay, class! Quiet down for the announcements." projected Mrs. Rickard.

The intercom crackled on and the jolly, meridional voice of the head of security for the building. Walter didn't hear what he was saying, however. He was physically at such ease that he might as well have been a sailor just landing ashore. Without concerning himself with what he was doing, he went into his backpack and pulled out a copy of *The Butterfly Club*. Rickard was going to instruct them to continue reading; he didn't need her command to know that. What he didn't know was what elaborate, roundabout monologue that she would deliver as she gave the class such a task. Besides that, the announcements weren't anything of interest to him. He wasn't doing anything for the school just as it did nothing for him. He cracked open the book to chapter five.

And on the ridge of the countryside was a patch of dirt that stretched from the well to the bent tree 500 metres out. If you didn't have your nose to the ground you wouldn't be able to pay attention to such a thing while walking along it, but twelve people had every step mapped out because of an incredible responsibility they had each taken on. "The Butterflies," the local villagers would call them. What they all really were was a collective bunch of vagrants that shared ethics as primitive as a Neanderthal's. They had taken on a collective debit – one that could only be paid in blood: resistance. There was talk of their hideout being somewhere remote and desolate, but the one fact that the rumors all had in common was that it was the last retreat for the stubborn and narrowminded.
For the Butterflies, however, it was a breath of air from a spot at the bottom of the ocean; the spark that sets off a campfire; in no uncertain terms, it was the thing that liberated them from the clutches of insatiable domination. They did not expect to overturn the rule of law, but they kept at the breach, riding in the wake of unprecedented upheaval and delivering themselves to the cusp of the times to come. Cresting perilous situations was what they did on their off-days – the main activity they engaged in was resurrecting men of the fallen empire. The rebels became the establishment with their victory, and after only a brief spell, they were faced by the reanimated corpses of their once-ruling, resoundingly-defeated enemies, taking up arms against them once more. The ones who were too badly dismembered or decayed couldn't be saved, so the newly-founded confederation took it upon themselves to chop up

every body that they came into contact with, just to prevent any new recruits to the army that sought vengeance upon them. It was commonly known across the land that they would continue to do their work and progress further towards the Capital with every trip out until they each met their own end. It was a suicide pact as much as it was a military effort. They knew that every minute that wasn't spent using their impossibly miraculous talent was a minute wasted, so they never slowed down, never avoided risks. Honestly, it was their only mistake to think that they thought they'd never have to rely on anyone but themselves to stay alive long enough to complete their tall task.

Walter took out a folder with notebook paper in it, as well as a pencil. He jotted down *Local populace doesn't like Club. Club are counter-rebellion to the current, newly-instated regime. Club brings soldiers back from the dead to fight regime. Only way to stop Club is to mutilate bodies or kill Club members. Club will have to rely on somebody outside of it to reach the capital. Club has all resigned themselves to death.* He went back to the book.

"Hey, Aleck," said a boy wearing a grey peddler's cap and overalls. *"Why do we have to wait for Dorothy and Rodrick to return from the grain silo? We should check on them in case they're in trouble, don't you think?"*

Aleck put down the charcoal pen that he was scribbling down a copy of a report with. "Ben, if you ask me to leave again, I'm locking you in the central chamber. No, we can't draw any attention to the field because in case you forgot since the last time you talked to me about it, it's just past noon. A boy starts wandering in one direction out in the open past the forest and people are going to notice. If they are right compromised as we speak, running out to join them wouldn't help in the slightest. They're there to check for any activity in or around the silo, so there's no need to back them up. They got there just before dawn and it won't be mid-afternoon until they return. I know you're ready to chart out the next few days so that you know what to prepare for, but hear me on this: restless and reckless are just two letters off."

The torches snapped and popped in their iron brackets that were bolted to wooden beams supporting the room. The walls were made of packed dirt held back by wicker fencing, and crates littered the room, each one containing supplies and serving as some kind of furniture. Aleck was both sitting on a small box and writing on one twice its size, and the bed behind him was a long crate with a hay mattress on top of it. The only decorating the place had to its name was the occasional trinket, skull, or map nailed to a post.

"Look, I know you're going to say no, but think about this for a second: if someone finds Dorothy, they're going to sell her back to Mortimer to be used as a slave. If someone finds Rod, they'll kill him and bring his brain to the Capital for testing. If I get caught, the worst they can do is use me to get closer to the hideout, but we've got so many decoys and traps set up around Blue Gulch that –"

"Stop," Aleck said, rubbing at his eyes, "you've made your point. I don't control you, lad. You run off and what happens next is I stay right here, doing exactly what I'm busy doing. Please just leave me be – and if you find out that either one of them has actually been captured, make sure they don't get taken away still living: we can't afford to have Butterflies out in the world being locked up and passed around like chattel."

"I'll bring both of my daggers," Ben replied eagerly, and then turned and headed for the doorway.

"And the blowpipe. And Ben – don't forget

The bell rang, immediately accompanied by sliding and clambering out of desks and into the hallway. Walter had been so immersed that he hadn't bothered to pay attention to what was going on around him – also he read at a lethargic pace whenever he was on any substances. People got up all around him, and immediately his vision snapped to his girlfriend.

"Brielle, I –"

She scoffed. "I'd say 'You'll see me at third block' but you only ever see yourself, so." Shrugging and flipping him off, she went to the door and became a part of the hurrying mob that was getting further and further away with every second.

Walter was stunned; moreover, he was sloshed. He could go for a Texas Tommy and a bag of hot fries, but lunch still wasn't for another two hours. Trying to get his bearings, he stood up and stretched, then grabbed his pack and went through the door so as to not be the last one out.

The clustered hallway seemed so desolate having to walk it alone compared to having someone with you to focus on. He wanted to tell himself that he was just one of many; a normal student who kept his nose relatively clean and didn't rock the boat too hard, but he knew on a carnal level that he was disturbed beyond redemption. No matter how relaxed or how good of a state he was in, he told himself, it didn't matter, because he had tossed out the one area of his life that had actual importance to him. He didn't know what had him in such a clumsy stupor, as normally he managed to be reserved and reactive rather than proactive in his triflings.

Gradually, claustrophobia of thought settled into him, and the body of people around him was his prison cell. He wasn't entirely certain how long it took him to get to the stairwell on the opposite side of the building, but he just remembered that in his mind, he should have felt as though he had a spot on death row, or that he had just found out that someone had been hired to put an end to him. Today, however, contrary to all that, he felt like dancing 'til his face turned blue and then singing a song. He wanted to drive a truck off a high-rise bridge above a river just to land on the other side, then get out and jump off the bridge, doing a flip into the water. It felt like how arriving at Valhalla must feel: satisfaction of one's girth and character and a lack of focus on anything but. He had no concerns for who populated the space he occupied because they could never relate to the selfish stubbornness that he was so entrenched in. Being your own person is marked by disregard for standards that others might impose on you, and Walter was more free-flowing than a flag, unhampered by the things that, if being socially considerate was important to him, he should be expected to feel for the collective, superfluous body of hallmates that he was sharing a space with – but one finds that there is never an opportunity to care about something that can't make them feel any sort of way. He went down the back stairs and stepped out onto the sidewalk, passing through the side entrance to the school. On the left was a wall that created a shady cove to wait around in and the street was visible to the right from behind a line of trees, quaintly square houses on the other side of the street.

"Fellas."

"Walt," said three voices in unison. Two of them were smoking cigarettes and the third was just lighting his.

Walter clapped his hands and then rubbed his palms together. "So… what are we having today?" he inquired.

"Rich Lights, if you've gotta know," Joe said between puffs, "Mary Poppins."

"Viceroy," said an effeminate boy. His blond hair was arranged in such a way that made he looked like a French flapper.

Walter walked up to the group and took a spot in their circle. "That's great, Shawn," he grumbled, staring at the ground. Suddenly, he looked at Joe and pointed. "Now, pass?"

"Can you ask in any way that doesn't make you sound like an ape or an infant?" Joe sneered.

"Apes can't talk," Walter remarked, a cheeky grin across his face. "Now –" he whistled, sliding up in pitch and flicking his first two fingers towards him as though he was picking a fight "come on and let me have it, please. I don't want to get into it but –"

"Oh, you're in it," Joe said grimly, and held out in front of his face the navy-blue pack that had the corner cigarette poking out from all the rest.

Walter snagged the filter of the loose cigarette with his teeth, standing close to Joe as he flicked out his lighter to allow him to burn its tip. Walter moved back and took a measured drag while fixating on the cherrying end of the cigarette, standing with his shoulders rolled forward and one foot against the wall behind him. After a few seconds, he shut his eyes, put the base of his index and middle finger around the filter and pulled all the way in. He took it away from his mouth, flicking its side to ash it. Looking around, he realized everyone was staring at him. "What?" he asked croakily, smoking billowing from his nostrils. "Oh – right, okay. Listen, I'm not one to spill my guts out, so –"

"Walter, don't play fucking stupid," Joe said. "*You* showed your cards – the moment you let us know something was wrong was the moment you opened yourself up for questioning." He tsked and flicked his head to the side slightly. "That's a rookie mistake if I've ever seen one."

"Brielle's pissy, alright? It's not that deep, really. She just wishes she had better control of me," he replied tensely, beginning to take long drags and shorter pauses.

Joe just laughed. "Oh Walt; you sweet, sweet summer child. It's a good thing that this conversation isn't a fist fight because if it were, I'd have already gotten you two times across the cheek. Brielle wants to *control* you? How would she feel if we shared that bit of information with her? If she ends up hearing that from me, it'll definitely sting – just considering how she always calls me her best friend." He was profusely enjoying himself with his little game.

The third boy stepped forward, causing his towering flattop of dense, curly black hair to wiggle slightly in the wind, and he put out his hand. "We wouldn't really do a thing like –"

"She'd probably take your side, because she doesn't keep a tally of *your* bullshit ready to throw in your face. But me, when I cross a line – doesn't matter what – she goes to war." Walter was biting his lip, regret draped around his neck.

"Well come right out and say it, Walt: what did you do?" Joe asked with the inflection of a prosecutor putting forth the last piece of evidence into place for the jury.

"Had a fucking drink, is what," Walter scoffed nastily, grimacing. "And she took it as some great betrayal, even though if she wanted it, she'd have already had two." He took one last long pull and blew the smoke all upwards from the corner of his mouth, creating a plume like steam coming out of a teapot. "You know what I think it is? I think that in her mind, everybody has worse intentions than she does, and she's perfectly justified in doing whatever in the hell pleases her and if somebody *else* does the same thing, it's beyond the pale because they can't be trusted. We could get arrested while committing a crime and she'd still claim innocence from the back of a cop car."

"Whoo!" cheered Joe as he pumped a fist. "That sounds to me like quite the confession. A round of applause for our unwilling participant!" He clapped by himself.

Walter rolled his eyes. "Relish it for as long as you can; her and I will still get back to fucking by Wednesday." He inconspicuously embellished Shawn's discontent at his statement, who appeared to have just heard something that punctured his mood like acne.

"Rasha is the same kind of way," the third boy said. Hands in his pockets, he held the cigarette in his teeth while he puffed on it, causing it bob around as he spoke. "I hang around Victoria or Lindsey and she gets all accusative just 'cause she sees us getting along. She must think I'm pretty stupid if she expects me to cheat right in front of her."

"Either that, or she thinks you're setting up for the rebound when you drop her," Walter said mischievously. "You'd be surprised how often people go down that route. Trust me Robbie, if you ever relationship hop, make sure you don't look back: it'll feel like you got away with murder."

Robbie frowned, looking at Walter, incredulous. "I'd never do that to her. I don't want anyone else, anyway, so what'd even be the point?"

"You might not," said Joe, "but Walt might be a special case. Our little man has the moral backbone of a goldfish."

"It is what it is," Walter replied flippantly, waving the back of his hand. "And if I cut off Brielle, I might just be the stupidest person I'll ever know; being with her is the best deal I've been dealt my whole life. I get all my schoolwork done with her, smoke and drink for free, rides, friends, constant copulation – she's the full package.

She's way out of my league, too. It's a wonder how I pulled it off; underdog story of the century, really."

"Why do you have to mention how much sex you have at every opportunity, Walt?" Shawn inquired, staring sternly out over the tip of his smoldering cigarette.

"I don't know, Shawn; if you ever try it for yourself someday, you might feel inclined to share it with people as well. Me? Fucking is the only fun thing that I'm halfway good at, so yes, I have a tendency to think and speak about it. Call me a hedon, but I find it interesting," Walter said like he was telling someone why he was against abortion.

"Well *I* find it nauseating. As I'm sure most people do: the ones who aren't nymphos themselves." Shawn dropped the butt to the ground and tapped it out with the front of his shoe.

"No opinion," said Robbie.

"Brielle talks about it to me, too, and I put up with it – so I'd be lying if I said it bothers me." Joe shrugged. He took out the pack from his jacket breast pocket and passed off a second cigarette to Shawn, lighting it for him.

"And also," continued Shawn, "I think it's disgusting that you'd speak about Brielle like she's a walking, talking VIP pass that you were just lucky enough to come in contact with. You act like relationships fall out of the sky and land in people's laps."

"No, actually, I don't think I just stumbled upon her. Relationships are work – they aren't just *similar* to work: they *are* concretely laborious. See, the way I figure it, I feel like I'm just sharing work stories. I have a good week with Brielle, she rewards me, and it makes for good conversation fodder. I think where *you're* going wrong is that you don't think it was a matter of tactics how I reeled her in. Think of it like like working in sales, or doing anything business-related that requires negotiation: the better your angle is, the better your timing is, the more you'll walk away with in your pockets – or in this case, rather, the badder the bit- I mean, the girl that you can land. All of that's just common knowledge."

"So one of said nymphos is like, a Christmas bonus," Joe chuckled. He tossed the remainder of his cigarette in the grass and got a new one.

Walter smirked. "Yeah, something like that…. Anyway –"

"Walt, come on." Shawn was squinting angrily like dust was in the air. "You give yourself so much credit that it's coming out your ears. Just admit it: you happened on her at a critical juncture of her life and landed a lucky roll of the dice. The same events could turn out a second time and it's more likely than not that you're unsuccessful the other go around."

"Nope – but, fuck it, you're not listening. And Robbie and I need new cigs; Joe can you –"

"Shut the fuck up," Joe mumbled around his cigarette, retrieving two more and holding them out. "Why do you think that Hope is being such a raging bitch all the time?"

"Gee, Joe, I don't have the first fucking clue, but if I had to guess: it's probably a mix of all the poking and all the prodding that you're always doing to her. Haven't you ever given it a thought that maybe she has a low ceiling for her patience?" Walter took a long drag from his cigarette and blew the smoke downwards, enjoying how fresh it was. "'Cause that would make two of you."

"She's always playing the victim!" he exclaimed.

"You want to know who really plays the victim?" Robbie asked. "Carley. Hear about what she did at Jenn's house?"

"The Mardi Gras party, New Year's, or last week?"

"Last week."

"That recent, huh?" Shawn muttered. He was standing with one knee bent and looking around hopelessly as if he had just missed the bus and was considering running after it.

"She was getting her coat from the walk-in closet while Mike and his boyfriend were in there, and they're not mad or anything when she goes in there, but instead of just getting it and leaving, she finds out they go both ways and *joins* them."

"Goddamn!" Walter cackled, smacking his hands together. "What's her fucking deal, seriously? I think I've heard her name twenty times in a week."

"She used to talk to me when we were lab partners. It's shameful that people give her the reputation that she's got: she really makes an effort to be a good person," Shawn commented wistfully.

"Well, as they say: if you don't succeed, you can't be sure that you're even trying," said Walter crudely.

Joe flipped his wrist around and looked down. "Alright, we've got a minute and a half."

They all dropped their cigarettes on the pavement and stomped once. Walking back inside the building was somewhat a relief; their little circles proved to be tiring and tension-building. The truth is that they all wouldn't want to do it if the other three didn't as well, but because the opportunity was there, they had no choice but to take it. They didn't hate each other; that much could be assumed. They just couldn't bring themselves to see eye-to-eye because the world was too riotous and painful to surrender one's point of view, so they each manned their position at each other's throats, always scouting out the next move of their peers. At least it was a free-for-all between the ones who counted; factions between them would only further complicate relations, and disagreements would be unavoidable. No, they had to remain free agents, otherwise their whole system would collapse. They'd never be able to decide on where to draw the lines, as well; they couldn't agree on where to eat, let alone who would get along with who for the rest of their high school careers. Did they really want the best for one another? Or was everything just a running charade that was kept afloat by constant sacrifice and compromise? He didn't know; he just knew that if he didn't survive his time in that building, none of them would stay back with him. They were all in it for themselves, and it would take a fate worse than death to stop them from walking the rest of the thousand-mile course that they were set down. It didn't matter, however – none of it did. He wouldn't quit; he couldn't quit. The world could melt and the Moon could crash down into the ocean but he would still have his mission and not even for the life of him was he going to be stopped. Love kept him propelled through the craggy mess of caves that was the oncoming future, racing against the clock and reluctantly praying for some meaning to it all apart from whatever he could gather from the moment.

IX – A

"Have you seen the one where Gavin Winchester is yelling at some guy in the backseat of that van?" asked a girl with a red ponytail who was in the corner of the classroom.

"*Blaring Sirens*. I was fucking on the floor during that scene: 'Bitch I am *gone* off that powder! My dick will be in and out of your face if I don't find out exactly where the mole stays at; you are about to get skullfucked like your eye socket was a tub of butter! 'Cause I'm more pissed than your dad without a dick! I'm ready to bust on your chin like I just got done taking you out to eat! You are fucking *fucked* in every hole that I can find or make! Mother Mary as my ever-living witness, I will not stop fucking you until you are a fucking éclair!" the boy in front of her energetically recited.

The girl was cackling the entire time, and caught her breath to say "I know, I know – but I didn't expect him to *actually* do it!"

Most of the room was carrying on in this manner, Walter sitting right next to the two of them and hearing all sorts of conversations about plots and characters and plot twists and quickdraws and headshots and car crashes.

"That shootout in the headquarters was fucking nuts."

"I know! They had that unreal shot when Abe used that guard as a shield and they stabilized the camera around the sights of his pistol as he was aiming it."

"Alright, class," called out the teacher. "If you all are ready, it's time to put on the radio."

The students excitedly cheered to one another and then went silent as the knob clicked and a voice cut on.

"Hello America; I'm Rockwell Stiller, but I'll also be brief, because I know you're all anxiously clutching at your radios in wait for the detail that reveals where Abe Carelin is and brings him back home. For those of you who may not be familiar with the name, Abraham Carelin is a breakout director who is headlining newspapers and theaters all over the nation following the release of fifteen films all at once that he shot and starred in himself as personal projects. Abe was last seen on Saturday while shopping at his local grocery store. Without further ado, let's dive right into it. Gav, are you ready?"

"O, I'm ready enough to burst from my skin."

"Spoken like a true dramatist; my friend here, Gavin Winchester, was perhaps Abe's closest partner in the film business, but also his personal confidant. Gavin here was such an influence on Abe, in fact, that Abe didn't even want to get into film in the slightest until the two of you met and you convinced him that he could do it, is that correct?"

"You're correct, yes Rock. He had always been a timid guy, Abe. He adored the public but couldn't stand to be in their glare. He wanted to hide behind a typewriter because he felt like it was in his best interest to not have his face attached to his work. I had to break it to him just how misled he was for thinking that; I could tell that he had a… an infectiously relatable set of expressions that would translate well to the camera before he ended up deciding to show me a professional photo of himself…. If he was going to capture hearts across the nation, I told him, it was going to be because he had stolen every shot with him in it just by his facial theatrics alone, and not by trying to produce the greatest literature."

"But neither of you had ever operated a camera any larger than a basketball before you first started shooting."

"No sir."

"Why take on the risk of filmmaking at all, then?"

"Well, I had worked on dozens of theater productions in my day as a student: first as an actor in middle school, but years passed and I gradually shifted to stage design. Every director I would work with said that I fascinated them in the way I could frame a scene exactly the way they wanted it, even before they had a chance to figure it out for themselves – it only felt like a natural transition to start filming."

"So what you're saying is that you knew you had the skill, but you just had to try and put it in practice to see if you were actually capable of dominating the film scene here in the U.S."

"I didn't set out to dominate anything… or anyone, for that matter. All I knew is that it would be worth the time if we could get an attempt off the ground."

"I think 'off the ground' would be viewed by most people as an understatement, because the last I checked, you and Abe have consumed the entire top 10 at the box office as of today – I think it's fair to say that your work has far exceeded what could be considered 'worth it."

"I don't think so."

"You don't."

"I don't think it was worth it in the slightest."

"How could that possibly be the case, Gav? Didn't you hear what I said about the box office profi–"

"One day when Abe and I were wrapping up production for all the films, I realized then that I had found the door that would put me on the other side of failure and obscurity, and the only thing I wanted from that point onwards was to step through it, close, and lock it behind me. It wasn't until I had already stepped into the halls of success and fame that I was able to fully understand what it means for my family that no one who shares blood with me will have to pay another bill until the 21st century…. But escaping life as an average nobody doesn't hardly even carry significance with me, compared to the way it used to, and that's just because the universe couldn't allow me to keep my most valued friend on the way out of those times. I don't want to be famous on my own... I never wanted anybody to repeat my name if Abe couldn't join me in on the conversation that would follow. He's gone; he won't be a part of anything I ever do again.... Just – Just let me go back to being nobodies with Abe, please God."

"Gav, you have me confused: one moment you say with certainty that Abe is gone for good, then the next you ask for the Lord to give him back to you.... Do you think that there's a chance that Abe gets found or not?"

"No, absolutely not, Rock. I don't know how well you knew Abe, but you couldn't make him appear anywhere unless he had already wanted to be there in the first place. He was a recluse; he had emotional barriers that kept him from being able to be properly normal or well-adjusted. He's avoided me at times in the past, for sure, but I was always able to wait him out just long enough for him to emerge from his shell, because I had a better sense of him as a friend than another soul on this planet could have even hoped.... So when the forensics report says he's vanished without another trace...? Rock, he's gone."

"Well hold on now; what about all the strips of cloth that they found stuck on the windows that had been broken at his apartment? What about the evidence that shows –"

"Evidence? Rock, you're being a damned fool – everything in his apartment had been left there on purpose after whoever did away with Abe was finished with their business. The cloth came from t-shirts that someone took from the goodwill and tore up, the shredded photos all had no prints on them, a single drop of blood hasn't been found anywhere on the property, and every room had been scrubbed spotless. As far as anyone can tell at this point, what happened was a group of maids went to Abe's apartment on Sunday to clean it, they stuffed him into a trashcan, rearranged and cleaned the place, then buried him forty feet deep. As much as that being the case would give me peace on what might my friend's fate actually might be, it's just as ridiculous of an explanation as any assumptions people are making: that it was the mob, someone from *his past, or if it's all just a ruse being purported by Abe himself. We'll never know – so let's everybody please just accept the fact that Abe is gone like smoke into the breeze."*

"Gav, it doesn't sit well with me that the investigation to find your friend has only just opened but you already seem to have this awareness that nobody will ever cross paths with him again. Now I understand your skepticism, but allow time for the law to do their work to find Abe Carelin – you must remember that he is a different person from yourself. Even if you think there doesn't need to be searches, it's the duty of the American police and public to try their best, regardless of any permission that they may or may not have from someone who was Abe's closest friend, even."

"I don't want them to stop searching, Rock – I'd want them to search until the end of time if there were any of the resources for that, because it would really take that long of a search to even dig up a single genuine clue. No – the sad reality is that people will give up in two or three weeks when they realize it's been just as futile as I'm predicting to you now. I'm just asking for anybody listening to consider the immense probability that Abe's final film has already begun airing in theaters."

"Alright. Well, that does it for our time here this morning. I'm dreadfully sorry, folks; it was my own personal hope that this interview would grant us all some hope for one another, but it seems as though our worst fears may very well be confirmed, if the prophecy that Gavin has given us here today turns out to be true. You can catch Mr. Winchester starring in Blaring Sirens, Miss Mallbory's Horse Races, *and* Tempered Expectation. *You coproduced twelve more films, in all of which you played smaller roles, am I correct?"*

"Indeed, Mr. Stiller."

"Quite right. Gavin will be on with us throughout the week to provide commentary on the mysterious case of Abraham Carelin. Gav?"

"Thank you so much, Rock. And thank you too, America."

"Until tomorrow, this is Rockwell Stiller, signing off...."

The classroom was aflame with a scattering of animated conversation that couldn't be described as anything less than full-scale hysteria. Walter raised his hand.

"Yes, Walt?" his teacher called out to him.

"Can I go to the library to read?" he asked.

"Sure, go ahead."

With that, he got up and headed out, glad to be away from the excess noise. If he didn't step away, it would've only gotten worse until the block ended. He went upstairs and into the library, going off to the left wing of it.

"Walter," said a boy who was sitting in a plush chair and reading the newspaper. He had light skin, full lips, and black, curly hair that poked out from under a plain baseball cap

Walter took the seat behind him and grabbed an arbitrary book from the shelf beside him, took out a paper from his pocket, overlaid it on the inside of the book and began reading it. He cleared his throat and then cautiously asked, "So, I assume you've been told that this week we're making friendly with Charlemagne's lot?" Both of them went silent, and after a moment, Walter spoke up again: "Well, it means that we've got to get along with Reno, and I need to make sure that you can restrain yourself when you see him."

"You talk to me like I'm some sort of animal," the boy replied from under the low brim of his baseball cap.

"No – I just know that you've got a particular grudge against anybody who's made any sort of move on Annabel, and if I were you, I might be inclined to take action against my better nature. It can't really be helped," Walter said coolly, skimming the sheet.

"I put up with Zeke well enough... doesn't that carry any weight with you?" He flipped the paper over, intently studying the classified advertisements.

"You've gotten pretty close – remember the soccer game at Palm Pastures?"

"He told me to 'just fuck off' and all I did was try to sit next to her," the boy said with disgust. "If I lack self-control, then he's just as bad."

"I'm just saying: losing your shit back on someone is even worse than saying the first thing, because at least if you ignore what they're saying and move on, nobody is the wiser and it just sounds like banter. The more attention you attract, the hotter you make the situation. Annabel was delivering some tabs that day, and the referee almost walked up the bleachers once you and Zeke got into it – imagine if he called someone else over and it got serious from there," Walter was trying to remain calm in his tone, but he was resolutely unwilling to surrender his position on the issue with a fervency that bordered on hostility. "I mean, Wyatt, it wouldn't be the first time you got one of us in trouble...."

"Yeah, it's so natural for you to bring up the Tomlinson's, but that's just 'cause you were out of the room when Rally came inside and started pushing the girls around," Wyatt replied nastily, on the offensive.

Walter sighed. "Come on – I didn't come here to argue with you about stuff that's long done and finished. Do you want to get into it or should I just leave?" He slipped the card off the book and into his pocket, then closed the book and set it back on the shelf.

"It's not even your spot." Wyatt replied. He looked up from his newspaper, analyzing the room around him.

"What does that mean?" Walter asked, sitting back in his seat to turn and face him.

As Wyatt turned all the way around to look past Walter's face, his heart absorbed all of the blood from his body, turning it pale and cold at the sight of Zeke approaching towards them from the back of the library at a moderate pace.

Walter faced forward again, cracking a wide grin and pumping a fist at who he saw. "My man!" he said in a whispering yell.

Zeke swiftly positioned himself in front of Walter, dapping him up in an instant. "You taking the noon slot for assignments?" He chose to mirror Wyatt, who was staring straight ahead, his head locked in. Zeke did exactly the same, both staring at the opposite end of the library in a parallel gaze. This, paired with Zeke's frozen stance, made him resemble a mannequin to the passing eye.

"Shit – my bad, man. I was going to go insane if I couldn't have stepped out of class," Walt gasped, mortified by the realization his unprecedented slight against Zeke. caused by a failure of memory – something that had been plaguing him that entire day, he noted. "I'll go, it's not a prob-"

"No, you stay. This one's crucial, but it has to be for you. Trust Wyatt, and trust me, kuya." Zeke said through a quiet breath. He placed his hand slightly to the left of the center of Walter's chest so that he could feel his heartbeat for a quick moment. "Because I trust you." He pulled his hand away like it had been burned just before taking two steps forward to be beside Wyatt.

Wyatt's eyes refused to so much as flinch as Zeke leaned into his ear, who began whispering into it in a voice so muted that Walter couldn't even hear him speaking. What felt like a minute but was more likely just several seconds passed of Zeke crouched over next to Wyatt's ears, his lips moving speedily but nothing audible reached Walter whatsoever. Zeke then snapped to, looking directly at the front entrance. He put his right arm out for a moment and flashed a thumbs-up to Walter without using his eyes to confirm Walter's reaction. Then, as if the front door to the library was the end of a wind tunnel, Zeke vanished from the library and around the corner.

An unsettling silence settled between the two of them after Zeke made his disappearance, with Walter being the one to break it: "Are you going to tell me the truth about what he whispered to you," he asked, "or what it is that you want me to think he told you?"

Wyatt took a measured pause, then replied "He told me that your first stop is Betty Donnelly: after you leave here, in fact."

"Is that what he told you?" pressed Walter.

"He told me that Betty's been dealing out of the school store today," Wyatt grumbled. "It's been a week and a half since she's had the opportunity to make any sells – so she stockpiled her cash and invested it in a special strain of bud. Shit looks like it has purple leaves when you shine light on it. That's something we can oversell like diamonds – so once we finish up here, you go find Donnelly in the school store, make the pickup, and don't think twice about it."

Walter bit his lip, trying to size up everything that Wyatt might be privy to. "Did he say why," he uttered as a statement and not a question, immediately regretting doing so The silence that followed did nothing to comfort him, as he knew the answer already – just as he already knew that Wyatt was about deliver it to him.

"Because you need someone to take revenge on," Wyatt finally said, nonplussed, and even cracking a slight grin to himself.

"Percy Donnelly," Walter mumbled with hostility, "tried to get his tongue on my shaft when we were passed out in the loft of Brax's dad's farmhouse."

"No, when *you* were passed out," replied Wyatt in an instant. "It doesn't matter why, but you're hitting Betty Donnelly and that's the end of it. She brought an entire QP with her to school today, and at least half of it is already gone – probably for dirt cheap. However much of it that you recover, the weed will end up being worth its weight in gold. So stop asking questions."

"If I go after Betty, Percy isn't even going to wait longer than a day to jump me. Imagine if it was *you* going up against this guy: six foot two and grabs you by the 'fro. Once he backs you into a corner, you're getting the scalping of a lifetime."

"I'm not afraid of having my hair pulled by some twink," Wyatt said repugnantly. "Come on, we need to get this over with. Get that book and take out your card already."

Walter's eyes darted from left to right across the floor in front of him, his mind absorbing the reality that his reinstated Fist List had become an open secret. Not wanting to lose his composure any further, he plucked a new book off of the shelf, opened it, then slipped out the card again and placed it on the page.

"Cal Ace," Walter read off in a stale tone. He covered the card with his hand and spoke his thoughts verbatim as they occurred in his mind.. "Cal's an interesting case because he doesn't have any friends or anyone to talk to for the first half of the day so he's a clear target for anybody looking for a quick jug, but the second half he spends every minute with the tennis team and they're the largest, most cohesive group of bitches that this school has," he stated.

"Doesn't a lot of fen-phen go through them?" Wyatt asked pensively.

"Like water through tissue paper," replied Walter.

"See them, today if you can." Wyatt went back to studying the space around them. Two bookshelves down was the circular front desk which the whole room was centered around. The ceiling was tall, resting on thin pillars, at the bases of which were tall pots holding a fern apiece. He went into his cargo shorts and rolled an orange bottle with a white cap under his seat, which Walter retrieved from off of the floor. "Sell that for two hundred. If we can get in with Kayleigh – and she should still be as big of a user as ever – then not only is she likely to take that whole bottle off of your hands for her and the team, but is also likely to be our ticket to Jose Billup's block party."

"Isn't that a bit overzealous?" Walter asked tentatively, observing the bottle as it rested at the bottom of his open backpack. "I mean, we know that Cal carries lots of cash on him because he flips cocaine in the evenings, so going after him would be easy money. We don't need Billup – his stuff usually gets busted by police, anyway."

"Trust me on this: we're going to want to go out there come next week. I can't say exactly who, but I know at least a few big-ticket names are going to be out there, and either we get off a huge sale or hit a fat lick." Wyatt snorted, rubbing the space between his eyebrows. "If we don't go to that party, we lose five hundred, easy," he plainly stated, without inflection.

"Okay, fine," Walter replied, rolling his eyes. Arguing it out with Wyatt only cemented Wyatt in his position further.

"Next?"

"That depends – can we pull more of a profit on vodka or bourbon?" he asked, checking the card again.

"Bourbon, easily: the baseball team has these ceremonies but without getting into it, they can put away a gallon in one night," Wyatt said with the professionalism of a lawyer.

"In that case, we need to go after Bronson: he sells Jim Beam out of his trunk during dismissal."

"Easy jug," he replied without giving himself even a moment to think.

"Uh – there's always tons of people out in the lot just before the final bell. If they see a robbery, they *might* be apathetic and let it play out, but they also might take on some spur-of-the-moment heroism. That situation needs to be avoided at all costs," Walter said, desperately trying to get through.

"Okay?" Wyatt scoffed. "Have you ever tried hitting a lick to the motto of 'be quick'? If you try it sometime, it teaches you that more than anything, people don't react if you're not there to stop. He's short, right? Just pull his leg out from under him, grab one bottle in each hand, and make yourself scarce. It's so simple that *you* could figure it out."

"Ease up, hotshot," Walter said contemptuously. "I'll do it but only because we need the profits. Any other situation and I walk."

"Great – I'm super fucking touched." Wyatt sneered, shaking his head. He had his cheek in his hand like a child in the waiting room. "Is that everyone?"

"Nearly – Minnie and Fiona Canaby," he read on the last line of the list.

"Doesn't Minnie go down on Pib Huxtable?"

"Couldn't say," Walter replied with a smack of his lips. "I just know that she does rounds for the volleyball team: Vicodin and Oxy like you wouldn't believe."

"So by process of elimination, Fiona must be the one who plays her guitar in the parking lot while she fishes for dates, right?" Wyatt asked, straining to remember.

"I'm pretty sure, yeah. She's a riot: you just can't look away – total train wreck for sure...." Walter scratched at his neck. "See, the issue is that once one of them makes an enemy, they both go commando. It's like a predatory thing: they have blood on their side, so if ever comes down to a two-on-one, that person's getting their ass kicked."

Wyatt was thinking intensely, weighing his options as objectively as a person could be capable of. "Alright, so you already have a full schedule for today with those three stops, so here's your plan for tomorrow: hold up Minnie, invest in Fiona," he said with haste and conviction.

"Fuck you," Walter exclaimed, barely able to keep his voice down, and causing the librarian to shush him. "What the fuck?" he hissed. "Didn't you just hear me? What kind of batshit logic makes you think that'll work out even remotely in our favor?!"

"Slow up for a second: doesn't Fiona have that shroom connect that everybody talks about but all of five people have access to?"

"Like hell we'll get to it by fucking around with her sister – seriously, Minnie's actually got a reputation for going after people and getting revenge for petty shit. I'm not making that up," Walter said insistently.

"Minnie's going to do her buying all at once: lift the pills off her before she can distribute them to the team and then let Fiona know if her sister wants to see a single tablet returned to her, she's got to turn over her shrooms plug," Wyatt instructed. "If Fiona really doesn't want to cooperate you can always perform... services –"

"Sick," Walter retched. "That's fucking horrid – I can't believe you'd even insinuate something like that."

Wyatt just laughed. "Well, that's all I've got. Catch you on the flip side, queer-o," he said jollily as he got to his feet and danced off in a trot with the spirit of a gingerbread soldier.

Walter sized up his list, observing the verdicts he had been given in the shorthand that he had messily transcribed. He didn't have the first clue what illustrious force made him stick to Wyatt's command: his role as the tactical brains of the group would completely evade all logic if it wasn't for his extensive history of success. Somehow that unassuming, fuzzy-headed nitwit had either arranged or weighed in on every stick-up, theft, beating, and deal that the lot had to their name. Wyatt wasn't just clear-headed and able to visualize situations laterally: he was so emotionally detached as a member of the society in which he was interred that he wasn't concerned for the well-being of anyone at all and only thought of others in terms of their capabilities, and that made for an exceptional skill at sizing up situations and organizing people. It was fair to say that Wyatt considered every person he knew with some significant severity and captiousness – all, except for Annabel. It was common knowledge that he lived with the preparation to go into a situation, didn't matter of what kind, important or meaningless entirely, and lay down his life to ensure her safety, just for the sake of having people say about him posthumously: "He was devoted to only one, single soul. He sleeps easy now that his eternal burden has been laid to rest." At least that was what wished could happen. Truthfully, he had no idea if he was going to end up a hero or not – it would all amount to the same if he met his end as a coward: sniveling in some dark, dank corner while everyone who was meant to defend him had already been done away with, merely waiting for the person to come along who'd do the deed at long last.

Realizing there wasn't any other choice, Walter went to the back entrance to the library and down the tucked-away stairwell, coming out at the side of the cafeteria, which was nearly entirely vacant in anticipation for first lunch, it being just minutes away. He went down the hallway to the side that led to the gymnasium and stopped halfway down it at the school shop that was inset in the wall.

"Walt," muttered a thick-necked boy with a buzzcut and meaty unibrow. He was manning the counter by himself.

"Tyler, hear me out," Walter said with the hasty and insisting tone of a real estate man trying to push condos in the projects, "You need to help me real quick,"

Tyler just scoffed. "If that isn't the Walter Monroe Special: 'Hey, guy, I'm a self-righteous, over-asserting, intruding, nonempathetic cunt who has nothing to do with anybody like you any hour of the day, but right *now*, you need to help *my* sorry ass because I don't know well enough to just fuck off and take care of my own business like any other self-respecting individual.' In short: no. Fuck no. Go right back the way you fucking came." He shook the backs of his hands at him to tell him to leave as though Walter was deaf and hadn't heard a thing he said.

"You know," Walter said, beginning to slip into an act, "we live in changing times. There was once a day in age that we worked in opposing directions, but it very well might be that we're both pushing the same current."

He grunted. "Fucking unlikely. You don't even know who I answer to. Now, if you'd kindly: shove off?"

Walter dashed forward for emphasis, holding out a finger. "Not so fast – you've been seen on the soccer field with Roberto Harrington and Amos Storm, and if you think I don't know what their affiliation is, then you clearly can't appreciate how large a scale operation we're all a part of."

"Where the *fuck* did you get that from?" Tyler spat, rearing back like he was a moment away from taking a hit to the face.

"I keep tabs – if I didn't make it my business to find out which athletes associated with one another, then I'd be missing out on a hundred different clients, and that's just the upperclassmen," Walter replied, relaxing in his position. "Do you want me to tell you how Ramsay and Lando are related? It's actually a pretty funny story, really...."

"I don't take orders from Ramsay."

"Yes, but he's the floodgates for Baker, and if Baker doesn't get supply, then all of you starve. You, Roberto, Amos, and everyone else on Caines Street – isn't that right?" he asked, trailing off as if he had just handed him a mic.

Tyler appeared disgusted like a pastor who had just caught his eldest son sucking dick. "... So, what then? I don't do what you say and you go to Baker? I really can't see you having any kind of power over me in this situation, so you can take your little FBI report and stuff it –"

"Wait – don't you know? Amos Storm and his brother are in the midst of repaying one of the worst debts that this school has ever seen; it's not every year that two guys get caught with a box of jewelry out of a friendly party's house – that's what one of us plainer folk call a 'great betrayal'," Walter said, speaking with emphasis.

"I've got nothing to do with that – I'm innocent," he replied harshly, beads of sweat forming near his hairline.

"Okay, so you do know. Well, it just so happens that Ramsay had quite the egg on his face when that story broke, and I shouldn't have to tell you that anybody who had even the most remote reputation for being loyal to him got put through the grinder: over two dozen people got jumped, and that's just accounting for the ones who are somewhat notable. I'm sure a whole lot of nobodies got put to the floor for Amos and his brother's stroke of bad judgment, and even more nobodies currently have their hoods pulled over their heads and their eyes to the pavement, just praying they don't get picked out of the crowd." Walter was staring at him: cold, punishing, and without remorse. "You don't work the school store. You never have. It was just... a spur of the moment decision to come down here, right? Or, no – I once heard that a coincidence purported by at least one desperate party is never anything more than a poorly-disguised conspiracy. Jay Gatsby didn't get placed across the lake by some twist of fate – he had every intention of doing what he did."

"Walter..." Tyler begged, beginning to break down, "whatever you're thinking about doing – it's not worth it."

"Look, Ty, I'll be straight with you because if I don't, then nobody will: you're a dead man walking – so, coming down here? The inevitable is named as such because if we can't reply on certain certainties to come about, nothing happens. So, yes, you're going to get held up by your ankles and shook for all the pocket change that might fall out... or...." He paused, rolling back and forth on his feet and stroking his left cheek with his right hand and posturing himself as if he had a cigarette at a photo shoot.

"If you're going to turn me in, have people come down here, then I say fucking go for it," Tyler exclaimed as he slapped his hands onto the counter. "I'm not afraid – I pay blood for blood. Everything that happens to me is just something that's going to happen to someone else." He was eyeing the door to the school store by his side.

"Well hold on – I'm not at the best part yet," Walter said, taking a step back and holding out his hands like he was showing someone how big of a fish it was. "The day after the news broke that the robbers, Amos and his next of kin, had been caught, Ramsay got held up at Dark Fern Bridge and lost everything he had on him. It was Lando that he called after he jacked the payphone there, and it was Lando that called down the cavalry: a hippie van that took him back to his safehouse. I was in that van. If Ramsay had kept walking, there's no telling how many vengeful strangers of the past he might have ran into, and from where he comes from, if you can't take anything material from someone, you take something that the other person can't take back. He's done away with more than a few people with that mantra in mind, so it wouldn't have been unreasonable for him to expect to run into someone who wanted to give him for as good as some friend of theirs might have gotten. In some uncertain terms, speaking in the realm of the probable and unlikely, Lando might have saved your middleman's dealer's life. And on that day, Lando saw a crumpled figure – one completely ravaged by the mistake of another – and he made a promise: if he couldn't be there to support Ramsay or his people in their time of need on any account regarding this greatly unfortunate situation, then one of his own people would be there for all and any of you. So, here I stand before you today, being someone who owes a particular… debt. Your safety is my payment to you. But all things come at a price, so if you could" he pointed at the door handle.

Tyler sighed. "You've got to be fucking difficult," he muttered under his breath, "that's all you ever fucking do." He opened the door begrudgingly. "There. Be quick," he ordered, standing back.

Walter entered the wall of the hallway, surrounded on all sides by racks and shelves that held different products and supplies on the walls of the inside, ranging from erasers to pencil pouches to backpacks to folders. He stepped into the backroom, turned the corner, and entered the storage room. As the door to it swung open with a creak, a crouched-down Betty Donnelly swung around from the box she was looking into, her expression shocked.

"Oh, uh – I didn't expect to see you here, Walt..." she said meekly, observing the stern, shadowed figure before her from her place on the floor. "Look – I'm really sorry about my brother admitting he tried to deepthroat you in your bed at Brax's farmhouse without permission. I can't control him though – he's my brother and not a part of me."

He kept his silence for another few moments, not moving a muscle and scarcely blinking. "That's not why I'm here," he lied, monotone.

"Yeah..." Betty paused, seemingly choking before taking a gulp and then a deep breath. "So, still – uh – need to cop still?" she asked carefully. She finally cleared her throat, and then waited for another few futile moments. "I thought you all were... buying... tomorrow."

"Yeah," he muttered, "we are. Donnelly, we can both be respectful about this. There's no reason for one of us to insult the other's intelligence."

"Why don't you have a heart?" Her voice was regretful and tumbling through shades of weakness. "You all aren't the only ones out here trying to make ends meet!"

"It's not about that – we have a vision that we're building towards. And if we don't succeed on this, all the work we've completed thus far goes the way of our good intentions. Believe it or not, each of us has a price to pay; mine's still coming. Don't be afraid – I'll put it to good use. Just be cooperative." He gestured to himself.

"'Don't be afraid.' That's a fucking stupid line to use: this is my *life* you're talking about!" Betty cried.

"Stop and listen to me, Don, nobody falls outside of our gaze. Our comb is as wide as it is thin-toothed, and you had to have known that being a dealer in any form puts you directly in our jurisdiction." Walter pointed to his feet and pursed his lips. "Just put it here," he murmured. "That's all I'm asking you to do; it really doesn't have to get ugly. It's a nice day – let's not sour it."

"My brother's going to find you! He'll kick your ass!" she shrieked.

"I'm not afraid of having my hair pulled by some twink," Walter quoted.

"Walter Monroe, I swear to you right now that if I don't sell a single sack for the rest of high school, I'll still get you back for this. You won't be safe: you'll never know who you're passing in the hallways that I've got ties with; who owes me back for something. You'll enter this building not knowing which flank to protect or what path to take. The more time that passes, the more you'll have to postulate what I'm really setting up for; what I'm putting in motion. Not a day will go by that I don't work towards that end goal, Walter Monroe. I will make it my only business to force you to pay for this – you won't escape me, you dingy fuck," she said, holding her tone stiffly like a fresh widow giving her speech at the funeral.

Walter leaned in close, getting right in her face. "Give," he mouthed slowly, digging his upper teeth into his bottom lip before he popped it out, all while holding out a hand like he had an expectation of receiving a low-five. She passed off a tight cellophane package about the size of a human heart. "Thank you kindly," he whispered. He went to the door but then stopped, holding one finger up on his free hand and flicking it around like he was trying to name the tune, and turned back around. "I'm not trying to give you the wrong impression, so I just want to come right out and let you know: I'd love it to meet the person who's killing me. I've been waiting for them for as long as I've known how to wait. It's not a desire to keep on that wakes me: it's a desire to ensure the final nail falls into my coffin when it's time and not a moment sooner. You think you're ending me? Better do it quick: I'm burning my candle at both ends in an oven over a firepit, and I'm more desperate to settle this whole issue than you, or anybody else is. You want to know the sad truth? All of this hatred; all of this vile, malevolent, sadistic, cruel, jaded, indulgent talk that's going to only amount to more of the same? All of it just gives me something to work towards. So long as I know someone out there is set to disapprove, I'm set to give them something to disapprove of. That's my job. I'm scum for a living, and if you don't like me, do something about it. Or don't. Either way, I get my fill, and you're just enabling me as much as the next guy." He stuffed the package into his backpack. "Tell your brother he can suck my dick any day of the week." As he passed Tyler on the way out, he merely absorbed his expression of absolute disgust. "Don't look so repulsed," he commanded him as he went back the way he came in.

"You're a slimy, skeevy gofer who's going to get his jaw stomped in the moment before he finds out what's good for him," Tyler hissed, teeth bared.

"And *you're* welcome," he replied, going through the door again and closing it behind him, then called back: "Don't say I never did anything for you."

"Choke."

"Only if it's on *your* cock, sweetie." At that, with a laugh and a skip, Walter made his way back down the hallway.

X – B

The hallways were all but cleared out when Walter reentered the building. He couldn't help but feel some kind of emptiness, brought on by his sudden isolation. It didn't matter that he didn't know anybody in chemistry because Fillius always would force them to do bookwork for the entire week once he was through with his lectures for that chapter. It was exhausting, because normally he had Brielle to look over his work for him and teach him the parts he didn't know, but she had Fillius on off-days, alternating with physics. She was still an invaluable asset to him outside of class, but making it through the 90-minute period could prove to be a gruesome task. So as he stared in front of himself from his position in the doorway all the way to the other doorway on the opposite end of the school and noted the occasional scrap of paper on the ground or empty bag of chips, he bargained with himself: he'd stop toying with Brielle if he could get her to promise him that she'll stop giving him flak for things that weren't entirely unbearable for her, so that he would know when to not unnecessarily provoke her and when it was alright. They were in a constant dance like two sparring partners out on the floor, barely parrying actual damage every swing and stab and lunge that they'd exchange and leaving caution to the worries of tomorrow. At times, it was greatly amusing how they'd play off one another and the banter would continue endlessly, but at other moments, it was grating and completely hostile. He wished that he knew how to bite his tongue and just drop

Crowe

issues, but he knew that if his mouth didn't keep up with his actions, he'd look like a child: afraid, helpless, and without a clue. It was all just an act really, being audacious in the face of impregnable odds. He couldn't say why they couldn't find a middle ground between being peaceable and giving into every passing impulse. Maybe it spoke to their true characters: mean-spirited and miserly, a distinct lack of empathy for the torment of another. It didn't please him to think of her that way, to consider the idea that she was a grouch who lashed out at the first sign of disorder. He was absolutely positive that she didn't have a sadistic bone in her body – even when she was plotting against her peers. Everything she did was calculated, somehow designed to bring her good fortune at some later date. It was why he trusted her so much with their future: she would have every step planned out from the front door of the school to the church steps.

Walter crossed the hallway and entered the classroom just as the bell rang. Thick black desks built for two filled the room, each one with nozzles for Bunsen burners, and the walls each outfitted with stations and glassware.

"Monroe!" Fillius called. "Is that you that smells like an ashtray?"

He froze up, stricken by the realization that he was compromised, and was only able to stammer back "Uh – I can explain."

"It had better be a goddamn essay!" he exclaimed. "See me after class, boy. For now, just get to work." His finger was directed to the blackboard, where page numbers were written in chalk.

Walter settled into an empty desk, sighing and biting his lip. He could've sworn that things weren't usually so unmanageable. It felt as though everything was coming at him at once and rather than react effectively, he flinched and merely covered his face, leaving himself completely vulnerable to whosever's nerves he was presently getting on.

The book creaked open across his desk after he pulled it out from the cubby at his feet. Immediately, the dense text was lost upon him; after reading all first period he had been left exhausted, sapped completely of mental agility.

'Hey, dickhead,' he thought at the same moment as him becoming ready to give up. 'You're rolling right now that you're so gone, but instead of productively using your being fucked up for anything and just generally bucking the fuck up, you're dropping the ball on every-fucking-thing. Slap your goddamn self out of it, you ninny. If Brielle could see you right now, she'd cold cock your ass; you've got to be that brittle to keep up with her – what was that she said? "Where are your balls at?" She knows when you're fucking up even better than you do. Think about it this way; you can either sit around and suffer alone for the next hour and a half, or you can suffer alone while you do the problems on the board and catch up in learning the chapter to her marginally, if at all. If you don't use your time in here, it probably won't matter in the long run, but you noticeably feel like a piece of shit and a half almost all the time, so it would be wise to fucking do something about it for once.'

Walter began reading the text, and due to his inattentiveness during lectures, he learned for the first time about how alkali metals were shiny, malleable, and highly reactive at 0 degrees Celsius and 1 atmosphere, how Alkaline earth metals were silvery-white all found in nature and relatively reactive at the same temperature and pressure, how pnictide compounds were usually exotic and particularly stable due to their inclination to form double and triple covalent bonds, how the stable, solid chalcogens were soft and poor conductors of heat, how halogens were highly reactive and have the potential to be lethally toxic to living organisms in large enough quantities as a result, and how noble gases had poor interatomic force, causing them to have low melting and boiling points. He had already known that noble gases were nonreactive – hence, noble – before he read about it, which to him was a moment that was equally gratifying and triumphant. This surprise didn't originate from him regarding himself as being unintelligent, it was just that when he took his knowledge and matched it up against reality like holding a paint swatch to the wall it was the case more often than not that he had no clue what the truth of the situation was. Learning was painful; when other people would talk about it being an uplifting and enlightening process he couldn't even imagine what caused them to feel such a way. To him, if he didn't already know something, it was more worth it to avoid the subject than it was to charge headfirst at the issue and hope that he was versatile enough to come out on top at such a sudden, unnecessary juncture.

Walter then went to the practice problems and tried tackling the first one. The two things he could remember from his teacher's lessons was that the law of conservation of mass says that matter is neither created nor destroyed during a chemical reaction and that you're supposed to begin with balancing the most complicated-looking group. It wasn't entirely unpleasant: he made a sort of game out of it. The further he got into it, the more compounds were being thrown into the mix, and the more complicated they were each time. A tip on the side said if you get stuck, try doubling the most complex compound and go from there. Eventually, he got to the point where he couldn't make any progress without deconstructing the entire problem and taking it one baby step at a time. He was reaching his breaking point when the bell rang and the room took to clearing out.

"Monroe," called Fillius. He pointed down at the ground in front of him.

Walter's blood ran cold, knowing his teacher was as unrelenting as he was prying. If he went up and got found out for his current state, he'd be in enough trouble to spend the next week at home. He weighed up his options while his teacher continued to repeat his name, and suddenly headed for the door.

"Walter. Walter!" he cried.

The last thing he saw when he looked back was Fillius grabbing his phone from off of his desk and quickly punching in a number. When he entered the hallway, a certain relief fell over him like apples spilling onto a blustery orchard. He was getting lost in the current of students, absentmindedly considering how he'd spend the rest of the day. For the most part, he was content with his position as a fly on the wall, unconcerned with the dealings of those more relevant than him and just riding along the wave that was carrying him. And that was how he carried himself: under the radar and going unsung despite all the promises of glory that are made once one tackles their involuntary, nonconsensual path through existence.

The loudspeaker clicked on. "Walter Monroe to guidance. Walter Monroe." It shut off.

"Fuck," Walter said out loud, much to the amusement of those around him who realized what had just happened. "Fuck," he muttered, "fuck, fuck, shit." He looked around, panicked. Realizing he was out of options, he accepted his fate and changed course from his third block to go down the other way towards the front office. On the walk away from the crowd, he couldn't help but to assume that if he kept his back against the wall, there wasn't much that could happen to him. It wasn't uncommon for him to be caught out and penalized by the faculty, but ultimately he was always able to squirm out of any real punishment. The hallways became desolate as he headed away from all of the classrooms, and he entered the guidance office in silence. Approaching the front desk, he peered down timidly at the woman behind it who was smacking her gum and had her face in a form.

"Whaddya want?" she grumbled nasally without looking up. The space around her was littered with family photos and baubles, a potted plant here and a stack of papers there.

"I'm Walter Monroe," he said.

"Congratulations."

"I was called down." He was beginning to wonder if he had made the whole ordeal up in his head.

"Oh – *that* Walter Monroe. Two doors down to the left; Jeremiah shouldn't be busy with anything so just walk right in." She was filling out lines and boxes at a breakneck pace, putting down her initials occasionally and laying down flurries of check marks with the accuracy of a competitive archer.

"Jeremiah?" Walter asked, put off by this new information.

"Mr. Bodwell." She looked up from her papers at last, holding her pen still as a conductor's baton. "Look, kid, will you get out of my hair? Just go see the man and be on your way. You look so nervous that I'm worried you might faint."

"Of course – I'm just out of sorts." Walter was rubbing the back of his neck.

She grunted, already back to scribbling away on her forms.

He walked with trepidation down the tight corridor, stricken with anticipation for the worst which would surely come. Prayer was a close friend of the superstitious, but in that moment, Walter didn't believe in anything: not himself, not justice, not mercy, and especially not divine intervention. He was going to have to face whatever was coming at him with gritted teeth and the tenacity to not flinch. Two knocks were all he put on the door before he turned the handle and opened it.

"Yes?" said a scholarly-looking man with silver hair, suspenders, and round spectacles.

"Fillius called me down," said Walter dropping his backpack on the ground and sitting in the chair across from his desk.

"Ah, alright...." He pulled out a scrap of paper and squinted to read from it. "Mister... Monroe, is it?"

"Walter – er, Walt." He was biting his lip, intensely dreading what was coming next.

"So, Mister Monroe: how can I be of assistance to you today?" Bodwell asked cordially.

Walter figured to himself that he might as well cut his losses and just come right out to get the whole issue out of the way. "Honestly? I'm not doing so hot today, so if we're just going to get down to brass tacks, you can write me a referral and send me on my way, please."

Bodwell looked at him quizzically and fixed his glasses. "Well, I'd be a fool to put down the hammer and not know what it is I'm striking. Give me your account – the stories that teachers tell can be so misleading. Students, on the other hand, are forthcoming when they know something is amiss. Wouldn't you agree?"

"You'd be surprised, Mr. Bodwell; I know more liars than a federal prisoner. But if I'll be straight with you, Fillius found out that I had smoked a cigarette with some friends," Walter said through a filter of wincing pain that was intentional perjury.

"Well, your first mistake was having a smoke break in the hallway," replied Bodwell plainly.

"No – we were outside. He could smell it on my shirt when I went into his class," Walter explained.

"Oh," he said blankly, clearly surprised by this new revelation. "So he didn't actually see you smoking anything?"

"Correct."

"So as far as we know, you didn't smoke anything at all?" Bodwell had his fingers together in a tent as if he was plotting. "Maybe you live in a smoking household, eh?"

"I... I guess?" stammered Walter. "I'm really not in a position to try and –"

"Well hold on now;" he cut in, holding up one hand, "work with me here, lad. Do you own any sweaters?"

"Yes...?" Walter surely felt more secure in that moment than when he had entered the room, but he was still on edge regardless.

"In the future, maybe pack a thin one, keep it in your knapsack, and the next time you have a little cigarette communion...." Bodwell gestured with his hands, telling Walter to finish the sentence for him.

"Put it on and then take it off when we're done and put it away. Mr. Bodwell, that's perfect!" he exclaimed. No matter what he was anticipating entering that room, he realized he had an ally exactly where it counted. He couldn't fathom anything else bringing him more relief than what he was experiencing in the present moment.

"If that's everything, then it appears we're done here." He held out his hand, which Walter shook enthusiastically.

"Thank you."

"It's what I'm here for," Bodwell replied with a nod.

"No, really; I mean it," Walter insisted as he retracted his hand and picked up his backpack. "You've been more understanding than any of the rest of the staff has ever been for me." He got up and went for the door.

"Cigarettes will put you in poor health!" he called after him. "Just so you know!"

Walter just chuckled as he exited guidance and reentered the hallway. He didn't know what was out there that kept him unscathed in the face of horrible castigation, but he was profusely grateful that he had been processed with such levity for yet another time.

"Walt – hey Walt! Wait up!" called a towering, slender boy sporting short, trendy hair and a black letterman jacket that had Japanese lettering down the bright red sleeves who had a lanyard around his neck with a small wooden block hanging off the end of it that had **RESTROOM** written in wide black marker strokes as he ran up to Walter and jumped into him, bodying the side of his arm with the side of his own arm.

Walter staggered to the side, got his balance, then spun around to face him. "Oh, Jay – what's up? I just got the break of a lifetime – not that you asked." He realized Jay might not want to hear about his business, even though the only thing he wanted to do was spread the good word of his saved ass.

"Just ducking out of Mrs. Hannis' class so I could rail some Bennies in the stall." He snorted and groaned.

"How do you feel?" Walter inquired.

"You ever been in one of those sensory deprivation tanks?" Jay talked like he was sleepwalking.

"No, but I can imagine what it's like," he responded.

"Well it feels like I'm going through a tunnel except my body is the tunnel and I can see everything I'm going to do for the next ten minutes. I'm gonna be so fuckin' bored…." Suddenly he snickered impishly as though he had just stolen a pair of sneakers. "At least I'll get some damn good head from Bethany in the backseat on the way home today."

"Shit – you can see that far ahead?!" Walter exclaimed, dumbfounded.

"Nope, I just found out from Soren that she wants a sheet of acid for the Southside rave and doesn't have the money to spend. Apparently she facefucks like she's missing her uvula. Goddamn do I want a cigarette: menthol, rich," he said with the upward tone of a high-end connoisseur.

"Well, I'm not a vending machine, so I don't know what to tell you. Wait – didn't Beth suck off Joe at Fishhooks last Easter?" Walter asked.

"I don't know about that, but I *do* know who gave top to fifteen dudes at the very least that night," Jay said, barely able to control his grinning laughter.

"You're not talking about –"

"That's right: Carley got belt-level with three linebackers, two outfielders, and both tennis champions – and that's just the athletes. Things got real freaky when she got around to those dudes in that jazz band and went off the rails by the time she had reached the artists," Jay said, practically cackling.

They rounded the corner and went to the right.

"How is it that every underclassman is not only aware of her body count, but a good portion of them have participated it its cumulation?"

"Listen, man, if I know anything about Carley, it's that –"

The door to Harrol's room flew open, Brielle standing squarely in its frame and grimacing intensely, shoulders raised, fists balled, and eyes slit. "Listen, *man*," she sneered, poking Jay in the chest, "if Carley knew anything about *you* talking shit on her name, *you* might just get removed from the list to Red's Weekends: I'm sure Red wouldn't put up with her little sister being picked on. She knows the Jualinciagas Riders, too, so you might just catch an ass whooping if you're not careful." She grabbed Walter's arm and yanked him in, then slammed the door.

"What the fuck!" Jay exclaimed from the other side and then ran off.

Crowe

Walter was mortified. "Brielle, that was –"

She quickly pecked him on the lips, then dragged him with her to a desk that had chairs on two adjacent sides. The room was occupied by a scattering of students working in pairs on classwork problems, but they were mostly talking. Mrs. Harrol was reading at her desk, fuming.

"What's got the teach so upset?" Walter asked, noticing her expression.

"I'll tell you later – it's kind of a long story," Brielle told him. "Why did you get called down to guidance?"

"Does it matter?" he replied meekly. "I didn't get in any trouble."

She cocked her head slightly to the side and halfway frowned. "When people heard your name being called on the intercom, I got made fun of: just so you know...." She huffed. "Do you already know what we're doing today?"

"Do I know what's going on at school? Nope. Do I keep up with anything math-related? No, definitely not." Walter massaged his eyelids with his fingers.

"Well I've got the whole classwork packet done for the next week, so just copy what I've got." She brushed his hair to the side gingerly, grazing his scalp with her nails like how she would with a dog, and then dropped her hand to stroke his cheekbone. "How are you? Not just 'how are you?' but *how* are *you*?"

"Uh – clearly intoxicated. But it's only obvious to me, so really, I'm only humiliated to myself and to everyone else it just seems like I'm tired, and you're allowed to be tired at school, so" he shrugged. "*How* are *you*? Still high?"

"HA! If I'm still high then Jimmy Hoffa is hiding in my boat shed. Hun, I've got enough tolerance to smoke all day and be sober by the time the sun sets," Brielle replied matter-of-factly.

"Oh," Walter said, surprised and disappointed. "Well, I'm sorry. That sounds like a great shame."

"No, it's alright – really. If I needed to be properly high, I could've ate those hash butter crackers that I've got saved in the icebox. Those would have me in Candyland." She continued toying with his hair, flicking around his locks, while he hastily jotted down the work needed to complete each problem and its respective answer. "Soo... let me read your mind," she said playfully.

"You'd just be looking at sheet music without notes or staffs. I'm as mentally active as tree bark." He yawned and shook his head. "You might think you'll uncover something interesting if you try and tell me what's going through my head, but interpreting me would be less productive than running your fingers over a basketball trying to read Braille."

"You're thinking about what Cosmo said to you," she said coolly, adopting the subtlety of a forensic investigator.

"What?" He appeared horrified, but then suddenly composed himself. "No, of course not. Don't make me think I'm thinking things that I'm not actually thinking. Cut it out."

Brielle giggled. "Kidding. But it was a good guess, though, wasn't it?"

"A good guess if you're you; for me, I couldn't be less focused on some bullshit that someone *said*. I'm permanently traumatized by things that I couldn't prevent, thank you very much, and as such I stay busy reliving terrible moments without break: it's a round-the-clock occupation." He flipped the sheet and continued scribbling speedily on its other side.

"I told you: I'm just playing around." She leaned in and looked at his face close-up. When he glanced over at her she kissed the spot on his forehead just above his eyebrow and then pulled back as he returned to copying her math work. Her fingernails tapped rhythmically on the desk with restless energy. "So what did you and the boys talk about for your little sewing circle gathering?" she hummed affectionately, yet still making her words pointed and accusative ever so slightly.

"We don't really talk about anything of any significance," he replied with the professional cadence and confidence of a politician, brushing her off her question as if it was a hand on his shoulder.

She dropped her head to the side condescendingly and then said flatly "You bitched to them about me bitching at you" in the manner of a parent letting their child know that they were onto them.

"OK, well, if you were there, you'd have seen how they pressed me for any information. I didn't want to talk," he admitted, speaking from the back foot.

"Shawn pressed you?" she scoffed. "Shawn just kicks at your ankles and tries to get on your nerves 'cause he's petty like that. Robbie is polite enough to be a Canadian tour guide. So by process of elimination, Joe was the only one who was ferreting you and even still just by himself it was enough for you to fold under the pressure." She was chuckling while lording over him as he was writing.

"Mind backing up?" he grunted without looking up.

She took an airy laugh. "Don't be bitter, dear."

"Don't be conceited," he flicked her knee, "dear."

"What would you do if I wasn't around to torment you?" She started to grapple with him while darting in and out to plant kisses on his neck.

He flinched away and swatted her off with the back of his wrist. "Are you fucking insane? What if Harrol sees you doing that?!" he hissed, then looked around to see if anybody around them appeared to be staring or disgusted, but the coast was miraculously clear.

Brielle cackled. "You know, the fact that you react just makes it all the more worth it for me. You're so good for cheap thrills." She gripped his chin, squeezing on his cheeks so that his lips parted and his bared teeth were showing. "Isn't that right?" she said in a babyish voice.

"Brielle…" Walter started, staring pure venom and slurring his speech due to the sudden impairment he was sustaining. "If – you – don't –"

She let go of him, cleared her throat, and began fixing her clothing extraneously.

He was split on how to behave, what to say next, and what mood to carry forward. Ultimately, he wanted her to know that what she had just done was unacceptable and wouldn't be tolerated any further, but if he got serious, she'd actually give him hell. So he rolled with the punch as best he could and made an effort to not be stern. "You're damn lucky that I'm enamored with you, but mostly that you're a girl who can't punch or block for shit," he snarled before making the decision to lean away from her so he had room to react if she reached out another time.

Brielle was just beaming, overwhelmingly pleased with herself. "That's payback for being such a poor sport this morning. I'll consider my vengeance sated – for now." She stretched and looked around the room that was active with chatter and festivity. It was the same as it was almost every day: the same few people talking to the same few people, but there was a certain charm to the orderliness of their fellowship. They were all only aware of the space that they themselves occupied and fervently ignoring anybody who had no directly involved with them, halfway out of a respect for their neighbors and halfway out of a desire to feel as if some asylum existed for them in this vapid place of being. In its sum total, the group had no desire to prove anything to itself, nor the time or patience to put on appearances that didn't directly affect their direct well-being. They were rogue, they were focused, and nothing could divert their attention from what it was they were striding towards. "You know, I do *love* our class," she said facetiously, "but I'll be glad once we can have a moment to ourselves. My mind can't help but submerse itself in fantasies about all the different ways that our evening together could play out."

"Slow your roll, cowboy;" Walter muttered, "Dad still has to say yea or nay on me being able to leave the house before I get done with –"

"Oh Walt," she said devilishly, "you think you're so slick but if you only knew how much you telegraph yourself."

"I don't follow," he replied, feigning ignorance.

"You know that you're coming over tonight – don't try to feed me any bullshit about how you're just going to do homework and choke your chicken 'cause *Daddy's* gonna be too tough and not let you out of the house. *Daddy's* going to be on his third bourbon of the afternoon, so you leaving will be just as convenient for him as anything else, and you need those damn flowers, Walt. We're talking about your mom here – you really think you're going to be allowed to just sit around, cock in hand, without being put to some kind of use? They'll be yelling so many commands at you once you get through the front door that you'll think you were a hard-of-hearing foxhound. You need to be more consistent in the way you present your appearance: you can't conduct yourself like you're having the time of your life when you should know full well that you're going to be absolutely miserable in a short six hours. Come on, shug; do you think we met just yesterday?" She was observing his stunned countenance, then tapped his nose with her finger. "I've got your every move written down on the back of my brain. The first thing I ask myself when I wake up in the morning is 'How can I break Walt's ankles today?'"

Walter, barely recouping himself mentally, sprang out from this sudden revelation that Brielle had just unveiled to him and just smirked jauntily. "Well, from the sound of things," he said, shifting in place how a card sharp would who had just been found out and needed to make a quick exit, "it would seem that I'm going to have to work even harder to put you over."

She giggled and punched at his shoulder. "You think I won't be at your heels every step of the way?" The two of them locked eyes, staring up and down one another like two feral hounds sizing up the next fight. "You're the only game I want to play, dearie, and if I can't be good at fuck all else, I'll win this one and rest soundly for all time."

"Yeah, you might think that," he said, appearing jollier than a musician on Friday, "but I'll whoop your ass at it just when you least expect it. I'm undefeated when it comes to our little toe-to-toes."

"You're about as undefeated as a boxer in a ring full of toddlers – just wait 'til I give you something you can't duck out of." Her face was overtaken by a mirthy smile that creased either end of her face and had her eyes squinted as though the sun was in them.

"Well, I hope for your sake that I never have to take us to that place, 'cause I'm enjoying our little-league games, personally." Walter was focusing intensely on her pupils, getting lost in the things that he knew that she knew that he knew.

"It'll be a sad day when we finally have to set aside our play weaponry and pick up something more lethal, but, you know: all things pass," she sighed, adoring the way he caressed her in his steadfast and rosy gaze, "don't they?"

If just a few moments more had passed like this and they hadn't said anything further, they very well might have wound up on top of one another, snogging as if they had never left the backseat of Powell's convertible. Instead, the bell rang, and without signifying the passage of their time together, they merely got to their feet and followed the class out the door. This was how things went most of the time – it was how they liked things to be, certainly. One goes back to the other and once they both have had a round in, everyone resets and has at it for a second time. The playful digging-ins that they made at one another let them know they were never too far apart in intentions or mood. It was a miracle that they kept the peace so consistently: they were completely uncommon, cut of entirely conflicting cloths, but still they found themselves winding up on the same page. They admitted it to each other often, but they never truly took it to heart how complete they each felt in their union; if it wasn't for their concord, they would both surely be self-loathing and purely bitter. There was no dodging the issue: they were together because they knew nothing else. It was true infatuation that bonded them, and they were tumbling together down the swerving tunnel that was endless risk and torment, never forgetting how close they came every day to toppling under the immense pressure to succeed as well as to stay on track, but remembering to always be hopeful that together, both of them would never have to fear losing themselves to madness in the clutches of the webbing that was rotten intentions and deception comprising the gnarled cage in which the two of them were trapped. There was nothing in their path so long as the other was there to clear it.

XI – A

Walter sighed as the bell rung, and he followed its command back past the cafeteria yet another time, this trip taking him to the other side where the auditorium was. For once, he was without his wits, as well as his scaly exterior, wandering around like a crab that had just emerged from its fractured shell. Truth be told, in that moment, he wished he could bring himself to cry. He knew what was about to happen: he would be thwarted like every time he made himself rely on the outcome of something that he didn't control. As the cafeteria passed and the auditorium doorway came into focus, he was immediately sentimental for the idea of Alina even being in the same direction as he was looking; just knowing she was in a definite place and that he could find her in just a few moments by walking was enough to set him at relative ease. It was the barrier between him and there that was unnerving him into pieces.

"…Yeah, so if he wasn't putting out all of his energy into being a linebacker, the team wouldn't have anybody to play around, and we wouldn't see even half of the amount of cohesion that we do when you all are out there," Couch Burgundy said. He had a pointy, cornered handlebar mustache that was the same faded blond color as his receding hairline.

"I completely agree," Davis said insistently, fixing his long, luscious locks ever so slightly. His shoulders were wrapped in the tough cloth of his golden letterman jacket.

"And frankly, if it wasn't for –" Burgundy eyed the sorry-looking, slouched-over boy who was steadily approaching him. "Hello, son – you lost?"

"Sorry, I don't mean to interrupt," Walter said in the tone of a funeral director.

"Well while you're over here, what do you think?" Burgundy asked.

"Huh?" he whimpered.

"Why do you think it is that we've had a good football season this year? We've really struggled at this point in particular during years past, if you remember still," the Coach stated warmly.

"Oh… uh, if I'm just being honest, I couldn't know less about sports even if I came from the arctic – I'm an indoor cat," he replied, genuinely apologetic.

Burgundy just chuckled. "You're a funny one, that's for sure…. Davis, you know this gentleman?" He turned to face the towering, fully-built athlete at his side.

"You're Walter: menace on the wrestling mat. I remember seeing you back when you used to hang around the swim crew," Davis said cordially as though he was on the deck of a country club, causing Walter to freeze up slightly, as Walter realized the only reason Davis thought that him and the swimming team were 'friendly' with one another in the literal sense of the word and not the euphemistic sense was because he was under the assumption that Walter had anything to do with anyone apart from the individuals who helped him with dope slinging – Davis was sorely mistaken. "You're Alina's better half."

"That's why I'm here, actually," Walter admitted.

"So what I'm gathering from all this is that you're here to get *into* lunch detention?" Burgundy huffed, causing his mustache to shake around the way rotating brushes of a car wash would.

"If it wouldn't cause too much of a distraction – I don't have any other opportunities to see her, so this is… important to me, to say the least," Walter explained with trepidation.

"What do you think of all this?" the coach asked Davis.

"I think that Walt's an old soul, and if we kept him from his betrothed," Davis said dramatically, grinning, "we'd just be doing him a disservice."

"So what I'm hearing is… just this one time?" chuckled Burgundy.

"Just this one time," repeated Davis.

Burgundy clicked his tongue, winked, and nodded his head to the side in the direction of the doorway. "Don't make us tell'y twice, boy," he said charismatically.

"Thank you," Walter tried to say, but the words were merely mouthed, not given any voice. For as badly as he wanted to speak, his strength was evading him, and before giving them a chance to point out his abnormal behavior to him, he went to his left through the passageway. The space inside was darkened, cold, and muffled. The hallway merged into the rows of seats like an entrance into the center of a coliseum. The stage was dimly lit with spotlights set to the lowest setting, the pit in front of it creating the stark juxtaposition of an open space below to contrast the cleared stage. The curtains were ruffled and thick, masking the back wall as if it was a quiet secret, told in whispers from one party back to itself, never revealing anything to the world around.

Students stirred as they noticed a new, unwelcome guest entering their midst. Faces of every affiliation put their gaze to him, all shooting condemnation in their collective piercing stare. He was sifting through it all like a rack of clothing, not halting for even a split second to consider the disdain or judgments of his peers.

"Oh, Walt," sighed a girl who had wild eyes and striking lipstick as he passed. "Doesn't it ever cross your mind that a nurse would never settle down with a dog like you? You should know that when people talk about you two, that's all they go on about. Just give her up – save yourself the time," she tittered.

Walter bent over, getting face-to-face with her. "I don't know, Aleah," he hissed, "I'm just surprised you're focused on anything other than your toe herpes – it sounds to me like it should be a full-time commitment."

Snickering, she nearly pushed him away in the moment before he walked off. "You're a clown with a target on his back, Walter Monroe," she murmured to him. "You know *exactly* what happens to your kind."

Walter looked up, away from the crowd that was around and behind him, up to the higher rows further in the back. There, halfway to the ceiling, completely alone, sat a girl with a gray shawl resembling chainmail over her sandy-brown outfit; ringed-fingers clasped together, hand-in-hand; her flowing hair pouring out from atop her amber features; and her gaze as constricting as it was addictive: she had the eyes of a viper and the coy grin of a hound.

With measured steps, Walter climbed row after row, slowly strolling under her comforting presence, trudging with the weariness of a soldier climbing the front stoop of his home after touching down in the nation at the end of deployment. He was holding his heart in his hands, staring into the things he knew weren't his keep, but still moving with the presumption that if he reached the end of his path, she'd be there waiting for him. He didn't want anything more than to believe that there was a place for him somewhere, anywhere, with her.

"Hey Alina," he said in a hushed tone as if there was presently a crowd around them and a performance being given down on the stage, and took the seat beside her.

"Hello, Sweet," Alina crooned. Her voice was fluid but carried weight like mercury. She was sitting properly and postured as though she was in an interview and was refreshingly aromatic like a candle shop.

Walter couldn't help but to be immersed in Alina's appearance, adoring the elegance with which she could arrange herself despite her face being held to the muck all hours of the day. Despite her regality, it was visibly apparent that she was only holding together by the thinnest of strings – not that he was in any position to brag, though. "You're dressed like you're set for a day in the park but you sound like you could use a nap until two," he commented warmly, trying to be affectionate while not sacrificing honesty or sincerity: the way that she preferred to keep things.

Alina gently took his hand, sparks flying from their touch as though he was leaning out the window of a departing train, promising her from her spot down on the platform below that he'd return someday soon. Her skin was as moist as it was smooth: she lived with gloves on at the hospital, so it never toughened up. Letting go of him, she sighed and shut her eyes for a moment. "Describe," she said airily, opening her eyes once more and shaking her head slightly, "to me the way the poem made you feel when you read it."

Walter sucked in a breath, shifting in his seat and moving his lips around, wondering if she already knew what was on his mind, as usual. "Don't –" he glanced around at the lower rows checking to see if anyone was watching them "– Don't you want to know what I think about it instead?" he asked, as though to appease her.

"No...." She was glancing from left-to-right, observing either side of his face one at a time. "I can already see what you think about it," she spoke with clarity. "It's all in your eyes – you need to know why that old man out in wild made all the mistakes he did." Her thumb was gripping her chin like she was a parent patiently listening to a child blather in circles.

"I'm tired," Walter replied, resistant. "I have tired eyes." He yawned, as though to confirm his alibi.

"No, these eyes aren't your tired eyes." Alina squinted, making her look quizzical and unassuming. It had him infatuated how picturesque her expressions were despite them being genuine and effortless. "You're looking out in a stare that's distant in the same kind of way as when you're tired, but your pupils look wily." Suddenly, her eyes snapped wide open and she sat back to look at him from a distance. "They're alert... and I think they're on the watch for danger," she said in a tone that seemed disapproving in nature.

Walter scrunched his face, trying to not appear irritated by her complete contradiction of what he had just told her. "What do you know about my tired eyes?" he asked dismissively.

"I know that last Halloween you fell asleep just about three times in Miss Nancy's kitchen," Alina replied, bobbing her head to the side like a gossiping Southern hairdresser saying 'mmmmhmm'. "You" she flicked his nose with her finger "might not remember all the fantastic photos she took of us having dinner, but I do 'cause I look at 'em just about every night and I have to say that she got some real expert shots of you chewing like a zombie who's too lazy to use his eyelids," she got quiet and leaned in "so I might even go so far as to say that I'm more familiar with your tired eyes than you are, darling."

The two of them experienced a moment of split awareness that they both wanted to grab the other and kiss them close and tight, but then he cleared his throat and sat back, causing her to do the same. "I think even if I tried I wouldn't be able to forget how much Miss Nancy used to have such a good time photographing us, but if you're asking me to remember dinner from last year then all I can say is that I'm not sure what I ate last week." He scratched the back of his head, putting his jaw to the side. "Before we get off the subject though, I just wanna say that I disagree with your use of the word 'lazy' to describe my eyes or anything in general about my behavior last Halloween, because I can't help but recall it being at least eight hours into the night and —"

"And the outside world was dark like the ocean floor but that didn't keep us from finding our way out past the other side of that park between the stone wall and that five-cluster of trees where we got to fucking like one of us had to die, but there was nobody around to hear it in a mile radius since everyone was over at the fire that went up on Pikeview." Alina took deep breaths, having said all that as though it was a three-word phrase.

"You took the words out of my mouth." Walter chuckled and fixed her shawl at the shoulder by pulling it all the way on.

"Does that night come back to you often anymore?" She had her head tilted to the side ever so slightly and her dimples were showing.

He rubbed under his nose. "I was brushing my teeth this morning when I thought about it last."

"Can you still feel it?" Alina asked sensually, reaching her hand out low and gripping on his shoulder.

"I've worn out the memory, I think," Walter sighed, suppressing an intense sense of melancholy grief as though he was in mourning. "I'm almost too ashamed to admit that I can barely remember what anything looked like from that long ago." He was staring down at the stage once more and put his hand over hers, rubbing her knuckles.

"Don't feel ashamed – you're just trying to hold onto better times while you wait on them to come back again." She was biting her bottom lip and her lower eyelids were raised in uncertainty.

"Even though I agree, let's not get into a conversation about 'waiting' and end up wasting the little time we have," he said from the corner of his mouth, contorting his face to try and thwart the frown that was finding its way between his cheeks.

Alina shook her hair and exhaled loudly, as though to calm the both of them. "How did the poem make you feel?" she repeated.

"I've never read anything with so much fear in it," Walter admitted. He just then noticed how cold it was inside the auditorium: his toes and fingers had gone numb and his knees were shivering some. Swallowing hard, he tried to toughen himself up, just long enough to be able to survive this conversation – then he could go back to being as stony and nonempathetic as a person could possibly manage.

"Dad started surgeries almost two years ago," Alina recounted, interlacing her fingers and fidgeting around with her thumbs, "and he wrote it just a couple of days before he had his first one. The doctor told him he wouldn't even be competent enough to use a pen once they began." She was staring back into the past, constricted by the inability to move past the moments that one can't help but to bargain with the universe for a chance at changing.

"Your dad wasn't writing himself as the old man, was he?" Walter asked nervously, trying not to offend her.

"No – Dad was too much of a diplomat to rupture any relationships he had with people who he cared about," Alina sighed. "The old man was just a figment of his anxiety." She closed her eyes and nodded slightly, just barely holding her composure.

Walter's right knee was supporting his left ankle and his elbow was resting on the side of his left knee, his chin in his hand. "But you think I'm becoming the old man then, don't you?" he asked in an attempt to be inconspicuous, so that he might not come across as either bitter or accusative.

"I think you just need to be really careful, Walt." Alina locked eyes with her boyfriend suddenly, lips pursed and hair flowing in the slight bluster caused by the air conditioning. If it was possible for someone to present a more genuine and passionate appearance, he couldn't create the image in his mind. Everything about her person suggested concern, level temper, and a caretaker's spirit. She was as much his margin of human goodwill as she was an arbiter of truth and integrity.

Walter tsked. "Alina, come on...." He rubbed at his eyes, trying to ward off impatience. "I knew from the moment I read the poem this morning that you were gonna tell me that I'm the old man, and I thought knowing that in advance would dampen the blow, but it didn't." He shook his head a little and looked away. "Not at all. I'm trying the very best I can – how am I supposed to take you telling me that I'm going to end up a complete lonely wreck of a human being? Can't you see how that's a pretty disheartening thing to hear from you of all people?"

Alina appeared stern in an instant. "I don't think you're the old man – I think you very well just might be walking on the same path he did. And I picked that poem for you for today because you needed to read it more than I think you could understand." She shrugged and put up her hands. "I'm sorry I can't be more loving or supportive in the way I express my concern, but that's because ultimately concern isn't supposed to be wrapped in love: it's love's way of heading off disaster."

"Great." Walter ran his palm over his forehead, dropping his head to the side. "Disaster. You know me more intimately than I know myself, and you're telling me I'm on track for disaster?" He sucked on his teeth and blew out a defeated gust of air how he would if he had just come up empty on the only wager that mattered.

"Who isn't?" she asked peaceably.

"Nobody," he replied with a roll of his eyes, "but that's not the point."

"If we're going to be discussing the points of things," Alina said with spiked decisiveness, "you should know that the point of criticism is not to criticize, but to prevent future criticism."

Walter pulled his top lip into his mouth and bit it. "I'm confused; are you being concerned or being criticizing? And before you say both –"

"Both." Alina gripped his wrist, forcing him to succumb to his girlfriend's presence. "Walt, you're on the ropes with yourself. I see it as being obvious that you're struggling, and nothing could be of higher importance to me than you winning the fight...." Their gazes were fused together, and nothing they could say to each other that would surmount the invaluable moments of sterling living that the two of them once participated in. They both knew how intensely they missed the days that truly mattered, and that every moment past those times had just been an exercise in licking wounds. "'Cause you're a fighter, and I'm a doctor, and there's no free surgeries in this world, so you better take my advice and take it to heart, or else you'll end up on the proverbial operating table of life with personal wounds you could've prevented and the tallest doctor's bill you've ever laid eyes on." She touched his collarbone then let him go.

"I'll see what I can do," Walter replied, looking down and away from his girlfriend. "I… I don't have the words to describe it, but I just want you to know that it's not my intention to be ornery and easily-provoked. I can't say why it is that I don't just get with the present and stop feeling as if everything is an attack on my character. I know that you're in my corner, and if the last thing I could say to you had to be about what I wanted you to take away from me as an era in your life, I'd have to say that my only desire had been to be as loyal to you as you are to me. It seems like the harder I try to be passionate for your sake, the surlier I become, and in between being unreasonable and bull-headed I hope there's at least brief glimpses into my intended nature. I don't want you to think that you're anything less than the better portion of my completed self." His eyes lifted once again to meet hers.

"Walter, if you could only just appreciate how damn disordered everything is. Not a day goes by when every expectation I have gets trampled over, and it's to the point where I'm so calloused that it doesn't even sting anymore. You have your spells – we've all got the same, if not worse. I just pray when the time comes for my patience that my sanity doesn't vanish with it." Alina appeared morose in an instant, her field of vision clouded by paranoia and unchecked speculation over the things that would soon dictate her existence. "It's a dark path that we're locked into, Walt."

"You said 'I pray' – do you still?" Walter inquired.

"Huh?" she snapped out of her stupor, giving her focus back to her boyfriend.

"Do you?" Walter repeated, touching the side of her chin with his thumb. "Still pray?"

"If I'm being honest," Alina replied, taking his hand off of her face and grabbing it, holding it low, "then I can only say that I've stopped asking anybody for anything. I don't expect anything – that's the only way I can manage to keep through life on a daily basis. The day that I get a break and the circumstances of it all ease up just long enough for me to breathe will be the day that my faith in

Holy power gets restored. Doesn't seem like there's any reason to hold out hope, though – just surviving takes so much grit and restraint that I feel as if I could be a child in the Middle Ages: an adult by default because of familial duties and running scared and filthy, responsibilities never-ending, debt and poverty as a way of life, and living in the barren hamlets of the outer countryside, looking up at the hills above through sickly trees and brambles to see a single hulking estate of some noble family built at the highest point, and holding that as being my only standard of satisfaction and security out of ignorance for what actually lies out in the world. I see the happy people, and it makes me wonder why I'm stuck as a servant to myself."

"That makes me sad to hear," Walter said, studying Alina's golden bib necklace which was made up of small rods that formed the shape of an owl with wings extended. "I always thought you took comfort in your spiritual connections."

"It used to be that I had foresight and could tap into other people and the world around me on a level that revealed to me at the very least that there was some plan in motion, but these days I'm so far in the dark that I can't even connect with my inner self. Every voice that once spoke to me has been silenced." Alina sighed. "But it's been that way for a while now, so it doesn't break me down nearly as much anymore…. Any news out of Portland as of recently?"

"I'm not really interested in Portland as a city anymore," Walter replied, putting his lips to the side again.

"What?" Alina asked, her head reared back and expression perplexed at his response. "Why?"

"I don't know. I just haven't been thinking about escaping at all lately. It's not important the way it used to be – I guess it just feels too far off, or too unfeasible." Walter went quiet for a moment, letting the whispering echoes of the room to be all that they heard. "What about you? Where do you want to go?"

Alina crossed all her fingers, fixating at the point where they were overlaid. Her teeth were bared down into her bottom lip, and she was humming gently to herself. "I don't know. To either coast, really – I can't stand being in the middle," she said at last.

"Well, which coast appeals to you more? It might be a tough pick," he replied, desperately trying to fuel a conversation that wasn't entirely grim in nature.

"I have no idea – wherever the grass grows greener, I guess."

Walter was suddenly overcome with something insuppressible by nature. "Alina –"

"Yes?" she exclaimed timidly.

"– I can't stand being reserved all the time," he said profusely yet shushed at the same time. "I'm so damn tired of living removed from my passions. I –"

"Walt, you don't need to tell me – my brain hasn't processed love in what feels like at least a year." Alina blinked solemnly as though she was announcing a death in the family and couldn't bear to make eye contact.

"It goes beyond that, though. Love is just a teething ring for adults, but we're becoming emotionally defunct: lacking heart and soul. When's the last time you've felt bad for someone else?" Walter asked shamelessly.

"Oh, hun; 'feel bad' is such an antiquated term. If you're feeling something, it's implied that it feels bad. People get hurt and I fix the ones that can be fixed – everyone else is on their own." Alina took a sharp inhale and rested her forehead on her first two knuckles. "I want to be able to feel that pang in my gut again when I realize somebody else is genuinely suffering," she whispered, "but it all just seems normal at this point. I don't mourn for other people's maladies anymore – not at all."

"I'm in a similar position, but instead of just being senseless, I'm vengeful over the most miniscule of insults – I get off somehow by pushing people to their limits." Walter sighed, frustrated. "I don't know if it's just a bad habit or if it's going to end up amounting to something that I can't control anymore...."

"Walt," she said, making him look at her, "you know what I'm going to say."

"It's not them," he objected.

"It's Lando, and it's Cisco, and it's Grover, and it's Annabel, and it's Zeke –"

"Zeke is more understanding than just about anybody I know," Walter cut in. "He has my back on every issue. If anything, he's a good portion of why I even care anymore."

"Well Walt, it keeps me up at night to know that you're going with them to that sale tomorrow… and I *do* know who all's going to be there," Alina said stiffly. "I'd be lying if I told you I wasn't fearing the worst."

Walter lurched forward in an instant, whipping his hands around her waist and kissing her with such fervor that she just dissolved in his loving contact, melting into the dim sunset that was their union, but still she gripped the moment like it was a railing one hundred feet up, rain pouring in sheets of fat, bullet-like drops that hit like the tears that do slip out. It wasn't enough to say that she would never forget it: she'd be back here again every day that week and for as long as her imagination could manage to supplant her into the present scene which was actively ending as it occurred. He removed himself from her at last, slipping back in his seat slowly.

"I'm so sorry," Walter blubbered, unable to maintain himself. "I'm fully aware: I'm playing around with a loaded gun in a dark room but it's all that I know." He glanced to the side, down at the rest of the detentionees, and realized in an instant that Aleah had been staring directly at the two of them for what probably was a good while, rocking back-and-forth in her seat with muted laughter at what had just occurred before her eyes. He just shook his head and focused on his girlfriend instead while biting his lip. "I have to do my Fist List again, even after I got told I was getting a free pass for the year – I'm so, so sorry. If I can't get revenge on at least five people who have fucked me over by January, Lando's going to give the word to have me jumped at least once a day until I get killed. It's not who I am, Alina… I swear to you that I'm not like them."

"Walter Monroe," Alina whispered with deadly barbs, "if you think I don't know who you are, you're the bigger imbecile than I am for loving you. Don't make me have to sit at your bed in the hospital after whatever happens tomorrow or any other situation you've gotten yourself into, because I promise I won't be nice with you. There's nobody who I have more confidence in because I've never looked at you and not seen the fondness of a saint, and if I'm not right on this one case this one time then all of Heaven can fall and the air can go up in flames and it wouldn't matter to me either way.

"Don't make me wrong on this one, Walt. You come around and you pull me all the way from out of the swamp that's had me by the ankles my whole life, and if you can't be my hero, then it's going to be sharp fall into Hell, and until I finally reach the bottom, I'm going to be cursing the day that I sold myself over to that boy who dropped into my world because I took that fucking waitressing job at Beanie's and I actually fell for his 'kind stranger' routine and before I knew it, he was mesmerizing me with the way he could make everything seem simple and silly, and for once I had a metric for serenity. There's never going to be another Walter Monroe. Don't –" Alina whimpered, "– Don't make me lose the only one I'm ever going to get."

XII – B

"So you really don't find Brenda and Patrick's relationship disturbing?" Walter asked insistently, having to project his voice over the clamor of the hallway. "I mean, he's pretty much made moves on her little sister *while* they were all in the same room, but Brenda's so desperate that she puts up with it and acts like she doesn't see it."

"Look, the way I see it, it's relatively harmless behavior: she acts ignorant, but at least she's got an eye on him, so if he *really* got out of line, she could step in whenever she would see fit," Brielle replied with confidence while dodging around incoming people.

"Okay, well that sounds great and manageable when you put it that way," he scoffed, "but imagine I was hitting on your sister as you watched: how would you react?"

"Well, A) my sister would never sully her honor by getting hit on by any boy that isn't wealthier than she is, and B) I'd beat your ass so quick that you'd fly sideways," Brielle growled.

"My point exactly: it's a relationship sin to offer yourself up to anyone else – being faithful isn't enough when you're behind your significant other's back, you need to be sure that you curb all interpersonal attraction in their presence," explained Walter.

"Try to think if you were me. You'd understand why I try to be empathetic to people who seem to be doing things in an unhealthy matter," she stated, lips pursed. "Because the things I've seen, the abuse I've witnessed; just simple cute talking is as harmless as a hug."

"Hugs are practically sex," Walter blurted, attracting the startled eyes of those around them who heard him.

Brielle gave his arm a firm right hook.

The hallway was tiringly busy as always; if it wasn't for the bustle of students rushing from class to class, there would be space to see more than just a few feet in front of themselves. Despite that, it was interesting to consider all the stories that surrounded them: panic, affection, excitement, uncertainty, and anything else anxiety-based. Everyone was hurrying down the fastest path towards irrevocable change, and there was nothing they could do to replace the need for cooperation on their way to whatever the end goal was that their sights were so hopelessly fixated on. If there was any worry that they might not be able to make it to the other side of destiny, it was because surviving school was about as unbearable as treading water with one's nose just above the surface.

"Who's that skank bitch that stays hanging off of Ronald?" Brielle commented, pointing to the other side of the stairwell. "She's always leaning in so her ass pokes backwards like it's actually fat or something."

"I think that's Ruth; she used to be talking with Joe," Walter replied, "if I remember correctly."

She scoffed. "Who hasn't used to be talking with Joe?"

"You," he answered plainly.

"I'd be talking with Joe if I wanted to be tied down with constant questioning – no thank you. Seriously, according to at least three girls, he's paranoid enough about getting cheated on that you can only figure he cheats himself, and that's not even getting into how he constantly has to check in on how his girlfriend – God help her – is spending her day, down to details on where and when she's having meals," Brielle stated with disgust.

Walter nodded at a guy wearing a red plaid sweatshirt with gray sleeves who nodded back at him as they passed one another, then continued speaking with his girlfriend, "Well, all that might be true, but he's popular and he likes me, so ultimately I cut him a break on basically anything that doesn't violate the Geneva Convention."

"Oh, don't get me wrong – he's one of my favorite people I know of! He's just rough around the edges, but" she shrugged.

"Hey, if I'm complaining about people I spend time with it's definitely –"

"Shawn," Brielle cut in.

"Er – No, I was going to say Harry," he said hesitantly.

"Harry? We barely spend any time with him. Are you sure you don't mean Henry?" she asked.

Walter grunted as though he had just been asked something intentionally ridiculous. "No, I definitely know who I'm talking about: Harry won't shut the fuck up about whatever the swimming team was talking about that week." He let the noise of the hallway around him to just be absorbed within himself: laughs, jokes, and rumors of the sort. "Wait, maybe I am talking about Henry. Hmm, hard to say."

"What's the most fucked up you've felt all morning?" Brielle asked, gripping his arm tightly for a second to emphasize her question. "I get the feeling that you'd have some interested stories for the shit you've been through already."

"Eh – sheesh, uh – probably when I had that cigarette, because I was on the trinity of alcohol, THC, and nicotine, and I was hyper enough to pick a fistfight 'cause of that inquisition I got launched into," Walter recounted. "Joe would've withheld my cigarettes if I didn't cooperate – he's done it before."

"Huh, I thought that you were going to say as soon as you had your little, enormous drink this morning. You didn't even wait before you went *right* to your book. You looked like a such a tool: too good to hear out the announcements with everyone else," giggled Brielle as they walked along the left side of the wall after passing through the central stairwell.

"Well *I* was immersed. I like that book – a lot. Something about it, the tension, maybe, distracts me from other stuff. So yeah, maybe I was fucked up then, but I was at peace, so I didn't really notice," he replied.

"Superb. I'm fuckin' pumped for you," She chortled. "Hey, when do you think you'll be able to get that gold-coated skull from your Dad's office? The play is coming up in three days so Mr. Lincoln's going to need it sooner than later."

"There hasn't really been an opportunity – him and Mom have been spending so much time in their room that I haven't had time to root around in there. Can't she just borrow a skull from the biology classroom? I don't think it'll matter if it's not golden," he replied.

"Walt, we've had this conversation already: the plot calls for the skull that had been to the molten gold crater to get dipped in because it's the only thing that the harpy will take in exchange for the baron's captured soul," Brielle told him like she was reading from an article.

"Gee shit," Walter snickered, "I wonder how I forgot something as important and urgent as the plot to a play that I'm in no way participating nor attending. I feel like that should've been my first priority for things to concern myself with."

The two of them went through the door and sat down near the back just as the bell rang.

"Okay class," said Mr. Lass, "we'll be covering the Khmer Rouge regime today. If you were absent Friday – Jacques – they were led by Pol Pot under what was referred to as 'agrarian socialism.' Whether his narcissistic experiment for economic revolution was inspired primarily by a fear of Capitalism versus foreign influence is a matter of political opinion – all that can be said for certain is that he succeeded in reverting hundreds of years of progress for millions of Cambodians. In the wake of hundreds of thousands, if not, millions, of cases of executions, live burials, purging, torture, and forced relocation was war with Vietnam. The Vietnamese invaded Cambodia and took down the capital, ending Pol Pot's reign and sending him further west, where he eventually lost his forces to defection. The main takeaway I want you all to get is that the slaughtering of the country's own people that occurred as a result of megalomaniacal military autogenocide is just another example of how Communist governments, not limited to China and Vietnam, influenced the rise of societal revisionism and eventual social collapse. Okay, let me know if you all have any questions."

Silence fell around the room as everyone started skimming their textbooks.

"Christ alive... they'd put spikes in the heel of a boot and force people to put it on so that their they'd never be able to walk properly again," Walter murmured.

"Says here that they'd put people in boiling water and lay them out with leeches all over their body," replied Brielle.

"Alright; they'd take babies and bludgeon them on trees," he gagged, "so I'm sufficiently disturbed – what do we actually have to do?"

"Says on the board that we've got to be able to write about it for the test next week," she told him. "So frankly, you can forget anything even happened at all in this class for about another ten days."

"Don't mind if I do – this stuff reminds me of the stories that Grandpa Torrance would tell me and Rachel about the fight in Okinawa. Apparently, he saw things there that he assumed had been retired during the middle ages." Walter had a thousand-yard stare, trying to suppress the memories of what he had been told about as a child.

"Isn't that difficult to even wrap your head around? We get born forty years earlier and I have to watch you get shipped off overseas, and where you become emotionally crippled while having to commit unspeakable atrocities. Or if the world wanted me to crumple under my own weight from grief, it would take you with it." Brielle looked mournful.

He took her hand, still staring out. "I couldn't let myself go off if the time comes: leaving you alone for the rest of your prime years is something I can't allow. Past that, anything is welcome to come take me."

"What does that mean?" she asked, shocked, gripping his hand tensely. "I'm with you 'til the end of it."

"I've got a lot of superstition about how I'm going to wind up. Sometimes I think about how easily Rachel got taken out, and it makes me wonder what kind of odds I actually have. I just can't ever make myself stand up to opposition – what's it take to be courageous against all else? I can't come to terms with it; I'm hardly hardy enough to ask for directions – how am I supposed to resist anybody who's already prepared to put another person away?" Walter asked hopelessly, regretting thinking up such a train of thought immediately.

"You need to stop criticizing yourself," ordered Brielle. "If you don't put trust in your resolve, you'll never have the chance to find out what your real limits are. You think honor is forged by chance? By luck? Walt, you've got to take chances with yourself and with others to know your place in the world. A firefighter who can't go into a burning building is just another concerned onlooker. I'm not saying that you *have* to go headlong into your destiny, but sometimes that's what it takes."

"That's easy for you to say: if *you're* not brave enough you can just smile and look nice and people will give you credit for trying," Walter replied, evidently aggravated. "Me? When I don't step up, I get told all the ways that I'm a coward, and it's an issue of character. Dad's always berating me for –"

"Walter, you need to take your parents' complaints and table them for long enough to really consider what it means to be independent and self-respecting. I don't hear anybody else trying to say that you've got poor moral fiber except for the only two people who are employed full-time to making you feel inadequate." Brielle was sitting with the posture of a sorority girl waiting for the arrival of guests, stiff but stately.

"You're burying the point: just because I don't have a list of every time someone's called me out for being too meek or apathetic doesn't mean it doesn't happen," Walter attested.

"Well, I could say the exact same thing – you don't know what people say about me," she sassed.

"You'd be surprised," he said mysteriously. "Speaking of things that make me feel inadequate, what group are we sitting with for the football game Thursday night? Henry is going to make us decide for him, and he's going to whine the whole time if he doesn't think it's live where we are."

"Whichever one of the two is closer to the field; Shirley or Sally," replied Brielle. "Frankly, I don't have a preference between them; I just want to be able to see Joe clearly. He's starting and it's all he can talk about these days, so if he can't see us cheering him on, we won't hear the end of it."

"Well you have to decide before we all show up, because Sally and Gustav have their whole row planned out and if we want to get next to people we know – and preferably not Henry – then we'll have to reserve spots with them. And that's not even getting into their obsession with loyalty ever since Shirley went with Mav and Wade to the water plant on her birthday."

"I swear on my beating heart if I have to hear the story about how they made plans that day to go to the Hayfield Hoedown one more time, I'm going to punch a wall. It's not as if I can't sympathize with being betrayed, but holy shit; like, sometimes it happens, and rather than dividing everyone you know into one of two camps, you could just chalk it up to them owing you one and be moving forward like decent human being," Brielle ranted. "Now we have to be diplomatic and understanding when either of them gets all possessive and claims ownership of each group of friends. It's some shit I'd expect out of middle schoolers."

"Well, you remember that Sally and Shirley did know each other from middle school? So, maybe it's fair to say that they never outgrew that phase of their friendship – just a thought." Walter was rubbing at his eyes as he said this, obviously bored by the tedious nature of making plans within their friend group. "Just remember that if we sit with Sally, Shirley won't bring her vodka to the full moon, and if we sit with Shirley, Sally won't save us front seats for Tomcat's Back Venue."

"Fuck! I forgot about that. If we don't go to the Sunday Venue Show do you think we'll miss anything? I heard that Joe Joseph and The Loving Hands are touring around the state so they won't be back for two months. Other than that, the only performer I want to see is Hard Davy – he's got that Baritone that hits all the right notes," Brielle replied, looking up and to the left as though she was visualizing past evenings at the one-room theater.

"Kone Kola is going to do five songs and then he has to get extradited the next morning to New Orleans for some shit he did on Mardi Gras, and that might be... time consuming for him," he replied. "I don't think we'll be able to see him for a while after this week."

"Alright, well that settles it: we're sitting with Shirley. If I have to miss Kola doing that high-pitched crying voice at the end of 'Don't Step to Me' for a second time, I might just break down," she said and then nodded slightly, as though to confirm it to herself.

"Okay, but what if we don't have enough liquor to use for poker during the full moon accounting for the jello shots we still have to make? Last time we were playing for like, an hour and we went through a liter and a half," noted Walter while he observed the dried bits of glue on the wall where posters used to be.

"If I really have to, I'll go to Robbie and get his brother-in-law to give him a bottle from his store – I think it's that time of month when they get rid of the stuff that isn't selling."

The bell rang.

"Thank God – this day is taking fucking forever," Walter exclaimed as the two of them went with the stream of people leaving the room.

Brielle tsked "Oh, don't even start: you're still fried, and you can't convince me of anything else. You're not having the same time that Cosmo is, but –"

"Fuckin' A: Cosmo again," Walter barked. "Do we really have to keep bringing him up? He was on some bullshit, it made for an interesting few seconds, but the truth of the issue is that he's already forgotten he even said anything – just as we should."

"Would you chill?" she spat nastily, provoked by his sudden attitude, as they exited the central stairwell and towards the front of the school the way they came, passing the office once more. "I was just bringing him up because he's the only one I know who's in a comparable state to either of us."

"Reggie told me he saved some serious downers for today and Miranda ate five grams of shrooms in some wonton soup – I talked to them about it in Vichy park on Saturday," Walter recalled. "I'd be interested to see how the two of them are interacting: I imagine they're in totally different places but talking about the same stuff."

"Last time Miranda tripped, I had to sit outside the bathroom at the Chinese bazaar while vendors harangued me and nosy little boys took turns trying to ask me out in broken English. I was forced to listen to her singing showtunes and relaying her astral projections to me in between retching, and she'd get louder if my response wasn't comprehensive enough for her," moaned Brielle. "It was the closest thing to public service that I've ever had to endure and it taught me if I had to live in the streets, it would be out in the country away from bored, wandering children."

"You might get eaten by the wolves," Walter remarked.

"The wolves might get eaten by me."

They entered the cafeteria, which was swarming with students moving from table to table, cheering and yelling and cackling over the noise of one another. They fought their way through the crowd over to the other side and got in line at the kitchen.

"I'm really sorry," Walter said suddenly as they settled into place. "Sometimes I forget that there's anybody out there that actually gives a shit about what I go through, and my ability to be respectful to people who deserve it is entirely defective. Really, you've got so much patience and I just want you to know that no matter what, I'm grateful out my ears that you give me so much slack. So thank you."

"You know… you're absolutely right," replied Brielle warmly.

"Really? You think?"

"Definitely – you couldn't be respectful if your hands were tied behind your back and a gag was stuffed down your throat."

Walter chuckled, as did Brielle, the two of them enjoying their personal solace in the chaotic wasteland that was the communal eating area.

"…I worry sometimes," Walter said, his tone strained. "See, I don't know what's pushing too far. I just live in shades of gray and assume everything is bound to work out, but truthfully, I have less of a clue as to whether what I'm doing is right than anybody else in the room. Just know that no matter what, no matter what I say or fuck up or anything else, I can't lose you. I won't. It just isn't going to happen."

The two of them quietly observed the other, waiting for them to make the first move like two birds sitting atop a rocky perch, drenching rain pelting them from above.

"I was furious," Brielle admitted, "fuming. I can't remember the last time I felt like you didn't care about my opinion." She reached her arm behind his waist as he put his hand on the back of her neck. "I wanted to say some crazy shit like 'You infuriate me,' or 'Why can't you ever trust me?' or 'Sometimes everything just feels like one big mistake,' but none of it felt right, so I just… held my tongue." The two of them leaned in towards each other. "Next time I'll just fucking cuss your ass out on the spot – just so you don't get another easy break."

"I'll count on it," he whispered.

The two of them embraced, kissing passionately, in their own personal haven that couldn't be interrupted by any disgusted onlookers – and the disgusted onlookers did in fact try to interrupt.

"That's fuckin' gross!"

"Ew! Get off each other! What the fuck?!"

"Hey, assholes: you're not in bed. Seriously –"

Walter turned to face the girl talking, who had a face full of piercings and baby blue hair. "Hey, prom queen: I like you even less than your dad does, so do me a favor and shut the fuck up." He tuned her voice out completely, cementing himself in the direction of Brielle.

"You know, that's going to get old at some point," said Brielle. "Grossing people out in public and getting combative can only entertain us for so long."

"Well, I'll be doing it 'til the last of my days, 'cause if it wasn't for easy kicks, I wouldn't have any way to entertain myself," Walter replied absentmindedly.

The two of them took trays of food from off of the counter, and then dropped a dollar-fifty each in front of the cashier, who was counting out bills for someone needing to have a twenty broken. They carried their food out to the central area, squeezing past people who were sitting pushed away from the table, leaning back in their chairs.

"What's crackin', pipe packin's?" Joe spoke through a mouthful of corn as they approached him and took seats around the table.

"I'm having withdrawal and I need a cigarette, but what's new?" Brielle replied.

"You could get some nicotine gum to help with the cravings," Hope commented, upbeat enough to be a kindergarten teacher.

"Yeah, but then I'd have to stop myself from munching on it long enough to eat, so it's for the best that I only can get the rush while I'm outdoors." She shoveled collard greens into her mouth while Walter ate bits of his cornbread. "Who are you sitting with for the game?"

"I'm sitting with Sally," said Shawn.

"I think she was asking Hope," Walter sneered.

"Well the question was going to get around to me eventually," he fired back.

"I'm sitting with Sally, too," said Hope. "I got into an argument with Shirley over whether Brenda and Patrick should break up, and I called her heartless for saying that Brenda didn't deserve any sympathy because she was weak and naïve."

"Told you!" Walter exclaimed to Brielle, his mouth stuffed with cornbread. "Other people think that them being together still is totally fucked, too."

Brielle scowled at him. "You don't know what you're talking about – Joe's with me that it's a non-issue."

"See," Joe said, gesturing with his hands, "if she really wanted him to stop, she'd make it so he couldn't come over anymore, they just meet someplace else from then on, and they'd have no problems. But, believe it or not, it's actually a fetish to watch someone else getting with the person that you're in a relationship with – something about the masochism of the situation makes for an interesting sensation."

"I can't get with that," Hope objected. "If you're in love, you deserve to have trust and stability. He's toying with her mental health by leading her on like this – imagine him *actually* leaving her for her sister. She'd probably have to take time away from school just to recover."

"Well, not everybody feels the need to be a complete prude," Joe grunted.

"Get stuffed, you insensitive douche!" she exclaimed, storming off in the direction of the bathroom.

"She's always fucking like this," Joe hissed. "It's so bullshit – how the fuck am I supposed to be honest if she's going to get her feelings hurt all the goddamn time." He was about to pound his fist on the table, then decided not to, then actually did it.

Walter jumped in his seat. "Same shit, different day," he whispered to Brielle.

"You think I don't know?" she murmured back. "If she loses it one more time, I'll get up and join her, because this is actually getting ridiculous."

"Hey Joe," Robbie spoke up while holding a forkful of teriyaki, which he aimed at him, "do you want Rasha to talk to her?

She might have more luck because she's got a bias towards her close friends."

"Rasha? Why do you think I can't handle this on my own? Why would I need someone to manage my relationship for me?" Joe asked, irritated.

"I guess you're right. I just thought that –"

"No, I'm legitimately asking: why would that be of any use to me?" he replied between swallowing mashed potatoes. "You wecommended it to me for a weason."

"She's just being difficult because the two of you have been having more disagreements than usual, right? So, if someone she has no issues with, and knows you, comes and tells her that you're really trying to make it work, she might be more willing to cooperate with you," Robbie explained.

"Actually, I think that she's mad primarily because you showed everyone that polaroid of her in a bra," Walter told Joe.

Brielle yanked his ear.

"Ow! – Shit!" he cried.

"Listen, fucker:" she snarled, "get nice or I'll ream you." She let go of him.

"Are we bringing beers for the game?" Shawn asked.

"Go ahead and bring all the beer you can find," Walter commanded, rubbing the side of his head. "Feel absolutely free."

"What he said," Brielle seconded. "We're barely going to have enough vodka for the full moon, let alone the game."

"We'll have, what, eight blunts for the moon?" asked Shawn, scratching beside his nose. "We should be fine for the night. Besides, any liquor we save goes into Sunday at Tomcat's Back Venue: Ben Billis and Zed Cali are playing 'If You Are Then Take a Shot' and apparently, they've got Bobbert on drums, so we're going to have to go all out for that in particular."

"Do we really have to go light on drinking at the moon?" Joe complained, dropping his fork into his pulled pork. "I'm going to need to be blackout by then and if I can't get drunk enough to balance out the high then I'm probably ending up on my back, singing scat like every other time."

"If I'm too drunk or not high enough, I might not be able to orgasm properly," Brielle noted.

"Fuckin' gross," gagged Shawn, staring down and away from Walter.

Hope came back and rejoined the table.

"...Hey," Joe said with trepidation.

"What?!" she exclaimed. "And don't say some dumb shit like 'nothing', because –"

"We shouldn't be at each other's throats all the time – it's really tacky and just unhelpful to either of us, not to mention that it makes for poor company. I don't know if you can accept an apology right now, but if it matters for anything, I only want to do right by you," he said with the measured pace of a diplomat.

"I'm pretty fucking pissed, because you've been nothing but rotten to me lately, so you'll have to forgive me for not waiting around to get put through any further shit." She took her backpack and turned away. "I'm going to the library," she scoffed as she walked off.

"See?!" Joe exclaimed the moment he saw her get out of earshot, throwing his hands out. "She's impossible to work with! There's no pleasing her – if I admit I'm wrong, it's just further confirmation for her to be a complete dick to me over the pettiest of shit."

The bell rang and students began clearing out in either direction, either towards the gym in one direction or the classrooms in the other. Walter headed off with Brielle and away from Shawn, much to his relief. It didn't matter that Shawn was brooding and bitter all the time: it was just the fact that he'd disrupt conversations so that Walter had no choice but to interject and set the record straight. It was infuriating how little self-control he felt he had around Shawn – just one word from him and it made Walter want to yell. Brielle put up with Shawn's moods because she got guilt tripped into being his one single friend back during freshman year, before her and Walter met. If Walter had gotten to Brielle first, he could've just told Shawn off at the first available opportunity and ensured he never got past a last name basis with her. But, by the time he had securely locked her down, Shawn had already been to her house and was going to the roller rink with the group.

Brielle and Shawn had drifted apart as soon as she and Walter first got together, because even though it was her core nature to never fully comply with the pressure that Walter might put on her, she recognized she had to make a decision, as loyalty is a pie that can only be doled out in portions. Forced comradery was the least of his worries – it was how intentionally malevolent Shawn was towards Walter that forced him to keep his hand constantly on the holster. Brielle hadn't been alone with him in months, but he knew that Shawn took on a strangely lewd and forthcoming attitude when Walter was missing. Walter didn't enjoy fighting, but if it came down to a fork that was split between violence and forfeiting control of the situation, he was always going to lash out, conquering the social territory he felt necessary, riding sternly and steely along the ridges of weekend negotiations amongst one another that followed movies at Robbie's house that followed group lunch that followed breakfast bourbon on the patio that followed a night of communal rest, the group gathered in the same room, crashed out on any surface that would hold them and hibernating from one day of juvenile degeneracy to the next.

XIII – A

"No, I thought she was just exaggerating when she said that they were canceling the charity walk.... I know, I know, but she's stretched the truth in the past.... Well, normally it wouldn't be a big deal for me, but Karen's been hounding me for a date and now I've got to – Walt. Walt. Walt? *Walt!*" Davis exclaimed.

Walter's swirling surroundings got swept away from him and the sound of the ocean washed from his ears, suddenly aware of where he was walking. "Oh shit – I mean, shoot," he said suddenly, looking over at the chuckling duo of Burgundy and Davis, who had watched him walk out of the auditorium and were both equally amused by his overwhelming grogginess. "I uh – I – Thank you, again," he murmured as he hustled off.

Every sensation, every input was blurry and faded-out. Just trying to chain himself down before he could do any real damage to himself, he went to the far side of the cafeteria past all of the commotion and bustling activity and took a seat alone in the corner. Sounds were piercing into him at the same tone and pitch, a uniform state of awareness strangling him. His vision was so scattered and hyperactive that vertigo had set in from everything he was taking in, but it was simultaneously blinded by the grief in which he was thoroughly mired.

A virus was burrowed within Walter, paralyzing his ability to relate with anything from his surroundings, and rendering him an invalid to his peers – not that they were paying him any attention, anyway. In the same instant, picking a fight with everyone within swinging range or instead fleeing to some blackened retreat where he could lay on his side with his knees to his chest seemed to be equally the most ever-presently desirable options for him to take. It was fair to say that his passions were gutted and he was removed of drive entirely; he had once read somewhere that a second wind find you just when you think you've been choked out. So if he was just to lumber onwards in the same direction then eventually some deposit of adrenaline and opioids would hit and he'd be back in the fight. Didn't seem likely, though. He was in a desolate land as far as he was concerned, and he couldn't even imagine a way to maintain any sort of conviction to himself. He had his temporary peace for the moment that it lasted, but his time to revel had come to a close and he was back to being as deranged and morally clueless as he always seemed to be.

It became apparent all at once that he needed some kind of an out: something that could occupy his focus so that it wasn't completely scattered and nauseating. Clarity passed over him like a cloud rolling in front of the sun, and it occurred to him: Cal Ace. If he couldn't be at peace, he could at least be working – frankly, he didn't know the difference, just that there had to be one.

Walter pursed his lips and considered his options as he got to his feet and strolled down the hallway in the opposite direction of the school store. Spacious and free of wandering, clustering underclassmen, he moved straight down the middle of the space around him, stopping at a door on the left to open it and then went through it. He ended up on the stage of the theater, the curtain drawn closed just as the auditorium's was. Walking around a piano and some flat wooden houses, he knocked on a door at the back end – from behind it was a scattering of chatter and overlapping laughter.

"Dead spiders," Walter said.

It went silent inside and a set of footsteps approached the door.

"Zeke?" asked a girl with an atrocious valley girl accent.

"Monroe," he replied. "I've got a full house."

The door opened in an instant.

The girl, who was dressed up like a soccer mom ready for brunch, hugged Walter into the room suddenly, shutting the door behind him with a kick of her high heel. "Oh Walt – have I ever told you how good of friends we must be?"

"Uh – No; I think it's always been implied, though. Thanks, Kayleigh." He patted her on the back twice and she let go. Peering into the dressing room, girls were scattered around the room sitting on chairs or the counters, every surface and pole covered with blouses and skirts and scarves and coats and all types of goofy hats. Behind a rack of dresses was a couch in the corner where a boy with chiseled features, floppy black hair, and a peacoat had his arms around two girls on the couch with him who were talking to each other.

Kayleigh grabbed her purse from off the box behind her and opened it with a click of the clasp on top. "How much?" she asked.

Walter held up two fingers as he took out the pill bottle from his backpack.

Slipping out two Franklins, she quickly exchanged them for the bottle. Popping the white top off of the foggy, orange container, she passed off some pills to a few of the girls in the room, and they took out a tube of lipstick each and used the bases of which to thoroughly crush them up on the counter closest to them, then they took to arranging lines of dust and rolling up a bill each.

Walter almost brought himself to laugh at how mechanically they took to snorting their meds: they were acting with such swift motions that it was as though there was a limo waiting out front for them and time was of the essence. In the midst of all the activity, he made his way past everyone and waved slightly at the boy on the couch.

"Walter," the boy said. "Last I heard, your bunch are set to become the largest little coalition in the school – is that what you're here about?"

Walter stepped over shoes and stools, going over to a chair in front of the couch. He dropped his backpack next to him and and sat backwards on the chair to face the boy, resting his forearms on the back of it. "Not this time, Cal, but maybe someday soon. You and the tennis crew are more than welcome to put a stake in our empire."

One girl who was bouncing a tennis ball across the floor to another on the opposite side of the room shook her head. "Can't trust Lando – he's always looking for ways to take advantage of people. Nothing good has ever come from him," she declared.

"Look," Walter started, "I'm not going to sit here and defend him, but –"

"Oh come on, Brittney," chortled a tall, Palestinian girl who was painting her nails a burnt orange and staring down at them, "you just don't like him because he won a bet that he could get you to put out in the same week as he met you. If he's so bad, then why didn't you see that coming?"

"I've got nothing against him," Cal said, "but no good person starts an empire. You get him and Charlemagne in the same room and one of them is going to start plotting, and the other is going to inevitably weasel into it in some way or another because they have about as much restraint as a couple of crack addicts." He thought for a second, letting the sound of snorting and snuffling and coughing being the only thing that they heard. "In fact, Walt, the apple doesn't fall far from the tree on this one."

"Huh?" Walter blurted, taken aback.

"Don't fucking 'huh' me – you know that you were a part of Brax and Candice stealing that bottle of Jägermeister from my truck while all of us were talking on the football field," Cal said accusatatively. "Your side was all in on it, so don't even bother playing dumb,"

Walter's eyes went wide and his expression turned blank, realizing that any presumption of innocence had went right out the window, and that he was presently a Blood in Westmont. He leapt to his feet, turning to sprint away when he was clotheslined by two girls. "Fuck! Stop-stop-stop-stop-stop-stop!" he cried.

About four or five of them grabbed an arm or a leg apiece and lifted him over to the couch, which Cal and his two girls had vacated, and they dropped Waler onto it upside-down.

As Walter scrambled to sit straight up, he realized three of them had pulled out either pepper spray or mace and were shaking up the cans while aiming them at his eyes. "Please – Please don't hurt me," he whimpered. "You're not getting anything from me, I can promise you that."

Cal was shifting from one foot to the other. "So you plead not guilty? Because if you want to claim ignorance, we're all ready to go down that route," he said venomously.

"Did Brax and Candy tell anybody what they were doing when they walked away from all of us and went to the parking lot?" Walter gasped. "All I can say is that if they did, nothing was said in front of me, but when they were passing it around later, they were talking like they had gotten it from the store, and I didn't think anything of it. You have to believe me – Lando doesn't let people steal from business partners. He's gotten in so much trouble in the past because of it that he's zero-tolerance when it comes to that kind of stuff, I promise you that. Just please... please put the spray away. It's unnecessary, I'm not going anywhere."

"Oh, you misunderstand us then, Walt," Cal said, flipping out a stubby blade and pressing the flat side of it against Walter's neck so that he felt the full, cold contact of steel.

"Cal..." Walter spoke in a soft whisper. "Cal... don't –"

"See, Walt: we're here to make sure that history doesn't repeat itself. The bottle was one thing, but do you know what really gets us? Cisco taking out debts on other people's names and walking. He's borrowed on Zeke's honor, on Annabel's honor," Cal pulled the knife away and pointed it directly at Walter's nose, pricking the tip of it slightly, "and you won't believe it, but he's taken drugs from us saying they're for *you*." He leaned back and analyzed

Walter's expression of horror. "Yeah…" he muttered, "yes, he did. And here we are: collecting."

"Listen, Ace," Walter said, gaining some mettle and trying to push back from his position of weakness, "if you can tell me exactly what he took and what his reasoning was, then we can at least start working on this today. I can promise you that whatever he took is his for as long as he stays on the run, but if we can assign motive to all this, then that should help clarify things some, yes?"

"What's going to stop you from lying?" Cal asked, slipping his knife away into his belt.

"What's going to stop *you* from lying?" Walter parroted.

"He took a half of Blue Dream from Mindy" Cal said, pointing to the Moroccan girl to his right who had owlish eyes and full lips in a harsh frown. "and he gave her a gold watch to hold onto while he flipped it for her. As far as we know, he smoked the whole zip. Turns out the watch was just painted gold, and it only worked for a day before the battery we found in it ended up dying. He tried to trade another three or four watches to Annie for her whole ivory necklace, but she had heard about the first deal and pulled out before one of us made the same mistake twice." The lanky girl he pointed to as he said that was inconspicuous and demure, standing in the corner, arms crossed and staring at the scene in front of her with emotional dismay.

"*That* was where the Blue Dream came from?" Walter exclaimed. "Cisco told us that his cousin mailed him some from California."

"And you all, being imbeciles, believed him," Cal growled, fingering the handle of his knife.

"He took the zip out of one of those brown envelopes that have bubble wrap on the inside," Walter said pleadingly. "What else were we supposed to do to make him prove where it came from?! Have him read the fucking serial numbers?"

"Okay, so he still has the wool firmly in place over your group's eyes. Good to know," Cal grumbled, his face in the palm of his hand. "What did he end up doing with it?"

"He traded it with Annabel for two sheets of Lucy," Walter recalled. "I know that because they were haggling each other around the campfire that night and nobody was helping to gather firewood."

"He gave me those two sheets for a safecracking kit," said a girl in the corner of the room who was looking through a photo album.

"Fucking *what*?!" Cal yelled out. "Is this *everyone's* first time hearing about this or is it just me?"

"He said that his grandmother died and he needed it to get a bunch of family shit out of a vault," the girl replied, nonplussed and not even looking up.

Cal exhaled loudly. "Okay, so just moving forward, anytime Cisco says anything about his family, feel secure in assuming he made his story up that same hour. Walt, did you have *any* idea that Cisco is cracking safes these days?"

"Jesus, Cal, if you think that Cisco shares stories regarding any of what he does in his time away, then you don't know Cisco," said Walter calmly.

"Well you've got to know what he needed with that key to the self-storage unit," Cal asserted. "He said that Annabel would be paying for that, and because we had just done a sale with her that day, we thought she was on board with the deal. When we checked a week later, she said she never heard word one about it – guess that makes it our fault." He saw pure confusion on Walter's face.

"I can tell you beyond a shadow of a doubt that Cisco not only hasn't told a soul what he's using that for, but he also has at least five made-up stories prepared for anybody who might ask him about it." Walter just laughed at the situation. "Ace, come on. You're hunting reflections. Every truth comes in a bundle of lies, and you're never going to be more devoted than any of us when it comes to –"

Cal's hand flew to his knife, but as he lunged towards him, Walter caught his wrist and kneed him in the gut. Cal dropped, doubled-over and wincing, his knife clattering on the floor.

Walter leapt to his backpack, picking it up and using it to cover his face as he darted through the room. Slipping through the door and sprinting across the stage back to the hallway, then rejoined the masses and hustled back with the current in the direction of the classrooms. Was it lucky that he didn't turn up dead while maneuvering the insidious dealings that were at the core of all of his activities? That was a word that eluded all meaning to him: luck. Either a situation is fortunate or it is laden with liabilities – to say that you're somehow favored by an intangible force around seems implausible at best. He reasoned with himself if he ever made it out and had relatively few scars to show for it that he'd have to genuinely consider if his survival was truly just a coincidence or anything more. For now, however, he did his best to dust himself off as always and moved with the crowd, trying to disguise his predatory inclinations and walk with innocence, claws retracted and affiliations hidden under the surface like a lone SS officer keeping his red armband in his coat pocket, cutting through one end of Warsaw to get to the other.

The cafeteria ended and the hallway past the front office started, after which Walter went back up the stairwell and to the left. He went into a room where girls were sitting on desks and fawning over boys who were leaned back in their chairs, taking turns being impressive and debonair. Sitting off to the side, he went into his backpack, moving the package from Betty down to the bottom and taking out a binder. He had begun flipping through some notes and took out a blank sheet of paper.

"Okay, class," said Mr. Bhatia as all eyes went onto him, "get back to your seats and finish your work from Friday. If you complete all the worksheets on torque, come see me about getting the next assignments."

A girl's hand shot up.

"Yes, you all are allowed to work in pairs," he told her, "so long as the volume is reasonable. Okay: get started and bring any questions up to me."

Walter, after having been watching his teacher, looked back down at his paper and saw a scribbled line of text in that familiar tiny scrawl:

Are you OK?!

He rolled his eyes, realizing he had forgotten entirely about the events of that morning with all the chaos that he had constantly been immersed in so far that day. It was more irritating than anything else that he'd need to protect himself from something that likely didn't exist physically – if he couldn't stand over whomever he was trying to subjugate, it made it hard to fend off any assailants. Blowing air from between his lips and shaking his head, he pulled a pen from his backpack. *What was that?!* he wrote, frustrated with this person's inconsistency. He shut his eyes and rubbed his temple as though he had a migraine, trying to focus in and meditate through the situation. Under no circumstances would he get flustered, lose control, or crack a temper, because he knew that something was steadily amiss about today, and butchering his connection with this 'Brielle' person would only reduce his odds of getting out the root of the matter. If Hell collapsed and everything was irrevocably overrun, it would be on his mind for all eternity how he had been too paltry to step up and make sense of all this bizarre pandemonium. He looked back at the paper.

Don't ask any more about the… thing that I told you about earlier today. It senses our connection that way and disrupts it. Ask me about anything else – just nothing related to it, or else I can't help you.

Great. Walter jotted down in a knee-jerk reaction. He checked his surroundings: he couldn't have been more invisible amongst either half of the class, one half talking and the other with their heads down in a book, working. *Things are pretty fucked right now for me, and I don't say that because I just got manhandled like a guitar in an orphanage, but because I'm losing track of reality. Do you know anything about that?* He turned his attention to a blond girl with crimson lips and a shirt the same color, cut so low that it left her shoulders completely exposed. She was holding her hand in front of her mouth daintily as she cackled amongst a group of jocks, all of their chests shaking with laughter. He checked the paper again.

Do I know that reality is slipping away like American birth rates? This might surprise you, but I've been figuring it out for longer than you have – and I've experienced even more absurdity than you as well, and if you don't believe me when I tell you that, then just remember that I was the one who reached out to you.

He tapped his fingers and sucked his teeth. 'She's got a point,' he thought. 'It's not an issue of trusting her, it's about gathering clues as to what's going on. So long as I stay methodical and deductive, it'll only be to my advantage to consider everything she's explaining as being valid information.' *Okay, so let's develop a starting point: when and where did any of this first take place and what's the most crucial discovery that you've made thus far? he penned.* His right hand went to his left eyebrow and it took to scratching, then he dropped it back onto his leg once more.

I'm not quite sure how to explain it, but I've become a bit… displaced. I've had one leg out the window of coherency and I'm just now starting to lean outside of it, and it's gotten to the point that I'm practically another person. The only thing that I'm lucid to is how blurry the lines are between one reality to the next. I've still got my childhood memories from when everything was simple and nothing was out of order, and I had about as much faith in God as I did in the federal government when it came to being able to do anything of significance. Fast forward to my teens and suddenly I started getting visits and spontaneous miracles would happen everywhere for no better reason than just to prove to me that there was something more in motion involving me than I could have ever perceived with my own senses. Now, though, I'm so disassociated from myself that I don't recognize any recent events as being real, because my head is so filled with far-off scenes that it's indistinguishable what I've been through and what I'm just watching occur from where I am.

Until he read the last part, he had completely forgotten about location factoring into this insanity. *Where are you, by the way – still at the movies? I wonder if time is passing at the same rate for the both of us.* he wrote. He experienced a moment of incredulity, becoming aware of how ridiculous any of the things he was insinuating must seem to anybody if they were looking from the outside without any context. It then occurred to him that if he didn't play along with the circumstances of what he was going through, at least just for the moment, there was no way he could restore order or sensibility to the condition of things. He sighed, lifting his elbows behind his head, interlacing his fingers, and shutting his eyes to fully absorb the sensation. His muscles twitched as they stretched out. He blinked and looked down.

I'm sorry, really, I am, but that was a lie. I was never at the movies – at least, not today…. If we can both be on a basis of full disclosure with everything from now on, then I should tell you that I'm not sure exactly where I am right now – and I don't think time is passing at all. I'm in some sort of… coma. I can't feel anything, I can't move, I can't see anything around me, but I'm able to direct myself places and watch what's happening like I was behind a window. It took some time, but I've built up the ability to take myself to different locations at different point in times. Like I told you, I don't think time is passing where I am, but it felt like at least several days had went by before I found you. the next part read.

He developed a new sense of terror when this revelation struck him: it hadn't even crossed his mind that her safety might be in question, and he felt a sudden sense of protectiveness that he couldn't pinpoint the source of. *I'll find you – you just have to give me some general directions. You'll be safe, I promise. Nothing's going to happen to you, just hold out for long enough for me to get to you.* he scribbled down as fast as he could manage. A group of boys out in the hallway were passing around a basketball while running along and whooping and hollering amongst one another, and Walter's eyes snapped to them before they returned to the paper.

It's not that straightforward – if you could just simply come help me, I'd be beyond grateful. There are stronger forces at play than either of us can imagine, and if we temper fate too much, we'll shatter it like hot glass in ice water. We're in a fragile situation, and unless we cooperate with the conditions we're beset by, then there's no telling what will happen; if things undo themselves any further, I'm worried that life as we know it might halt entirely. he read. He bit his lip while scratching his head, shaking it. *You're going to have to forgive me, but if we're still on our basis of full disclosure, then my only response is that everything you just told me went right over my head. This is all confusing enough without getting into any conjecture. What do you know is in danger objectively?* he wrote, then checked the digital wall clock: **1:12**. More had appeared when he looked back:

I can't speak to 'danger' as a definite outcome that would result in any kind of damage, but all I know is that people are more pugnacious and easily-provoked. It seems like everyone has collective paranoia about something that's out of their control and even their perceptive capabilities entirely. Try to take that into account in any future confrontations: you might not be able to control the situation the same way as you'd have been able to before this drastic outbreak of aggression. It read.

'Okay,' he thought, 'so this means she's seen more of you than she's admitting to. This doesn't mean you can't trust her – it's just that when she tells you she's not sure about something or that something is outside of her awareness, she could be lying by omission just to keep me compliant. It shouldn't be an issue so long as I ask all the right questions, though.' He put pen to paper. *So, if nothing's coming for anyone, and nothing catastrophic is in motion – not beyond a shadow of a doubt, anyway – then why should I be needlessly careful and give in if I'm a position that's forcing me into conflict? I feel like not stepping up is the only way to fail here.* he wrote, then started rubbing his forehead as if he was making a wish and analyzed the palm of his hand before moving it out of the way of his line of sight.

I know that you're eager to dive headlong into all of this and be done with it, but I can assure you that if we're not careful about what we do and especially about what we say, then one of us will certainly slip up, and any casualty will be enough to sink the both of us. So just have patience, please? As for your dealing and antagonistic tendencies, I'd say you should be safe until I see something that makes me think otherwise – just be sure that when you're interacting with people that you're certain you're really you in that moment. It read.

He was put off by this, getting the impression that she was implying he was vulnerable of succumbing to psychosis, or a mismatch of planned intentions and what he'd do in practice. 'She doesn't know you,' he thought, 'so there's no reason to take her advice personally. If she really is afraid for the both of us, then it makes sense that she expects me to make some mistake, because that's the surest way to keep herself safe. Just go with the act and work with her.' He pulled his bottom lip into his mouth, fitting it behind his top row of teeth. *Does that mean you're afraid I lack self-control? Because if you can't trust me to keep a stable mental compass, it'll be hard to trust me with any information that might put either of us in peril. I can assure you that I won't ever forget our mission to take back our respective lives – I couldn't, not for my beating heart.* he wrote. Popping his neck, he closed his eyes for just long enough to refresh his patience. He opened his eyes and read:

I promise, you seem like a competent individual – in fact, you might be the only person I've met who's competent enough to stick through this until the end, but something's coming over people…. It seems like somehow, all of a sudden, the same kids that I've known for years are behaving completely out of line in terms of what I've come to expect of them, and it almost resembles something out of a case study how ignorant everyone is of their former nature. The strangest part of it all is that they'll come to occasionally, and for a spell, they'll be back to themselves, if not just for a brief period. Do I think that they're weak-minded? Probably, but that's not the point: I'm afraid that I might end up getting this affliction as well, and you of all people are definitely capable of succumbing to something that preys on your emotions – the more your moods flare up, the more you can be sure something is amiss. It's like getting rabies and trying to not turn primal: you only have so long.

While he was somewhat unnerved, he was more so concerned with sickly sensation in his gut, which had become so sensitive that it felt like he had just taken a punch there. Again, he was beginning to experience the same sensation from that morning when his senses were blotted out and he was face-to-face with his unbridled conscience. *Okay, look, I know that my behavior might seem suspicious in the face of this... disease, let's call it. Regardless of it: I'm not a monster. I do vile things and talk the part, but if I'm evil then fuck it anyway. Right now, I don't have any commitment to anything but what's in front of me, and anything else is amoral at best. So I'm going to keep behaving with a poverty of ethics because it's a means to an end, and I'm not going to think about the social impact of my behavior because it's above my paygrade to be efficient and considerate at the same time.* he scribbled down in crude, frustrated lettering. He shut his eyes and inhaled sharply, filling his lungs, holding for long enough to hear snippets of conversations around him, then losing interest, he blew all of the air from his mouth. His eyes opened.

Are you telling me that? Or are you telling yourself? the next line read.

He shook his head, frustrated with this person's nippy attitude. *You've got a deficit of faith in me? Fine, but as far as I know, no one else is out searching for you, so considering I'm your lone savior* was all he wrote before he blinked and a new line had appeared below what he had been writing:

IT'S CLOSE. DEAR GOD, IT'S WATCHING ME.

Shivers gripped the meat of his back, his cheeks dropped, and his fingers gripped his knee so hard that the nails bared into its skin. There he sat, strung up by his intestines over indecision as whether to write back or not, because realistically, he couldn't do anything to help her even if she gave him instructions, and trying to communicate might direct 'its' attention to him, and if she truly was compromised, it would be incredibly foolish to voluntarily give himself up as the next target to hunt down.

Walter reprimanded himself, feeling cowardly in some chauvinistic sense, as there was no reason to want to protect this person apart from some primordial desire to save a member of the female sex just to be the one to do it. He didn't owe this person anything, she had nothing to do with him, and if it took her, then maybe that just meant he had a better chance at survival, because as far as he knew, this thing had some sort of hunger or could be sated. Frankly, he was somewhat relieved that his sudden responsibility had been diverted by some outside force: if he didn't have to fulfill his commitment to her by default, then that just made his own life more manageable – or rather, equally unmanageable as it always is, but above all it would shed the unnecessary burden of being a part-time hero.

Rattling breaths and a dead stare were what characterized Walter as he waited through the dense anguish that was his time alone and isolated, but then, the bell rang, and as the class filed out of the door, he packed up his binder and went with them. He didn't want to feel any sort of fault for whatever might have happened to befallen that person, who or whatever she claimed to be. The hallway came and passed around him, and he felt a certain connection to the students around him: the young and the lively, all marching right into the insidious clutches of destiny, not taking into account how hopeless and devoid of glory the whole process of it truly was, for they had their unwavering egos and personas to hide from their peers as well as the veracity of the matter. It wasn't that they weren't aware of their collision course with rampant doom and destruction, but if nothing mattered, then there was nothing to lose, and it was all just one foot in front of the other as far as they were all concerned.

Wherever the Grass Grows Greener

XIV – B

Walter and Brielle were staring intently at two students in front of the library on the other side of the stairwell. They were wearing large posters fastened at the shoulders with duct tape. On one sign read the words **SOCIETY OF THE PARANORMAL** and the other one **DUES MUST BE PAID 10/18**.

Walter grimaced. "If I have to see or hear another thing involving ghosts and shit, I'm going to fucking pop off: Christ as my witness."

"Apparently it's not all bullshit – the club's really popular, so there's lots of falsified reports and sightings that come out, but a few people do communions with the dead and they encounter pretty clear apparitions. Imagine being on some sugar cubes and seeing that shit," Brielle said, giggling and playfully hitting his arm.

Walter was just gritting his teeth. "Brielle – I'm only going to say one more fucking –"

"Sorry."

"Wait, I see Jay and Cosmo talking to those two guys – let's go over." He started walking in the other direction and beckoned her to come.

"Okay!" she said giddily and hustled after him.

Walter dashed through a gap and jumped into Jay, bodying the side of his arm with the side of his own arm.

"Oh, shit!" Jay staggered to the side and looked down. "Oh, hey Walter." Then he looked around. "Wait, I'm in the stairwell. Huh."

"Cosmo, what did we talk about this morning?" Walter asked.

"I haven't seen you since yesterday – you're tripping," Cosmo scoffed.

"Look! See?" Gripping Brielle's shoulder, he pointed to her and then to Cosmo, and then back again. "Right on cue, he has no idea."

"Whatever – I know better than to start this conversation again," Brielle replied flatly, holding her hand up to him.

"Are you coming to the meeting tonight?" asked the boy on the left.

"Me?" Walter frowned and shook his head as if he had just been asked to pay for someone's spilt food. "No, I can't say that I am."

"Well if you want to join up," the right boy said, "then next week will be the last opportunity you'll have to be there for free."

"I know," Walter said eagerly, "I can read your sign." He pointed at it and clicked his tongue, raising one eyebrow.

"We were just talking about the full moon," said Jay, energized through his haze. "Miss the clocktower – it's going to be desolate. Listen to this: Jenn's got ten kegs and 200 names on a list for Friday. Malcom Van Davis finally got the word of Jarrod Carter that they'll run 30 there, and Carter's powdered ass never fistfights so that's a wild sentence just to say. If you don't go, don't expect anybody to ever stop talking about it without you."

"It's for the best; I hate it when the clocktower is crowded. It's so open out there that there's no privacy," Brielle joyfully replied. "I hope Malcom gets to run 30 a few times with Carter – he's my boy and I don't want him getting soft."

"Be careful if you're going out to Cobey Pond or anywhere near the clocktower," said the boy on the right. "Our contact out in San Bernardino says last full moon was the worst for sightings and attacks they've ever had on record, and predictions from out that way are that we're seeing an uptick in –"

"Alright, well I've had my fill of conversation for now," Walter cut in, adjusting his belt as though he was making room for his gut. As he strolled off, Brielle ran up beside him and grabbed his hand, listening to his griping all the while. "See, the issue I have with all *that* bullshit is nobody ever asks before they start rambling endlessly about whatever nonsense that it is they're on about. If they got permission first, I'd at least have patience with them, but as the way things stand I feel violated intellectually when I have to endure it," he ranted.

"…You done?" Brielle asked loftily. "Ceasefire?"

"I'm pretty heated. But fuck it – I should've expected them to talk about it," groaned Walter in the tone of a bratty child, dropping his tense expression. "I don't know what I was thinking."

Brielle was eyeballing Walter cheekily from the side, even though he was staring dead-set forward out of frustration. She sighed sweetly, "I think it'll get better once the full moon passes and everyone has a chance to get all the excess curiosity out of our systems."

They entered the classroom on their left, greeted by the wall-mounted faces of Freud, Skinner, Piaget, Pavlov, Jung, and Maslow made in 3-D papier Mache with written quotes sprawled all over them. Jeb had accidentally knocked Mrs. Bertow's enormous ceramic brain display onto the floor and made all of the faces for extra credit so she could display something in its place.

"Walter, Brielle: homework," their teacher ordered. Mrs. Bertow was a woman with a mature face that still retained much of its youth. Her light blue button-up blouse complimented her navy-blue pencil skirt – black heels being her personal necessity and not a choice.

The two of them went to her desk where Bertow was shuffling through notes from her seat, a filing cabinet to her left, a bookcase behind her, and a potted fern next to her typewriter. After depositing their respective worksheets in the black plastic tray on the corner of her miniature office, the couple went to the other side and filled the two seats against the wall.

"Alright, that's everybody. Okay class, so we're doing our unit on the DSM-III still this week, and we'll be doing schizophrenia today and tomorrow, psychotic disorders Wednesday, and dissociative Thursday and Friday," Mrs. Bertow spoke. "Schizophrenia is" she went to the whiteboard, uncapped a marker and wrote *auditory hallucinations, thought withdrawal, insertion and interruption, thought broadcasting, somatic hallucinations, delusional perception, feelings or actions experienced as made or influenced by external agents* "what happens when the barrier between subjective personal experience and worldly occurrences dissolves. The schizophrenic has to stop and consider everything they are hearing, because what is actually a voice speaking in their head might be mistaken for a recording being played on tape somewhere around them, or noises that sound as though they could be made by the environment are actually just being generated by their own brain. Where it goes from being benign or relatively manageable is when nonsense becomes passed off as genuine perception. This is how someone becomes unable to stop themselves from saying things that don't have any outside context to anyone but themselves. Furthermore, people who lose control of themselves further might assume their very thoughts are being read, and potentially distributed, by some outside force: either a person, a group, an organization, or something completely unknown. There's no way to trace back the origin of such a belief because said person can't think objectively enough to consider why they have this distrust for the world around them. Conversely, it can cause a person to think that their thoughts are not their own, but have been supplanted by said outside force instead. The word 'delusions' refers to the state of being in which the person cannot understand anything other than their own beliefs, resulting in hostile and antagonistic altercations between people who can't comprehend why the other one is behaving the way they are. That's the scary part about this disease: to an outside observer, it's no more apparent that the afflicted person even has a mental disorder than if what they had was just simple depression, and this goes for the outside observer as well as the one with the disease. Without constant awareness of one's disorder, it can seem overwhelmingly straightforward why one feels the way they do, but the reality is it's much more complicated and requires patience – not confrontational actions." Bertow checked her watch. "Alright, that's all I've got memorized. Do homework. Don't talk too loud," she commanded, then went to the window, which was gaping wide open, and lit up a cigarette while perusing a copy of Cosmopolitan.

"Fuck – the smell of that smoke. Walter, I need a cigarette, I *need* it." Brielle fell over him, draping her arms around his neck and on his shoulders. "Oh, Walt – why does my life have to be full of tragedies? Why can't good people just get the things that are their God-given right?"

"Beats me," Walter spoke to the air in front of him, while patting his girlfriend on the back and resting his cheek on the top of her head. "Hey, what do you think about all that reality-being-imagined jazz?"

"Why? You thinking about studying people for a living?" Brielle asked, scrambling to get up all of a sudden to get a good look at him.

"I'm dying for a living. No, but I only mention it because I think I have something somewhat similar to hallucinations," admitted Walter.

"Holy shit – you see people, Walt?!" she exclaimed.

"Lower your voice and wash your mouth out with soap when you get home, Brie," Bertow called through her cigarette from the other side of the room, not moving her eyes from her magazine.

"Holy shit – you see people, Walt?!" Brielle repeated in an airy whisper.

"No, of course not," Walter said, tsking and pushing his mouth to the side as if a cousin had asked him for a loan and he didn't have the right words to turn him down. "I've just got this weird déjà vu, except it's not – instead I'm seeing double when it comes to myself. I've got this one frame of reference for what's real and what I've lived through, and then a random memory will drop in of something that's never happened – like I had just seen a television program and was thinking about it still."

"Are you *sure* you aren't actually just talking about some program you've seen Brielle insistently inquired, tapping at her cheek restlessly. "It wouldn't be surprising if it was something you had just halfway forgotten about since? 'Cause really it almost sounds like –"

"No, I'm positive it's all new. Every time I visualize something that's unfamiliar I have this moment where I register it as being made-up, and I've got to convince myself somehow that it never really happened," Walter explained, going into much more length and depth than he had anticipated at all.

"Well shit, Walt – this sounds serious," she said intensely, leaning in and gripping his arm.

"… It's serious like a black hole: sure it means something, but from where we are, how're we supposed to determine anything by it?" he rationalized, trying to play it cool in the face of the unfamiliar and unpredicted.

"How long have you had this?!"

"Honestly? I can't say that I have the first clue when any of it started. But let's stop talking about this – it makes me feel like a freak." He was rubbing the space below his eyebrow and biting the inside of his mouth, unnerved.

"Okay, babe," she sighed, dropping back in her seatand toying with her hair. "I want tea and knee socks and the drawing room couch and us and the whole Bummarum album playing with the filter on the record that pitches it down slightly."

Walter was staring under his desk, counting to himself on his fingernails. "Give it a few days and we'll be doing that and more – no need to rush," he vacantly replied.

"Why can't we just do it today? Why do we have to put everything off?" Brielle insisted. "What's wrong with living in the moment?"

"Let's be frank, dear: the two of us aren't going to remember this conversation in two hours' time," he meandered through his words, taking time to glance up and around the room.

Brielle giggled. "Okay, you have a point. Still – I want to do something sweet and couple-y. It's been so long since we've had a quiet afternoon to ourselves when we only had ourselves to ramble to." She paused, let her eyes close, and sniffled slightly, filled with memories on a dime. "Or better yet, just lay in silence."

Walter's eyes snapped back onto his girlfriend. "What do you mean?" he asked, helplessly confused. "We just spent Friday lounging around at the Duck Park Docks and we even managed to smuggle some margaritas off of the deck of that yacht – I was so faded that I was sleeping with my eyes open, but I was watching myself sleeping from a distance as I dreamt that I had sleep paralysis. That and when we got up I had pins and needles so bad that I lost all vision for a second and fell into the water – don't ever let anyone know that happened, by the way."

"Elaine already knows," Brielle said, laughing daintily like a little old lady who had just had her heart warmed. "I'll never forget the way you just dropped: it was as if someone had cold-cocked you in the back of the head. And all of that was great and everything, but I still want to have a room to ourselves where we don't have to worry about anybody bothering us – it has to be vacant enough for you to start hitting it."

"We fucked for twenty-three minutes in the hammocks by the Corners bungalow just this Thursday...." Walter's eyes were slit. "Brielle...? I feel like I'm the only one remembering all of this."

"I know; I said it has to be vacant enough for you to start hitting it – not actually doing it. You were talking about fetishes earlier today? I get off by being able to have sex and just lying around peacefully instead," said Brielle matter-of-factly.

"Huh..." Walter murmured as he sucked in his lips. "So that means you get off by –"

"By not getting off?" she finished for him, unable to keep down a grin that stretched upwards across her face so delicately.

"Yeah, I've thought the same thing myself. I love a good paradox – especially when it makes my crotch sizzle."

The final bell rang and the class cleared out. The afternoon announcements came on, talking about clubs and sports practices that have been moved or canceled and buses that have been changed, but ultimately, no one in the hallway heard them over the collective shouting and hollering going on in it.

"This is fucking insane," Walter exclaimed, barely able to speak audibly over the clamor.

"Wait," Brielle yelled, "Walt – do you hear that?"

He tuned his ears, then realized some of the yelling wasn't joyous, but angry and strained. "Look!" He lifted her up off of the floor at the waist so she could peer over the crowd.

"That has to be Toby and Rich!" she called out as he dropped her back onto her feet. "Come on, we're checking this out."

They rounded the corner of the hallway and pushed through bodies to get to the center of a tight circle that had formed against the wall. A cleared space in the middle held two boys, one with the other in a headlock, the headlockee slamming his body back to hit the first's head against the lockers behind them.

"Fuckin' brain him!" one voice said.

"Choke his shit, Tobe!" another commanded.

The boy in a headlock reared just forward enough to snap his head back and smash Toby's nose with his dome; Toby dropped him and clutched his face instead. Rich, just then getting free, gasped for breath and swung out. Toby slapped the punch away as it was coming In, lifted his knee towards his chest, and then flicked his ankle out and put the heel of his boot square into Rich's gut as though he was kicking down a door; Rich's knees buckled as he cried out in pain and doubled over. Toby then jumped back, spun around as he extended his leg, leaped into the air, and made full contact with his toes against the side of Rich's head, holding one fist up and the other one out in a signature martial art pose. The crowd erupted in roars as he landed on the ground, getting his balance and dusting himself off. Hands reached out and lifted him into the air, carrying him around as he laid on his back, his smushed nose still gushing blood down his chin onto his neck. "Toh-bee! Toh-bee! Toh-bee!" they chanted.

Walter and Brielle followed them, but when they reached the corner, they carried him off to the left as the two of them went to the right, away from the herd.

"Does Toby do that often?" Walter asked. "I've never heard of him getting a clean KO before – didn't know he was capable of that. I just always remembered how he got his leg swept by Sam Roswell and knocked off the lunch table that they were grappling on."

"I think Toby Warner used to get whooped pretty consistently, but then he started taking Taekwondo classes and joined the basketball team," Brielle replied. "Joe was telling me about him – apparently the only person who's won more fights than him is Bill Potcher, and it's expected that they'll fight if for no other reason than to let people bet on the outcome. Apparently the last time something on that scale has happened is when Jax and Luke had that Muay Thai square-off, and Luke made five hundred bucks off of the one-fifty that he had put up."

Walter had his lips pursed. "When the time comes, do you want to –"

"Watch from the front now? I wouldn't miss it for an ounce of shake – I'll tell our grandchildren about the outcome, down to the last brutal moment," she declared with fascination.

The two of them strolled with the crowd past the cafeteria and through the auditorium hallway, relieved that they had survived yet another day of turbulence and uncertainty. It was like jumping a ramp on a motorcycle and landing on the other side: you can do it five thousand times and still have no clue how you're supposed to survive the next one. There was no glamor or glory in it, however: making it through was its own reward, and that felt incredibly meager when you considered how the only real consolation prize received for running the gauntlet that was the dire straits of young living is that it means you probably have a decent chance of making it through the next go-around. A refugee in a foreign land coming from a state that had disowned them must first be thankful that they had made it out at all, because nature doesn't produce victims: either you're the prey or you're the preying and anything that any creature gets away with on another can be considered to be deserved by both parties. Being self-pitying is just a roundabout way of expressing how malleable one is under the conditions of daily life, so it takes either a despondent or provocative individual to say that they'll take the scenic route to Hell just to make a trip of it. Neither of them had the resolve to tread water on their own: they were tethered to one another in the open ocean, buoyed at the shoulders and ankles and merely drifting together through whatever harbored them for the day.

"Wheels," Walter said to Powell as they walked up to him.

He was smoking and leaning up against a pillar outside with one foot on it. "Romeo," he replied, standing straight up and flicking away the half-spent cigarette.

"Hello, dear," Brielle cooed.

He merely nodded back at her.

"So Walt," he started, walking up beside him and nearly touching shoulders, "I hear the two of you are going to the Rich-Park townhouse this week? Need a ride?"

"Wednesday, right?" Walter asked Brielle.

"I think so," she replied, "and Joe offered to give us a ride, but if you'd rather do it then him –"

"No, that's fine with me," Powell said. "What do you think we're going to find in there?"

"If you're asking me if you think we're going to find a ghost, let me just say that you're going to get less out of me than a Japanese P.O.W." Walter grumbled, irked yet again.

"Sorry for asking," Powell replied nastily, "fuck."

The three of them boarded his car and the ignition cut on with a twist of the keys. Music was blasting and cheers and whoops could be heard all over: the sound of a day's work closing down for yet another afternoon that had been sealed shut, welded by time, and it couldn't be reopened with a fortune and a crew of a million people. They were the youth of the hour, never stopping to question their nature or contradict the paths that seemed to be automatically laid out before them. It wasn't a labor of love that they survived through their trials: it was a miracle gifted by the universe that would be repossessed before long.

"I want," Brielle said, looking down at the match she had just pulled from her pack of cigarettes and then struck on the pack's side, "to see something incredible; astounding. Something that'll take my attention away from whatever boring fucking mire has my mind trapped right now."

Walter observed her as she held the flame to the exposed tobacco, turning it orange. "What if we went to the Golem's Cove someday this week? I have to see Rachel's carvings so I can add this year to the list of her dates."

"I'd like that," Brielle replied through her cigarette. She appeared as a model off of a poster: poised but mysterious, stunningly aristocratic in her eloquent appearance, and familiar in a way that was somewhat nostalgic, strangely enough. "What dates are you going to put on there?"

"Well, last year I did our trip through New England, winning that game of manhunt with you in South County that had five dozen people playing in it, and nursing that eagle from your backyard to health... oh, and I started with the accident happening. That was the first date I ever had to put down in her place, obviously," he said, frowning intensely as though he had just ingested a sour grape and shaking his knee.

"Let's just forget about everything for a bit," his girlfriend spoke softly. "I think it's fair to say that we've both had full days, so something that's not hard to handle should be a good change of pace."

"Okay – but what?" He scratched his nose and tried not to look morose.

"Tell me a story?" she gently suggested.

Wherever the Grass Grows Greener

Walter cracked his neck to either side, rolling his shoulders and shutting his eyes. Brielle gripped his left hand with her own, and slung her right arm over his right shoulder, giving her full control over his torso. He wouldn't have been able to break free even if she had only been doing one or the other, as he was deep in the ruffles and ridges of his brain, plunging to its furthest reaches to dig up anything that he could remember the start and finish to. The trance ended after quite some time – the amount of which he had taken not being of his concern – and his eyes snapped open. "Alright – I think I've got one," he spoke as he began to put on a sober and pronounced inflection. "Once there was a kingdom ruled to the ends of the Earth. One man owned the largest metalworking and wood manufacturing complex in all of humankind, and he wanted to become king instead of whomever else was in charge. So one day, he had an idea, and he ordered a pillar to be built to the roof of the sky, and from there he had a flat surface built from ocean to ocean, leaving only a small circle at one spot out over the forest. When the king woke up the next day, he saw that the world had turned pitch black. In a panic, he sent out scouts in all directions on horses to search for light. When one rider found the hole, and brought the king out so he could see for himself. There, the man was waiting for him, and he told him he had stolen the sky and had it stored away. The king asked how he did it, and the man said he had pulled it all down in pieces and given it away so that the king could never find all the individual bits on his own. The king, who was considerably greedy, wanted to know if he could have the last piece of sky for himself. The man told him he could have it, but only if he went up to get it for himself by climbing a rope he had tied to it. So the king took to climbing, and when he reached the top, he saw the sky for its entirety and realized he had been duped. By then, the man had the pillar cut down with a drill at its base, breaking the whole covering into pieces as it dropped to the ground, but the sheer speed at which it fell burned every bit to ash on the way down. The entire land was relieved to return back to their lives as they knew them, but by the time night had fallen and the next day arrived, word had spread that the king was missing. The man went to the center of the kingdom and told of how the king sacrificed himself to save the daylight, and that he made a promise that if the man would rule in his place, he would give his life for the good of the population. The people believed him, and the man had a long rule as king and a life full of love and plenty." He took a deep breath and had a few soft, staggered coughs as a result of recounting the tale in record time.

"That was refreshing – thank you." She looked around. "I miss being able to come down this way to the country and having picnics. It's a shame that the lake got infested with mosquitos." The neighborhood formed around them. "And, it's over." She tossed her cigarette butt into the street as Powell stopped at the curb out front of his house. As Walter had leapt out over the side of the car, she grabbed hold of his backpack, yanking it from him.

"Hey!" he whined, swinging around to face his girlfriend. "Brie, I need my backpack – my dad might not let me leave without my homework being done. I'm actually serious right now."

Brielle was stoic as she held both of their backpacks down with her knee. "Having to bring your backpack over to my house will just slow you down. Your dad understands what you're doing, Walt. You're an adult now." She lurched over and pecked him on the lips before pushing him away from the car. "Just trust me," she whispered. As Powell's car revved, the last thing he heard her call out to him was: "I'll meet you in the woods, dear!"

Walter watched the red convertible disappear down the street in a matter of seconds. Sucking in a firm breath of air and bracing himself, he merely turned and went up the walkway to his house. In a swift motion, he opened the door to find his father at the bar yet again after a day at work.

"Walter..." he said, slurring his speech and rolling his eyes around to meet his son's. "What did you learn today?"

"That Pol Pot got away with some of the worst atrocities I can conceive of – oh, and that Toby Warner has a clean tornado kick," stated Walter, trying to cooperate with his father who was fading in and out of reality.

"Your mother left the office early to spend the rest of the afternoon with Rachel, so I'm going to be next door with the Caulfields while she's away," replied his father absent-mindedly, his head hung forward as it bobbed from side to side like he was a mannequin being dangled over the roof of a skyscraper. He began grumbling and griping. "Where's your backpack? Don't you have homework?"

"Am I allowed to go and get the flowers before the sun starts to set?" he blurted out, teeth bared and lips intensely frowning as he cringed at the very words he spoke. "I *do* have homework and it's not all the way done, but –"

"Walt *hic* Walter, you need to recognize that you're the adult now," Walter's father spoke with a certain drunken snappiness, the whole sentence coming out as one word, syllables smashed together like two grilles at the middle of an intersection. "That means if you're going to walk around with your shoes untied, you can damn well expect yourself to trip – and I'm certainly not going to try and catch you. I'm powerless to make you conduct yourself the way you need to be conducted. Am I right, boy?"

"Absolutely so," Walter replied insistently.

"So instead of doing your work, you want to go pick flowers and rail your uppity blonde little Bourgeois bitch at her parent's estate –"

"Brielle's house is barely larger than ours," interjected Walter.

"– then go ahead. Don't even wear a rubber, fuck –" he burped "– fuck it."

Walter knew better than to argue over passing comments that his father would end up forgetting by that evening anyway. "Tell Mr. Caulfield that the two of us need to face off at shuffle boarding again sometime and the missus that I miss her pork roasts." He didn't wait for a response – his father rarely would direct his attention to what he said, so it was pointless to try and have dialogue because anything he could think to say would just get talked right past – like a ship in the night.

As Walter reunited himself with the outside world, he felt a strange relief; Frankly, he hadn't expected to leave without some kind of fight, any kind of fight. It came into his system all at once that he was free: utterly unrestrained by the shackles that others could put on him. He was alone, he was alive, he was in his youth, and no past traumas mattered because he could walk down the block with vibrant trees and well-dressed, dolled-up houses on either side, hands in his pockets and his head in the clouds. He could've whistled, or sang, but he didn't want to ruin the tranquility for himself. He honestly couldn't tell whether he was under the effect of anything or not anymore, but it didn't matter because he had the one assurance that he was soon to see the one person who carried any weight in his heart. He wasn't sure when exactly, but it wasn't long before he broke into a jog and transitioned into a full sprint no slower than a man chasing his stolen wallet.

Powered by adrenaline coursing through his system like an electrical current through copper wiring, Walter blew through block after block, crossing several corners and not paying attention to any onlookers he might have gained. It didn't concern him – it couldn't, frankly. He had one goal, one mind, one motivating force. He wasn't just running towards a destination: he was burning the barn merely for the sake of it. It was an obsession, an addiction truer than anything else he could ever possibly manage to form. Eventually, the sound of soles flying off of the pavement with quick scuffs and pounding footfalls became deafened to him. His mind was merely a concerto of disbelief and excitement at the prospect of him getting his way so tremendously. He could've been smuggled into an obscure nation, gambled his life with someone rich enough to not have anything better to do with their money and won the right to do anything his heart could conceive of and he'd put himself right exactly where he was right then.

Pain was just a word for the upset and dejected who didn't want to appear to be easily surmounted. Pain, to Walter, was an opiate that turned him superhuman in terms of his physical tolerances and constraints, and he moved like he had to outpace the methed-up battalions of Nazi soldiers in the midst of Blitzkrieg, solely as a result of the immense amount of pain coursing through his body and the eroded mental awareness of a beast. His state of being fueled into itself, making him a self-propelling engine that had no concept of becoming overwhelmed or accepting failure. Failure at this point would require a complete and entire change in his core human nature; what he was doing right then was as primal and carnal as fornicating on a grizzly bear pelt.

The street began to border on a dense forest that had an opening in the form of a dirt path, which he leapt straight down. Suddenly, his ears opened to the sound of birds calling one another and bugs buzzing like a microwave. They were all cheering him on: telling him that he was so close to victory that the only thing he had yet to do was don the crown. Leaping over brambles and ducking under branches, he moved like water through a pipe. He had become something noble, something meaningful. He knew in the pit of his soul that he couldn't be anywhere else on the planet right that moment for the life of him. The path came up on a ridge, which he leapt atop, looking below to see a girl walking down the path in front of him whose shiny, golden hair was so silky that it resembled a tapestry, the disposition of a feature in some classical Romantic portrait, and a smile that could make his ankles fail. She mouthed 'Hello,' and waved slightly.

Walter hurled himself over the edge landing several feet down, tucking his head in and rolling forward over his back to properly curb his momentum. He came up on one knee like a man achieving knighthood, taking a moment to look above him and into her eyes, then pounced at her like a cat spotting a dove on the railing. He wrapped her in his arms, leaning both of them over and kissing her with such suction from his lips on hers that he could feel their surface being tugged on and stretched. Her scent of sweet, fresh rose petals filled his nostrils and evoked vivid connotative memories. There they stood, interlocked and breathing raspy, ragged breaths. Both of them moaned and sighed, completely engulfed in bliss and serenity, unable to register anything beyond the overwhelming sensation that the present brought. They detached faces, still hugging and just looking at one another tentatively, both waiting for the other to make the first move.

After the better part of a minute that they had spent just staring at one another, Brielle stepped away to turn and point behind her. "There's some foxglove down the way that I came," she said at last.

"That'll work great," he said coolly. "You were right: you found something that'll please my mom." Walter embraced her with one arm over her shoulder, holding her tight and quickly planting a peck onto her temple. "Thank you," he whispered, as he clasped his hand with hers and began walking down the leafy path.

They didn't talk much while they were out there – they had said just about everything they wanted to say while they were in class that day. They didn't have any unrestrained desires; no inclinations that were tugging at their focus and demanding attention. They each had the one thing that was relevant to the other, and it was with levity that they strode down the leafy path, hand in hand, their dreams projecting around them and the barriers that kept back the impossible all melting under the intense heat that their collective strength of spirit was coming together to form, and it wasn't their resilience that kept them in the fight: it was the conviction of their position in the world as one who belongs to the other, and they were traveling at breakneck speeds along a bridge that they'd someday have to jump to the other side of, but still they floored it at top gear, snarling with unrivaled hunger that kept their mouths wide open, screeching in the face of steadily-constricting cataclysm, and they would make all the noise that they could muster until old age stopped their tired hearts or a tragedy cut them down. Defiance is the fuel that powers every reluctant decision, and they were ready to slit the throat of whatever king presided over them if that's what it took to keep capitulation at bay. They were

Wherever the Grass Grows Greener

brawling in a packed room with studded knuckles and spiked knees,
and it was the only love that they'd ever know.

XV - A

"No, I mean it's fine and everything, but if Ciara doesn't put us on the list to her house party, then I won't have a chance to see –" The girl talking stopped and looked up as Walter entered the room, then donned on a stern expression and pointed to the empty seat to her right.

"Fuck," Walter grumbled to himself, and pushed past the group standing in front of the row to the furthest side of the classroom, then dropped down into the seat that had been selected for him. "I'm sorry, Annie," he told her. "I'm sorry from me to all of the fucking tennis team – I'd kick Cisco in the nuts if it would get your shit back, but it's gone." He sat back. "So there, are you happy? Isn't that what you all want from me: an apology? Or does it have to come with some top until I make you cum? I don't get the inclination that anything satisfies you lot, so you'll have to forgive me for assuming you're only out for more."

"Do the worksheets and read chapters 23 and 27 when you're done," Mr. Morris called in his flat, nasal tone from his desk, face scrunched and jammed in a dense book filled with nine-point text.

Annie just laughed. "You're a riot, Walter Monroe. I know you won't believe me, but we don't actually want anything from you – you're a reliable source and we'd be morons to throw you away. You wouldn't have expected it, but once you had fled the scene, we were cackling wall-to-wall –there's a reason why we keep Cal Ace of all people around us, and that's because he pulls off funnier shit than any of us could imagine on our own."

"I'm sure it must be hilarious from where you all are, but considering how close I come to getting maimed, it's hard for me to be anything but more antagonistic, and that's bad for business. So you see how this is all a vicious circle that I'm trying to break," Walter stated.

"Look, this really goes beyond simple street-level dealing: we're gearing up for a full-scale conflict," Annie replied.

"Wh-What makes you say that?" Walter asked, taken aback by this sudden prediction.

"Cisco is working steadily towards his goals on his own accord, without anyone's knowledge, and what he's doing even goes against Lando's intentions, if what you were telling us today was the truth. When the time comes, he's going to grab his stake and run for the hills with it: I'd be surprised if you ever see him again after just a few months. You all are so flighty, it almost won't even come as a surprise to the rest of us when it happens," Annie said with clarity, self-evidently thinking laterally.

"Well when the time *does* come," started Walter, "then it's safe to say that we'll end up in opposing trenches. You've got commitments to people who look at me as a back-biting, opportunistic double agent. If it gets to the point that I've got to actually protect someone who I roll with, the odds of us ever patching up any kind of acquaintanceship that might have existed beforehand are going to bottom out. It's fair to say that we're chasing conflicting outcomes."

"Are we?" asked Annie. "You won't believe it, but *I've* got a connection to Charlemagne… if you can imagine such a thing."

Walter's jaw dropped. "No – you're kidding," he said, dumbfounded.

"You know Rudy Dormer? Well when he delivers the concentrated wax he gets from Canada, he goes by their operation before he gets to us, and sometimes we get asked by proxy to do favors on credit for all them when Dormer comes around the next day," Annie said slyly. "We've actually got more than a few owe-us-ones saved up, and if we ever get into any kind of conflict, it's going to be with a swift and decisive presence that his crew will come through and make everybody cooperate." Chuckling, she fanned out her fingers and put them over her chest as though she had just absorbed an insult.

Annie's face then dropped, and she grimly muttered, "If Cisco butts in, however, suddenly the game changes. Any kind of funny business on either end will only lead to a quick termination of alliances, and things could easily become heated in what might feel like mere hours. I only talk to you because I believe that it'll be fortuitous to establish some kind of understanding before it's too late."

"I don't know how to get into it," Walter began explaining, "but if I don't keep everyone placid enough to prevent any kind of confrontations – let's just say that there's a lot at stake and we can't afford to lose on this one."

"No, I know what you mean," Annie replied warmly. "I've never been so concerned for anyone the way I am now – and if in the months leading up to all this I got even the most minor idea of the scale that all this is going to develop into, I'd have moved back to Arizona while I still could've: it's fair to say at this point that this issue encompasses two hundred people, easily."

"Well, I'm glad that we're on the same page here, but what should we realistically expect ourselves to do when the floodgates crack? If we don't a comprehensive plan that puts us at a definite endgame, it's likely that we'll end up with regrets more extensive than a beehive. I'm not trying to go the rest of my life not being able to forgive myself for letting people close to us getting their lives irrevocably mutilated," he said solemnly.

"That's why I wanted to speak to you: we don't have to sit around, hands glued to our crotches waiting while everybody we care about suffers or worse – no, we can remedy the whole situation," she said with a steadfast intonation like a commander to his officers. "Kayleigh is getting dick from Reno, and I don't have to tell you for you to know that no one's closer to Charlemagne in this city than him. The day's going to come soon that my side meets with his, and when that happens, you should be around to make sure Cisco's true nature gets some exposure to Charlemagne, just so he knows what's going on in your corner."

Walter scoffed. "It might not matter here in a day or two: I won't have to come along to jack shit and I'll still end up tied to a chair in a walk-in freezer with two of his goons telling me what I can and can't do. Corbin told me I'm getting a visit, all because Lando won the lottery with that crate of bullets, meaning now he's in a position to flood the market and sweep prices and apparently, they all want to find out what's he planning on investing into, presumably so that they can turn the largest profit possible as Lando makes his decision either which way. So basically, I'm in charge of insider trading for a whole faction that I don't have any affiliation to – can't say I'm particularly anticipating what's inevitably going to happen to me for being involved in this kind of detective work."

"That might not be such a bad thing: if Charlemagne finds something that he needs in you, he'll let you give him counsel, being a business partner and all. A Charlemagne that is aware of all the chess pieces on his board is always going to take the wisest path of action, and cluing him in on Cisco's under-the-table plotting will make him surprisingly manageable, I would think," Annie said.

"OK sure – all of that sounds great and everything, but the hard truth of the issue is that doing anything involving hidden intentions is inherently fatal on a social basis out past our side of the tracks. Full stop. Anybody gets wind of me going out and setting up schemes..." Walter paused "I'll be exposed that same afternoon just for the sake of absorbing my reputation – from there, I'm immediately set to become targeted by thugs on an even greater scale than how I'm going to be when I don't get my Fist List completed this year," Walter said emptily.

"Wait, you don't mean... Lando went back on his decision to not have you do your List?!" Annie cried. "That's so fucked! How can he do that to you?"

"He didn't say the reason when he made the call – he just implied that I've been pussyfooting lately and he wants to see if I can still keep formation with the pack. It might not be entirely hopeless, though: Annabel wants to pull a Hail Mary and try to complete it all at once, so that nobody has time to sabotage my doing so," he told her, lips to the side. "If that does happen – and this is a big 'if' – then I'll have immunity from harassment and I'll be safe to play both sides of the court at my leisure. I'm a bit more skeptical than Annabel is, though – much more skeptical, in fact, so I'm preparing for my life to descend right into Hell, just on the off-chance."

"Are you sure that Annabel has intentions that match up with yours?" She interrogated him. The ridicule in her tone was daring him to try and get a lie past her. "She's kind of a disagreeable personality and just generally socially repulsive."

"Annabel is just an extension of Zeke, and if Zeke ever did wrong, I wouldn't be any the wiser of it because in every case I would've done the same, just two times as bad. He's got my back, so as long as she keeps his nose to the grindstone and makes him pitch into hitting licks for just that one day, we'll be safe beginning, middle, and end. He sees things out," Walter attested.

"You're so gay," giggled Annie.

"Yeah, I guess," he replied with a shrug of his shoulders. "I just keep track of who's worth trusting, and trust gets a lot of mileage with me."

"You really trust the company you keep?" Annie asked, as though to spark a revelation within him that might change his mind.

"I didn't say that anybody except for Zeke gets much of any mileage with me – you're putting words into my mouth," said Walter with a click of his tongue. "I have trust for them the same way that a lion trusts the hyenas that surround it: they're ravenous and bloodthirsty, but not for me – at least, not for the moment, anyway, as long as we all keep moving and nobody lies down for too long. So I assume that they just want to do respectable business and I try to make it work as best I can. I don't see my situation through any shades of danger."

"'Respectable'?" she scoffed. "Walt, you all have your rounds collecting from prostitutes on a weekly basis for rent fees: you're pimps."

"Whores are respectable because if you don't respect them, then nobody will respect them, and that is the sad fact of the matter." Walter was rubbing his cheek just under his eye, staring blankly out in a random direction, barely focusing on what he was saying. He pulled his hand away, and while fixating on the tips of his fingers, rubbed them together, then dropped his hand. "Somebody has to choose to do business with them and it might as well be us. There's no difference between helping the homeless and the people paying out their body for a living: if I worked in a soup kitchen, you wouldn't cast my behavior in such an immoral setting."

"You're enabling their perpetual cycle of poverty rather than doing anything to help them break their miserable habits: you're not holding a gun to their heads, but you might as well be," Annie said, beginning to dig in.

Walter snapped to. "Whoa, wait – we're in a philosophical discussion all of a sudden; Annie, I'm sorry, but I'm not the person to have this sort of talk with. I'm thoroughly apathetic."

She dropped her face of mounting irritation and began laughing again. "You're a strange bird, Walter Monroe," she said sensually, fluttering her eyelids.

He smacked the insides of his cheeks against his gums. "I... do not know what that means," he said, then paused, then chuckled with her.

"It means that I'm sorry about Cal," she said, dropping her voice closer to a whisper than not, "because if he did anything crazy, none of us were going to take the fall. That was some dangerous shit, and –"

"Pfft." Walter shook his head, grinning artificially just to keep a grimace from between his cheeks. "Let me get a knife put to my body…" he replied with the same volume as hers while he looked away from her and kind of ducked and weaved slightly to emphasize what he was saying, "let him put steel right to my neck and all of you just had mace to my eyes. Fuckin'… I'm fuckin' lucky that I didn't get blinded back there. But it's all just 'sorry'. 'Sorry we toyed with your bodily integrity like it was a keyring.' It's all just – you saying that it's not all one big joke just makes it all the fuck funnier the next go around." As he spoke, he couldn't help but to take up bargaining with the universe again for the ability to spark a cigarette.

His eyes were straight ahead, so they didn't catch Annie tearing up slightly, sucking on her lips and looking low. "None of that was planned," she whimpered meekly. "The girls – they all just go along with him. It's a subconscious-connection-between-people thing, basically. And I can't help feeling protective of you in some idiotic sense but even if I had stepped in and said something, they'd just have –"

"Oh, I already fuckin' know: they'd have –" Walter glanced over to watch one drop slip out from off of her eyelid and begin dragging down along her cheek as she sniffled. "Oh, fuck, Annie," he gasped with the guilty weight of a lifelong sinner. He had a thousand-yard stare as though a ladder had just toppled off of his roof with a child at the top. "I have a fucking girlfriend," he said with so little voice that he almost didn't even hear himself. "Why?" he asked gravely, as though he had just been diagnosed as being terminally ill. "Why me? I'm chickenshit: fuck me and anything about me, Annie – go for anybody else. Regardless of that, I'm a burnt out wrestler and a dead man walking; you'd be chasing a used-up corpse and that's a shit way to spend your youngest –"

"Don't," she snarled, wiping her cheek off with a swift drag of her fingertip across it, "fucking tell me what to do with my heart and what –"

Walter held out his hands face-down in front of him and was patting the air as if it was 4 AM and he was trying to silently tell the band to shut down because the police were parked outside. "I – have – a – girlfriend," he growled through gritted teeth. "If she gets word that we're talking the way we are with each other, do you know what's going to happen to me? Do you? I'm out on my fucking ass, is what, and for you it's just another failed attempt at nabbing up some quick pipe to help pass the time. So fucking forgive me for not wanting to reach my hand out while the fan blade is still spinning: I'm not interested."

She just shook her head, frowning and looking him up and down. "You'd think we didn't just have a conversation about the duty we have to the people that surround us. We've got to work fucking together, Walter, and that's whether we like it or not."

"Yes, I agree: we need to work fucking together and we will, but not if you've got your heart spilling out all over the place," He said crudely. "Forget you have one, at least for a little bit – if you end up having to put it away permanently, I hear ignorance is bliss, so maybe feeling nothing at all while the two of us wade through all this horseshit will work out in our favor,"

"Walter Monroe, if you don't hear me out I will make you regret every decision you've made up until this point of your life," she said with the potency of an adder.

Walter put up his hands and shrugged, his lips one long crease across his face. "Doesn't sound like I've got jack shit when it comes to choices here," he tsked.

Annie inhaled deeply and shut her eyes for a second, readying herself for the gauntlet that she was about to force herself to run. "Alina," she started, eyelids snapping open and her eyes going right to Walter, "doesn't have to be afraid of anything. I don't want to do anything with you – or anything to you. It's a story that's as layered as it is deep why I feel the way I do right now, but in all honesty, I'm intensely desperate for a person exactly like you and no one else. You're not unnecessarily adventurous, nor prone to wandering: you set out for something and by the time you've come back you've got it. You're a man, Walter, and a man of character – no matter what you say to the contrary. I don't know what love is; I'm too broken to have a sense for it, but when I think about you being out there, alone, without someone to keep an eye on you… let's just say that I know what I want and nothing could be clearer."

Walter just blew air out of his mouth, letting his lips flap around. "Welp, if anybody is going to tell Alina that we're talking, I'm skewered lengthwise twice over – fuck the doghouse, she'll just chop my dick at the base and gouge my fucking eyes out. So at this point, what's it matter? We might as well pick out the color scheme for our wedding, then, right?" He was trying to not be intensely condescending, but it was hard to have any sympathy for this person.

Surprisingly, she began giggling at his string of comments. "It's crazy… I feel like we've known each other for years but we've only had a few exchanges at most," Annie said wistfully, completely brushing off his continued mention of his girlfriend.

"I didn't think I had heard your voice before today," Walter replied, contradicting her, "so are you sure that we've talked before?"

The two of them were deep in a stare that had their eyes welded together, searching for all the things that they were too afraid to uncover, but still they fostered their connection as if they'd someday be able to return and reclaim the fond feelings that they might have been experiencing in that instant. "I couldn't forget talking to you if I had a handful of Ludes with a box of wine – and I say that from experience." She took his slight grin as a sign that she was on the right path.

"I mean… okay, I can give it to you that we might have passed each other a few times before now," he said through a smirk that he very badly wanted to suppress, "but you're still doing nothing to explain how anything about me makes you feel any of the way that you're describing. I mean, this all sounds awfully similar to something that someone would say when they've been dared to lead some dumbass on for a date."

"Well…" she reached behind her neck and unfastened the necklace that was hidden under her jacket, then pulled out a metal cord with pieces of polished ivory strung along it "I presumed you were bound to ask what I'm putting up in this gamble, because right now you're the only person with any chips in the pot, so I thought ahead and I conjured up a way to show you I'm in it for the long haul." She slipped off the largest of all the pieces, which was at the very end and was shaped like Libya, and then dropped it into his palm before reconnecting the necklace behind her neck and slipping it back under her shirt.

"I really don't need this," Walter objected, looking back and forth between it and her.

"That used to be Chuck Reals's," she said with the vacant longing of a forsaken bride. "He always carried that piece because he said it was good luck – that he was safe so long as he'd have it on him. Then Rally got to him… and now there's no more Chuck Reals." She sighed. "He was the love of my life; I feel like a widow who lost her husband overseas to some war that she couldn't even begin to comprehend, except he didn't die for a cause of any kind: just money and territory." She gripped the hand that he was holding the ivory in, fondling his knuckles. "As long as you keep this on you, I'll always be with you, seeing you through your every conflict, your every struggle."

Walter sighed himself and put away the ivory into his backpack. "That would be great and everything, but I'm no Chuck Reals – not by any metric of comparison. That guy was your fiancé, practically, and he played things by the book – I'm entirely off the record. Because from what I've learned, you can get away with anything so long as nobody's around to tell on you." He scanned the area around them briefly before whispering, "Does the phrase 'body count' mean anything to you?"

"Jesus!" she exclaimed, gripping the back of her neck with her nails.

He cackled. "I'm kidding – holy shit, I didn't think you'd fall for that. No, but really, I'm consistently the absolute worst, so you'd only be doing yourself a disservice by having any kind of investment in me, and not even getting into how immensely self-destructive it would be to think of me in a romantic frame of mind. Don't do it to yourself."

"I knew what I was getting myself into when I thought about it at the first chance I could take once I had the time to myself. If we can't be anything, let me at least know you, Walter Monroe. You fascinate me," she said in a hushed whisper, her defenses lowered so drastically that his dropped as well, both of them so exposed to one another that it was just like the afternoon he spent facing Alina down at Fragile Falls Creek in a sweltering June when they both stood bare, not an article of clothing between the two of them, hands clasped in one another's, the water rushing past the riverbank and their toes submerged in the sand; protruding from the middle of the forking rush of water was a tiny, shrubby island that served as their personal Eden, and as they looked on at the world around their naked bodies, a sinking feeling had surfaced inside their respective hearts, as they both knew the moment that they were sharing had already passed. And it had. And here Walter and Annie sat, staring at each other the same way, the past still warm in its grave.

"I'm leaving early," said Morris from the doorway, "I'll be around the corner – come get me if anybody needs something."

"Annie..." he whispered. "This is wrong. This is the wrongest thing I could imagine myself involving myself in, and I rob –"

"Rob people," she cut in, looking guilty yet pleased like the cat who ate the canary, "you rob people. Walt, there's nothing you can tell me that's going to change the way I consider you in contrast to my perception of every other guy I've ever had access to – I mean, how many sports functions do you think I show up for? Every single one that gets scheduled: that's how many. I meet hundreds of boys on a monthly basis, and that's not even including all the pill-snorting blowouts where enough people hook up to fill two nurseries come nine months later. If I wanted any one of those meat-headed, party-hungry, horny brute then I'd have someone new to talk to every moment of the day from now until I die a miserable death. They don't make me feel like I'm taking any kind of risk: you get me worked up enough that I figure to myself that if all this didn't matter, there's no way I'd get the sensation that takes me over when I think about... us."

"This is getting too freaky for me," blurted Walter. "I think you're either misled, or purposefully overblowing my image to excite yourself: seriously, don't expect anything from me. I've got nothing to benefit anybody." He got to his feet and went for the door.

Horrified, she checked the clock, noting that it was fifteen minutes before dismissal. "Walt – where are you going? It's not time to leave!" she called.

"Please," Walter begged from the hallway, "get a grip: for my sake." Fuming, he trolled down the hallway, thoroughly disoriented and without a frame of reference for how to conduct himself for what only seemed to be the tenth or eleventh time that day – and it wasn't getting even more remotely tolerable, at that. He really ran it over in his head: what came first in this situation? Was it the intense disrespect that all of his peers collectively possessed towards him, or his capitulating nature that forced him to respond to every situation with his trademark defusing attitude of passing as a free target to harass because he couldn't bring himself to retaliate, or his smarmy and bad-mannered nature that forced people to lack empathy for him by default? Reason would suggest that one birthed the other two, but it was irrelevant anyway, because he was stuck with all three until he bucked up and started trying to take command of things. The only thing he knew to a certainty was that he was such a forgettable character that nobody cared if he got rolled around or stepped on, as no one would shed a tear for his suffering.

As he exited the building and went out into the back parking lot, he scanned the area around him and searched for familiar faces amongst the packed rows of cars where small scatterings of friends were standing in groups conversing, enjoying the end of another long day. He made eye contact with a boy sitting behind the wheel of a tan Dodge Ram 50. The boy had a blond mullet and a red mesh ballcap on his head, and a smoldering Black & Mild between his lips. Bluegrass was blasting from the stereo and reverberated throughout the parking lot: two acoustic guitars played a plucky beat over the gnarled groaning of the singer on the boy's radio.

'I'm sick with these re-grets that have me feeling lost,
and if faaate permits then I'll pay the cost,
but not if I become a herrrmit and wind up on my... cross,'

Walter went over and opened the door, sitting shotgun.

"I checked your schedule; you seem to be everywhere today," the boy remarked as the shaken-up basket case entered his truck. He flicked open a lighter for Walter, who had slipped a cigarette into his mouth.

"Huh?" Walter grunted, smoke shooting from his nose like a cartoon bull. "Oh, fuck," he said suddenly, appearing frustrated, "I don't even want to know what that means." The palm of his hand rubbed his eye. "Good to see you, too, Brax."

"I'm sure you don't," Brax replied, his laughter unrestrained. "Trevor told me your autism spiked this morning: you walked the fuck off after saying you didn't know what you've been up to lately. I almost couldn't believe him when he told me, but I've come to not expect anything less from Walter Monroe." He had to stop himself from cackling too hard so he could continue smoking.

"Yeah, don't forget to breathe, asshole," sneered Walter, just before taking a lengthy drag of his own, and then pulled the cigarette from his lips, blowing the smoke out the window from the corner of his mouth. "It was the crack of dawn and there was four of them."

"OK OK, yeah," Brax continued, "whatever. Cal is looking for you." He was reveling in Walter's discomfort at these reminders of his not-so-distant past. "He was his usual ass-for-a-head self, but I don't think I've ever seen him that worked up, so good job, whatever you did."

"He held a fucking knife to my neck and I kneed him in the gut: it's not that deep," Walter grumbled, flicking his cig a few times before putting it back in his mouth.

Brax began roaring with laughter. "Alright, I'm officially fucking done. You're a goddamn oil spill of a human being – I just want to let you know," he said, gasping for air.

He just shook his head, opened his backpack and passed off the cellophane package as well as the two hundred dollars, smoke coming through the spaces in his teeth around the cigarette he had stored between them. "I just want to get this shit over with and be done with my day: I've fucking earned a break," he said.

"Quit your griping; either you're giving me steady head or you don't get to take my time complaining." He coughed deeply into his fist.

"I'm surprised you don't have Candice glued to your dick by the mouth," Walter remarked.

Brax ashed his cigar and glanced around the lot, making sure that they were still invisible to the public eye. "Are you worried about hitting any snags?" he suddenly asked in a much lower voice, looking at Walter from the corner of his eye and leaning around. "Don't get in there and start floundering, 'cause in that event, I'm leaving: rescue missions are for suckers and the military."

Walter tsked. "When's the last time you've seen me flub a smash and grab? I was born doing these," he asserted plainly as the two of them set their focus on the stumpy boy with a buzzcut going into his trunk down at the other end of the lot.

"Okay, well you can either jack yourself off some more, or you can –"

Walter swung out the door and closed it gingerly behind him. His soles scraped the pavement as he crossed the row of cars and made the long walk across the lot, ashing his cigarette and smoking it intermittently.

"Thanks, man," said a boy with dreads to his shoulders as he walked away from the trunk with a bottle of whiskey.

"Walt," said the boy with a buzzcut as he was approached.

"Can I see what you've got, Bronson?" Walter asked, rubbing under his nose and looking around in an attempt to seem inconspicuous while taking drags.

"It's whiskey, Walt," Bronson objected. "Are you buying or not?"

"Why can't I look at the whole selection before I pay?" he insisted, gesturing with his cigarette.

His face scrunched with incredulity. "It's Jim fuckin' Beam – it's all the same."

Walter put his lips to the side of his face. "You've got flavors though, right?"

Bronson sighed, exasperated, and rolled his eyes, then flipped open the trunk. "There. Fucking pleased?"

"Is that Double Oak in the back?"

"No – it's Black."

Walter nodded. "Yeah, I'll have some of those."

Bronson just looked at him strangely. "Sure… whatever." He leaned over, reaching as far his stubby arm would permit.

Walter grabbed his ankle and flipped him forward, sending him headfirst into the trunk.

"You fucker!" he yelled, tumbling in place to pull himself out and screeching in pain all the while.

Stashing one bottle in his backpack, he yanked out two more and sprinted back the way he came, cigarette bouncing up and down in his lips as smoke trailed behind him like a locomotive. He passed the bottles through the open truck window to Brax, then pulled the one out of his pack and gave that one over as well. "There, easy," he panted. "Take me to the bus stop?"

"HA! That was great," Brax chuckled. "Yeah, hop in the bed."

Walter leapt into the back of the truck, pulling himself over the opened gate. As they rode off and the final bell rang, he observed the swirling scene of students flooding around them, all of them running and racing from the back entrance to the school. Their strides covered the ground that served as the barrier to their proper selves, the future just one marathon away – the victors of which would be the quiet and unassuming, for only a placid, humble figure can handle the stress of excellence and standout performance. Like the waterhole that connects two endless sections of savannah, beings of all shapes and sizes; ranging from the tall, peaceable giraffes to the hardy gazelles to the bold, commanding lions; took over the space as if they had been born right there, and the world could carry on and be unyielding as ever: under no circumstances would the youth lose track of their stake in young society and it would be the one thing that they could say they held strong for in the face of it all.

XVI – B

"Yeah, so it turns out that going second at Griffipa basically fucks you right out the gate if you don't get a hand that can combo break." Brielle was steadily pulling on a thin, rolled cigar as they strolled down the block as well as playing with a pebble, lobbing it up and leaning from side-to-side to catch it with both hands as they strolled along.

Walter reached out and snatched it from the air right over her head, then plucked the blunt from her lips and stored it in the corner of his mouth. "Yeah, but if they just draw a face then they get out of the vicious cycle – what's the problem?" He began throwing the pebble overhand up into the air and letting it fall into his palm, then turning his hand over to flick it back sharply so that the pebble launched into the air, letting it land back into his upturned palm after it came down and thus repeating the process.

"They were playing Strip Griffipa – or Strippipa for short, and in that the one big rule is turns are make it take it. So Beth and Harver were screwed right from turn one."

Walter stopped in his tracks. His hand froze and the pebble clattered against the concrete. He was merely staring straight ahead, apparently at nothing. "That's fucking stupid," he said at last. He grabbed the stone from the ground and hurled it in the opposite direction. "I'd be pissed – I'd probably just walk out."

"Well they were fucking that night at that house so...."

"So just find another house?"

"Harver has roommates from hell and Beth's dad has a shotgun."

"Oh." Walter passed off what was left of the canoe and peered to the side, observing the sunset dropping behind the row of houses they were walking parallel to. "You ever think about all the people who saw the sunset and wanted to take it and keep it all for themselves? Conquerors and the like – anyone who took something and only craved more. I bet each and every last one wanted to freeze the moment and put it up on a shelf for all of time to admire. Now they all swim in dirt. Isn't that hard to believe? We look at the same celestial bodies that Marc Anthony and Cleopatra spent their nights under."

Brielle burst into snickers as she finished the roach, dropping it in the dirt. "Walt, it's a good thing that we'll be drunk soon, 'cause this weed has you talking like an accomplice with two broken thumbs." She stood in front of him as they approached the house. Walter leaned against the wall on one shoulder, his hands in his pockets, as Brielle bent down and began punching numbers on the keypad.

"Why can't you take me seriously?" he asked through an exasperated scoff.

The metal clamps on either side of the garage door let go with a hiss and retracted into the ground. "Door," she said sweetly, grinding the toes of her left sneaker into the gravel driveway to appear ditsy and bubbly.

"Brielle."

"Dooorr," she hummed upwards in tone, walking up to Walter, bearhugging him and planting a fat kiss on his cheek. She gripped his biceps using either hand, took in a sharp breath, and stood back to look at his face, airily sighing, "Door."

"My name's not Door."

"Have I ever thought about how every power-hungry maniac to ever exist has looked at the sun and the moon and the stars and wished it was all theirs to keep but now each and every one is bones or ash or both? Yes, all the time, and it fucking scares me, Walt: it scares me." She took a step back and clapped her hands energetically, chin up and a beaming grin thrown across her face fitting of an activity coordinator giving the campers their schedule for the day. "Now – door!"

Walter grunted. "Fuck it." He reached down, slid his fingers under the foamy lining of the garage door and peeled it from up off of the ground. With a heave, he pushed it over his head, up and under the inside of the roof.

"What?" she asked with incredulity, her creased brow and wrinkled nose forming a sour expression. "Is there anything more I could have said? Walter –"

"No, just forget it." He walked into the garage and turned to face his girlfriend, who was standing timidly and clutching her coin purse in both hands. With a bow, he gestured for the kitchen door, pointing towards it with both hands.

"So that's it then?" she continued, taking on an edge of aggression. "We're just going to keep going back-and-forth about this?"

"No; let's do one better and just forget it," he said, still waving her over. "Come on – wine."

Brielle squealed. "Your name might not be Door, but I will answer to Wine!"

"Okay, okay, okay," he spoke in a rhythmic cadence. He held her by the shoulder and herded her towards the door. It creaked open with a twist of the knob and a slight push.

Walter peeked inside, analyzing the posh cooking stations as the lights flicked on. "Huh – the house is a lot more peaceful without your dad acting out scenes from the British War Room."

Brielle socked him in the arm. "He just gets excited whenever he has someone to brag to. I'll kick your ass if you keep making fun of him."

"I'm surprised he hasn't written for Broadway the way he pieces together all the little details. Seriously, he should make a –"

Brielle kneed the top of his thigh from the back.

"My ass!" he cried. "Fuckin' – AGH, goddammit, you gave me a Charlie horse!" Walter bent over and began hobbling across the kitchen, clutching his leg with both hands.

"Holy shit, are you serious? Oh my God!" She began cackling, cupping her mouth with her hands. "Are you okay?"

"No, it fucking hurts!" He collapsed into a chair, holding out his leg as though it had been broken. "Why – Why the fuck would you do that?"

"I've got to be a lady of my word! I'm sorry, hunny." She twisted her legs around one at a time. "If you want you can take the first shower; the hot water should ease up the bruises."

"Yeah… urgh – please, let's go."

She helped him to his feet and he limped after her on one good leg as she strolled into the dining room and through to the foyer.

"Just so you know, my dad's no Ernest Hemingway – he might drink like one, but he's not able to decide what to have for breakfast, let alone able to sort out some as intricate as a plot." She gripped the banister gingerly and took slow steps upwards so that she wouldn't get too far ahead of her staggering boyfriend.

Walter scoffed. "Uh, yeah, haven't you ever heard of a joke?"

"I mean, even still… I'm just saying."

Brielle's house was vacuous enough to be an airplane hangar and decorated like a fresh grave. Wall ornaments ranging from plaques to animal pelts to ornate gilded crests lined the pinstripe surface of the wallpaper. Small tables peppered either side of the halls, each with their own crystalline lamp and assorted framed family photos that rested atop colored silk banners draped over the outwardly-pointed edges, the cornered ends of which were fitted with knotted string tassels. A certain spirit presided over the premise, watching from the painted eyes of the massive portraits that hung on whatever space could fit such things and breathing through the tired creaking of the foreign-made air conditioning. As they moved over covered stairs, an ancient breeze swept up from down below and carried itself above to the ceiling, sweeping along fragrances from yesteryear and emitting a low whistling akin to what would be heard at the top of a valley.

"You ever think that your house might have ghosts?" Walter asked.

"Ghosts?" Brielle parroted like a toddler. "What's a ghost?" She had to suppress her intense giggling while she took to mocking him for his complete reversal in character and airheaded hypocrisy in comparison to his attitude that entire day all after just a single blunt.

"The leftovers of a person's wants and wishes when they can't complete them in time."

"The only people who ever lived here were a family of corporate dentists," Brielle commented, shifting into light chuckling, "so I don't think anybody died with regrets on the brain within the four walls of this house."

Polished wind chimes played a mournful melody out on the patio behind their backs as they rounded the corner that led to the second half of the staircase.

"You'd be surprised," Walter replied halfheartedly.

The light from inside of Brielle's room shined out of the crack under the door out onto the cerulean carpeting and walls of the hallway, drawing them in like a siren's call. Brielle gripped the crystal knob and pushed delicately, allowing the teak door to rotate inward ever so slightly. The two of them stepped inside to find her bed that's frame was made out of polished wood and resembled a statue, complimented by an array of furnishings.

Everything in there appeared to be haphazardly littered around, but it all was actually placed with individual care and precision. To her, that room was a personal bastion from the stubborn, unrelenting world in which she was trapped. Their backpacks rested against her bed like two bundled-up napping babies. She reached down for the hem of his shirt, beginning to pull it up.

"Whoa – hey, what are you doing?" he exclaimed, and yanked her prying hands off of him.

"Don't you want to take first shower?" she asked innocently.

"Yeah, but I can manage to undress myself. Thank you, though." He walked tensely over to the bathroom door and let himself inside.

Brielle went over to the life-like sketch of her and her sister Ashleigh that the street artist in Chinatown had done for them and tugged downwards on the frame. A light click sounded off and the framed picture swung outwards, revealing a safe guarded by a combination. She punched in 1-9-1-7 and the safe door opened to reveal a small circular light shining down on a large tin bucket filled with ice holding a half-dozen different bottles of liquor, each varying in size, color, and rarity. Two frosty chalices decorated the opposing walls. Her nails clinked against glass as her fingers settled around the necks of two wines and yanked the sweating bottles out from the ice that held them, the cubes rustling. She popped the cork on the Balidarci and poured out a half glass, then began taking sips.

"Oh – That's so *fucking* good. Walter, I don't know what I'd do if I didn't have this booze locker," she called, having to speak up over the rushing of water from out of the showerhead down onto the tile.

"What did your parents want you to use that thing for again?" he replied before slinking behind the blurry shower door.

"It's supposed to be for things that I want to save in case of a fire, but if I really value something and I don't want it destroyed in a fire, then why would I stuff it into my wall and not be using it every day?" She sat down on her bed, studying her fingertips on her right hand as well as the silhouette of her boyfriend, who was shampooing his hair. After she finished talking, she cocked her head back and finished the glass in one gulp.

"Don't you have some photos or small decorations that have some sentimental worth to you?" Walter inquired

"Do you?" Brielle fired back.

"Pfft – no."

"Then why would you expect me to?"

"Because you're filthy rich;" he tsked, "I don't know."

Brielle deposited her glass onto the nightstand behind her and pulled both of their backpacks up on the bed with her. She procured two binders and laid them out in front of her, sifting through papers. "Harrol didn't assign any problems out of the book, right?"

"No, I don't think so," Walter replied, his feet thudding around as he picked them up to scrub under them.

Brielle began solving chemistry equations, deciphering the missing elements on either side of each reaction. "Chemistry bums me out."

"At least you can do it.... Just have some more wine and make a game out of it."

Brielle paused her focus, looking around herself with blank eyes as though there were a light show going on. "Make a game out of drinking wine or doing the homework?" she asked in lethargic, measured syllables.

"...Both?"

"I can't drink any more for the time being or else I'll get complacent – how about we talk about something interesting?" She put her elbows up, stretching out the joint between her arms and her shoulders, the indentation of her bra poking through the fabric of her shirt.

"Only if you come up with the topic."

She dropped her arms, exhaling deeply. "Shower thoughts."

"Oh shit – I pass."

"Hell no; now we're definitely talking shower thoughts." She pointed a finger at Walter, merely for emphasis, as he was effectively blinded by the shower door.

"Mine are about as embarrassing as they are psychopathic. I get all obsessive over whatever person who's been bothering me lately and start imagining made-up scenarios where I'm forced to defend myself from them." Walter spoke with sluggishness and thick guilt,

"Wait, really?" asked Brielle, incredulous.

"Sadly, yes."

"Holy shit! I thought I was the only one!" she exclaimed. "What are yours like?"

Brielle twisted the end of a lock of her hair between her fingers. "Whenever I'm all worked up by someone who's been lousy to me lately, I wait 'til I'm all lathered up and relaxed before I play out an impossible situation in my mind that involves me cornering them and then I do some crazy shit like claw their face or pull out their hair. It's really twisted."

"Jesus...." Walter grimaced. "Yeah, mine are a pretty close second to that, but I don't imagine myself tracking people down and torturing them. Something just prompts me to start making up hypothetical scenes that pit me against somebody I'm on bad terms with and things get pretty brutal most of the time. One time it was me and Joe and we were in a prison yard, us two caged in by cheering inmates, having to fight with our wrists tied together using metal forks someone had stolen from the guards. I made all the right movements, but it was pretty easy 'cause I was making up the whole thing for the both of us."

"That's fucking insane – what did Joe ever do to warrant that?"

Walter sighed. "Well, do you remember that one day when you were wearing that silver pencil skirt that makes your ass absolutely pop and you had to sell a half to Joyce in front of her locker?"

"Fuck – Don't remind me," Brielle groaned. "That shit was way more stressful than it had to be."

"Well, when you were using the bathroom at lunch, Joe was saying things like 'Brielle's ass looks unreal', and 'I'm going to grab those buns like they were a stuck door handle'." Walter dropped his voice to mimic Joe's tone.

"That's pretty funny, actually. What stopped him?" She paused, waiting for a response. "Don't tell me you actually intimidated him?!"

"Hell no – he was talking all of that good shit and suddenly you emerged from the other side of the cafeteria, and he got all silent and reserved and just kept his eyes right ahead and his hands on his legs." He paused, the weight of the fresh memory impressing itself upon him. "It freaked me out real bad though – I don't know what I'd do if someone disrespected you like that."

"You wouldn't have to worry about it; I'd take care of it." She flipped her hair over her shoulder.

"Yeah, well, I was still fearing it like the devil. I'd say the most grotesque shower thought I ever had was Shawn pulling a knife on me in an alley, and I had to wrestle it from him and cut him pretty nastily to just get him away from me." Walter struggled to speak while explaining himself, obviously ashamed of what he was saying.

"Actually no, *that's* fucking insane," Brielle cackled, "How on Earth does Shawn make you feel threatened like that?"

"No, it had nothing to do with feeling threatened – it was because he made this one comment to Geoff about how he has this switchblade that could cut a finger off." He grunted, twisting his torso around and popping his spine.

"He was probably bulllshitting," Brielle asserted

"Probably." Walter cleared his throat. "Didn't stop my active imagination, though."

"What are you thinking about right now?"

"Mostly? What life's going to be like when we finally move away."

Brielle thought for a moment, suddenly becoming immersed in the pattering of water that had been coming from her bathroom since the shower cut on. "Yeah…. What do you imagine college is like?"

"It's probably… college is probably like high school except it lasts all day and nobody cares what drugs you do, or whomever you end up banging. That and I've been told there's not a single campus where you can find a fridge lacking a full stock of beer."

Crowe

"Do you think everyone is sad all the time there, too?" she asked like a student on the verge of uncovering crucial information.

"I'd be surprised if they weren't. Drinking only makes you happy if you can occupy yourself with something that interests you...." He pondered for a moment. "Same with everything, I guess."

"I just hope we find a large group to get baked with. Not a thing makes my day brighter than feeding off of each other's high and giving back to it by being thoughtful company. I want to be able to get done with a long day of classes and sit in the woods with people laughing and merrymaking, passing around bottles of Irish whiskey and crisply-rolled blunts. Nothing would satisfy me more," she spoke, mystified by her own imagination.

"Do you want to try and get fucked up with our professors?"

"HA! That would be hilarious. Now that you mention it, it sounds like great fun. I can only wonder what stories they'd have to tell."

"We should live in a cabin down by a lake like Thoreau. Imagine fucking and being able to scream as loud as you want 'cause there's no one even halfway in range of earshot." Walter was grinning from ear-to-ear, pleased by his proposed fantasy.

"You've got smut on the brain."

"It must'a rubbed off from you."

Brielle's mouth gaped open as she yawned loudly. She smacked her lips. "What was your favorite shag?"

"It had to be our first – banging it out in the back of Joey's van while everyone was in the tents sleeping," replied Walter. He reminisced as he flicked a page of *The Butterfly Club* over. "I wouldn't trade that experience away for the better part of the nation."

"OK, but would you change anything about it?"

"No – Definitely not.... Why, would you?"

"Yeah: personally, it was really strange being piped to 'Black Suit, Black Tie' by Jerry Righteous." Her nose was scrunched as though she were smelling something pungent.

"What?! You don't like Jerry?" His fingers snapped, making a beat, and he sang,

'It's a cold, cold day for a funeral,
and it's a bold, bold way to go out sooner
and; you're watching from the sidelines,
we're talking to the white bride,
they're dropping out the timeline,
and I'm popping out my sleeves:
black suit, black tie, black suit, black tie.'

Brielle scoffed. "Yeah, see, unlike you, I can't stand music from just a few years ago – let alone six. Our bus driver used to play it over the speaker almost every day for months when it came out back in fifth grade."

He snorted and then spat a fat wad of mucus onto the drain. "Well, what about 'Cash Crop' by Quarters?"

"I practically broke you to that song," cackled Brielle. "I felt a little bad for you, honestly."

Walter snapped to attention – losing all interest in the book. "You didn't wear me that thin."

"Oh, dear," her laughter echoing out of the shower, "it was concerning. You were throbbing like a sore thumb and ended up clawing my back to shreds...." She took Walter's silence as a sign of embarrassment. "But I guess it was alright; you're just lucky that I had my first orgasm to that."

"Was I lucky?" he asked jauntily. "Or just naturally talented."

"Well, you certainly haven't gotten any more skilled," she giggled.

"Hey!"

Brielle gave a hearty laugh, wholly satisfied at getting the exact reaction she desired. "Kidding; you do just fine, honey. For a boy a few months younger than me, I can appreciate that you keep up."

"Thank you." He paused and thought for a moment. "Do you think some people have less of a capacity to fuck than others? Or is is all trained skill?"

"I have no idea – ask a porn star," she replied flatly.

"Very funny."

"No, I'm serious. Either that or ask Carley."

Walter gasped. "Oh, shit! You did not just say that!"

"What?"

"You bitched Jay *out* today for making a comment about her – what was the deal with that?"

"Honestly?" Brielle picked up all of her hair in her hands behind her head and dropped it all at once to feel it fall against her neck, then shook her head to lay it out evenly again, like a duck flicking around its feathers to dry them out. "I just wanted you back and I was jealous that the two of you were being so chummy. I don't actually have any respect for her: she slept with this guy who once had me absolutely enamored, and he ended up dropping me for her like I was a dead hamster."

"Well, it all worked out for the best though, right?"

"If you're asking if I would trade you out or another boy, I couldn't get rid of you even if the fate of the world hung in the balance," Brielle told him.

"Where do you get all that from?" he asked, genuinely confused.

"All what?"

"All the you're-worth-the-planet talk," Walter answered. "What have I ever done for anybody to warrant that?"

"You resist me too much – you know that, right?" She leaned back, holding herself up on her hands that were planted behind her. Her knees were bent up into the air, one over the other, her posture being that of what she would otherwise use if she were down at a populated, chattering beach in a white bikini under a searing sun and sitting on a pinstripe towel.

"I resist just the right amount," he assured her.

"See; you're resisting me even right now," she spoke in pointed words.

"Okay, I'll stop resisting if you can just answer me."

"Lovely," she said, tilting her head back and closing her eyes for some time in momentary victory. "You know how bees pollinate flowers and from there, the whole world thrives?"

"I... I guess?" he replied in more of a question than an answer, intensely confused.

"Well, I have a theory that we're all the bees to each other's flowers."

"... Explain," Walter asked of her.

"I think if it wasn't for all the other people, life wouldn't be possible, even if you had all the keys to survival in the palm of your hand, 'cause if it wasn't for the failures and successes of the crowd around us, we wouldn't have any fuel to keep us going. That's how I see you: just because you're out there trying, you're as important as the sun is for light. You give everyone around you a reason to keep on, no matter what things look like." She talked with a certain charming cadence at a rate that made each syllable hit with its own individual emphasis.

"See," Walter started, carrying a wave of energy, "I feel that way about you, except I don't think it's some big cosmological coincidence that you keep everyone marching onwards: I think that you're such a radiant soul that anyone put in contact with you will be awestruck by your commanding presence. Seriously, you've got the grace of a swan and enough affection to fill a room. I don't think I've ever seen you smile and a person and not receive a smile back."

"Well... agree to disagree," her defiant pessimism replied.

"What do you mean?"

"I think that you see what you want to see when you look at me," Brielle asserted. "If you asked anyone else, I think you'd find that I come across as overwhelmingly ordinary."

"Don't say that!" Walter exclaimed in shock. "You're so much more captivating than you'll ever give yourself credit for."

An unnerving silence set over the room, broken only by the pouring of water onto the shower floor. Suddenly, the handle flipped and the water shut off, resulting in the slurping of water down the drain and then… quiet. Outside, an owl hooted over the sound of bugs clicking and chirping. The shower curtain whipped to the side and Walter emerged, a towel around his waist.

Brielle got up off of the bed, stretching her legs out one at a time. "I love it when your hair is all wet and tangled like that. You look like Tarzan." She walked up to him and wrapped him in her arms, planting a flurry of kisses across his chest and soaking her clothes in water.

"Whoa, hey, alright –" he peeled her off of him "– thanks but no thanks."

She pouted. "You're no fun."

Walter dodged around her and went to her closet. "Are my black jeans and red cardigan still in here?" he asked, fingering through her dress shirts.

"Check the middle drawer under my blue slippers, silly." She collected her clothes up in her hands and dropped them to the floor with a soft thud.

Walter bent over and pulled the wicker knob to find a variety of his possessions. "How was I supposed to know that?"

"Darling, all of your stuff has always been in there." She flipped on the shower and stepped in, closing the door behind her.

He fixed the collar of the cardigan around his neck and buttoned and zipped his pants. "Right – I don't know how I forgot."

"What did you have to go down to guidance for today? What even was that?" Her hair was soaked, plastered to her back and shoulders. She scraped into her scalp with her fingernails.

"Mr. Fillius could smell the cigarette smoke on me, and he snitched to the office about it. I talked to Mr. Bodwell, who just wanted to know what happened, then he gave me some advice and let me go. Overall, it was one of the easier situations that I've had to handle – I guess the guidance department care more about burying problems than solving them." Walter was skimming a copy of *The*

Butterfly Club and jotting down the occasional quote. "Bye the way, how the fuck did Harrol not send you down to the office for losing your shit on me and slamming the door? I thought you were about to get a week of detention."

Brielle giggled, "I asked the teacher for permission: we all knew you were coming back from guidance, so she agreed that you needed a little fear in your heart – just until your behavior improved." She lathered her hair with shampoo and then turned to rinse it all out under the shower's spray. "It's a shame that you weren't there for the first few minutes of Harrol's class, 'cause that shit was hilarious."

"What happened?" he asked absentmindedly, his focus poured into the book.

"So you know how Clarence rounded out his wooden block flute with a knife? Well, he still needed to carve the square mouthpiece into a regular flute-shaped one, but he couldn't remember exactly what it looked like. Peter spoke up that he *could* remember *exactly* what a proper flute head looked like, he could easily carve it into one using his own hunting knife. Clarence was so eager when he passed it off, and Peter just held it under the table and was working like a lunatic. A moment before Harrol walked back from the teachers' lounge, Peter passed Clarence's flute back to him – and its square mouthpiece had been carved into a photo-realistic penis head. Clarence was totally stunned, but as Harrol was letting Quinn to get up in front and do his weekly jig, Peter asked her if Clarence could play a song to accompany the dance. So, Clarence got up like an inmate reaching the end of death row, and when Quinn began hopping around, he *actually* put that thing to his lips and started blowing into it. He went on for about thirty seconds when Peter yelled 'He's sucking flute dick!' and the class started rolling. Harrol called it off and made everyone calm down, but Clarence's face was still red like the sun."

"Holy shit – I can't believe I missed that," Walter cackled. "Why does all of the gold have to happen when I'm not there?"

"Because confirmation bias," she yawned.

"I think I'm just casually unlucky, but we can have differing opinions on this one." He gripped the end of the pen in his teeth, pondering and shaking out his free arm. "How come Peter always calls me a bum?"

"'Cause he hates stoners," she replied. "He'd call me one, but I think he's got too much of a crush on me, so I guess he just settles for the next best thing."

"It doesn't make any sense, 'cause he could poke fun at Albert for his floppy beanie that's glued to his head, or Maurice with his chin scruff and moles, but he picks on me. I look like a little kid – how am I a bum?" Walter asked, more rhetorically than anything.

"You look like a man," Brielle said proudly. "A manly man."

"You're a goddamn riot, you know that?" he scoffed.

"Resisting me again."

"Oops. Force of habit." Walter shrugged his shoulders to himself. "I'll feel like a man on the day that I can hold my own on a wrestling mat with Joe – so never."

"Do you ever miss your wrestling days?" she asked, her interest piqued in an instant.

"Eh," he replied. "It was fun at first, but I'd much rather just be lazy now instead."

Brielle wasn't listening, caught up in freshly-uncovered memories. "Watching you at meets, seeing you flip snotty upperclassmen perverts back when we were just freshman…" she mused with enthusiasm, "those were the first times I've ever felt my pussy throb while just sitting around. It'll stay with me forever the way that the crowd cheered for you at regionals: the way you beat your chest after coming off of the mat undefeated was enough to make my ovaries explode."

Walter recalled how his ability to physically dominate was enough to make his girlfriend swoon. "Well hey, why don't we go to the weightlifting room tomorrow?" he suggested. "We need to catch up with the athletes, anyway."

"I'd like that," she answered, buzzing with a soft energy. "Just know that I'm going to hold you to that promise."

"I'll count on it."

They both stopped talking and let the fresh, chilly evening air be undisturbed by their presence. It happened on occasion that two of them agreed on moments of peace without having to communicate it. Quiet time designated a period of mental relief, giving them a minute to themselves to have their own mental space out of the long hours that came with each passing day. The rush of water was shut off, causing the sounds of the outdoors to trickle in once more.

Brielle called from the shower: "I want my J&G tights and the blue and yellow scarfsweater – think you can manage that?"

"Oh damn, I couldn't hear you – the condescension must be really thick in the air," warily replied Walter, acting as though he were on a car phone going through a tunnel and the connection was going out.

"Please?" she begged.

"Right away." He gathered the clothes from her closet and proceeded to approach the bathroom doorway, catching his girlfriend in lime-green boyshorts and a red bra with white felt hearts inset over either breast. Dropping the outfit at her feet, he dashed forward and leaned her back, passionately fitting his lips into hers.

A few seconds passed, but then she jerked away in a snap reaction and gathered her crumpled wardrobe from off the floor and stomped past him into her room. "If you were going to just throw it on the ground I could have just fucking got it myself, fucking –" She groaned angrily and quickly slipped into her tights.

"What?" Walter asked, stunned by her reaction and still holding out his hands like she had never left them. "What's wrong? What the hell? Am I not allowed to see you like that?" He turned around to face her. "Fuckin' sorry."

"I'm okay being frisky fully dressed or fully nude – I don't like getting felt up while I'm halfway. Makes me feel like a kid, and you don't want to know how uncomfortable that gets me." She slipped her scarfsweater over her head and tied the tassels around the front.

"Well I think holding you in your drawers is unbelievably arousing," he testified.

Brielle picked up the two bottles of wine and popped both of the corks with her thumbs. "Looks like it's getting to be that point in the night when I've got some serious shit to repress, so let's do our best to blackout."

Walter took the Balidarci and saluted her. "See you on the other side."

They interlaced their arms, each holding their bottle over the other's mouth, both of which were wide open. Their eyes connected and lit up in a moment of synchrony, and they began gently pouring it out down their significant other's throat, but then gradually ramping higher and higher, until the bottles were fully bottom-up. Their arms unwrapped and they stood back to look at one another. Brielle's eyes rolled back and she went limp, dropping downwards but still holding the empty bottle.

Walter caught her on the way to the floor, looking at her peaceful, slumbering expression with horror.

Her free hand reached out and caressed his cheek. She started mumbling inaudibly.

He put his ear to her mouth, beginning to hyperventilate.

"... Foot... rub," she whispered.

He held her back, the two of them staring at one another and Brielle smiling goofily, the better portion of her tongue poking out through her teeth.

"You know, just asking works fine, last I checked." He lifted her up onto the bed.

"Yeah, but that wouldn't be fun," she tittered.

"Right – 'fun'. Heart failure sounds like a great way to pass the time." Walter got down to his knees, the room swirling around him. He pressed his thumbs into the firm muscle of her foot as though he were rubbing off a thick coating of eyeshadow, occasionally gripping her ankle with one hand and pinching the thin part of it between his thumb and the knuckle of his pointer finger. He would switch off to the other foot every minute or so, working tediously to do a thorough job. He was sitting on his feet, and his eyes were glued down in the direction of the floor so that he could see exactly what he was doing. The deep breaths his girlfriend was taking served as motivation for Walter to continue pleasing her, as he knew how rare it was for her to feel satisfaction. As he labored, he considered her gratitude for him, and he found himself aghast at how undeserving he was of her affection. She would look at him like how a child watches an adult: with adoration and wonder unlike anything that anybody else could conceive of. When she would tell him about the way he makes her feel, she spoke to his virtues that he wasn't even aware existed, and just his mere presence could cause her to break out into smiles as sunny as the summer sky. He only wished that he could manage to keep up with her emotions for the rest of time, because nothing would turn his heart more vacant than her being disappointed in him.

Brielle was laid completely back, her hair splayed all around her and her legs hung over the edge of the bed at her knees. She was melting under the pressure being applied on her feet, the feeling of each press of her boyfriend's thumbs being amplified by the rush of alcohol in her blood. Ever so slowly, she slid her fingers into the waistband of her tights and took to massaging her clitoris while digging her middle finger down and in and then taking it out and pulling upwards, only to slide it back in again. She began squirming on the bed, her eyes scrunched shut and her neck contorting as her head flipped from side-to-side.

"Oh God, oh fucking – fucking – fucking – fucking –" she whimpered.

Walter began rolling his knuckles into the meat of one foot at a time, using his other hand to hold it in place. The thick skin of her foot bent inwards, contorting to the force he was exerting.

Brielle began to climax. "Oh – oh – OH!" she exclaimed.

He dropped her foot. "What was that?" he blurted out, suddenly anxious.

"What? Uh – it was just –"

"You've got a right loony fucking sense of pride – you know that, right?" echoed the yelling voice of a woman from the foyer downstairs. "You could have just taken a little criticism but instead you *lose* it in front of the crowd."

"Oh sure, play the victim and then start listing off all the ways I'm awful for ruining our night at the opera. That's rich – are you the innocent one or not?" replied a male voice, equally as loud.

"Shit!" Brielle hissed. "That's Mom and Dad! Walter, quick: out the window!"

The two of them hustled to the other side of the room.

"Shoo, shoo!" Walter said, flicking his hands in the direction of the owl sitting on the branch just outside of her window as it took off.

"Okay, so I'll ask if you can come over – just wait a few minutes outside and then climb back up."

"You sure you can do it?" he asked back, one leg out of the window.

She got next to him and sat down on the windowsill, "It'll be tough to calm them down enough to make them consider anything else other than their collective rage, but I'll try my best."

Walter climbed out, balancing himself on the branch. "Good luck." He leaned in and they kissed fiercely and loudly. Pulling his lips away with a smack, he began scaling downwards.

XVII – A

"See, what I think you're forgetting to take into account is that now, the sin tax on cigarettes has doubled!" said a lanky, long-faced man with a gray suit and hat as the bus he was sitting on roared through a turn. "And the excise tax on telephone services is even three times what it used to be – so I'm not sure how you can say that the lower classes aren't feeling the burden of the Tax Equity Act,"

"That's a very narrow scope of thinking," replied a short fellow with a tambourine necklace who was sitting on a long bench near the door. "The Economic Recovery Tax Act has been highly beneficial in how it reduced income tax rates, yes, but it's self-evidently not been enough because of all of the loopholes that it leaves open for Big Business to avoid paying taxes, almost entirely, in some cases. Without the Tax Equity Act, we can't move forward – this is about long-term thinking."

"Listen friend, they're calling it the largest tax increase in American history; if this doesn't reach the poorest of the poor in the end and force them to bear the brunt of the cost, then I'll eat my hat," the gray-clad man rebutted.

"It's just not possible the way it's set up," objected the second one. "If ERTA didn't remove tax breaks for the business sector, they'd be receiving far too much accelerated depreciation, let's say, that they'd be able to deduct throughout the year. If businesses aren't forced to pay their share, a potentially enormous budget deficit could form over time." The short man got to his feet while stretching and prepared to disembark as the bus groaned to a halt.

"Well..." said the tall fellow with guilt in his tone, "if I'm being honest, I only dislike it because it makes cigarettes more expensive – I can't afford them no more...." He looked to his side, making eye contact with the boy sitting next to his backpack and smoking out the window. He nodded slightly when their gazes met and smiled.

"Me?" Walter asked, pointing to his chest with the thumb that held his cigarette and thoroughly disbelieving the situation he had just been put into. "I can't afford them either – this isn't mine," he admitted.

"No cigarette is ever ours," said the first man with a sly grin. "Whaddya say? Willing to help me out, comrade?"

"Look, you seem like a pleasant enough fellow," started Walter, "but it's nothing personal – I wouldn't give my grandmother my spare cigarettes." He started taking fuller, faster-paced pulls to make it burn down faster.

"I presume because you don't want her to get cancer," the man replied with a chuckle, attempting to sound astute as he peered across the bus.

"No – because I'm shamelessly addicted," Walter stated, biting his lip. "Don't try to come between me and my self-medication: it's about the most futile battle you could undertake."

The man held out his hands. "Well hold on now: don't you believe in the law of attraction?"

"I don't like physics," he said with a cough.

"Ha-ha!" He slapped his leg, leaning in. "You're a funny man, friend.... No, what I mean to get at is that some people say that wanting something can be understood as just another form of working to get it."

Walter frowned. "I don't follow – this sounds like some motivational malarkey."

"No, not at all!" the man exclaimed, beginning to backpedal, his expression desperate. "It's scientifically backed! They've shown that people who focus on their desired outcome can reach them through pure persistence and strength of mind!"

"So it is self-help!" He thought for a moment. "Wait – your goal is to successfully fish for cigarettes on the downtown bus?" he asked as he tossed the finished butt out the window. "I couldn't think of a drearier objective to focus on if I had a gun to my head."

"No, no – I said 'desired outcome'! My *goal* is to get this job at the Blackrock Motel once I stop off there," the man said confidently. "But that's irrelevant – until I get my first day of commission, I've got to reach out to the public for my cigarettes."

"Commission?" Walter repeated, dumbfounded and unable to mentally piece together what he was being told just then. "You're a cleaner then? Or some kind of catering?"

"No, of course not: I'm working the front desk, but I'll have to do a quick interview with each guest and then direct them to the right room for that person specifically and I get a percent of whatever tips they leave," the tall man replied matter-of-factly.

"You need to direct the guests…?" Walter paused, bouncing around this information in his head. "Wait, let me guess: you're not actually picking out the rooms themselves for them; you're matching them with girls." He absorbed the man's suddenly-pale, low-hanging face and gaping mouth. "Yeah, I'm not surprised; my Mom used to work a motel – I mean, not *work* a motel, but work work a motel."

"It's just something to get me through the present," the man objected to him as though Walter was questioning his morals – on a bus, no less. "And it doesn't make it any easier that usually-kind strangers have suddenly turned cold and defiant to goodwill."

"So you're going to be the foot-pimp to fat gangsters sitting in some tall, pointed building downtown who are collecting on your whole awful operation – and assuming the scene gets busted, *you're* going down, but *they're* just going to go overseas until things get calm again," Walter postulated without inflection. "Well, you might not believe it, but I'm rather involved in the pimping business myself."

"Shut your mouth!" he exclaimed. "You're what, fourteen?!"

"Give or take a few years," replied Walter. "If I can give you any advice it's that you can't let any of the girls actually spend the night with the clients, no matter how much they beg and offer; don't let them do anything outdoors, again, even if you get large offers – basically anything that involves a sizeable bribe is likely going to get everyone on the property arrested that same day."

"Well! ... Why are you even working a daytime job? Shouldn't you be rolling in dough around the clock, being such the young business prodigy that you are?" the man questioned. "That is, assuming you aren't riding the bus to your pimpery right this very moment."

"I'm going to my work work currently, but I'm in school, too, because it's not worth it to spend long shifts down at motels or any place of the sort: you've got certain times of the day when lots of fights break out, and if you stick around too long and a dissatisfied customer from earlier that day shows up to recollect the fee he paid for an appointment that he was in fact dissatisfied with, assuming he recognizes you, you had better be light on your toes and have a firm swinging stance," Walter recounted.

"Could you... put in a word for me?" the man requested meekly. "I'm worried that they won't like me at the Motel because of workplace disagreements."

Walter squinted and his eyebrows pointed inwards like someone had just delivered a feeble insult using his name. "You're not even working there yet – fucking exactly how in the world could you possibly have any disagreements with the guys working there if you haven't worked with any of them yet? You're not that unbearable, just needy," he told him.

"Well, you see... I have this bad habit of falling in love," he admitted.

"Oh Jesus," Walter exclaimed as he stared out into the empty space of the bus. His expression turned grave like he had just been asked to take the stand. "Do anything else – and I'm not even saying that as a suggestion, that's me commanding you to –"

The man scoffed. "Now, c'mon, guy, just because you've got it all figured out by being a gloomy Scrooge doesn't mean you wouldn't be surprised what some living can do for a person: I bet you don't even do lines bigger than –"

"I get through by having a girlfriend. Just get a girlfriend: it's easy, pretend like you don't want anything and soon you'll be surrounded by all kinds of type-A nutcases who want you to stabilize their desperate lives so badly," Walter explained. "The one thing you've got to watch out for is getting fucked with by people who know you'll lay down when they tell you to: they'll treat you like a child because it's a riot when groups give the same person hell and everybody's in on the joke."

"Well gee, kid: you sound like prom king the way you have everybody figured out. I'm sure that the broad you're chained by the ankle to is nothing short of a supermodel," the tall man chortled facetiously, finding Walter's act to be disingenuous and starting to peer out the window absentmindedly.

"I'd say she's pretty close, but no – I don't think you've been listening to me: I get picked on for sport. I'm notorious for being a weakling that isn't going to get back at anyone for anything. I won't say that I don't have my place and that I don't earn it, but I make an effort to keep the peace," Walter replied, much more relaxed with this conversation now that the man had stopped haranguing him for free shit. He got up and put on his backpack once the bus stopped for the sixth time since he had gotten on. "Don't let anyone tell you what you can't do – but you really shouldn't panhandle for cigarettes: imagine someone you know catches you," he said while departing.

"You're walking a crumbling bridge;" the strange, gray figure called to Walter as he took his first steps away, "don't let them take you on the way down! Don't let them take you, now! Not without a fight!"

The doors jetted out air in a screeching pop and the bus's engine shrieked as the bus tore away from the corner. In an instant, Walter was stunningly alone and away from criticism – only for the next five minutes. He shook off the second comically unbearable bus ride of that day alone; it was stunning how he was actually able to *tell* that man of how everybody used him as cheap target for harassment and in that same instance, he was in that very moment being used as a cheap target for harassment by the man he was informing his problem to.

The ashy color of the pavement complemented the sky which was of a slightly lighter shade, and sandwiched between the two were the pale faces of tall, corporate suites. The downtown scene always instilled a particular sensation of densely-packed terror: Walter had come that way a handful of times when he was a child to eat out or visit the museum, but the bustling roar of an infinite number of people passing another one always gave him the impression that if you had nothing to offer, you were just in the way. He didn't want to think of life as being one long walk over six streets and down four, multiplied a hundred-thousand times over, but as far as he was capable of perceiving, the only thing that moved people was the threat of unfulfilled obligations. The traceless remnants of the lost and forgotten who never escaped that stretch of the city forever stained the pavement, constantly trampled by the up-and-coming, over-embellished generation of the future that was marching onwards every hour of every day, trudging through rain, sleet, snow, and tragedy alike.

He went three streets down, around the corner and into an alleyway formed between a drab square building that had a bulky, square sheet-metal door inset on its backside and a massive brewing plant. The door swung out with a concerted tug, his ears being assaulted by the hissing of pipes and machinery coming from within the brewery behind him.

"Walt," said a voice from the corner of the room.

His eyes snapped to the side to see his co-worker labeling outgoing mail: a man with a buzzcut of black stubble, whose smooth and lustrous light skin shone in the dull lighting like brass. The man looked up from an assortment of stamps to reveal his roof-like mustache that came together at a sharp angle, causing him to resemble Lionel Richie.

"Hey, Emmett," Walter muttered with trepidation as he observed the clock and dropped his backpack by the door. "I'm... pretty late," he commented, scratching his eyebrow and sighing to himself. "Fuck," he said under his breath.

"What do you mean?" Emmett asked, sliding a box full of packages and envelopes down the chute in the wall that was next to him, then got up and walked over. "You were back here with me helping me label." He tapped Walter's arm with the back of his fist, giving him a coy grin.

"Really? You'd do that for me?" Walter exclaimed eagerly. Noticing Emmett's suddenly serious and incredulous wide-eyed expression, he softly whispered, "You're a lifesaver."

Emmett reassumed his calm countenance and then flicked his head in the direction of the door. "Let's go see about it." As the two of them went through, he turned the other way unexpectedly. "I have to get more PS 8076 forms from the paper closet – just go clock in," he instructed him.

"Wait, Emmett –" Walter started, but he was already gone. He swallowed hard and was launched directly back into his initial feeling of fear: facing Ross and Derek alone meant he was in for a thorough scolding. He crept down the darkened hallway, past the water cooler and the noticeboard and leaned against the door at the end, holding his ear to it.

"If Pat asks Doug to cover for her one more time, just come straight to me and I'll lay her off that day," said a weaselly voice from the other side.

"Just fucking get rid of her," growled a deep voice. "She doesn't deserve to have both Monday and Thursday morning – and once she's gone, we get Walter to start closing so I can work entirely daylight hours."

"Walter…" the first voice cut in suddenly, a pause emerging from the other side of the door. "Where the fuck is Walter? – Hold on." Footsteps started thudding in his direction.

Powering through the door in an instant, Walter nearly collided with his boss. "Oh – Derek, sorry, I didn't know you were there."

"I'm always there," Derek murmured to himself, walking over to the schedule on the opposite wall. "See this, Monroe?" The lanky arm of Walter's boss pointed a bony finger at the spots on the mounted piece of paper where two red circles were with numbers inside them. "Tuesday: 20 minutes. Thursday: 5 minutes. And now" he took a marker from the table and scribbled on the calendar for that day then circled it as well "Monday: 15. Three strikes in two weeks is the rule, so I've got to be consistent and let you know that you're free to go home whenever –"

"Derek – what are you doing?" Emmett asked, coming from the hallway with a stack of papers. "Walt was just helping me match serial numbers. He's been here." He walked to the other side of the room, passing through two doorways in total and emerging in the front lobby from behind the counter and then dropping the stack into a tray.

"Why would you think that it would be okay for him to start working without clocking in first?" Derek fumed.

"I asked him to," Emmet replied with the candid innocence of a drunk man explaining his new haircut to his wife.

Derek slunk his gaunt frame up to the punch clock, lazily set it back, and punched Walter's card, placed it back, then finally reset the time to what it properly was. "Just this one time I'll play stupid and go along with this little charade: next time rolls through and you're out on your ass, no questions asked, no questions answered." He grabbed his accordion binder and stormed out of the room. "I'm in my fucking office."

"Walt: get more packing tape from the storage room," ordered Emmett as he slipped between Walter and the deep-voiced, lumbering man to make his way to the back room.

The grim-looking bear of a man drifted from his side of the break room, passing Walter, and going over to the counter. He unwrapped a package of popcorn and dropped it into the microwave, turning it on. It began whirring as Walter stepped towards the storage room, but when he did, the man stepped directly in front of him and held out his hand to the side, still watching his popcorn beginning to unfold the package so that one half of it lifted into the air and landed on its other side, flattening it out. "You don't need to go get your tape right now," the temperamental behemoth snickered, finding himself a bit funny.

"Uh, that's hilarious, Ross," Walter said, his tone strained as he tried to get around but was held back by the lone outstretched arm. "I might be late but I'm still here to work – you can at least respect that, can't you?" Suddenly, Walter's collar was being gripped for the second time that day, this time by the hand of Ross, and he was taken face-to-face with the snarling Aunt Nancy who was towering over him.

"Okay, so you're going to go down the 'respect' route. Well, I can *'respect'* that you're completely –"

"Ross," Walter whimpered, fear-stricken, "come on, don't do this."

"You're just another cog in the machine: nothing protects you because you're nothing special," Ross hissed. "You stay consistent with your fucking-ups? I'll start keeping a tally, just so that we can know how often you're stepping out of line."

"The fuck does that mean?" he exclaimed.

"It means, for once, you're limited on the number of fuck-ups you're allowed to cash out on, bucket boy. In a word: no more free passes." Ross let go of his collar and pushed off of him by his shoulder as though to get a boost, then disappeared that way around the corner into the mailroom to continue bathing in letters the way he spent every other spare second.

Walter barely had a moment to look behind him before Ross had already slinked off in his comfortable shoes, and he didn't stop to wait for him to come back. Quickly going down the stubby hallway to the side of the schedule, he opened the door and retrieved the tape by the handle of its plastic holder; glancing around the dilapidated storage room, he took note of how some shelves were broken and the rest covered in broken containers and bins filled from the bottoms to the tops with nothing but useless plastic packaging pieces. That rusty cubbyhole he was standing in was the epitome of the whole building: outdated, on the way out, and only around because nobody had any incentive to replace it with a modern space for the sake of the people who worked there. The clear explanation for the horrid state of affairs all around him was that he wasn't in a place that people move into, but rather, one where people move back to. Once the high-sailing antics of the youthful townsfolk hits the wall of reality, they settle back into their parents' old way: whatever drudge it was that they were reliable with to sustain family living. Only after the extra energy dies off does the reality set in that a person's time on this planet is only marked by the progress they made.

Was it sad? Who's to say – but when the kids all did finally settle down with the meager sums of bread that they each respectively came home with, and when they did settle into their recliners, the women felt matronly creases developing in their faces and the men touched their heads to find their hairlines had receded, and it was all too obvious that if there was supposed to be some redeemable existential tragedy of unfulfilled prospects, it went completely unregistered in the conscience of whatever Holy Keeper presided over them. They weren't the exception to the ocean of nonentities that they presided in – they'd never have anything to do with the celebrities that they had spent the better part of their golden days imagining themselves as being, and in whatever universe they were fortunate enough to realize their dreams of prominence, the celebrities they'd become couldn't possibly have anything less to do with all the people that they no longer were forced to be one of.

"Thanks again," Walter said to Emmett as he entered the back room and dropped the tape on the table that he was working on.

"No…" Emmett replied, trailing off as he rapidly taped several packages shut in mere seconds, "problem. Can you take over labelling while I print out order receipts?"

Walter went to the desk, sat down, and started checking labels to match up the serial numbers with packages he was taking from the shelves behind him, dropping them into the open container sitting to the side once he got a match.

"How many years again did you say it'll be before you get out of this deathtrap of a city?" Emmett asked with comfortable rapport that he had self-evidently rehearsed down to a science.

"Uh –" Walter began to panic as he blanked on coming up with any coherent information "it might be five years, it might be ten – hard to say," he stuttered. "But 'deathtrap'? Really? We've got neighborhoods full of tweakers and a pretty frightening issue with crime, but other than that, it's habitable."

Emmett scoffed. "Yeah, okay. Tell that to Missy Ginger," he said gravely.

"Somehow I don't think that I'm actually able to tell Missy Ginger anything," Walter replied, slightly shaken up by this change in mood.

"She had four boys and they hung out on and around the block," Emmett recounted, "and they were about three years apart each. Well, when the oldest was seventeen, one night he brought some friends over, who brought some friends over, and so on. It only took all of twelve minutes for the mob to end up stripping that house of all the belongings it held inside it. The neighbors called the police, and when they showed up, the looters trampled Missy on the way out, and she died on the way to hospital. I could go on: I've got dozens of stories of innocent folk just trying to pass the time and getting robbed, handcuffed, beaten, or some combination of the three. This city is just one tragedy following the last that wasn't even far off in the time it occurred from the one before that, and that's why I'm picking up my wife and the next paycheck I earn and getting as far away from this state as my conscience tells me to drive for."

"Jesus…" Walter grimaced. "That's awful. I'm sorry to hear that, though – you're the only person here who has more than an ounce of respect for me." He thought for a moment. "I've been having some… strange encounters as of late. Do you – what do you think is going to happen to me?" He realized how strange his question said after he had asked it. "If you have an opinion any which way," he amended.

Emmett chuckled. "Do I look like a soothsayer to you?" he asked humorously.

Walter laughed back. "I mean… I've had teachers who used to be street fighters, so I'm really not surprised by anything these days."

"Oh, you said 'surprised'?" He yanked his sleeve up his arm, revealing markings in the shape of a captivating set of eyes set just above his inner elbow – the irises glowed green, in stark contrast to his chestnut skin. "Surprised?" he asked.

Walter jumped. "Holy shit!" he exclaimed. "Is that infected?! Are you okay?" He shuddered under their pointed stare. "Why would you even get a tattoo like that?" he asked weakly.

"That's the hardest part to believe: I don't have any tattoos. I fell asleep in some woods around here in a tent when I was eighteen, and when I woke up, the tent had been torn to shreds and I had this imprint in my arm – see?" He held his arm close to Walter's face for the two of them to examine it, and sure enough, it wasn't ink on his skin, but indentations set over charred lines of flesh arranged to convincingly appear like two eyes. "It didn't even sting – I still don't have the first clue how I slept through my arm being pressed into like a brand on a cow's hindquarters, but I've still got it, to this day. And I believe it to be the integral part of my decision to leave this place for good."

"What does it mean?" Walter asked anxiously, going back to labeling to try and shift his focus away from his mounting dread.

"You might not be foolish enough to take me at face value when I say this, but they only glow green when something bad's on its way," Emmett told him while he took a load of receipts out of the printer and deposited them on the shelf beside it. "The first time it changed colors, my Mom died in the hospital that same month. The next, my house got broken into – it seems to go off a few weeks before the trouble comes. That's why I'm taking my warning and not letting any more of this unfettered evil seep into my life: there comes a point when a person has to check in with themselves and really take a close look if they're doing right by them. You'd be shocked what will reveal itself to you when you stand still and let your base instincts take hold."

"…How long's it been since it started glowing?" Walter stammered. He was already quivering in his shoes, and consciously flagellating himself for asking anything related to superstitions while in his current state as of that day.

"Twelve days," he replied, squinting one eye and baring his teeth like he was in pain. "Yeaaah… Something like that." His face went back to normal. "Yeah, but normally the delay on it is three weeks, so as long as there's no error in my check going through, I'll be out by two and a half."

"Wait, you never answered my question: what's happening to me? Do you have any idea?" Walter asked pleadingly.

"Hear me out, Walt, you seem pretty thoroughly shook up," Emmett firmly told him. "There's no masking the issue, so I'll just be honest with you – I'd want someone to do the same to me if I was in your shoes. You have to stop questioning what it is that's happening and think about what options you have available to you. If you wall yourself off and block out the whole world just to make it through the moment, you'll survive to find yourself too underdeveloped and vulnerable to stand toe-to-toe with what's really out there. Don't expect to just coast through anymore: it's about to be some of the roughest times of our lives. That's even true for me as well – doesn't matter that I'm getting away. I know I'm not dodging fate this time. We're all coming up against the test that'll decide how everything shakes out, and I know that just as well as you should." He shut off the printer and put on a front-brimmed, cotton cap. "Don't sit around and ask too many questions: you wouldn't want to get caught waiting when your time finally reaches you. You don't get a second try with these kinds of things." He went to the break room to clock out before leaving the building through the front entrance.

And like that, painfully as ever, Walt was isolated from any kind of interpersonal distraction and forced to cope by pushing himself to fulfill his purpose; to give his employers a single reason to keep him around. Being a disposable worker bee was a lousy motivating force, so he was trying his hardest to immerse himself in the names and addresses on each of the packages and parcels that he was handling, making little stories and scenarios for what might be the cause of them being shipped in the first place, imagining the characters of the people who were relying on him to get their mail delivered. Maybe the dense, plump package was some piece of valuable art that a high-end socialite was sending to their newlywed nephew, and maybe the bundle of pink, dolled-up envelopes was being sent by an adoring grandmother who only desire is to know what activities her child's children are engaging themselves in for that week, and maybe the wide, rattling box was a gilded chess set, being sent between collectors concerned solely with maintaining the most desirable layout of the show houses that they toiled long, excruciating hours to outfit in a way that immediately connotated excellence to anybody who came in contact with it. Some time went on this way, but he tried to put the amount of however much of which was passing out of his mind as best he could, because if he couldn't rely on himself to do the work that was required of him to sustain himself, he couldn't rely on himself to do anything. An hour and a half later and a few hundred pieces of mail later, Derek appeared in the back room and slung his keys on the desk, them skidding across it and in front of Walter.

"Uh, Derek?" Walter asked, taken aback. "You dropped your keys."

Derek gave what was halfway a scoff and the other half a chuckle, peering at Walter out of the corner of his eye. "The nightly comedy hour with Walter Monroe; you're closing tonight."

Walter's blood went cold as he remembered Brielle's warning. "I really don't think that's a good idea," he protested.

His boss raised an eyebrow. "There's nothing to steal: everything's locked up. All you have to do is go out the back, dump the contents of the cart into the dumpster, and lock the door then slip the keys under. If you can't manage that, then I'm sorry, but your time employed here is likely face a sudden termination," he said, then thought for a moment. "Well, you're not going to get fired tonight, regardless of what you decide, but if Ross has to close for you, then not only am I giving him the last half hour of the evening, but I'll give him the first one of your shift. You want to go without a full hour of pay? It's your call."

"Fuck..." Walter murmured under his breath, shaking his head. "I guess I don't have a choice," he replied at full volume.

"That's what I like to hear." Derek went out the back door and called back to him: "See you Wednesday."

After a half an hour of moving one box to another room and then depositing its content into its respective bins, Ross hustled past him, not looking anywhere near his direction, pushing through him by the shoulder as if he had been blocking his path in any way at all. Walter sighed, relieved to be so close to the finish line, but still incredibly tense for what was soon to come and only imagining the worst as he continued his work for the rest of the hour.

The back door creaked open as he backed into it, his hands loaded with of dozens of collapsed cardboard boxes. He dropped the load onto a short cart and tossed his backpack into the alley, but as he went to close the door back again, in the light shining from the alleyway into the back room he saw a shadowed figure, knees bent so that its feet were directly behind it and arms down by its sides, at the same height as if it had been standing as it floated in a split second straight across the doorway on the other side of the room that led into the hallway from the right side of his vision to the left. It moved with such velocity that a gust of air could be felt after it passed, sweeping all the way from across the room and pressing into him, causing him to jump with considerable theatrics. In an instant, he slammed the door shut and locked it with the keyring before slipping the ring back under the doorframe. He shook his head, breathing deep sighs at a rapid pace and pushing the cart down the alleyway. It was unbelievable how many inexplicable occurrences he had experienced just that day alone, and it was really putting him over the edge in terms of his tolerance and patience for such phenomenal terrors.

A pipe on the left wall protruding from the brewery was pouring out thick steam straight out onto the opposing wall from it on an interval of about ten seconds, so he pushed the cart up to the billowing cloud of sweltering heat and paused for a moment before it shut off again. He made a dash to the other side, so as to not get hit by it at the last moment as well as to be done as quickly as he possibly could manage in the same instance. Picking up and throwing the broken-down cardboard boxes into the dumpster, he went back up to the wall of steam, waiting once more. This time, when he passed in front of it, a pair of pale hands shot out from between the bars of the grate. Their gangly skeletal fingers interlocked behind his cranium and yanked him inwards.

Walter was narrowly able to brace himself against the stone lip of the pipe and not get his face smashed into metal fixture inside of it. The spindly hands that held him in place were dwarfed by the length of the thin arms that followed them. They were coated in fur blacker and thicker than any bear – but as the steam came back on, full force, the coat remained bone-dry despite being engulfed by a cloud of steam.

He had covered his face with his hands in time to save his eyes as he wrestled to free himself, crying for help and feeling boiled alive in the cloud of steam that was soaking his entire upper body. The arms tugged on his head with firm and measured force that seemed to toy with his physical limits rather than outright crush them. An echo from inside the wall turned into a horrible groan, sounding something like the death rattle of a lifelong smoker or a toad the size of a basketball: **"EYEURRRRRRRRRRRRRR."** Struggling back in the opposite direction away from the pipe and losing as he was being drawn in gradually closer, he came within inches of making contact with the searing hot bars, but suddenly as the steam shut off, the arms retracted in a flash, letting go of him and disappearing into the blackened depths of the pipe.

Toppling to the ground just moments before he clambered to his feet, he sntached his backpack from the ground, soaked from the waist up by the steam from the pipe. He never looked back: breaking into a sprint and exiting the alleyway, he bolted down the block and as far away from what was the continuation of a fever dream unlike anything he could've imagined, moving at a velocity that can only be achieved by being on the drug of either love or fear, and between the two, it was fair to say that he was only ever affected by just a single source of pressure and nothing more – by such a metric, he was a machine that only new one form of fuel, and it was that ignorance that blinded him.

XVIII – B

Walter slipped, losing his footing for just a second and falling back onto his rear. He groaned and stumbled to his feet, wobbling around like a schooner in a typhoon. The wine had punched him in the nose, laid him out flat and left him for dead.

A car whooshed by in a flash of light and passed within an instant, leaving him in the glow of the moonlight. Streetlights buzzed a low buzz and dogs barked and yipped from the distance.

"You just *love* watching me fumble in front of others – and I'm just *so* happy for you! It sounds like your superiority complex is functioning just fine!" he heard Brielle's father shout from inside.

Crouching, he snuck along the side of the house, weaving between large, fluffy shrubbery and the jutting brick wall. Coming up to a window, he peered through the gap in the curtains and looked into the dining room.

A woman wearing a tan, layered dress with a long, thin face and tightly pulled back hair that came back into a plump bun was holding her purse on her forearm which was held out like how a falconer would to be able to hold their bird. A man with slick, dark hair parted down the middle and a dandy mustache was wearing a vertically-striped dress shirt complimented by suspenders and forest green slacks was pacing across the room. Brielle hustled down the staircase, boasting pearl earrings the size of marbles and dressed in a button-up blouse, miniskirt, and knee socks.

Crowe

"Mother! Father! Can Walt come over?" she hastily called from the sixth step on the way down, rushing up to her parents and standing between them.

"Walter? At this hour?!" exclaimed her father. He used his forefinger and thumb to rub his chin as his eyes glanced the ceiling.

"His dad has had him chained at home, so he can only leave now. Please? He has a ride." She had her hands clutched together, fingers interlaced.

"I like Walter," her mother commented.

"Er – right; of course he can come," her father declared, standing erect with a wide smile and, like he was ordering a drink from across the bar, pointing a finger upwards to signify a magnificently orchestrated resolution on his part.

Walter crept back around to the side he came from and began pulling himself up the tree, reaching above him while his legs gripped the trunk and then letting it go so he could lift himself further into the air. His swung his hands overhead and did a pull up on the branch to find Brielle dreamily leaning on the windowsill with both elbows, her head in her hands and her eyes low, thin, and foxy because of the amount of alcohol in her system.

"Good work," he grunted, and crawled along the branch.

Brielle darted out of the way as he tumbled inside. "They're in the basement right now, so everything is going according to plan."

"The plan that came into existence just a few minutes ago."

"The best kind of plan," she remarked with mischevious energy.

"So what all are we going to do in the basement?" he asked as he dusted himself off. "The usual?"

"Yep. You good with playing maid for a bit?" she replied.

Walter chuckled. "Only if you're good with playing bartender."

"Always am," Brielle giggled back. "Just need to finish my makeup." She took a seat at her vanity desk and pointed her lamp at her face. Her eyes stared deep into their reflection in her rounded mirror, not even noticing as Walter walked up and gently placed a hand on her shoulder.

"Want me to braid your hair?" her boyfriend candidly offered, fluffing her wet blonde curls in his fingers; the sweet smell of her lilac shampoo was enough to melt his insides.

She opened a tube of primer and squeezed out a small dollop of thick tan liquid onto her finger, then applied bits of it to the corners of her cheeks, nose, and forehead. The primer spread evenly along her skin as she stroked a sponge across her face. Tossing it aside, she dipped a thin brush into a small glass container of foundation and began dusting it over her cheeks with sharp, light swipes. A moment passed, and she realized he had been waiting for an answer the entire time. "You serious?" she asked him, finally glancing over.

Walter was meekly standing around. "I'd like to," he spoke in an unassured tone. "It always reminds me of when I used to put Rachel's hair into Dutch braids."

Brielle's expression went blank, and she merely turned back to her mirror. "I would love for you to Dutch braid my hair, dearest. My ties are right here," she said sweetly as she pulled open the small drawer next to her. He grabbed two ties from it and closed the drawer as she continued blending her foundation. After setting aside her thin brush, she picked up the wide one for contouring and opened a pallete of highlighter. Picking up a thin coating of the powder onto her brush, it only took a few strokes to get the bridge of her nose to shine; then her cheekbones, and then under her eyebrows.

All the while, Walter was separating her hair into strands, focusing intently on his girlfriend's golden locks as he switched his hands around to gently weave them together. He was being visited by a memory of his sister – Rachel had been callously killed by a truck on the highway almost two years ago – but her energy was so familiar and corporeal in his mind that she could have been sitting right next to him. Her few times training him was still enough for him to easily use his thumb to interlace new locks of hair as he braided down along the side of her head. After he tied off the bottom of her braid, he prided himself on how he had managed to fit all of the hair on the right side of her head into it, how he had with his sister's hair so many years ago. He was going to ask if he did a good job, but the look of glee when she checked the mirror and saw his handiwork told him that she liked it. Moving to the left side of her head, he waded back into his memories as Rachel explained to him how to do it again.

The eyeliner pencil rested in Brielle's fingers as she slightly stretched her right eye. She then drew a line from the inside of her top eyelid straight across to the other side. After a quick trace back over part of it, she switched to her left eyelid. She pulled down the bottom eyelid of her right eye, tenuously tracing the eyeliner pencil along the outer edge of her waterline to leave just a thin coating, then let go to do the edge of her left eye. Finally setting aside all of her eye makeup, she looked in the mirror again to see that Walter had finished her second braid, and that he was standing off to the side: proud as could be. Beaming, she placed a dab of lip gloss on the tip of her finger and rubbed it onto her lips. Making a loud pop with her mouth, she turned to Walter and puckered up.

"Your makeup is fit for Debbie Harry," Walter remarked.

Brielle laughed through her nose. Giggling, she roped her boyfriend in using her arms. "Shut up and kiss me, you fool," she murmured just before the two of them began sensually smacking lips and tongue wrestling.

Their faces glued together, he pulled her from her chair and she jumped up into his arms. He held her firm and close as the two of them tightly pressed together. Their hands were grabbing and rubbing on the body of the other; frantically shifting around and just trying to feel as much skin as possible. She shifted her weight to make him stumble in the direction of her bed, and the two of them toppled onto her foamy mattress. Making sure to keep him under her, Brielle mounted Walter and held his shoulders back against the bed.

Sneaking his hands up, Walter undid the middle buttons on her blouse and slipped his fingers through the bottom of her bra. The warmth of her breast sent jolts of ecstasy through his palm as it felt along. He watched as she tilted her head back slightly and shook her two braids around like she was a floppy-eared rabbit; she then leaned forward at a crooked angle to allow her boyfriend's hand to rest comfortably inside her bra while she sucked on his neck. He shifted his head to put his mouth against her ear. "Let's have sex?" he whispered through light moans, still fondling her chest. "We probably have more than enough time."

Brielle's lips smacked off of his neck. She hummed, grabbing his hand and pulling it out of her bra. Holding him by the wrist, she used his pointer finger to pluck on her bottom lip, making the noise of a dripping faucet. "Mmmm, now?" she responded.

Walter cleared his throat and said with the utmost seriousness, "Or maybe tomorrow during drama class." As Brielle scoffed and gave a massive grin, he lost his composure and had to hold back his laughter just to say, "If we do it on stage, maybe Mr. Lincoln will even give us bonus points."

His girlfriend cackled wildly, jumping back off the bed and grabbing him by both his wrists. "Come on and get up, you freak," she said between giggles. "I bet you would want to fuck me in front of Mr. Lincoln, too." After pulling him off of the bed, she buttoned her shirt back up as he stretched.

Walter cracked his neck either way. "What do you think your dad's going to talk about this time?"

"Hopefully not his safari trips – if I hear about the pride of lions that was crossing through Tanzania during a blood moon one more time I'm going to scream," Brielle replied, adjusting her braids.

"Even with the least amount of makeup on, you really do look enchanting," Walt doted.

"Thank you, dear. Contrary to popular belief, I do try." She skipped to the door. "Let's go."

As they descended down the darkened stairway, the sound of a record being played from the basement became audible.

'And I don't want to give you misgivings
and I don't want us to hear ourselves forgiving
and it's scary to sit and watch you when you're grinning
but – if – I – don't – give you another chance
then our time left together will – be – our last.'

"God dammit," Brielle sighed, stepping down onto the polished wooden floor of the foyer, "they're listening to Lotus Bushes again. She's so boring."

"I like it when your Mom sings along though – it always entertains me."

"I swear to all that is holy, if you keep talking shit about my family I'm going to floor you."

The two of them passed the kitchen and went to the basement door, opening it and walking through.

"Do it – maybe I'll feel something for once," he commented flatly.

Brielle looked back at him and glared at him nastily, her eyes especially slit.

Starting from his seat at the booth, Jules went from sitting and nodding head to the song with his eyes closed, up to his feet when he heard the footsteps slapping against the cold marble stairs. His pupils sparkled and his thumbs were dug under his black snakeskin belt as he rolled forward on the balls of his feet in place. "Ah, Walter! So good to see you, lad."

Brielle rushed behind the bar to put on an apron. Reaching around a cloth that covered a cubbyhole in the wall, she began pulling glasses and polishing them before placing each one into an arrangement on the counter.

"Hello there, Mister Monroe," said Beverly, who walked up to him. They kissed the air next to each other's left cheek first, then the right, their arms down and extended outwards, holding hands. She stepped back to look at him. "How are your folks?" She spoke in a tone that was punctually enthusiastic as though she were recording herself for the answering machine.

Jules walked up and put his arm around her waist.

Walter bit his bottom lip. "Drunk – but what's new?"

The two of them began tittering at the comment.

Jules suddenly stopped, put the top of his fist to his mouth, shut his eyes, and cleared his throat. "No, that's not funny. My sincerest apologies for your loss; I couldn't imagine the grief you all must feel." His tone was somber and low.

"It's all pretty much numb…." He stared vacuously ahead. Suddenly he snapped to attention and walked off. "Let me start cleaning up."

Beverly clapped her hands together. "Ah! You're such a dear, Walter honey."

"It's the least I could do, really. Is the game of the evening going to be billiards, darts or Ring the Bull?" He slipped clean dishes from off of the bar through the cloth that covered up a cubbyhole in the wall.

Jules looked at his wife. "Bev?"

Beverly had her thumb to the front of her chin and squinted eyes. "Hmm…. I'm feeling particularly tact right now. Let's have ourselves a game of darts!"

"Cheery! Let's get to it!"

Brielle's parents got to one end of the room as Walter put on an apron and tucked his cardigan in, then took the dartboard from under the counter and balanced it on the nail on the wall. They each took one dart from a bone cup behind them on a brass bookshelf. Brielle was puling bottles from the ice locker built into the bar. All the while, a lilting woman's voice sang from the record player to the tune a melodramatic orchestra.

'And you've got me – running scared!
I searched for sanity and there was – nothing there!
I just wanted my shot but I should've realized – nothing's fair!
And if you think I'm acclimated to the daaarkness
just because I'm a starving aaartist
and that my heart has a certain haaardness,
but even if I make myself an easy taaarget,
know that nothing will ever be the same regaaardless."

Crowe

"You know that I once beat the Duke of Borchastaire in a game of darts?" exclaimed Jules like a child let out for recess.

Beverly rolled her eyes. "Oh Lord above; this story again."

"Cease your prattling! It's new to Walter! Isn't that all that counts? Walter...?" he asked, trailing off in the anticipation for a quick answer.

Walter hesitated. "Er – I think I've heard it before. But I'd like to hear it again!"

"A good sport, like always!" He swung out his arm in a jolly gesture.

Brielle was working hard, mixing small portions of liquor and carbonated water and the occasional dollop of fruit juice or syrup. Her hands were flying around, twisting bottles to put out just the right amount of liquid each time. Finally finished, she poured out the finished product into two mugs, sprinkled shredded ice over the top of each of the drinks and used it to line the rims. After dropping an olive in both of the mugs, she brought them over to her parents.

"Thank you, Brie," her mother hummed as she gripped the bottom of the thick, frosty glass container. She was sitting back in a chair, her legs folded daintily.

Jules was flaunting his dart in one hand like it was a microphone and swung his glass around in the other like it was a stage prop. "So I was travelling as a part of a tour group and I was in charge of planning the places where we would stop, and I ran into the host of the Borchastaire Games Hall at the bar! He told me that the Duke was stopping in for a charity event, so naturally, I convinced the tour guides to allow us an evening in the Hall. Never before had I seen such a fantastic underground room, complete with pillars and arches stretched over the ceiling. And there was the Duke, wearing a long white coat with amethysts fixed to its coattails, his fine brown hair like a horse's mane."

The Duke let me take the first turn and would you believe it – a bullseye. The tour group could hardly contain themselves, but the charity crowd? The charity crowd was rioting at this point. Anyway, we had a close few turns after that, and I barely eked out a few points over him. There was no reward for my victory – all the proceeds went to the homeless in the audience. We all got a fantastic photograph, however – it's in my album of the tour and you can see me holding the board with my single dart on it, right smack in the middle. Ha-ha! It was a fantastic way to round out the week, I'd say!"

Beverly gingerly grabbed the edge of his hand. "That's an incredible thing to be reminded of, love. Do you want to go first?"

"Er – Yes, of course!" He stepped in front of the dartboard and closed one eye while he balanced himself, bending his knees slightly and bobbing up and down. As he aimed the dart, his elbow was bent, extending back and forth as he made the motions of throwing for practice. He took a sharp breath in and shot the dart out towards the board, where it landed firmly in the outer ring, just missing the number '2'. "Ah! Bollocks!" He took a deep swig from his glass, then looked at it accusatorily. "This thing put me off-kilter." He settled into a chair, huffing.

Beverly stepped up and swung her arm out, sending it into the air and just barely next to the bullseye.

"Sloppy form," Jules remarked.

Brielle was pouring brandy over sweetened seltzer water into crystal goblets, then ground up slices of limes and dropped some bits of pulp in. She brought the delicate cups to her parents and set them next to the mugs, then went back over to the bar to face Walter and sat on a stool, dropping her elbows on the counter. "That foot rub was really good for me," she said under her breath, leaning in with glowing eyes and childishly revealing all her teeth across an immeasurable smile.

"Anytime," Walter replied at the same volume. He was polishing cups with a rag soaked in special cleaning fluid that put a shine onto it. "You drunk?"

"Time is moving at half speed, so I'd have to say yep, yeah."

Walter chuckled, observing the sparkle coming from inside of the glass that he was holding at an angle. "I've got a skewed sense of setting, so it feels like I'm in the middle of a bar right square in downtown Manhattan. It's exciting."

Brielle giggled. "You always say the funniest stuff when you're drunk or high… especially both. You hungry?"

"Yeah, a little bit."

"Mother? Father?" she called. "Should I prepare something to eat?"

"Do we still have rice and tuna in the freezer?" asked Jules, taking his third turn and landing another dart on the right side, just on the verge of hitting a 13 but instead getting a 6.

"Oh, and Chamomile?" his wife chimed in, swinging around her leg that was over her other knee.

"Let me check," Brielle replied, and hustled to the far side of the room past the pool table and slid open the door on the top of a steel container. "We're in luck." She filled a pot halfway with water from the tap, placed it on the burner, put a coating of olive oil onto a pan, then flipped on the gas-powered stove and began boiling the rice as well as filling a teapot with water and putting it in the back. She cut a slice of butter from the stick that was in a silver container surrounded by ice and dropped it in the middle of the olive oil. She sprinkled salt and cow-horn pepper on the steaks she had just pulled out and smacked them onto the pan, beginning to fry them with a sharp sizzle.

"So Walt, have you done any painting recently?" Beverly inquired thoughtfully.

"Oh – uh, I've been pretty busy lately." Walter replied, nearly forgetting that he had any interests at all. "But I'm having a pretty bad artistic cramp right now, and it's hard to translate having a vision into something concrete, you know?" He was pausing intermittently as he considered what he wanted to say next.

"Keep in your mind that theme is the most important element: without perspective or contrast, even the finest work can look drab. That's not to say that a little flatness is a bad thing – it just comes down to the consistency in your art. Any scene can work with the proper angle. Get perfectly in-tune with how its structured, and the small details will fall into place as you develop a color scheme. From there, build steadily and patiently outwards," she explained.

"Thanks," he said, awestruck.

"Of course, dearie." She landed a dart in the ring just over top of the bullseye.

"No, I really mean it – thanks so much. I've been trying to get back into it but I've been struggling harder than ever before. It's like I can't even hold onto small, single ideas that I'm planning on using later: I come up with them and then it's out of my brain just a day later." His eyes began trailing off as soon as he got to the end of his sentence.

"Brielle tells me you all have started reading *The Butterfly Club* in your English class?" Jules asked the moment before a sip of his sweetened Brandy reached his lips.

"Yeah, just a week ago we did. It's pretty interesting but I'm freaked out at how often Dennis threatens the mayor and steals from the Local Fellows." Walter was wiping and polishing silverware that had jeweled handles.

"Oh, he'll gets his comeuppance, just you wait," he chortled.

"Well hey, don't spoil it now," protested Walter.

"I still remember the day that Darcy Smythe published it," Jules loftily recalled. "I got an invoice from him asking me to come down from Olemiss and help direct the local camera crew that was recording the press conference he was holding at Butcher's library. There was a crowd as thick as jungle brush, and the temperature was crisp and even-keeled with pearly white clouds peppering the sky. A few people had already asked a few innocuous questions when a boy with thick glasses and hair parted down the middle got on top of a crate in the middle of the crowd and cried out: 'Was Joseph's induction into the titular Butterfly Club an allegory for Chiron willingly rescinding his own immortality to allow him to finally die?' See, the reason he believed Joseph had relation to the Greek mythological centaur was because of the climactic scene in the novel in which he –"

"Jules!" exclaimed Walter. "Please, have mercy!"

"Huh?" Jules looked around him like he had just lost his mother in the supermarket, perplexed. "Oh! Right." He downed his mug and took aim for the dartboard, hitting the wall beside it. "Hell and mortar! Well, it would appear you have me beat, dearest." He picked up Beverly's hand and kissed the back of it.

The teapot began whistling harshly, and Brielle walked over with a platter of tuna steaks and two bowls of rice. "Dinner is served!" she announced triumphantly as she set the table for her parents. She put out two glasses filled with ice and poured scotch over them, then put out two more with teabags in both and filled them with boiling water.

"You're an angel, Brie," crooned her mother.

"I'm hungry like an ascetic and ornery like a cracked beehive!" Jules announced. "You know just how to appease the beast in me, love." He then tuckered into the plump section of meat on his plate, occasionally shoveling in a spoonful of rice.

"She definitely has a talent for taming wild animals – I'm still surprised that she's able to keep me leashed," Walter stated plainly, studying his reflection in a goblet.

The room fell into peals of laughter. Brielle moseyed over and placed a plate of tuna steak on the bar for him to eat. Walter grabbed a set of silverware for the two of them and they sat next to each other on stools, ravenously consuming the meal.

"This is incredible," Walter said through a mouth full of flesh, pointing to the food with his fork.

"That's an understatement!" replied Beverly. Her fork and knife were clattering against the plate as she struggled to keep up with how quickly she was eating.

Walter cleaned off his plate and dropped it into the sink, then began wiping down the bar with a rag as he listened to the record player: a lethargic violin played as an elderly singer bellowed out a melody in a croaking Southern accent.
'I'm aaall by my lo-nesome,
and it's an e-ternityyy making it through the mo-ment,

and my paaath is littered with bad o-mens;
I only hooope someday soon I reach a-tonement,'

Jules pushed his plate across the table away from him. "Walter – come on now, chap and give me a hand with getting the next round kicked off," he said with a swing of his pointer finger.

"Of course, Jules; my apologies." Walter leaned across the counter just far enough to be able to whisper into Brielle's ear. "I give your mom fifteen seconds before she asks for another drink," he murmured with a smirk. He then walked up to the board and pulled all the darts out, as well as the one in the wall.

"Brielle, darling, could you please top off my scotch?" Beverly asked, lightly tapping her fingers on the table to the tune on the record player.

"You don't even have to ask, mother," Brielle replied in a way that was cordial and genuine as though she had just woken up and was being asked what she wanted for breakfast.

Beverly and Jules took turn after turn, landing low scores primarily in the outer ring. Jules finished his scotch and stepped up lackadaisically, just wanting to get the round out of the way so he could start working on his tea, when suddenly he landed a bullseye. "My word!" he cried. "You all – did you see that?!"

"Yes, sweet; we'd be hard pressed to have missed it," Beverly said, snickering slightly at her husband's over-enthusiasm.

"It's been a long time coming that I've gotten one of those! I was convinced I was on quite the streak of black luck, but it appears I was mistaken. Huh.... Oh! It's your turn, my love," he said, quickly turning around and bowing.

A slight grin stayed etched into Beverly's face as she sipped down the last of her tea and went to take her husband's place.

Jules finished his as well and went over to one of the booths, lying down on a cushioned bench. "Whoof – I'm stuffed. Give me a second to get up." He propped himself up against the wall on a pillow and closed his eyes, his face gradually reaching a state of rest.

Beverly took her turn and went back to her seat. "Jules? Jule," she called, pathetically waving her hand up and down at him. "Oh, forget it." She yawned and went limp in her chair, tilting her head back. Soon enough her eyes drooped closed, and her and her husband were intensely snoring.

"...Oh," Walter said. "Alright, I guess. Well we're on our own now, it would seem." He wiped his knuckles with the rag and replaced it, taking off the apron and putting it up, then pulled his shirt out from his pants.

"We can't leave them like this – they'll be beyond furious when they wake up. It'll be worse than when they got home," said Brielle, watching their napping faces.

"Who first – Jules or Beverly?"

"Mom."

"I've got her shoulders – you get her knees."

They picked up Brielle's parents one at a time, bringing them upstairs and laying them on top of their bed over their covers, being sure to turn them on their shoulders facing outwards away from each other in case they got sick in their sleep. When they finished, they stopped and took a second to breathe, admiring their handiwork.

"So..." Brielle said, panting slightly, "still wanna fuck?"

Walter's arms were towards the ceiling and he was standing on the tips of his toes to stretch out his calves while lightly grunting. His heels touched back down onto the floor as he hummed through pursed lips. "Well... I did want to, but I get the feeling that my mom and dad expect me to be home. Sometime soon, though; I promise." He observed his girlfriend's parents as they slept in their opulently-decorated bedroom like two toddlers on full stomachs, and it filled him with the urge to nail Brielle someplace risky and raunchy – just probably not in front of his future in-laws. "Someplace fun," he added.

Her doe-eyes stared him down as she kindly inquired, "Well we can at least joyride for a bit though, right?"

"Just because you asked," Walter replied seductively in his deepest tone.

Brielle giggled. "I'll go grab the keys and the box of joints."

Walter hustled down the staircase and went to the garage. The record player in the basement was still going, playing an ethereal pop tune from down below.

'Your love – was a crime of passion!
I couldn't – help but stare at the glaring distraction.
My heart – now I have to ration,
because now – in my life there is an awful, awful chasm.'

The singing echoed through the halls and reverberated off of the hollowness of the atmosphere that filled it. The house was eerily alive with energy, propped up like a corpse attached to a cross. He couldn't help but to feel like there was always eyes over his shoulders, checking to follow his movements step-by-step. Low breathing rattled behind him, a remnant of the past that refused to wilt. His spine was subject to insidious shivering, his very being at the mercy of the collective presence lurking all around him. The low rumble of an airplane overhead reminded him of the groaning of rocks grinding around deep inside caverns, haunted by the forgotten residue of a time long passed. The air around him settled into an unnatural stillness, complete silence falling all around him. A hand reached out and gripped him by the shoulder, yanking him around. "Jesus fuck!" he yelled.

Brielle slapped him firmly across the cheek. "Hey dumbass: Mom and Dad are asleep. You forget already?" she hissed.

Walter was breathing heavy, obviously unnerved and looking around timidly like a squirrel.

"Uh... are you... okay?" she asked when he didn't respond.

"Let's go," he sputtered. "Please – I want to go."

"Yeah, okay... we're going." She walked to the garage, Walter following in her shadow.

The garage door creaked open, the light coming from the street illuminating the inside of the room, revealing a cherry red Lancia Rally 037. Brielle popped open her door, as did Walter. The two of them settled into the car and she started the engine. She passed him a small wooden box with colorful roses carved into its surface. The tires pressed into the tiny stones that made up the driveway, creating a crackling sound. The car whipped around and began flying down the street.

"Matches," she said sweetly.

"Er – right," he replied, taking off his shoe and removing the sole. "I think I really need this," he said, short of breath.

"Really?" she asked, interested like a farmer discussing the end of a civil war.

"I'm just really – really freaked out, and I can't make any sense of it." He removed a match and lit it, taking a deep inhale. "Like, fuckin'… ah, goddamn; I could just melt," he said, rubbing his shoulders against the leather seat with his eyes closed.

Brielle looked over, laughing at the sight of her placid boyfriend who was completely still between puffs like a monk pausing to have his bread and water. "Hey come on; pass it, you hog." She began pinching his arm.

"Yeah, alright, alright," he protested. As Brielle plucked it from him and began hitting it, he cracked open his eyes to observe the street around them.

The world was whizzing by, blues and yellows and reds of lights flashing in synchrony all around them. The windows were open slightly to let the smoke out, causing the blustering wind leaking into the car to blow over the upbeat big band that was playing over the radio.

'Don't you want to go back to the first time we – had – our – own?
Don't you want to shine again like you were – a – cut – stone?
Hearing you whine is just something
that I can – not – con-done.
But you've got me confined and it's a lie
that you're leaving – me – all – a-lone.'

The air was sweet with dreams, floating around like wisps in the night, invisible but giving the darkness a certain charm that couldn't be equated with words. There was a primitive crudeness to the atmosphere, drawing upon the ancient civilizations that once roamed the earth that they were now driving over. All things were happening in unison, the overlapping of the never-ending past atop the promises of the future, wrapped up and stored away for a later date. As they passed people in the hundreds resting inside of their houses by the minute, a variety of scenery whooshed by, stone walls and small ponds and tall, reaching trees were all intermixed around them, leaving a trail of visual memories in their wake. Eventually, they made their way to the countryside, where they went through the forest on a firm dirt road.

"I always feel like something's going to jump out of the brush at night," Walter said, watching the moon through the tree line and hitting the joint.

"Really? I find the woods to be extremely calming," she replied as he passed off the remaining half of the joint over to her.

He was studying the fireflies that were lighting up the thick bushes that lined the ditches on either side. "The tall grass reminds me of the stuff we had to hide out in when Joe pissed off security at the Stetter festival."

Brielle snickered. "You mean where Joe got his boots stepped on and he just started shoving people around like nobody was going to notice? You were absolutely mortified, Walter," she said, looking over occasionally and smiling wide.

"I was about ready to curl up and die when Joe had shoved the third or fourth person and someone started yelling, making the guard from two stands over start pushing his way over, causing more chaos. It was like sitting in the middle of the street watching a continual wreck going on all around me." Walter took more pulls from the joint, his thoughts spacing out and becoming more delicate and streamlined like cotton being woven.

The music was piercing the space around the car, expanding outwards and reaching the far corners of the streets. Nobody else but that pair of lovers heard it, however; every last one of the street's occupants were deep in peaceful rest. They were lone riders on the River Styx, a serene body of souls collected all around them, each of them cursed in their own right but all carrying on through the vast nothingness that was the past, present, and future. Doom filled the air, but they could only feel the sharp rush of life that coursed through the brightly-lit car and that bounced back and forth between one another as they talked in proud, raucous tones.

Brielle was cracking up. "No, the best part was when the guard got up real close to Joe: they were eye-to-eye, brow-to-brow, and he snarls 'I reckon you ought to just make your way to the parking lot, boy', and immediately: POW! Joe plants his forehead right into the guard's nose, and then... havoc."

The two of them were cackling at this point, slapping one another and bouncing around in their seats, rocking around as they struggled to breathe. Their mouths were gaping open in wicked smiles akin to what a madman would wear upon learning he would only have to wait until the next day for apocalypse.

"It's a good thing that he had those six beers before he did that, 'cause he was out like –" He whistled upwards like a slide whistle and snapped his fingers. "It still blows my mind that we actually herded him through that mass of people. There must have been how many out there just around us – two hundred?"

Brielle finished the joint, tossing the browned roach out the open window and pulling a new one, swiftly aided by Walter in sparking it. She was commanding the smoke around her like a dancer playing with fire, being at once a conduit of its energy but also a recipient of its tender touch, caressing it within her lungs how a mother bear would sleep with her cubs. "Aw fuck, baby: I don't know – I just know that everyone erupted like a beluga whale hitting the surface, and as fast as we could scatter, we were cutting from one end of the festival all the way over to the thicket of reeds by the horse pen. How much time do you think it took to make him come to? Fifteen minutes? Twenty? I just remember him moaning in this really low voice and that welt on his head looking like some nasty-ass beef curtains."

Walter took it from her and drew in deep inhales off of the fresh joint, feeling sharp and crisp like a wild, blustering breeze filling the sails of a clipper ship, riding without worry for the outcome of the world around it. "Yeah, I don't know – that bruise did look awfully like some fat pussy lips. Poor Joe. He probably didn't think that he was going to get the whole event shut down for the weekend while they sorted out the security situation. I don't think anyone got fired, but fuck me, if that wasn't the loudest group of shrieking individuals I've ever encountered."

They watched as the forest melted behind them, becoming a quaint country road with a t-shaped wooden fence to their left side and the occasional cottage to their right. A pinkish-purple shade colored the scenery, the vibrant hues of the day being boiled down into the somber display that was the frigid evening. It was as though time had sped up irrevocably, and they were at the doorstep to oblivion, finally forced to face the inevitable demise of their time that was now expended. The woods suddenly had disappeared, gone like the flesh off of an arm that was absorbed by gangrene. Instead, they were replaced with the smug countenance of the seemingly modest suburbs that made up the neighborhood in which Walter's existence was rooted. Their breaths slowed, and the music faded out into silent static, irrelevant to their collective focus. Come to think of it, there was nothing that seemed relevant in the moment; just that they once had all day to spend in each other's infatuating gaze but now they were set to deal with their own respective curse for the better part of the next dozen hours. It was all a cruel exercise in what could be endured and what wasn't worth surviving through, and they both knew that they would brace themselves for hellfire if that was what it took to save the other, but there was nothing they could do to save themselves the agony of parting ways in the dearest, most carnal moments of their lives. The few times they had actually slept together were also some of the most glorious of times: there was the instance in which they had the penthouse of Richard Rallous all to themselves as the whole host of adults were spending all night in a club that was supposedly coming apart at the seams with activity, or the evening when they were at McAller's barn and they were allowed to sleep in the dog room together, covered in puppies on a basket stuffed with hay in the corner – and of course, every full moon down at Lake Cobey, as well. Despite the phenomenal memories, it all seemed trivial – irrelevant, even – in the present. It felt as though it was some kind of twisted test, like the invention of a despicable aristocrat who had nothing else to do with his wealth than to push people to their mental limits. But there was nothing evil, or malevolent in the slightest about what they were forced to endure: it was all perfectly ordinary. And the brutal reality of the situation was that nobody would ever know of how they suffered on their own; that nobody would wake up the next morning sorry that the two of them had lost their privilege to the only thing that held their waking interests. It was like a Shakespearean-style screenplay written by a janitor: laughed at by crowds and jeering colleagues; completely worthless to the eyes and ears of anyone with a voice and an opinion, but representative of the infinite qualms that plagued the lone brains of the most isolated and deranged regardless. There was no essay that could encompass their desperation; their dripping anticipation for a change in their lives that might let them have the comfort of one another for the hours that brought them to their knees. It was having to go without water, caged at the foot of a river.

Brielle pulled up in front of his house and shut off the radio, giving their ears relief at last. "Well…" she started, having no intention to finish her sentence.

"Do you…" Walter muttered. He swallowed hard and cleared his throat like he had just drank a bug. "Do you want to say it first, or should I?"

Brielle reached out, cupping his cheek in her hand. Her lips were poised and ready to speak, full like a flower in bloom. Everything about her face seemed assembled by some concerted force, trying to forge serenity and order in a land plagued by hell and despair. To call her a mere oasis would be like receiving relief after a hurricane and just softly sighing, "Aw gee, what a pleasant surprise" – there was no overstating the personal sanctity she provided for him

She stared at him with deep eyes that couldn't help but be fascinated at the sight before them. "How about neither of us say it – wouldn't that be nice?" Her voice cracked slightly, and she held in her tears like the gut of an elderly mistress of ceremonies strutting across the stage, aged far beyond her capability of such a role.

"You know that if we don't say anything that we'll both regret it 'til Powell comes back for the both of us again? You're aware of that, right?" he asked like a surgeon trying to coax a child away from the room in which his parents were being operated on.

Brielle lurched forward and gave him a profound kiss, pulling on his lips like they were a bow on a Christmas gift. She peeled them off of his face in an audible smack and observed him as though he were an art exhibit, her hand caressing the back of his neck. "Come on, Walt; we're not kids anymore – eventually we've just got to say die, you know?" she asked weakly.

Walter mouthed the words to her, cut of voice and unwilling to shatter the veil of peace that surrounded them. Mournful, he swung open the door and pulled himself from the car, took his backpack with him, and made the long walk away from all of his hopes and passion.

XIX – A

At some point on the way home, Walter had taken off his soaking-wet work shirt and swapped it for the one he had in his backpack; but he didn't remember what landmarks were around him in the moment that he did. The blocks of quaint, handsome houses blurred past him in his mad dash through the dense suburbs that filled the space between the downtown cityscape and the wide-open countryside. He dried off as he had passed neighborhood after neighborhood at breakneck speed, before finally taking a sharp turn that took him down the winding road that meant home. After finishing his journey to the heart of the lowly trailer park, made his way up the steps to his house. He was sapped of all awareness as he pulled out the screen door and pushed in the front door. The weak stove light was on in front of him in the kitchen as he entered his house – but when he locked the door behind him, the entire space was in complete darkness. His eyes flashed to the left, where the TV was faintly glowing in the living room, allowing him to see the outline of his mother laid out on the couch.

"Walt!" his mother exclaimed. "Come here, come here! You have to see this!" She waved him over like she was telling one of her friends to come meet somebody.

"Really?" Walter sighed under his breath, not in the mood for further antics. He went to the side of the couch, dropped his backpack, and stood up against the wall, leaning on it and viewing the television from a distance.

"So we've got Josie dead in the stables, the Marin twins are missing, and the guests are starting to leave their seats because the shit going on down around the track is more interesting than the race itself – am I getting everything?" said a pale man who had long black hair and a full beard that stretched all over his face and was in a bloodstained tuxedo counting with one hand while he dabbed his forehead using a yellow-stained rag with the other. He was sitting on a bench in a locker room with one other person, two lockers open that had an assortment of rifles, pistols, and submachine guns lining the walls of both of them.

"The records are missing from Mallbory's office – if we don't get those back, they'll release all the scheduled race fixing we set up," said a shorter Filipino man with neat hair and a tuxedo as well, his shirt being torn up and covered in fur. He was pacing furiously.

"They've been in the office?!" the first man exclaimed as he sprang to his feet. *"That's the doomsday situation: if they get the office then they'll have Mallbory not long after, if they don't already."*

"I found Mallbory dead a half hour ago – headshot," said the second man with a heavy sigh. He was holding his chin in his forefinger and his thumb as he walked.

"Jesus H. –" the first man started, then twisted side-to-side like he was being shot from different angles, throwing around his hands and stepping in either direction as if he was dancing. *"Okay, so the doomsday honeymoon has officially expired – we're dead and have gone directly to hell."* He kicked his open locker door. *"Fuck! – No, wait, this is alright."* He held out his finger straight up and stood still. *"We just give everybody a refund as they go out the back exit and cancel the races indefinitely. It'll give us time to recoup our… losses in management."*

The second man stopped in place, turned to face him, and held up the back of his hand like he was about to slap him. *"A refund? Danny, we're down a half-dozen crewmembers – what are we going to do without that money?!"* he yelled.

"Mallbory was in the process of secretly selling the racetrack and the rights for using this space to gamble – if we can survive this ordeal, we'll be out with a fair sum," the first man said impishly, completely placid as opposed to moments ago.

"What about the Morton Gang? Somehow I don't feel like they're about to just give up today's pot. If all that money we'd be refunding doesn't go directly to them, we'll be buried faster than we can get away," the second man replied tensely, very apparently thinking through situations in his head.

The first man loosened his collar, swallowing. *"If we offer to give them a stake in every race to be held here from now on, they'll be able to get back the revenue they need. It'll just take some… gentle – gentle negotiating."*

"Is this all it is?" Walter asked, overwhelmingly bored and ready to go to sleep at this point in the day.

"Well, hang on!" his mother insisted. "It's ramping up – you've got to give it time." She giggled. "It's so exciting; I guess you just don't appreciate how engaging this is, which is your decision."

Walter suddenly realized he had an out for this situation for about the third time that day. "I'm having a cigarette," he said as he went back to the door and let himself out.

"Where did you –"

"Friend," he cut her off as he closed the door. Going back to the curb that just twelve hours ago he was occupying, he began doing the exact same motions of retrieving a match from the matchbook under his shoe sole. After replacing his shoe and pulling his cigarette from a thin metal case in his wallet, then replaced that within his wallet and replaced his wallet within his pocket. Sighing with his hands at his sides and holding the match between his left index and middle fingers and the cigarette between his right, he stared ahead into the dimly lit horizon of houses that resembled shoeboxes, subconsciously processing the random assortments of ornaments that were scattered around each of the lawns – or sections of grass beside the houses, rather. Some houses were extensive in the decorations it had, others were more conservative, but everybody with signs and words being presented chose to press some philosophical viewpoint and were intentionally attempting to evoke some kind of emotional or inspirational response, if for no other reason than to cheer people up as they passed by. Not wanting to be wrapped up in his surroundings so unbearably, he stuck the butt of the cigarette in between his teeth and struck the head of the match on the pavement and scorched its tip. A single puff made him feel more reserved and upright, as though he had just hit emotional puberty. He rocked back slightly, holding his knees so he could lean halfway over while pulling from the cigarette out of one corner of his mouth and exhaling from the other, his eyes closed.

"Walt!" called an approaching voice. A sudden squealing sound caught his ears, grating them and forcing his eyes open. The bike he had heard stopping parked right in front of him, and a boy with a circular head, one large swish of hair put to the side, a collared solid-red jacket, and nice brown leather boots dropped off of it and let it clatter to the pavement.

"Oh – Matthew it's just you," Walter blurted out, sitting up reactively and holding his cigarette in his hand, ashing it while chuckling. He scoffed, "Scared the shit out of me, Thew – damn. You fuckin' race around like that everyplace you go?"

"Only the places that don't have more than two cops," Matthew gasped for air, hands on his knees as he caught his breath. Swallowing deeply, he stood straight up and regained his voice. "I was trying to catch you on your way home from work – how'd you get here so fast?" he asked, awestruck. "Are you trying to make cross country as a senior?"

Walter was ashing his cigarette on the pavement and blew out a gust of smoke. "Something spooked me on the way out of work. When I get scared, I more or less stop thinking." He placed the cigarette back between his lips.

"Well, I'm glad you came back out to have a smoke – I thought I wasn't going to be able to find you," Matthew said, clearing his throat.

"I'm glad you found me too, Thew," Walter mumbled around the cigarette that was still dangling loosely from his top lip. "Keep me company."

"Yeah, OK," he muttered back. He was scanning the area around them to check for witnesses. After finding the coast was entirely clear, he said in a nasty and pointed tone, "Just for your information, everybody knows Fiona is the next one on your hit list. You all do your cycles and you just repeat the same order every time through, so... just know that she's not taking any of your shit."

Walter eyes scrunched with suspicion at this sudden accusation. His mouth held his cigarette as he let the noisy crackle of the burning tip be the only sound in the air. Picking it from his lips, he held it out in front of him and spoke as the last of the smoke poured out his nose: "Let's just step back once or twice here, Matthew," he said with his words being directed by points of his cigarette, "and not forget that the only reason you bring up Fiona Canaby is because she took your virginity and you thought you took hers, but then you figured out the ugly truth that you're as prone to getting hoodwinked by other people as a redneck lotto winner. Don't feel bad because you're gullible – we all are when life's shit, and let's be honest: you're not exactly rolling in it right now, man. Common knowledge."

Matthew bit his bottom lip, barely able to hold himself back. "You want to fuck with someone I used to care about and start taking things that you have no right to?" he spat, stepping forward slightly every now and again. "Then all I can say is that anybody is justified in doing anything to you, because your side is so far beyond the pale by being punctually sadistic in a way that's so strict you all might as well qualify as being mobsters, if your side just wasn't so goddamn unprofessional."

"'Mobster', as a word, is really loose in terms of definition," Walter remarked, grinning and taking a light puff.

"You're such a total asswipe – I'm surprised I caught you smoking and not sucking yourself off," Matthew said, tilting his head back some so that he was staring down at him from a sharp angle.

"Anyway, I didn't come all the way out to this tin can ghetto for no reason. Get up," he commanded, and kicked at Walter's shoes.

Walter got to his feet, turned around, and held out his hands to either side, his cigarette in his right hand. He was laughing and shaking his head as Matthew patted him down, checking his shoes, pockets, belt, shirt, and shoulders.

Matthew removed his wallet, and began to flip through its contents, checking pictures and receipts for hidden cash or cards. He then opened it to have searched the entire thing without finding any bills at all. "You've got fucked up pictures in there – and Alina has great tits: nice beady brown nipples," he said as he passed the wallet off to Walter, who had turned around to face him.

"Thanks – I pride her on them, but she thinks they're too small," Walter remarked, returning it to his back pocket.

"If I haven't heard that line being used by at least a hundred different girls, then I'll just say that it feels like I've heard it from at least two hundred," Matthew responded, the two of them chuckling. He gestured to himself suddenly and dropped his expression. "Now, pass?"

"Can you ask in any way that doesn't make you sound like an ape or an infant?" Walter recited.

He tsked and rolled his eyes. "You're being a fuckwit – quit being a fuckwit." He grabbed the cigarette from him and went right into a deep, lengthy drag. "So," he mumbled around it, "have any comments on the Charlemagne situation you all are getting yourselves involved in?"

Walter looked around absentmindedly, his only focus just being not looking at him. "You say that as if being around his people is like catching a virus," he scoffed, taking out some gum from his pocket suddenly, popping it in his mouth, and chewing ravenously. "You think that we don't all know what we're doing?" he asked, smacking his teeth on the gum as he tore into it.

"I" Matthew exhaled a large cloud "think you're ridiculous to serve under the equally-corrupt minds of Lando and Charlemagne." He was ranting now, and moving inches closer to Walter with each statement he made. " Both your clan and his are all lambs to the slaughter: every one of you. If for even a moment you're actually able to see the chaos coming and it strikes you as a quick profit and nothing more, then you're just as irredeemable as the rest of them. You intentionally make getting started on life – as in getting out of *school* – impossible for the same people who need the money and possessions that you *steal* to even cover the cost of survival. Doesn't matter if someone can't make ends meet because you all need their acid from them and are too psychotic to even consider paying for it, because, what is it again? 'Nobody falls outside of our gaze'?" Matthew was inches away from Walter.

Walter's mouth had been gaping open the entire time as he chewed in circles with the speed of a washing machine. At last, he stared into the eyes of the smug boy in front of him. "Sounds almost like you want an apology, or something," he said between making the grunting noises of chewing, "friend."

Matthew scoffed. "Not exactly; it's pretty obvious that you're convinced you can just coast by with the rest of your people," he said with a sly intonation, "without expecting some kind of retaliation, so consider me whooping your ass as being the surprise of the cen– oh – fuck you! What the fuck?!" he screamed out when Walter's gum shot from his mouth, landed on the toe of his right boot, at which point Walter's left foot stepped down onto it, just pressing the sole of his shoe into Matthew's boot at first but then putting all of his weight into his foot in an instant, crushing Matthew's toes. "I'll fucking kill you!" he cried through his high-pitched whining. He managed to grab Walter by the arms and then shoved him back, but not before Walter had plucked the cigarette from his mouth.

Walter staggered back, the gum snapping at the point where it had been connected, leaving behind a wide, circular light blue stamp of sweet, rubbery tack. He took a split-second drag from the burnt-down cigarette as Matthew had looked at his boots to observe the damage, and then Walter pulled back his hand and made a calculated toss at Matthew's face, hitting his eyebrow and making embers fly off in all directions, causing him to begin screaming wildly.

"You're fucking dead – I'm fucking – fucking killing you!" Matthew was screeching as Walter sprinted the other way behind his house, cutting around more houses and heading towards the woods, as Matthew ran off after him, in close pursuit, considering how close he came to getting blinded just then.

Walter bounded over a line of thick bushes and began running at about the same speed as he had been just an hour or so ago, cutting straight through the forest of thin, spread-out pine trees. As he sprinted at top speed through the spacious woods, he pondered what it was that kept putting him in these sorts of situations: it seemed as though danger was attracted to him above all else because if he wasn't around for people to unload their built-up malice, then they'd have to find someone who might actually stand up for themselves in a fight that's at least worth a damn – or, better yet, just get outside assistance. He was a maverick, poor of heart and propped up by long-expired ambitions, but still he made his best attempt at keeping on, just extending beyond the grip of life as a cripple, among other incredibly painful possibilities if he ever got caught by the wrong person with the wrong weapon at the wrong time and place – he had caught beatings before, and he thanked his Lord above for not letting any of them escalate into anything real or permanent, and he still had intense gratitude for his lucky tidings in that regard.

The light in the forest grayed out and minutes later it was so dark that you could only see trees as you were coming up on them. Walter held up and slapped his back up against one of the cylindrical pines, panting intensely and trying to ignore the taste of iron in his mouth. The forest was almost entirely silent, but apart from the noise of small chittering mammals, singing birds, and the common bugs that reside in tall grass, he was able to make out the furious panting that was slowly approaching him from behind. Matthew's gasping breaths were hitting like a drumbeat, half time: "HUH-hah HUH-hah HUH-hah."

Walter jumped out and threw a flying punch, but Matthew pulled his arms to his face and just ran through Walter, bodying him entirely, and tackling him to the ground.

"You didn't have to do this to yourself," Matthew's raspy cry sounded-off as he began climbing on top of Walter and taking jabs at his head, forcing him to hold up his fists to counter any hits. Matthew held both of Walter's wrists back with one hand and reared back his other fist to throw a quick dart of a punch aimed at Walter's nose.

Faster than Matthew could land the blow, Walter dropped to the side and back, swinging his legs all the way around and knocking Matthew off of and away from him. Both of them staggered back as they got up to their feet. A distance of a few paces had been created between them, which was broken by Matthew after pausing for a moment before charging Walter. Walter dashed forward as well, and Matthew made the decision that he would jump and throw an elbow intended to catch him in the throat or face, but Walter stopped in place and took a step back the very moment after Matthew went forward into the air, causing Matthew to stumble as he landed back down on the ground. Walter ran through him, picking him off the ground by the waist, carrying him in a sprinting burst of movement, and slamming the entire back of Matthew's torso and head up against a tree before dropping him.

Matthew slid down the trunk with his back against it, instantly concussed, and was rolling his head around, eyelids drooped and pupils staring in different directions. "You're... I'm – I'm coming... you're," he mumbled, making his neck bulge as he fought to breathe.

Walter's chest was heaving and his heart was pounding but, as he also gasped for air, he watched his fallen assailant from a distance, ready to take up the fight again if it was time for a second round. Barely, out of the corner of his eye, he noticed a pine tree in the distance disappear at the bottom – except the bottom part had folded back and at a 90-degree angle to the side of what appeared to him to be the tree. Walter squinted, but due to the darkness he couldn't make any details out, when suddenly shining like that of high noon flared up from all over, the forest becoming blindingly light, the air completely white and every tree illuminated so brightly that colorful patterns in the bark were visible. The tree, as he knew it, didn't become the ashy-brown shade of all the trees, but it remained pitch black instead, thick fur covering its body that all was flowing to the side in the wind. It was an enormous man with broad, muscular shoulders and legs that were pulled behind it at the knee. The only detail of all this that mattered was its head: a white, melon-shaped dome that was also covered entirely in long black fur, except for the face, which was hairless in a ring around its facial features like a full moon against the night sky. Its eye sockets were gaping, deep, and black, it was without a nose, and it had an inhumanly wide-open grin that exposed its black, bottomless maw; its spaced-out jagged teeth filled exposed, bloodied gums that were contorted upwards in a strangely joyous smile from cheek-to-cheek, making the figure look comically pleased.

Walter couldn't do a thing but examine it in the moment he had because it was so drastically unlike anything he had ever looked at in his life. A low, upwards whistling could be heard, droning out all other noise as it got louder and higher in pitch. It halted suddenly and the eye sockets began to glow white in two small white circles out of the massive black caverns that were its eyes, resembling the headlights of a car shining through the dead of night. The only sound he heard was his own: a sharp inhale… and then **"EYEURRRRRRRRRRRRR"** was the call of the horrible groaning that echoed all the way to Walter, piercing his ears, and as soon as the thing began to make noise, it's head spasmed wildly around, snapping all the way back and then all the way forward as it shifted left or right, resembling a car antennae that had been yanked to the side and was flapping in every direction as it slowed down and returned to its resting position. But this thing's head didn't slow down, and it continued to growl in its guttural, nasal tone while its whole body stayed still as stone suspended in the air in contrast to the head that was bouncing with the speed of a striking hammer, each complete movement from one side to the other happening in the blink of an eye. Without notice, it leapt out, breaking its frozen position in the air, holding its head still and launching itself in his direction, shrieking **"RRRRRRRRRRRRAH-AH-AH"** in an inhumanly strident vocalization and at such a low pitch that it could only be described as the kind of noise that a silverback gorilla would make in a fight to the death.

Walter got a hold of himself as he regained awareness of where he was and what was happening, and he turned and tore away from the scene at a velocity that even he couldn't have anticipated. As he got further away, the unbearably bright white light all around him faded back to the black of night, but in the moment that he had made it back all the way back into the darkness, he heard Matthew's agonizing screaming, who was making noise in the form of senseless, bloodcurdling cries, and that noise echoed at full volume just until the street became visible through the tree line, and as he exited the woods, his voice phased out and the quiet song of the night was the only thing he heard. Trotting back up to the path in front of his house at a leisurely pace so his breath could catch up, he picked up the bike from out of the street and stashed it under the front stairs of his house.

As he gripped the doorknob, he forced himself to treat the past day of monumental chaos as just being what had to be done to move on in life, because if he didn't put every instance of his highly implausible escape out of mind, he'd never be able to let go of how immensely the odds of him remaining personally intact were stacked against his favor, and yet still he was returning home after another full day, nothing missing from his person that he couldn't go without. Despite all this, he was thoroughly convinced against the idea of him being 'fortunate' in any sense of the word – there was just no way that he could describe the tumult of his personal life in any terms that didn't directly connote to burden and unease, and no matter how thoroughly the world proved to him that he was making his place in it one step at a time, he knew in his heart that it was all one continuous mistake. The door shut behind him as he pressed it back into its frame.

"Oh, Walt!" his mother exclaimed, looking frenziedly back-and-forth between him and the television. "Sit down, sit down! You absolutely have to see this part – it's what I wanted to show you!"

Walter, too emotionally and physically demolished to resist, went across the room and dropped down next to her.

"AHHH!" cried the man who had the full face of black hair as he dug into a bullet wound in his calf using a pair of Lineman's pliers. "FUCKIN' – AH – AH – AHHHHHHHH!" He yanked a slug out that was covered in gore and let the pliers clatter to the ground, then fell back on the baby changing station that he was lying on, gasping. Tearing off pants at the knee, he used the bloody suit leg to tie a hasty tourniquet. After catching his breath, he called out, "Pritch." The tall man got onto his good foot and began limping across the bathroom to the exit. "Pritchard," he mumbled out as he stumbled over hunting rifles and giant dead men wearing leather vests. The bodies were scattered around in random positions on the floor, each in his own pool of blood. "Pritch," he repeated.

The baby-faced man with nice hair entered the room and reached his arm around the first's shoulder, who did the same to him. The hobbling man using him as a crutch, the two of them walked slowly out of the bathroom. "They're raiding everything," the short man told him. "The offices are long gone, a group of guys are leading all the horses out to the parking lot and riding away with one apiece, and anything with a door or a cover is getting torn open."

The tall, crippled man grunted as he struggled to speak. "This place – hrgh – This place is still valued at a fortune; we've just got to get to the truck before anybody catches us."

The two of them stopped in their tracks, the sound of their dress shoes scuffing the tiled floor ended abruptly. The only thing audible was the noisy buzzing of the ceiling lights.

"That's smoke," the short man stated after a pause. "I'm smelling smoke."

"Fuck's sakes," cried the wounded man, *"that's the stables."* He let go of his support and propped himself up on the wall to keep from toppling over.

"I'm going to –" the Filipino man started to say as he walked off, still looking at the tall man but pointing in the direction he was moving.

"Go, go," he cut him off, *"sprint, if you can."* He saw his comrade fly off down the hallway, and then pushed off the wall and began walking one foot at a time in the same direction.

The scene cut to a shot from the center of the racetrack, which was entirely devoid of living occupants other than three people: the short man on the ground while he scrambled backwards over dead bodies and getting kicked by a man in a white tank top. Another man was in the top story of the stables, the roof of which was completely engulfed in flames, and was dropping black duffle bags onto the ground below from out of the window while he sat in the sill so that the burning roof above him couldn't fall on his head. Two shots rang out, dropping the kicking man and the one seated in the window, his body falling into the inside of the burning stables, and the limping man emerged from the building next to bleachers, pointing a handgun with one hand and holding his leg with the other as he moved.

"Well," said the short man as he got to his feet and hustled over to help support the injured man, *"so much for being out with a fair sum."*

"Not entirely," he grunted. *"Take me to those packages he was tossing out of the window."*

The two of them made their way over across the track.

"Whose are those?" asked the man who was dusty from being kicked around in the dirt.

"Miss Mallbory's," the tall man replied. *"And Miss Mallbory"* he dropped to his knees and unzipped two of the bags, one full of plastic explosives and the other with sealed duct tape packages each the size of a textbook *"was the largest distributor of C-4 and cocaine in all the southeast United States. The only issue we have*

is that we've got lots of dead bodies, and they'll be looking for us if they find any remains, so if we take the cars out in the parking lot and scatter them around with what we've got here, all we have to do is"

The scene cut to the two of them sitting in a truck, the dirty man behind the wheel and the crippled man shotgun. The two of them had an arm out the window each and they were faced forward, calmly observing the back of the bleachers from their spot in the far end of the parking lot. Two three-inch lines of coke rested horizontally on the dash in front of either of them.

"Ready?" the driver-side man asked, clutching a small clicker in his left hand.

"Go" commanded the right man, and the two of them lurched forward, holding one nostril shut and pressing their faces down onto the end of their respective line while inhaling from their open nostril as violently as possible.

Halfway through his own line, the left man pressed his thumb onto the red box, making a light clicking noise as it connected with the body of the clicker. A sudden shockwave shot out and shook all of the remaining cars in the lot as the buildings around the track all blew outwards, debris colliding with debris as modestly-sized fires exploded in the air like a small-scale firework show, and a moment later, an aftershock occurred when the cars' engines had time to detonate. The two of them looked up, finished, to see the scene of the racetrack cleanly leveled, a thin layer of rubble and ashes scattered amongst a flaming car here or there.

"Alright" sniffled the wounded man, *"We should probably"* and the screen went to black, credits rolling.

Walter's mother was cackling. "Wasn't that great?!" she exclaimed. "Everything he makes is just so funny, I find. It's a great distraction..."

"Who made that?" Walter asked.

"Abe Carelin," she replied. "That was him in the tuxedo with the shaggy mop of black hair. I was watching one of his movies this morning before I nodded off."

"Can't say I know who that is," he remarked. "Hey, it's been an... eventful day. Do you know anything about seeing things you can't explain?"

"You mean like special effects?" his mother asked. "The way his films are shot and all the colors he uses, you can't tell that what you're watching isn't actually happening, it's –"

"No, Mom," he said, irritated, "I'm talking about my *life*. It's been stressful in ways I can't accurately describe with words."

She scoffed and replied flippantly, "Well, Walt, we're all stressed about *something*."

Walter just pursed his lips and nodded his head. "Kay," he said, got to his feet, took his backpack and went into the hallway bathroom in an instant. When he stepped into that shower, his entire body aching from a day of involuntary physical contact, and the cold water swept over his naked frame, he became melted down with closed eyes, not having anything to do with what's happened to him or where he was. He was free, and he was without guilt. The frigid shower was a good reminder that he could push himself and still make something positive out of it, even if it was something as simple as struggling to stay warm. He shut off the knob, dried off, slipped on his boxers, and took his clothes and backpack to his room, not stopping for even a moment to let his mother get in a word before he could get away. Dropping everything in the corner, flipping on a lamp on his dresser, and shutting the door behind him, he wanted with his whole being to just let himself pass out right away to be able to forget about what he was forced to endure since the time he left that room, but instead, he fought himself and pulled up his mattress before he fell onto it, and removed a note that was stored there. He flopped down and took to reading it:

Oh Walter, I'm so sorry.

I couldn't apologize enough if I took up the whole sheet. I don't get sick – I never get sick... but on the night of the homecoming dance that also marked our one-year anniversary? – dear God, Walter, if I could've done anything to hold it together, I'd

have made myself stay, but I just couldn't. Thank you – really, thank you for the patience you must have had to say "Sure, I didn't want to be here anyway" when I asked to go. That's something I'll never forget – not even on my deathbed will I let it slip from my mind. I don't know how anybody could be attracted to me once they've learned me the way you have, but then again, nobody has ever come close to learning me compared to the way you've got me figured out. I didn't know what to do to make it up to you, so I figured I'd go someplace I had never decided on before and try some artistry, just because I think your strange dedication to me calls for a strange decision on my own part. Anyway, here goes:
And below was a meticulous, lifelike penciled depiction of the blackened cafeteria illuminated by the Chinese lanterns that the SCA had put up for the theme, and there they were, in a space at the center of the crowd that was comprised of other boys who were in dress shirts and the girls in dresses, Alina's skirt swirling gently around her and her perfectly-straight hair glossy with a shine like a window in the sun, Walter's chest popping out the buttons along the center of shirt and the pleats in his pants pointed like a roof, the two of them in mid step with each other, his hands around her waist and hers behind his shoulders, and the two of them looked so suave and gratified in their faces that he couldn't picture them actually being the people that she had drawn, but he liked to think that whoever these two people were, they were enjoying themselves well enough in the place of him and his girlfriend. Even still, the gray scene of shadowed pillars in front of the auditorium doors was so visually captivating that it resembled what Dance Hall in Arles would have look like if Van Gogh had decided instead to set it in the eating space of a run-down high school, but as he scanned from the top down to the bottom, his eyes went to an unfamiliar small line of text in the bottom right corner: *Be very careful in the coming days… it has your scent. But she really loves you; give her some patience -Brielle.*

XX – B

Walter watched the swishing of the trees in the breeze out front of his house, the red shutters creaking back and forth. The night was still like a petrified rat; vacant of activity and desolate enough to be a cemetery. How tired the world must have been from the bickering antics of its daily population; now it lay dormant, ignorant of what reality had in store for time to come. It was true that certain days were just more difficult than others to endure; that if nothing else became of the hardest hours of our time spent on this planet, we'd go someplace distant for at least a few hours that might not be so concerned with the terrors of yesterday. The peace that instilled the world around him was just happenstance. The remnants of our most severe discomforts were just the garnishes that lined one memory to the next, and while it didn't matter that there was nothing but silence all around him, Walter was stricken by the cruel nature of his captor. He found himself unable to relate to the purpose that was set out for him; it all seemed as though the cycle that each person was subject to was just a reflection of what could be in the most optimal of existences. The darkness was calling him, but he could only find himself wanting to resist out of some futile desire to correct his poor position as a human being.

"Hello?" he called into the ghostly foyer of his house as he slipped through the door. "Mom? Dad?" He tuned his ears, seeking out any sounds that might signify some form of life apart from his

Crowe

own sorry state. Gradually the noise coming from a bonfire came into focus, coming from behind the house. He stumbled through darkened corridors, merely trying to make his way through the confusing maze that was his own intentions. Through the glass of the kitchen window he saw his mother wearing a thick shawl and staring longingly into the firepit, and then went out the back door.

"Oh, Walter," she said in a tone that was almost disappointed, as though she had wanted an ultimatum delivered to her the instant she heard a disturbance behind her, but was thwarted instead by the appearance of her son. "You surprised me."

"You don't sound surprised," he commented. He was studying her shadowy figure, wishing for a reaction from her like a student wishes for enlightenment from his master.

A disconcerting silence settled between the two of them. The crackling of the fire was the undercurrent to the unnecessary tension that the two of them were forced to endure. If anything could be taken for granted, it was that he wouldn't have to worry about her doing anything other than continue to stare into the flames with hollow hope and long-lost aspirations. The wonderful shrubbery and decorative layout of the back patio were all but forgotten, irrelevant as a backdrop to the quiet scene of conflict going on around it.

He trotted up to her slowly, so as to not disturb her, and zipped open his backpack, retrieving the flowers. "These – These are for Rachel," he said, speaking like an inventor presenting the final failed project of his career.

She took the wildflowers from him, staring at their vibrant colors in the orange glow of the blazing embers. "They're beautiful, Walt. Thank you. Thank you so much," she said as though he had just given her the opportunity to see her daughter one more time.

Walter was stoic and unexpecting, trying to remain as neutral as possible for his fickle mother, as he knew that she was as liable to show him love as she was to lose herself in her perpetual sorrows. As he noticed her wavering in place, he dashed forward to hold her in place.

"Huh?" she muttered. "Oh – Uh, thank you. I guess I'm a little bit out of sorts right now," she said, trying to save face.

"It's the least I could do, mother. Let's get you inside." He guided her towards the door, from which point he laid her down onto the couch, making sure to only let go of her once she was safe and secure. He then flicked on a lamp, went to the kitchen, filled the pail from the counter with water, and went out back to dump it onto the fire. It went out with a sickening cry, and he placed the wire covering over it afterwards. After replacing the pail, he went back into the room and watched his mother, who was wiping tears away as she took sips from a glass of wine that had been left out on the coffee table.

"I'm sorry – I don't know why I'm so worked up," she said, regaining her composure. "I really do appreciate you doing this for me, darling. You're very thoughtful. Rachel would be delighted to have received these – you're doing her spirit great justice."

"You don't need to apologize; I'm just glad you appreciate them," he replied. He was squeezing her hand and leaning in like a therapist being paid by the quarter-hour.

She finished her glass and took a deep sigh. "It feels like the harder I try to move on, the more I'm reminded of why I don't deserve respite. Losing her was like hearing about Kennedy over the radio: first I didn't know how to react, then everything set in and I could only just pray for some certainty that wasn't just ever-present doom." She put her free hand over her face, beginning to sob as she shook her head. "I just can't grapple with it: why do the things we can't control have to dictate our very happiness?"

Walter was struggling to think of a reply. Instead, he took the glass, went to the kitchen, and filled it with water. He took it back to her and observed her carefully like a zookeeper who had been kept up for a week caring for a diseased koala.

She thanked him quietly and took to drinking.

Scattered light fell in from the windows and settled on the gilded plates and pottery that decorated shelves all around the room. Sometimes the house felt like the manor of some fief, representative of a wealth that was never enough to match the desires of its prideful occupants. The ancient clock in the hallway was ticking its characteristic measured song, providing a backdrop of activity to the deathly stillness that encompassed the space around them.

"If – If I might say," started Walter, "I'd like it if you could just go to sleep. The rest is the best thing for you right now."

His mother cackled. "Oh honey; nothing is best for me right now. That's the sad fact of the matter: I'm caught in limbo and every push from the universe around me feels like the continuum of some sick joke that I'm not in on. I just don't know what I'll ever do; I'm falling apart from top to bottom." She finished the glass.

Walter got up and refilled it. "I know you don't believe me, but you're strong. Stronger than you've ever been. One day you'll wake up and it'll be like something came through the window and lifted all your burdens from your shoulders. It happened to me just the other day: I was caught up in this comment that Joe made about my physique, when suddenly, it was like it just didn't matter anymore – I'm not saying that his criticism was untrue, but it was like I had made peace with it, you know?"

She scoffed, incredulous. She tilted the glass and held it in front of her face, poised to take a sip at any point. "Somehow I think the opinion of your little friend is dwarfed in size by the torment I go through over Rachel, but it sounds like you're trying to relate to me. If you ever understand one day what a tragedy feels like as it touches down in your life, you might be able to speak to me on like terms when it comes to such a subject."

Walter was hunched over, his fingers interlaced and his head bowed. "Do you really think my sister dying wasn't a tragedy for me?" he asked, desperate to reach his mother.

She shook her hair around, lifting the cup up like she was giving a toast. "I think that being a parent is the first time you ever get a chance to be in tune with your own nature, and losing your child is the first time that you get convinced we're all just pawns in a maelstrom of chaos. When you finally reach the point where the unbelievable becomes mixed with the ordinary, you'll understand what it's like." She chugged her water down and placed the glass away from her so that her son wouldn't fill it another time.

He sighed, biting his lip and looking to the side for some sort of reprieve but finding nothing. "Sometimes it feels like you only want to hear me agree with you."

"Well, I'm sorry; if you don't like what I'm saying, we don't have to talk." She motioned towards the bar. "Bring me the screwdriver."

Walter's eyes fluttered at her command. "Mom, are you serious? It's the dead of night and there's not a person in a hundred-mile radius who's not out cold."

She snapped her fingers and then pointed to the floor. "I wasn't asking," she said.

He got up and shuffled over to the other side of the room. He was shaking his head and murmuring swears to himself under his breath. He popped open the wide freezer that was built into the back of the bar and reached behind rows of frosty bottles to grab one filled with opaque yellow liquor. The door shut with a sliding creak and the bottle was dropped off on the corner table.

"How was the visit at Brielle's?" she asked between swigs.

"I thought you'd never ask," Walter said, relief in his voice.

"Why does telling me about your day matter so much to you?" She was slumped over, her hair messily covering either side of her face.

"Call me self-centered, but I *also* happen to enjoy discussing things that have some sort of relation to me." He was rubbing his eyes, then slid his hand up over his forehead and fixed his hair. "But anyway, she's doing well. We got our homework done and I gave her a foot rub and then we hosted a game of darts for her parents. So overall I'd say it was a successful use of my evening."

"A foot rub? That's unusual." She flipped the bottle up like a lever to down as much of the sweet alcoholic nectar as possible.

"It was her idea. I think she was stressed out, so it felt good to do her a solid. She's got issues feeling alright, so this was a big deal for me."

"I know; you tell me about it. Why do her parents make you cater for them like a servant? Shouldn't they be the ones butlering around for the two of you?"

Walter bit the inside of his cheek, plucking its bumpy surface. It was unnerving how his mother could turn an inconspicuous conversation into a one-sided string of criticisms. "I don't know. Maybe it's a cultural thing."

"Well it's just strange, that's all I can say for certain. Whatever happened to Ashleigh? I thought she was rather charming. I miss having her over for bridge." She had her head cocked and was staring blankly upwards, in a relaxed stupor.

"I've told you: she's married to that Egyptian banker all the way out in Nevada," he told her. "I don't think Brielle's seen her since she was still home for high school. And she's a rather nasty person, if I have to be frank."

"I thought her manners were impeccable."

Walter yawned loudly. "Well, was there anything you wanted to talk about? I might just go hit the hay." He waited on a response, and when he received none, he got to his feet and began to walk out.

His mother reached out and grabbed him by the arm. "Don't leave me here all alone," she whimpered.

Walter was taken aback, not even aware that she had a vulnerable side to contrast her usual barbed attitude. "Mom, I'm sorry, but if our conversation's over then it's over. I don't know what else you want me to say, but I've been sleeping poorly for as long as I can remember, so *really* it's for the best if I just –"

"What's the first thing you want to do once the new year rolls around?" she asked like a beggar requesting pocket change.

"Honestly, I have no idea. I'll be lucky if I make it to the end of December – let's not get too far ahead of ourselves here, mother." He pried her hand off of his arm and took his seat once more.

"Why don't we plan a trip to see Uncle Marcus again? He's always such a superb host, and the scenery around the cabin is gorgeous in the winter," she said, mystified.

"Er – Yeah, that would be great, but don't Uncle Marc and Dad have a long-running feud? I think it goes back to something about an investment gone wrong that neither of them want to own up to." Walter's eyes were struggling to stay open.

"Oh, they're just a couple of rabble-rousers. Once the holidays roll around, they'll be ready to sing Kumbaya and chug bourbon; you'll see." She was talking as though she were being interviewed, strangely airy in her intonation.

"Well I'm glad you're so optimistic, because the last thing I remember Dad telling him was 'You're going to freeze out here all alone on this heap of ice. Patricia left you, and there won't be anybody around when it's your time to go.' Somehow I feel like Marc's not just going to let that one go, but what do I know?"

"They're just bickering like usual – I can promise you that there's nothing that a hunting trip and an evening in the hot tub can't cure. You remember how mad Cousin Robert was when he came to Thanksgiving at the cabin and found out that Tillie had been invited? He was livid, but it just took a bit of hiking up and down the trails for a few mere hours and suddenly the two of them were the best of friends." She grunted softly while she stretched, putting her elbows far back and bending her spine around.

"Yeah, but Bobby hated Tillie because she accidentally told his mom that he wasn't in the air force anymore. Dad and Marcus have issues with each other that are business-related, and I shudder to think what an argument between the two of them could avalanche into. You'd have both of them throwing numbers around to try and figure out who cost the other more money, and it would all just be one big exercise in hostility. Personally, I'd rather not be involved with it, but I don't know, I guess I've been wrong before."

His thoughts were becoming light and less coherent as he struggled to elaborate the points he was thinking up.

"I think I'll bake a wonderful red velvet cake; I know that's always a big hit." She clapped her hands together enthusiastically.

"If you really think so, Mom," he said, unable to believe the words coming out of her mouth. "I guess there's nothing I can say that'll change your point of view."

"There was this remarkable evening when Jeremiah Doughty fixed that man's car on the spot after it had broken down in the middle of Houston on a scorching hot afternoon. He was off the road for maybe five minutes before the engine came back on, and let me tell you, this person was beside himself with how grateful he was for the good deed. Turns out, his brother owned a chain of restaurants around Texas and Arizona, based just a few miles away, and we went to the largest of the franchise and all ate for free! Your father ordered the most enormous, juiciest lobster I had seen in my life, and the red velvet cake they served for dessert liquified in your mouth," his mother rehearsed like she was talking from a script.

Walter was in further disbelief that their conversation had devolved into light party chatter – sometimes he wondered if he was just another person for his parents to impress. "Mom, I was there," he said, trying to quell his fuming attitude.

"So you remember Rachel's pink lacy dress? She looked like Jackie O. I picked it out for her, you know. We were at Barners and she needed one for homecoming, so naturally I asked what the theme was, and she told me Candyland. It only took me one scan of the store from wall-to-wall to find it, and if she wasn't completely impressed from head-to-toe. I don't think she thought that I had such a strong nose for fashion!" She chuckled, closing her eyes and gesturing with her bottle. "That homecoming was a proud, proud night for me, I'll tell you...."

Walter huffed. "That's great – I'm going to sleep." He got up and hustled away, looking away from his mother out of spite.

Again, she gripped his arm and pulled him around. "One last thing," she said with a smack of her lips. "You have to go get the Fat

Feather Tequila and have a glass with me." She giggled. "Oh! At the bar, actually, at the bar."

He was horrified. "Mom, that sounds like an awful idea. I need to sleep, and you *really* need to sleep. And I've got no business drinking during the week, let alone a school week. Why would you suggest such a thing?"

"Because if you were at the bottom of the pit known as Hell, you'd be clawing at the walls just the same way I do," his mother hissed. "You want to talk about sleep? You've got your whole life to sleep. I've got at most a good two decades; past that it'll be daily agony until my time comes, that is if I age anything like my folks. Your sister sleeps from dawn 'til dusk for all eternity because someone else chose for her how she'd spend the rest of her life. You want to make that decision for me? I wouldn't even trust you to make it for yourself. Now get my goddamn liquor."

Walter's blood was icy as she released her grip on him. He sputtered out a few meager words, but they didn't form anything sensible, and he merely went to the bar and retrieved the bulbous orange container that had a skull inset on the side. Uncorking it and placing ice cubes in two glasses, he filled both of them halfway.

"Nope," his mother said as she walked up, "nuh-uh. All the way to the brim."

"Mom… you can't be serious?" he mewled in a wounded tone.

She took it from him and doled out the drink herself. The glass flew off the counter as she plucked it up and scooted his across the bar to him. "Come on: up," she said, holding her glass out for cheers.

Walter turned his eyes away, grimacing. He clinked glasses with her and put it back. As the fiery substance inflamed his throat on the way down, he felt himself return to the days when he and Brielle hung around the Box Star Club and he had to pound cinnamon whiskey cut with grain alcohol to keep his seat. He only ever put up with it for her, because of how much it mattered to her how they spent their Sunday afternoons, but deep down, if anyone else had even asked him to grin and bear it through such a task, he'd have broke all association with them the very next moment. It seemed to be irrelevant that his suffering went on; no one seemed to notice him wincing to himself, just trying to hold himself together in time to face an irreverent future.

As Walter's stomach turned over again and again, trying to extinguish itself like a man covered in flames rolling around in the street, he wondered what his empathy might be for his family in five years, or maybe ten, or maybe even twenty. What does one do when they walk away from every avenue of torture that they were forced to endure for their waking existence? Does it call for triumph or sorrow? Is there any point to weep over the time that vanishes when we care about someone who ends up being starkly indifferent, or to beg for another opportunity when an epoch of one's life closes on conflicted terms? He wanted to flee to a place that hasn't yet seen its first house, just so he could forget what it was like to be a part of society. He was a beetle scurrying in the muck, mixed in with all the other festering creatures that were competing for the next chance to feast so as to prolong the trouble that is another day. The polished cars and aristocratic houses were poor disguises for the truth that was a race of shame and despair. No amount of covering up could change just how isolated he currently was as a survivor to the constant bombardment that was being his parents' son.

"Ahh," his mother exclaimed, refreshed. "That did wonders for me!" She chuckled as she went back to the couch and settled in.

Walter stumbled over to his chair, disoriented and sweating. "Mom, the room is spinning," he said in a low, scared tone as he dropped into the seat.

She cackled obnoxiously. "That just means you're at Stage 2. Once you reach Stage 4 you'll be good to go."

"I'm serious, Mom – it's like I'm in the hull of a ship," he sputtered, breathing disjointedly in rattled gasps.

"You know, you're not such a bad sport, Walt. Your father criticizes you for never putting up a fight, but the Walter he knows would never have been up to the challenge." She was rubbing the silky fabric of the couch, playing with its texture.

"If Dad was awake, he'd throttle me. I don't know why you're painting him as being impressed by any of this." His forehead was buried in his hands.

"You know what I'm in the mood for? I could absolutely go to the aquarium. The lionfish there are so noble; it looks like they're covered in pointed armor like a Renaissance knight."

"Mom, the Renaissance didn't have knights. That was the point of it," he mumbled, fighting a headache.

She reared back as though she had just had her honor questioned. "I didn't know that Brielle was teaching you history, now."

Walter looked at her angrily. His ears were red, partially from embarrassment and the rest from the tequila. "You know, Brielle isn't the source of all my knowledge. Sometimes she even learns stuff from *me*, and believe it or not, I've read up on a fair bit of European history, but you don't hear me bragging about it."

Her head was leaned back and her eyes were cracked open ever so slightly, staring in two directions like a frog.

He slapped his thighs and shook his head at his open-mouthed, snoring mother. "I'm leaving while I can. Goodnight." The stairway was twisting around as he made his way up it; the wine had loosened him up, but now he was fully dismantled by the single glass his mother had forced on him. He didn't know why his parents made him uncomfortable for sport. If they weren't being unnecessarily critical then they were being purely pejorative. He was caught in a limbo of never being enough in their eyes as well as being a blank tablet full of future prospects but needing someone to carve in the important parts for him. Sometimes it seemed like they wanted to live through him, to once more feel the successes that one encounters as a youth.

The large portrait of their family seemed to call out to him as he passed it. He didn't know why, but he felt guilty as he spotted the detailed figure of his sister out of the corner of his eye. Call it survivor's guilt; call it whatever you want, but he knew that he didn't deserve something that she did. He wouldn't play the game that was imagining what things might be like if this or that or the other happened, because he had already wallowed around cumulatively for hours upon hours doing exactly that. Their family seemed to consider the brief time that she spent breathing with a certain filter of glamor, like she had been some sort of rough-riding cowboy, living fast and loose and meeting the only end that such a person inevitably meets.

He grumbled to himself, irate that the drink had perked him right up from the brink of sleep. His heart was palpitating in a complete contrast to the quiet darkness that possessed the hallways, shadows falling all around the corners that weren't touched by the gaze of the gaping windows. The energy of his surroundings had been sapped entirely, and he was filled with grim dread at the prospect of mortality: if the day wilted so easily, what bodes for the bumbling generation he was a part of? He couldn't help but to imagine what the equivalent of the evening would be for his own existence; what he might be concerning himself with as his own sun set. He hoped that he'd be smart enough by then to have done away with all of his regrets. He'd pray for his soul, but he didn't want to give God the false impression that he ever had faith.

Walter pushed open the door to his room, listening to its weary creaking. He flicked on his lamp and took another moment to marvel at his room. Nothing looked the same as he could recall. From the feeling of things, he was something more for once rather than just being something occupying a space – that he had some humanity. Between his flashy posters and the wondrous arrangement of photos of him and Brielle, he actually felt sanctuary. It couldn't never be fully described how intensely he wanted to provide for her and give her anything she might want one day. Funding her smile was the only goal he could think of that was worth achieving, because if his work might eventually bring her gratification, he would labor all night and into the morning until his fingers bled just to have the privilege of hearing her ramble to him as the late afternoon came and passed. Her presence was a warm embrace from a cruel, cold capsule of space and time.

Frustrated, he went under his bed and procured an easel and a canvas. Setting it up, he studied the canvas, which had scuffed bits of drawn and colored patches. It looked like the half-completed scaffolding of a house: vaguely resembling its finished state, but still a primitive model of what was to hopefully come. It was neverendingly frustrating how little capability he had to harness his creative intuition. He remembered enjoying painting the small pack of dogs, all of different breeds and playing with their owners – the rest of the picture was much more morose, however. A young boy wept down by the waterside. A group of teenagers were consumed in a brawl between one another. Down in a small ridge off to the side, a lady stared into the sky, wailing. He had imagined the chaos of a Baroque painting, but the overall level of activity was so disjointed and spread out that it lacked thematic cohesion. It was as though he was looking at a variety of smaller scenes that had been smashed into one another.

Walter traced out the details of the jackets on the cluster of fighting youths, making patches and pointed shoulders and folds and buttons and zippers. It took him minutes to form mere corners that had fullness and depth, as he had a poor grasp on his creative capability. It was like floundering for the surface, caught somersaulting in the undertow. The harder he fought to muster his focus and make meaningful progress, the further he was pushed back by his physical constraints. It felt like being an elderly ex-basketball pro: fat around the waist and banged up at the knees, unable to make any use out of his skill and knowledge. It broke him, how little power he had to translate his wishes and visions into anything sensible or pleasing.

Stepping back, he analyzed his work in the dim light of his lamp and tried to get a fuller image of what he had made. At first, it was entirely unnoticeable that he had even made any progress, but as he continued to look, he noticed the minor details that had come into existence that night. Still, he was ashamed of himself for being so struck in the same place, complacent like he was on a ten-year contract. Did he really believe in himself? Probably not. As best he could tell, every attempt he made at proficiency wasn't anything more than him grasping wildly at whatever it seemed like someone actually talented would do. His effort projected a vacant cry for acceptance; for a place among others even if there wasn't any substance to the crowd. It all became the one-dimensional obsession to rest easy amongst the masses, forget his place and stature and lose all form.

After a twitch of his eye, Walter became aware of something that he thought for certain hadn't been there just moments before. He reached out and felt the top story of the clocktower, which was covered in a thin coating of black fur. It was coarse and rugged like fuzzy leather. He suddenly pulled his hand back, overtaken by fear. In an instant, he dismantled the easel and placed everything back in its spot under his bed.

Walter shed his clothes and shut off the light. His eyes observed the ceiling emptily, the noise of toads outside filling his ears. What was Brielle thinking about right now? Probably that summer when they spent a week going down to Brackets Creek until they found out they were getting ticks from that end of the woods. It was great, though: they brought a boombox down and blasted Southside Symphony and the acoustics were such that the sound bounced off the boulders and came back to them like they were in an amphitheater. They'd sing along to the loud, droning vocalists, hitting all the high notes and staying strong from one end of the scales to the other. She'd say: "This makes me want a music room for our future manor. Think about it: all the instruments you could spell and some that we still haven't learned the names to yet. We'd just sit around and chain joint after joint while playing out our every frustration."

Walter liked it when she'd get thoughtful like that. It reminded him that there was still innocence in the world; that if you could just believe and hope you won't get your hand bitten off when you reach it out in the direction of approaching fate. It was his dream to fumble a risk and not be immediately disciplined.

He began drifting towards a blank pearly sky, searching for the other end of a desperate journey. There was nothing there for him, however. 'Submit, submit,' the walls chanted. He winced, trying to resist the grasp of the inevitable. Giving in at long last, he searched for a familiar face as the world swirled around him, but all he saw was a mouth without eyes, ears, or a nose. She had nothing to say to him.

The Story Behind the Story

I was actually upset when I stumbled upon the concept of two stories being told from one viewpoint. One day in November of 2015, I had just got back to my dorm after a tough day of classes. While I was washing my hands in my hall's restroom, I considered what it would be like if I could go to sleep that night and wake up in another life – just for a day. Then I'd go back to sleep and wake back up in my normal life.

My initial reaction to having this thought experiment was 'That would be cool; it would definitely give me perspective if it was possible.' My second reaction was 'It sounds like the idea of a cliché YA novel about high schoolers. That would be such a cheap story to write.' I had been ashamed, frankly, about even having the idea of not someday outperforming J.R.R. Tolkien and George R.R. Martin with the scope of an epic fantasy novel but instead settling for corny dialogue and prose about how much daily life as a teenager sucks. After swallowing my pride, I continued to indulge myself in this thought experiment: there were so many questions that formed in my mind that served as creative doors to be opened for further exploration.

How would these two separate but identical high schoolers meaningfully interact with the world? How can I prevent them from just Googling their name or reverse image searching a picture of their face? How can I explore the confusion of not knowing who you are? How can I depict environment shaping behavior rather than the way someone is born? How can I show that growing up with access to different opportunities can affect a person's emotional maturity and outlook? How can I show that class and wealth affect a person's ability to rationally self-analyze themselves?

The thought experiment had turned into a viral takeover within my brain. If I was ever having a creative insight, it always looped back around to this idea of two duplicate people in two different lives. So, after twenty months of stewing on the details about how a novel like this could even possibly work, all I had to my name was around 10,000 words. By August of 2017, I was sick of not being able to make any use of these ideas. I sat down and got to work: four months later, I had written over 100,000 words and completed all twenty chapters.

To make a long story short, this novel and the series that follows it are inspired by an idea for a new type of noir fiction. The tension of ordinary life can often be hard to capture, as contemporary society is so complex that any one plot will never break more new ground than it misses. By using only one person's viewpoint in two unrelated stories, my aim was to contrast them against one another to make an overall greater and more exciting experience to read.

Andrew Zacharich
Crowe

Contacting the Author

Email:
azcrowewriting@gmail.com
Website:
azcwriting.com
Instagram:
zacrovve

THIS SERIES IS DEDICATED TO
THE VENUE ON 35TH STREET
WHERE I LEARNED TO BE AN ARTIST

Crowe

colophon
Brought to you by Wider Perspectives Publishing, care of James
Wilson, with the mission of advancing the poetry and creative
community of Hampton Roads, Virginia.
See our production of works from ...

Gus Woodward II
          (MC G2)
Tanya Cunningham
          (Scientific Eve)
Terra Leigh
Ray Simmons
Samantha Borders-Shoemaker
Taz Waysweete'
Bobby K.
          (The Poor Man's Poet)
J. Scott Wilson (TEECH!)
Charles Wilson
Dezz
Catherine T.L. Hodges

Cassandra IsFree
Jorge Mendez & JT Williams
Sarah Eileen Williams
Stephanie Diana (Noftz)
the Hampton Roads
          Artistic Collective
Jason Brown (Drk Mtr)
Martina Champion
Tony Broadway
Ken Sutton
Crickyt J. Expression
Lisa M. Kendrick
... and others to come soon.

We promote and support the artists of the 757
  from the seats, from the stands,
  from the snapping fingers and clapping hands
  from the pages, and the stages
  and now we pass them forth to the ages

Check for the above artists on FaceBook, the Virginia Poetry
Online channel on YouTube, and other social media.
Hampton Roads Artistic Collective is a charitable extension of WPP
and strives to simultaneously support worthy causes in Hampton
Roads and the creative artists.

www.ingramcontent.com/pod-product-compliance
Lightning Source LLC
Chambersburg PA
CBHW030634260626
47157CB00007B/2321